SURROGATE SERIES

OMNIBUS

(ALSO KNOWN AS THIRD WHEEL)

HALEY RHOADES

Surrogate Series Omnibus
Copyright © 2023 Haley Rhoades

All rights reserved.
The Surrogate Series is a work of fiction. Names, characters, and incidents are all products of the authors imagination and are used fictitiously. Any resemblance to actual events or persons, living or dead, is entirely coincidental.

Any trademarks, service marks, product names, or named features are assumed to be the property of their respective owners and are used only for reference. There is no implied endorsement.

Cover by @Germancreative on Fiverr

❦ Created with Vellum

DEDICATION

I dedicate this book to my family.
You allow me to chase my dreams and inspire me with your achievements.
You are my rocks.

TO ENHANCE YOUR READING

of The Surrogate Series,
read the Trivia Page near the end of the book
prior to opening chapter #1.

No Spoilers-I promise.

TRIGGER WARNING

Trigger warnings for all my books are available on my website.

www.HaleyRhoades.com

PART I
THE PROPOSAL

1

TINY BUBBLES

Taylor

A text alert ping startles me from my candlelight meditation. I reach from the soothing bubbles for my cell phone. *Where did I put it?* I crane my neck left then right around the entire master bathroom.

"Crap!"

Tiny white bubbles race down my torso as I rise from the tub. I run through the hall to the kitchen. When I hit the tile floor, my feet slip out from under me.

"Shit!" I shout as my feet fly up, and my head falls down.

Slowly, I assess myself.

Legs, feet, and ankles? No pain.

Arms, wrists, back, and neck? No pain.

Butt? Smarts a bit, but not broken.

I can just hear it now. The doctor at Urgent Care asking how I fell. Me explaining I was covered in bubbles, running naked through my house to find my cell phone because I received a text.

I am such an idiot. I was relaxing in the tub, washing away all my stress. I was enjoying a moment of long-needed self-care. Why do I care if I miss a text? Cell phone in hand, I return to the master suite.

Deciding to read the text later, I lay my iPhone on the edge of the tub.

My to-do list for the first week of July enters my mind. As I mentally organize my priorities for the day and week, I wonder if I might be able to buy a new plant for the apartment. My mind moves to the items on my 'This Month' to-do list. I vow to check some tasks off my list while I run my errands today.

I slap my cheeks. I'm in a bubble bath. I need to relax. Now is not the time to think of all my lists. I need this break.

I focus on lying back, submerged in warm bliss. As I slip under the bubbles, I am distracted by tingles on my bare breasts. The warm bubbles pop in the cooler open air; a pleasant prickle floods the surface of my skin. I lightly trace my index finger from my chin down my collarbone. This heightens the sensitivity of my skin, and goosebumps appear. My finger finds my hard nipple just as my phone rings beside me.

"It's your best friend...dah, dah, dah...Best friend..." My assigned ringtone for Kennedy blasts.

Startled, I knock the phone from the tub's edge to the tile floor below. Water splashes over the side. Before I finally grasp the phone, my ringtone ends, sending the call to voicemail.

Caller ID displays Kennedy Hayes. I quickly scroll to favorites and tap her name.

"Hey, you!" I greet.

"How is my dearest and oldest friend doing today?" Kennedy asks.

"I'm fine," I lie. "I'm just soaking in my tub." *Without any toys,* I pout to myself.

"Good." Kennedy's voice nervously shakes a bit on the other end of the line. "At least you're taking care of yourself."

"A girl's gotta do what a girl's gotta do," I tease.

"Jackson and I have a present for you." She pauses for a moment. I am about to speak when she continues, "We have a plane ticket in your name waiting at the ticket counter. We arranged for you to fly to Kansas City. We'll meet you at the airport." Speaking fast, she must pause to catch her breath. "We'd like you to fly down for some rest and relaxation." Her voice sounds more relaxed now that she's made her announcement. "Jackson says we won't take no as an answer." Kennedy waits for my reply.

"Wow! You guys." Tears threaten to stream down my cheeks. "I am doing okay. You really don't need to look after me."

"It's not a pity gift. Jackson and I miss you. It's been over two years since we last got together. I miss my best friend. Besides, you have no reason not to come now." From Kennedy's tone, I imagine her lower lip juts out in a pout.

I run my hand back and forth across the dwindling bubbles floating in the water. My first reaction is to pack now and go. But I wonder... *If I go, am I running from all my problems?*

"Here's the deal." Kennedy's voice slices the silence. "If you don't use the ticket, tomorrow, I am flying up and dragging you to Missouri kicking and screaming." She's serious, but there is laughter in her voice. "You can do this the easy way or the hard way."

"Okay!" I answer. "I will fly down for a few days." I attempt to conceal my excitement. For the first time in the past year, I'm actually looking forward to something.

"Pack light. I have a shopping trip planned." Her excitement is contagious. "How soon can you be at the airport?"

"What?"

"Well, there is a flight leaving in four hours. You could be here in time for dinner." Kennedy pauses, hoping I'll take the bait.

"I guess I could make it."

What am I thinking? This is crazy. I'm soaking in a tub of bubbles, planning to fly to Missouri in less than four hours.

"But I've gotta let you go now. I'll call you when I get checked in at the airport." My thoughts are already shifting to the many things I must do and pack before leaving. "Kennedy, are you sure Jackson won't mind?"

She assures me Jackson purchased my ticket before he shared this plan with her. She urges me to hang up the phone, pull myself out of my bubbles, and pack.

I try to gather my thoughts before I hop from the warmth of the tub. *Maybe a break from my surroundings will help me make plans. A break could be good.* With my right foot, I release the stopper. I lay motionless as the warm, soapy water level retreats. Relaxing waves flow over my entire body. My skin prickles with the sensation of the tiny white bubbles exploding and the cool air connecting with my warm flesh.

I slowly skim my fingers over my bare breasts, down my abdomen, and between my thighs. I don't have time for this, but it feels divine. My sensitive clit assures me I can quickly award myself with an orgasm before I rush to the airport. I press my thumb against the swollen bud as I delve my fingers into my warm heat. *Pop. Pop. Pop.* The soapy bubbles explode upon my heated skin as the water retreats. My thumb circles, and my index finger thrusts over and over. Soon, my muscles clench as I climb closer and closer...

My cell phone's generic ringtone sounds, interrupting my sensual moment.

Ignore it.

Two fingers now working; I increase my thrusts. I grind against the palm of my hand, and my hips lift off the bottom of the tub.

Ignore the ringing.

The moment is lost...

Ruined.

2

THE THREE HORSEMEN

Taylor

I close my eyes tightly as I withdraw my fingers from my folds. My orgasm will have to wait. Opening my eyes, I grasp the phone from the edge of the tub. I check the caller ID. It's Grace. I rise, grab my robe, and let voicemail take her call.

Toweled off, I tap play and the loudspeaker on my new voicemail.

"Taylor, are you there? Please pick up," Grace urges then sighs. "I know it is all over now between the two of you, but I want us to get together one last time. I have something for you."

I press end and delete to block out the whiny pleas of my recently ex-mother-in-law-to-be. *Kansas City sounds even better now. I won't have to tell anyone, no one will find me there, and that is what I need right now.* I quickly pack a carry-on bag with only my make-up, a change of clothes, pajamas, a bikini, a couple of pairs of Converse shoes, flip-flops, and my vibrators. I create a mental list as I pack. *Gas, cash, gum, and download a book or two.* I grab my favorite white, scoop neck tee, my favorite pair of jeans, and my gray and black Converse for the flight.

Glancing at my iPhone, I realize I need to step on it if I am to check in and clear security for my flight. O'Hare is always busy.

Minutes later, with carry-on in hand, I step through the garage door. I begin to press the wall-mounted garage door opener when I hear my generic ringtone. I decide not to answer; instead, I escape while I can. *If it is important, they will leave a voicemail.*

A smile slides onto my face as I turn the key and my Mustang roars to life. I roll backward into the driveway. As the garage door closes, I realize I am free. Free to fly away from it all. I so need this trip. I unlock the roof then press the button to lower the top. A convertible ride on the highway is the perfect start to a Fourth of July vacation. I crank the radio. Not in the mood for The Black Crowes, I press two on my presets to find Ellie Goulding. On preset three, I find Bryan Adams; on four, Shaggy; and on five, commercials. Just not hitting the spot. I tap the audio-in button and connect my iPhone. I quickly tap playlists and choose my heavy playlist. *Five Finger Death Punch. That is more like it.* I pull from the driveway, singing along to my favorite bands.

I arrive at the airport just over an hour after Kennedy's invitation phone call. I packed light; that sped up my arrival. I browse the long-term parking, Lot E, for a protective spot for my baby. It is worth a few extra steps to ensure she doesn't get a door ding or a fender scrape.

Perfect! I spot an opening near a light pole. Hurrying with my carry-on, purse, iPhone, and keys in hand, I climb aboard the shuttle.

The airport is busy. I knew it would be. I make my way to the American Airlines counter, finding the line not too long. While I wait, I text Kennedy, letting her know I arrived and will text when I clear security.

"You are booked on flight 1362 at gate 73. Any bags to check?" I shake my head as the robotic counter person continues her memorized talk without using much brain activity. She makes eye contact and smiles her fake smile. "Thank you for flying American."

I grab my carry-on bag and boarding pass. Sighing, I head toward the security screening area. At my turn, my shoes and belt are off, my loose change and lip gloss are in a tub. After my body is scanned, my shoes are on, I grab my stuff, and the TSA is done. Now through security, the stressful portion of the trip is over.

On my way to the gate, I pop into a newsstand for gum. I debate the purchase of a magazine and decide to download a book instead. Glancing at my phone, I have over an hour until boarding. I look left then right. Busy travelers urgently bustle here and there while duty-free shops beckon shoppers.

Ah-ha. I dart into a bar. I spot a high-top by the window in direct view of the television. I scan the area, finding I am the lone customer. With his back to me stocking bottles, the bartender asks what I would like as I attempt to walk by. I pause at the bar opposite his back.

I order, "The Three Wise Men."

The bartender turns, making eye contact with a sly grin upon his warm, chestnut face. His coffee-brown eyes crinkle at the corners. His jaw is dark with the hint of a day or two without a shave.

I shake away the handsome haze his devilish good looks have trapped me in. "What?" I question.

His smile grows wider, reaching up to his hypnotic eyes.

"Do I have something in my teeth?" I ask.

His brown eyes move from mine to my mouth. I unknowingly lick my parted lips as a warm heat rises in my core.

"You stumped me. That almost never happens."

"Excuse me?"

Am I in a parallel universe? I think I'm speaking English. He seems to be speaking English. Why doesn't anything make sense?

"The Three Wise Men?" he questions. "I've tended bar for four years, and I've never heard of that one." He washes and dries his hands, then he jots "The Three Wise Men" on a napkin. "What's in that?" His eyes reach deep inside me, hoping to pull the recipe to my lips.

"Umm..."

Suddenly, I can't recall his question. His eyes heat my lips; his body heat seems to be radioactive, reaching through the solid bar to me. I slowly tuck a stray lock of hair behind my right ear as I survey his strong shoulders straining the threads of his black tee. I follow his dark right arm with a tribal tattoo and script leading to his wrist. His large fingers point to the napkin.

"Oh. Um, it's three shots." I will myself to meet his eyes. "Jim

Beam, Jack Daniels, and Johnnie Walker." A head tilt now accompanies his smirk. "The Four Horsemen adds a shot of Jameson or Jose Cuervo." I gulp. "Like the Four Horsemen of the Apocalypse." I prattle on.

"You're an enigma."

"Excuse me?" The more we talk, the more I need my drink.

"You ordered a drink I've never heard of." He turns briefly, grasps Jim, Jack, and Johnnie, then places them on the bar. He shakes his head, smiling widely, then excuses himself to pull a plaque from the back wall near the register. He rips the paper reading 429 from its clear pocket. On a Post-It note, he writes a large, thick zero then slides it under the plastic. Slowly, he spins the plaque to face me.

I read aloud, "'Zero days since Jorge has been stumped. Oh!" I gasp.

"Yes," he smirks. "Four-hundred twenty-nine days of perfect. You walk in and stump me with the name of your drink. Then I assume it's a frilly drink with more than the usual rum or vodka." He shrugs. "You stump me again. See, it's kind of my thing. I'm supposed to know every drink recipe. I have a gift for predicting a customer's favorite types of alcohol, too. The regulars and staff like to challenge me." He's not bragging. He's embarrassed. "Now, a personal favor. Can I snap a picture of you holding the sign?" He points to the plaque. "They will have a million questions about you and how you stumped me," he explains.

I nod my permission while taking the sign from him. He snaps two pictures with his cell phone. Still shaking his head, he returns the plaque to its place on the back wall of honor.

When he returns to me, his sexy smirk still in place, he asks, "Can I get your name and phone number?"

3

RELENTLESS

Taylor

"Can I get your name and phone number? They are relentless."

My imagination is working overtime. There's no way he asked for my numb—My eyes feel as though they might pop from my head.

He keeps his eyes on the bar napkin with "The Three Wise Men" written on it, pen in hand.

I recite, "Taylor T-A-F-T, 7-0-8-5-5-5-2-5-5-3." I watch carefully as he transcribes on the napkin.

"Now about that drink." He grabs a glass. "We can't serve shots, but I can pour you three glasses with a finger each." His head tilts, and his dark brown eyes search mine for acceptance as he awaits my reply.

"One glass is fine. You can serve it separately as three shots or as an all-in-one drink." I smile, loving the weight of his dark eyes upon my face while he listens attentively. *Hmm… Bartenders really are great listeners.* "I'd like two fingers each, please."

"Hold up!" He looks left then right. He walks to the back then quickly returns behind the bar, his hands empty.

I glance around, trying to understand the cause for his actions. I raise an eyebrow.

He leans his cellphone against an empty glass. I squint to see as he presses record. He smiles at me and explains, "I'm going to record this. They will not believe this drink is what you," his eyes roam from my head as far down as he can with the bar between us, "order. And they will never believe that you drink it when I describe you to them." He pours two fingers of Jack first, then Jim Beam. He pauses with Johnnie in his hand. His eyebrows raised, he awaits my affirmation. I nod. He pours two fingers of Johnnie then slides me the tumbler as he ensures it is displayed clearly on his recording cell phone.

I swing the glass in a small circle, stirring the caramel liquid. I rest the rim on my lower lip, look into his curious eyes, then down it in one long, drawn-out drink.

As I place the tumbler upon the bar top, he asks, "Will the lady have another?" His eyes are wide. His grin is gone. It's as if he truly has no clue what I will do next.

I wipe my mouth with the back of my left hand. "I'll take a Jack and Coke please." I risk a glance up.

A sexy smile greets me upon his chiseled face. "Shall I change the channel?" he asks with his slight Latin accent crossing the lips of his smile. His head tilts toward the flatscreen mounted behind the bar.

"I really don't mind," I lie, absentmindedly spinning my ring around my left ring finger. I stare as he turns to make my drink. His black pants cling nicely to his muscular thighs and tight butt. I do my best to not be obvious as I watch him. His rippled arms reach overhead for a clean glass. He turns his back towards me as he clutches the bottle of Jack Daniels Whiskey. He casually runs his fingers through his wavy black hair as he fills the glass with Coke. I nervously look away as he will be delivering my drink.

My eyes dart to my hands. I suddenly realize that I am spinning my ring. Tears begin to well up in my eyes as I remove the engagement ring from my hand. I place the diamond carefully on the used cocktail napkin and then quickly try to wipe the tears from my cheeks. The bartender places another napkin in front of me and then gently places my fresh drink on it.

"Is everything alright?" he quietly asks. "I'm sorry. I couldn't help but notice." He motions towards my tears then to the tiny diamond ring lying on the napkin.

"I'm okay," I slowly assure the stranger. My words do not sound believable. I turn away, wiping more tears from my cheeks. Thoughts of John enter my mind. His sandy blonde hair pulled into a man-bun on top and freshly shaven on the sides and back. Him shirtless as he loved others to witness the rewards of his hard work at the gym. Him proudly crossing his arms across his chest, drawing attention to the dragon with skull tattoo and full sleeves as he strides toward me. His washboard abs flexing, drawing attention to his low-riding jeans. With each step, his abdominal tattoo, 'Take No Prisoners,' flashing like a neon sign. I loathe that tattoo almost as much as I detest his knuckle tattoos, which spell out. 'Hell yeah." Who even says hell yeah, let alone permanently adorns their very visible hands with the words?

I jump as Jorge stands beside me. "You look like you could use someone to talk to." He glances at the bar then the TV. "I have a 15-minute break. Would you like a little company?" He pauses for a moment. Smiling, he states, "Trust me. It's not a pick-up line. It's been a slow day, and I would welcome the conversation."

I say, "Okay." Then I immediately wonder what I am thinking. Nothing I have done today is the norm for me. He introduces himself as Jorge, pointing to the nametag I had already noticed. I shake his extended hand, stating I am Taylor. His eyes stare at the engagement ring on the napkin between us. I tell him I just realized I was still wearing the stupid thing.

"I am still wearing mine," he says, showing me his left hand, complete with wedding band. "Rosalynn left me six months ago to move to New York for her dancing career." His slight smile, droopy brown eyes, and wavy, coal black hair lead me to wonder how anyone could ever leave someone so gorgeous. "Rosalynn was my first love. I just can't admit she isn't coming back to me." He twists the gold band. "Besides, it keeps some of the barflies away." He is trying to lighten the mood. "What about you?"

"My story is not as simple." I try to find a way to summarize the last year and a half of my life. I explain I moved to Chicago for work, bringing along my younger college boyfriend. While I speak of our four-year mess of a relationship, he pours another Jack and Coke. He slips away the empty glass I was playing with, replacing it with a fresh one.

"I broke off the engagement about two months ago." Our eyes meet. I see no pity in his.

"What brings you to the airport today?" He lifts my glass to his plump lips and sips.

I quirk a smile his way.

His brown eyes spark to life as he smiles. "This one's on me." He points to my glass now parked on the bar napkin.

"It'd better be," I tease. "You make a habit of sharing drinks with your customers?"

He chuckles shaking the now empty glass. "Let's share another."

I'm on vacation. I might as well. I explain how Jackson and Kennedy bought me a ticket to distract me in Kansas City. Jorge states that fun with good friends is probably exactly what I need right now.

He glances at his watch. "I really must get back to work. Not that anyone else is in the bar." He saunters behind the counter again. He walks towards me and leans across. "Another drink before you fly to KC?" he offers.

I look at the clock. I have 30 minutes before boarding starts. "I should really get to my gate," I reply.

"Stop by and see me when you return. Let me know how everything goes," he pleads.

I want to say no. His sexy smile and the spark in his eyes seal the deal. I know I will stop by upon my return.

I slowly gather my bag and purse. I am acutely aware of his eyes on my back as I prepare to leave. My drinks have warmed my insides and only slightly affected my ability to think and walk. They have taken the edge off. I embrace the feeling. I grab my ring from the napkin, tucking it into my jeans pocket.

With my iPhone in hand, I slowly turn to meet Jorge's milk chocolate eyes behind the bar. I thank him for the drinks, slide two twenties his way, and promise to drop in next week. He slides me a bar napkin as I walk by. I nervously grab it and head for the terminal without a look back.

4

MY JACKSON

Taylor

Did I just cry with a stranger? Did I, looking at the unfolded bar napkin, accept his cellphone number and promise to see him next week? I haven't been single for two months yet. This is not me. I don't take these risks. I do not share private feelings with strangers. I do not meet men in bars. I don't go to bars. I work. I plan. I scrutinize and calculate all my decisions before making them. I have at least three to-do lists going at any given time. I live to plan and organize everything. Deciding to fly to KC at a moment's notice is not something I do. Accepting the number of a bartender I just met is even farther from the norm for me. What am I thinking?

I find my gate just in time for boarding. The agent scans my first-class ticket, and I secure my carry-on in the overhead compartment before I plop into my spacious seat. I smile at the thought of seeing my friends. Jackson and Kennedy know about my screwed-up mom, my life with Grandma before she passed, my desperation for scholarships, my desire to find someone so I was not alone. They know all my secrets and love me despite them.

A few moments pass. Then a young couple takes the seats between me and the window. They giggle, coo, and are constantly touching. It is easy to see they are very young and very much in love. Why can't I find a love like theirs? My true love, my good guy? Where is my Jackson?

I flag the attendant on her way by. "May I have a Jack and Coke as soon as you get a chance?"

She smiles at me then scurries off. This is just my luck. I am running from my failed relationship, and fate puts a young, newlywed couple next to me for my flight. I have nowhere to escape them. Suddenly, my seatbelt feels like it is shackling me to my failures.

On her way to assist another passenger, the flight attendant delivers my drink. I thank her twice. She tilts her head to the right and smiles a knowing smile at me before excusing herself.

As I place my glass to my lips, I hear, "My name is Mark. This is my wife, Sarah. We're headed to the Bahamas for our honeymoon." He turns to grin at the giggling Sarah then back to me. "Will you take our picture for us?" He urges his cellphone towards me. I set my glass down and accept his phone with a forced smile.

"Perfect." He glances at the picture on his cellphone screen. "Thanks." He turns, and the couple's lips connect in a tender kiss.

I sigh and finish my drink in one attempt. As the attendant works the area, I signal for another.

During the flight, I do my best to block out the cute couple's coos on my left as I finish my second drink then move on to plain cola. I busy myself by reading the latest, number one best-selling romance novel I downloaded from Amazon for the trip.

I don't normally read for entertainment. I read for work, for research, or for news. I thought this would make for good vacation reading. It was overwhelming, trying to choose the perfect book. I was not looking for sappy fantasy relationships where the world seems perfect. I chose a rough guy, a spunky woman, and a relationship of opposites full of turmoil. I am five chapters in as we land in Kansas City.

I browse anxiously through the crowd for Kennedy. Not seeing her,

I find a nearby seat to relax and wait. I pull out my compact to check my hair. I raise the open mirror. There, in the reflection behind me, is Jackson. I stand and turn just in time for a tag-team hug from Kennedy and her husband.

"Sorry we are late," Jackson greets. "I couldn't find a parking spot." He grabs my bag from my hand, kisses my cheek, then motions me toward the exit.

Kennedy wraps her arm around my waist as we follow him. It feels like home, being back in the company of my true friends. "You. Look. Fabulous!" Kennedy takes me in from head to toe. "How many days a week are you working out?"

"Three to four," I admit. I straighten a crease out of my white cotton T-shirt. "I just threw on the first clean thing I found when you called. You know, I didn't have much time to prepare."

"You look like a model. Just threw it on, my foot. Those Converse are to die for. How much did they set you back?" Kennedy refuses to shut up about my selection of travel attire.

"A model?" Jackson butts in. "I believe you must be five foot seven to be a model. Even in those shoes you are under five foot one."

Without thinking, my middle-finger flies into Jackson's face. Looking around the concourse, Jackson grasps my wrist, lowering my hand to my side.

"What's this?" I tease back. "You are slipping in your old age, Jackson. I've been on the ground for ten minutes, and this is your first zinger."

"Come on." Jackson laughs while pulling me tight for a bear hug," I tease because I love."

"Yeah. Love has nothing to do with it," I reply.

Kennedy steers the conversation to a topic of more importance. "What's Taylor feel like for dinner?"

"Whatever is closest," is my reply, grabbing my growling stomach. Sandwiched between the two of them, I am guided toward the exit.

Inside their Chevy Impala, Jackson drives us from the airport towards a restaurant Kennedy chose. It seems like no time has passed. I set the two of them up on their first date and spent many a trip in the back of Jackson's car as he drove Kennedy and I here or there. They are the perpetual couple; I am perpetually single.

"Taylor," Jackson's voice interrupts. "Earth to Taylor. You okay?"

I smile at his eyes in the rearview mirror then at Kennedy. "I'm sorry. I had drinks during the flight. What did you say?"

Jackson shakes his head while mentioning that things are moving quickly back to the time before John if I am consuming drinks. This causes me to pause.

"I drank while I was with John." The sound of his name off my tongue causes me to cringe. It's over. I no longer have to deal with him. I am moving on.

"Taylor," Kennedy answers, "you might have taken a sip here or there, but you never drank."

"You were drunk when you met John at the team party," Jackson reminds me. "But I don't think we saw you take more than a taste or two while you were with him." Jackson's eyes in the mirror convey his sadness.

I don't want their pity. It's over. I made a mistake, I chose wrong, and I wasted four years of my life.

Kennedy continues, "Honestly, we knew he became overly controlling. We just thought you chose not to drink so you could try to keep him from losing his temper." She, too, looks at me sadly. "You changed everything for him. You gave up so much."

"Enough!" I yell. "This is a John-free trip. I am single. I need to heal and move on. I can't do that if you two are pointing out all the mistakes I made."

As I talk, I fail to notice that Jackson has pulled into a large parking lot and stopped the car. I become aware when he opens the back door, takes my hand, and pulls me out. I barely have time to unbuckle before he has me in a tight hug. Tears sting my eyes. Where did they come from?

Kennedy also wraps her arms around my waist. Jackson's deep voice interrupts the group hug. "We are not pointing out your mistakes. We are not against you. We are your friends. We lost you to John. We lost our fun-loving, daring, life-of-the-party best friend." He brushes the tears from my cheeks. "It didn't happen overnight, but you withdrew from us. You cut us off. You avoided our calls and invites. You changed the way you dressed, the way you acted, and even the way you talked."

"You were a Stepford Wife," Kennedy states.

"Ouch!" I bite back.

"This trip," Jackson continues, "is an intervention. We are going to bring back Taylor."

5

YOU HEARD THAT

Taylor

"I didn't change. I grew up," I argue.

"Bullshit!" Jackson states, his brown eyes wild with rage. "He was an abusive, overbearing, insecure ass. You changed everything to prevent his anger."

He's cursing. That is rare for him, and I'm the reason. He's fuming to the point of swearing, and it's all because I didn't have the balls to drop my loser boyfriend when I graduated college and moved to Chicago.

I wish I had known then what I know now. The past two months proved I am capable of living on my own. I let the fear of adulting in a new state and large city get to me. I thought taking John with me would prevent my loneliness. It did not. I now know he made me lonelier than I would have been on my own. I neglected to make new friends, to go out, and to explore the city in order to avoid his wrath.

"You couldn't hide it all from us. We heard everything; we know everything he wouldn't let you do," Kennedy states, twirling her index finger nervously through a strand of her blonde hair. "We heard him make you change clothes more than once during senior year. He controlled what you wore, where you went, and who you spoke to."

"You heard that?" Fear envelops me. I went to great lengths in my attempts to hide things from the two of them.

"Yes. We heard him call you a whore, slut... You name it." Jackson struggles to rein in his over six feet of balled up anger. He fights the urge to pace. "He wasn't as quiet in your bedroom as you'd hoped. We tried to act like we didn't hear so you could still go out to eat with us." He runs his hand through his dark brown hair then down his dark, stubbled jaw. "It killed me to sit across the table from him. The way he treated you behind closed doors... You didn't deserve that. I should have stopped him." Jackson's hands on my shoulders grip tightly, burning my skin as I look up at him. "I know it had to be even worse than we ever knew."

"We wanted to help," Kennedy claims. "We thought if you were out with us, you would open up to me. We thought you might ask for help. We just tried to be there for you as often as you would let us."

"You mean when *he* would let us," Jackson interjects, his voice laced with venom. "The asshole didn't tell you when we called. He sent our birthday cards back with 'return to sender' written on the envelopes." At this memory, Jackson releases me, turns his back, and paces a few steps.

"What?" I can't believe this. "I never knew you..."

They are right. I was a Stepford wife. I became his robot, doing and saying what he allowed me to. I became the exact opposite of the woman I was prior to meeting him. I let go of my fortitude for a loser.

"We have the cards in a box at home. We will show you later," Kennedy states, assuring me Jackson speaks the truth. "When I'd call, he'd say you were out of town or busy getting ready to go to a work event. I'd ask to leave a message, and he'd tell me you were too busy to bother with a phone call."

My legs feel like rubber. I thought my friends had forgotten about me. I thought they'd moved to Kansas City, gotten interesting new friends, and didn't need me. I thought I'd lost them forever. I felt so alone for so long.

Suddenly, I feel lightheaded with this new knowledge that he hurt me more than I even knew. The pain his actions caused seems to grow instead of fade. I vaguely hear Jackson's deep, concerned voice. I feel like I'm underwater and listening to him. Heavy. My eyelids and limbs feel heavy.

"Get the front door; I will carry her to the sofa."

"Should I call Reagan? She's a nurse; she might be able to determine if we should go to the E.R.," a voice I think is Kennedy's asks.

Jackson assures Kennedy it's stress, the flight, and too many mixed drinks with no food. My limbs feel stuck in mud when I try to move my hand to my head.

"Taylor," Kennedy calls. "Honey, are you okay? We think you fainted."

Jackson's large, warm hand cradles my neck, lifting me to a sitting position. I struggle to open my heavy eyelids. I slowly take in my surroundings. I am not in the Impala. I am in a family room. I'm on a sofa. Wait! No. I'm on... I turn my head; I am on Jackson's lap. I quickly try to scoot off.

"Easy, honey," Kennedy calmly encourages, her hands flying to my shoulders to stop me. "Sit still and take a sip of this juice." She reaches out one hand and offers a glass of grape juice.

"Juice?" I croak.

"You didn't eat lunch, did you?" Jackson asks, his brow furrowed and eyes concerned.

I shake my head slowly, my foggy brain spinning.

"The juice will help until we can get dinner into you," Jackson prompts. With a slight chuckle, he states, "Just like old times."

"Jackson!" Kennedy admonishes him.

"What?" he teases. "How many times did the two of you skip a meal and start drinking, and I'd have to babysit one or both of you all night?"

"Babysit her maybe," Kennedy corrects. "I always had a few and spent the night vomiting in the bathroom."

I successfully scoot off Jackson's lap to the corner of the sofa. I flip him off before I snag a throw pillow, pulling it tightly to my chest.

Jackson extends his long legs, putting his feet on the coffee table. Long, dark hair accents his sun-tanned legs. He folds his arms across his golf shirt-covered chest. A smug grin dawns on his golden face. There is a hint of a sunglasses tan line around his brown eyes, extending toward his ears and dark brown hairline. His six-foot frame causes me to shrink into the cushions. He is strong but not ripped. He does hard work and has no time to work out. He's not fat, just a bit soft compared to John. He is much more handsome than John.

I quickly slap my cheeks to draw me out of my wayward thoughts. John is out of my life for good. No need to compare others to him; he is so not worthy of my time.

6

THAT'S A GREEN VEGETABLE

Taylor

I take the barstool across from Kennedy as she prepares the salad.

"What can I do to help?" I ask.

She slides three more saltines my way. Rolling my eyes, I push them aside.

"No. Thank you. Five crackers was enough." I see the concern in her eyes. "Ken, I'm okay. I was so excited to fly here when you called; food was the last thing on my mind." I rise from my perch, pacing to the refrigerator and back to the island. I feel anxious, caged. I need to move. I pace while Kennedy rinses the lettuce. Her soft, natural blonde hair is swept into a messy ponytail. She's still slender, just not emaciated as she once was. Her eye makeup accentuates her blue eyes. Her white blouse loosely conceals everything from neck to wrist. Her gray capris are at least one size too large for her frame. Cherry red polish draws my eyes toward her fingers and toes. She's come so far, but some habits remain visible. I mentally add, "Chat with Jackson about her eating disorder," to my to-do list.

On my way back to the fridge, I pause. "I drank too much today." I meet her eyes. "I was distracted," I say with a shrug.

"Distracted?" Jackson's voice startles me as he emerges from the patio door behind me.

Kennedy laughs, and Jackson smirks. "Distracted by what?" he prods.

"I, uh..." I slowly slide back onto the barstool at the kitchen island. "I, uh, was so excited to get here, I arrived at the airport too early." I shove a carrot from the salad bowl into my mouth. As I crunch, I hope they will move on to another topic. I risk looking up for an instant and am greeted by four concerned and prying eyes.

"Okay!" I scream. "He's a bartender. I just popped in for a quick drink. One thing led to another..."

Jackson slinks out the back door, shaking his head.

"My stomach was empty. I had three or four drinks." I snag another carrot. "I'm not sick. I just drank too much."

"A bartender?" Kennedy asks, perfectly-shaped eyebrows raising.

"I thought you were worried about my fainting."

"We are," Kennedy assures. "But you mentioned a bartender." She raises her hands, making air quotes around "bartender." "Did you, uh, you know?"

"Oh, my god! No!" I screech.

Jackson darts into the kitchen, ready to fix whatever he can find making me yell. He looks between the two of us in question.

I meet Kennedy's stare. "We just talked and drank. I did *not* sleep with the bartender I just met at the airport." I mimic her air quotes. "I just kicked my deadbeat fiancé of four years to the curb. I'm not ready to bed the first hot hunk I lay eyes on."

"Hot?" Jackson teases. "How hot?"

"A hot hunk..." Kennedy turns her back to her husband and fans herself with a plastic lid. "Details. Now!"

Jackson kisses her neck. "Details can wait. The steaks are ready." He pats her behind. "You still prefer yours mooing, right?" he directs my way.

"Just north of mooing," I correct. I search the cabinets until I find plates. I grab three, placing them on the island. Next, I plunder the drawers for utensils.

Jackson strides in, proudly displaying the grilled steaks. Kennedy places the salad near the plates. Jackson snags another platter, disappears, then returns with grilled asparagus.

"Um," I pause. "That's a green vegetable."

Kennedy giggles. "It won't kill you. You'll give it a try." Her tone suddenly reminds me of my grandmother's.

Jackson senses my apprehension. "I coat it in olive oil and lemon juice." He places two sprigs upon a plate and hands it to me. "Just a bite. That's all I ask."

Plates full, the three of us walk to the family room. Jackson turns on the local news. We eat as we casually discuss the current events. Hoping they were distracted by the weather forecast, I nibble on the asparagus. I nibble a bit more. Before I know it, my plate is empty.

"Song of the Day time," Jackson announces during a commercial.

I forgot all about this game we started back in high school. It was Jackson's and my thing. We would try to sum up our day by using lyrics to a song. We would also try to stump each other on naming the artists and titles. My love of music has never left me. I just quit playing the game.

"Taylor..." Kennedy prompts.

"Let's see..." I already know my song. I tap my finger on my cheek, pretending to think. "I'm unsure..." I take a long pull from my ice cold Bud Light bottle. "Where my path leads." I stand up and pretend to pace. "I remember all the places before this."

Kennedy giggles. "I'm lost." She never was good at lyrics. Even when she likes a song, she can't think without the music to accompany it.

Jackson stands, takes my right hand in his, singing the first five lines of the song before he answers, proudly beaming. *"Here I Go Again* by Whitesnake."

Together, we sing the song through the end of the first chorus.

I clap mockingly at Jackson then excuse myself to the kitchen. I grab two more sprigs of asparagus as I place my plate into the sink.

"I saw that," Jackson whispers from the island behind me. "I knew you'd like it," he teases.

I spin, steak knife in hand. "Don't get any ideas. This is the only vegetable you'll trick me into trying."

"Easy now," Jackson calms. "Let's put down the weapon and discuss this."

"There's nothing to discuss. I eat lettuce, carrots, green beans, corn, pickles, and potatoes. Those are my only vegetables. So, don't." I swing the steak knife in his direction. "Don't try to force any other veggies on me." I swing the knife in a Zorro-like Z-pattern then drop it into the sink.

"You forgot asparagus on your list," he corrects as I place his plate into the sink.

Kennedy joins us. "You're pushing it, Jackson."

"Yeah, Jack," I tease. His eyes grow hard, and his smile retreats. He hates being called Jack. I love this tidbit of knowledge. I use it to signal he's teased me enough. He always gets the message.

"My turn," Jackson states. "You are unsure of yourself, and I don't know why."

This one is too easy. I quickly state, "One Direction, and the song is *What Makes You Beautiful*."

Kennedy suggests we grab beers and head to the deck. Conversation flows easily as do the first and second beers. Kennedy places a bucket of beers and ice between Jackson and me. She stopped after consuming one Lime-A-Rita.

They fill me in on Jackson's work at the grocery store, Kennedy's job at the YMCA, the forecast, and their plans for the Fourth of July.

As Jackson opens our last beer, he suggests we move inside before mosquitos eat us alive. We quickly gather all our beverages and empty bottles before ducking indoors.

Kennedy grabs four more beers from the refrigerator in the garage. She leaves one in front of me then places the rest in the kitchen refrigerator.

Jackson smiles and slides my new beer to the side, replacing it with a shot glass. He places one in front of him before asking me to pick my poison.

"I'm an American girl." I state.

"Jim or Jack?" Jackson nods, approving.

Kennedy looks confused by our conversation.

"Ken," I prompt, "join us in a shot?" I laugh knowingly as she shakes her head. "Not the hard stuff. Another Lime-A-Rita?"

Kennedy is a lightweight. Always has been; always will be. She sips a beverage now and then, but there are too many calories in alcohol for her. "One more," she agrees. "I need to be lucid for the two of you tonight." She nods to the bottles of Jim Beam and Jack Daniels in front of me. "Seems it'll be a long night."

"ABC order," I announce. "Jack first with beer chasers," I challenge Jackson.

"Two shots then we move to the living room," Kennedy demands.

Jackson and I fill the shot glasses as Kennedy and her Lime-A-Rita move to the sofa.

"Ready?" I tease. Jackson isn't much of a drinker either.

"Go!"

Two shots and half a beer later, I grab two more cold ones as we join Kennedy. I snuggle close to her on the sofa as Jackson chooses the floor in front of us.

I commandeer the remote from Kennedy. I scroll through too many channels before I give up. On my phone, I scroll to 80's rock on Spotify and press enter. I turn the volume up loud enough to hear but low enough we can talk over it. I place my cell on the table in front of the sofa.

With Guns-N-Roses playing in the background, Kennedy begins, "We will talk about John tonight and tonight only."

My eyes quickly dart to Jackson to save me. On his face, I do not find my rescue. "We'll talk about it tonight. Tomorrow, we will return to life before and without John." A small smile climbs to his lips. "I'll make it painless." He passes me the bottle of Jack, prompting me to take a swig.

I sigh deeply. Three gulps of the warm, amber liquid soothes me from the inside out.

"Fire away," I encourage.

7

GREEN STOCKS OF STINK

Jackson

"When did it get bad?" Kennedy asks.

I inwardly cringe. I introduced John to Taylor. I did nothing when I first witnessed him controlling her, changing her. This will be an excruciating conversation for Taylor and me. Kennedy looks cool and calm in her corner of the sofa. I realize we rehearsed this conversation and brainstormed Taylor's reactions, but I am a nervous wreck while Kennedy seems fine.

"Where to begin..." Taylor repositions herself on the sofa, leaning on the arm. She clutches a blue throw pillow to her chest. I want to be the pillow. I want to be the comfort she needs. I will be. We will be. Kennedy and I are back in her life to stay. I will never let some guy come between the three of us again.

"Last March, I chaperoned the eighth-grade trip to Washington D.C." She swallows hard. "I do it every spring. I was gone for seven days. When I opened the door to my apartment, I nearly fainted. My words can never express the disaster I found." She closes her eyes. "The mini-blinds must have caught on fire. They were mostly melted, charred black, and had left dark burn marks on the window sills and walls. Red Solo cups covered everything and most of the floor. My bowls were used as ashtrays." A low chuckle escapes her throat. "I guess I should be thankful they used ashtrays at all." Taylor shakes her head. "Food, trash, and used condoms littered the tables and floors. I had to scoot my feet, moving the trash out of my path. There was no way to step around it."

I take a sip of the Jack Daniels then hand it up to Taylor. She parts her lips for a short sip. She hands it back, and I return the bottle to the coffee table on my right. I take a deep breath as she continues.

"It's stressful, chaperoning a field trip. Keep in mind the trip included 100 13- and 14-year-olds, both boys and girls. The boys are starting puberty. The girls act like 18-year-olds. For the hundred students, we took two teachers, the principal, and eight parents. They were great kiddos. They were so excited to witness and learn."

Taylor beams with pride for her middle school students. A twinkle returns to her eyes, and her smile is contagious.

"The ratio is ten to one. That's good. However, parents don't think like educators. So, the three of us watch our ten students plus all the others, too. We caught some couples making out in secluded parts of the hotel. I caught a parent allowing boys and girls to cuddle on beds while watching a movie." Taylor chuckles. "I know I was no angel, but I wasn't this advanced in eighth grade. We couldn't allow anyone to go home pregnant or violated under our watch."

I can tell she's a great teacher. She wants the best for the students.

"So, to say I was exhausted upon returning home is an understatement." Her eyes are sad once again, and her dazzling smile vanishes. "I slid my way to the kitchen. I poured myself two shots from the first bottle I grabbed. I didn't need salt or limes, just tequila." Taylor pauses for a second.

I can't imagine what she found next. *If this happened over three months ago, how much worse did it get leading up to last month?*

"Next, I slid my way down the hall. There was a couple passed out naked near the bathroom door. The door was ajar, so I nudged it. A guy with two naked ladies lay in the bathtub. My bedroom door was closed. I didn't knock. John was passed out on the bed. His dick was still in some blonde. His hands were on the tits of yet another blonde."

Taylor takes a long pull from the bottle of Jack. "No offense, Ken. These are the kinds of blondes I loathe. They are tall, skinny, and big-boobed. They do and get whatever they want without a care for anyone else."

"Time out," I interrupt. "You're getting off topic." I smile at her. "We are bashing John, not the entire blonde population."

"Yeah!" Kennedy fakes anger.

"So, I found my man attached by dick and palm to two women, and none of them were me." She sips Jack. "I mean, I'm just as fond of a threesome as anyone, but this was not..."

"Allowed!" Kennedy interjects as her hackles rise. I'm glad she is angry. I'm glad she cares this much for our friend.

"Right! I wanted to castrate him." Taylor sips some more Jack.

"What did you do?" Kennedy prompts.

"I nudged his foot with my boot," Taylor chuckles. "Well, really, I kicked his bare foot, which was hanging off the bed. He woke up screaming in pain."

He got off easy, I think to myself. I chug the end of the bottle of Jack Daniels.

"I cussed like a sailor. Threw everything I could find from the dresser at them. I didn't realize until much later that there was white powder on several surfaces of the house. He yelled at me as I kicked naked people out of my apartment."

Kennedy giggles. "No way! Naked?"

"Oh, don't feel sorry for them. I tossed the few clothes I found and a couple towels out with them," Taylor brags. "I'm not that heartless. They'll remember this walk of shame." Taylor hops from the sofa. "I need to pee."

I offer to grab some more beers and water from the kitchen. Kennedy grabs some snacks. *Who needs television? This is real.*

"Guys!" Taylor hollers from the guest bedroom. As she enters the family room, she states, "I think I need to find a doctor or Urgent Care." A frantic look consumes her face.

"Why?" I ask quickly, walking to her side.

"My pee stinks so bad." Taylor crinkles her nose and forehead. "It never smells bad. Ever."

Loud belly laughter erupts from Kennedy. I try to contain my own laughter. I cannot keep a smile from my lips.

"You really don't eat veggies, do you?" Kennedy teases. "It's the asparagus. It's a diuretic that causes urine to smell."

My smile fades as I remember Kennedy's eating disorder, the reason she knows about asparagus.

Taylor glances from Kennedy to me, judging the truth. "Seriously? I don't think it tasted good enough to tolerate that smell again." Her face still scrunches with distaste.

I offer an ice cold Bud Light to Taylor. "Enough of your urine talk." I motion to her corner of the sofa. "You have a story to finish." I hope my smile conveys my love and support as I prod her to spill her dark memories.

Taylor plops onto the sofa, secures the throw pillow in her lap, then huffs. "If you promise to never serve me those green stocks of stink..."

"Alright already!" Kennedy shouts too loudly. "You kicked the naked people out. What did you do to John?"

8

TOMORROW, WE START OVER

Jackson

I shrug at Taylor. "Need more of the hard stuff?"

Taylor shakes her head. A veil of sadness slides over her features. "I told him to get his ass in the shower before I could speak to him. I let him think it was to wash their scent from his skin." Taylor's blue eyes briefly connect with mine before looking away. "I really needed time to calm down and think." She giggles to herself. "I made a list."

"You and your lists." Kennedy laughs.

Although I thought Taylor would brandish a knife and threaten to castrate him, making a list is not a surprise.

Taylor continues, "I told him he had to clean up everything before I returned to talk to him at 8:00 a.m. I couldn't sit in the stink and filth. If I threw him out, I'd be stuck cleaning, and that was not going to happen." Taylor shrugs. "I drove to a hotel for the night, and I visited the hotel bar."

Kennedy prompts, "Was it clean?"

"Yes. He claims he did it all himself. I still don't believe him. The jackass had picked up breakfast and roses. He tried greeting me at the door. I pushed him away."

Taylor stands, beer in hand, and paces towards the foyer then back. "It got really ugly really quickly. I ask him to move out. I told him I couldn't let him do drugs and cheat on me in my own house." She plays with her ponytail absentmindedly. "He got mad, and he blamed me. He claims he wasn't doing drugs. Not that I believed him, but I told him he couldn't let his friends do drugs in my house. I could lose my job. He begged and pleaded. He claimed he had nowhere to go and no money. He said he only came to Chicago because of me, so I couldn't throw him out."

"So, you let him stay?" I growl.

"I gave him a week to find a place and a better job. He took that as a challenge to win me back in a week. I made him sleep on the couch. I locked the bedroom door every time I was changing, showering, or sleeping. He offered to run errands for me, he cleaned, and he even cooked. We also fought a lot. He kept asking what I needed to forgive him. I answered I didn't think I could ever forgive him. So, he would yell, and we would fight."

This all happened over spring break, but she didn't kick him out until May. *How does someone so awesome attract such losers?* Taylor never sought out the bad boys. Her high school and college dates never seemed anything but normal. She always found the losers, though.

Hours later, I lay staring at the shadows on the ceiling while Kennedy lies sound asleep beside me. Visions from Taylor's tales haunt me. I keep seeing John following her to and from the middle school. I envision him peeking around doorways. I watch as he reads her emails and checks her cell phone. I even imagine her looking out the window as he feels the top of her car hood, checking for heat to see how long she had been home.

Taylor's stories of John's stalking prevent my sleep. I give up, quietly tiptoeing from the room. I take the stairs slowly. I hope they refrain from creaking. As I pass Taylor's slightly open door, I pray she found the sleep that eludes me.

I round the corner into the kitchen to find it occupied. Leaning on the island, Taylor eats ice cream from the container.

Taylor

"Not a word from you," I warn as Jackson arrives in the kitchen at 2:45 a.m. At least I'm not the only one who couldn't sleep.

Jackson grabs a spoon from the drawer behind me. Without a word, he spoons ice cream from the container.

"Want to share?" I tease.

"My house," he reasons.

"True dat," I state.

Laughing, Jackson claims I've been around middle schoolers so long they've penetrated my vocabulary.

"Kennedy kick you out of bed?" I tease.

"You just get off the phone with Mr. Bartender?" he teases back.

I point my loaded spoon at Jackson. "Not right now, Jack."

He hates when I call him Jack. It's our code. He knows I'm serious.

Jackson wraps his arm around my shoulders. "It wasn't easy sharing with us tonight. We didn't want to open old wounds. We only want to know everything so we can help."

His long black lashes frame his brown eyes. In them, I see his concern. *Am I the reason why he can't sleep?*

"I'm safe now. It's over." I take large bites of French Vanilla ice cream. With my mouth full, I state, "I'm a big girl. No need to lose sleep over me."

"I'm pissed at you," Jackson confesses. His arm leaves my shoulders. His spoon plays in the ice cream tub. "You had a stalker. You were in danger, and you didn't ask for our help."

"I went straight to the police," I defend. "What could you do? Would you have burned a week's vacation to babysit me? I would have still called the police."

"I'd have flown you down for a week or two."

"I had to teach. I only get two personal days," I argue.

"You could have called in sick for a week or two."

"My students need me, and the community relies on me to teach."

"Your safety is more important than that. They would understand." Jackson paces to the back door then to the island again. "Argh! You are so stubborn. I could have helped."

Tears well up in my eyes. "I thought the two of you had forgotten about me," I confess. "I hadn't heard from you in two years." I swallow hard, trying to refrain from crying. "It's like you married Kennedy, we moved to Chicago, you two moved to Kansas City, end of friendship." I risk looking into his eyes.

Jackson throws his spoon into the sink then stomps from the kitchen.

Was it something I said? Or something I did? Maybe I did something two years ago to upset him. Did Kennedy lie to me? Did Jackson ever want me here? I quickly put the ice cream in the freezer. I need to run to my room.

I jump as a large shoe box is thrown on the island. Confused, I spin towards Jackson.

"These are the cards and letters we sent to you for two years. There are even emails for the only address we had for you." His face is stone serious. Jackson grabs the bottle of Jim Beam and takes a long pull.

I blink at this new information. I finger through the papers and cards marked "Return to Sender." I watch as Jackson takes a second sip then replaces the bottle on the counter between us.

I take a sip as Jackson speaks. "After a couple, we realized it wasn't your handwriting. So, we sent some emails. They went unanswered, too." He sighs. "We kept mailing and emailing, hoping one time you would be the first to the mailbox or to read email."

"What you must have thought of me," I state, unable to hold back my tears.

Jackson moves around the island. His arms capture me in a hug. As I sob into his chest, he states, "We knew it was John. We were anxiously reading your blog and Christmas letters to keep tabs on you."

"How did you know?" I ask.

"In college, he started keeping you to himself. It took a year, but we figured it out. Your blog was about your students and school. Rarely, you wrote about events with John and never with friends. In May, you blogged about your school less. You were going to movies, out to eat, and to bars with friends or colleagues. We were excited to read that." Jackson squeezes me tighter. "Your line at the beginning of each post no longer stated, 'John is out tonight,' or 'John is working at the bar tonight, so I'll write to my internet friends.'"

Jackson holds me at arm's length. "So, Kennedy reached out to you. She sent you a birthday card with our email address." He smiles. "And you know the rest."

"I'm a..." I fan my face, trying to collect myself. Tears flow like rivers toward my chin. "I'm a terrible friend," I declare.

"No." Jackson hugs me to his chest again. "No, you aren't."

"I don't send birthday cards, and I never call," I state.

"He would not have allowed you to." Jackson rocks me back and forth. "He would have watched you as you wrote or talked. That's if he didn't fight with you until you decided it would be easier not to even try."

I don't deserve my friends. I abandoned them for two years. I gave up on them, but they never gave up on me.

After several long moments, I withdraw from his arms. I need to change the topic. We need to move on, or we will never sleep.

"Song of the Day," I prompt. "You have major feelings for the sociopath in the seat beside you..." He has no idea, so I continue. "You have major feelings for the killer in the seat beside you."

Jackson says, "I know it's from a DC Comics movie, but I don't know who sings it. I think the title is *Heathens*."

"It is Twenty-One Pilots," I inform him.

"Phone me once and I am there to make the sunny hours all better..." Jackson whispers softly.

I know the answer, but I want him to continue.

"I'm as good as Clark Kent. You only need to phone me once..."

"*One Call Away* by Charlie Puth." I grin. "I absolutely love that song."

He wraps me in a bear hug. "It's been a long night," Jackson consoles. "We've learned a lot." Motioning to the shoebox, he continues, "Now, you've learned a lot. Tomorrow, we start over."

"You mean today," I correct, pointing at the clock. It's now 3:30. "What do you say we down the rest of that bottle and crash for what's left of the night?"

Jackson offers me the first drink. After two each, he disposes of the bottle, and we pour ourselves into bed.

9

HAIR OF THE DOG

Taylor

I clutch my pillow to my face and scream. I don't hold back. I let a scream start in my lower abdomen and creep up my chest. I can't control it. This scream hid inside the pit of my stomach for years. As it tapers off, I worry I will be hoarse. My throat is dry.

Lying on the bed, the room spins. My day replays as I close my eyes. A hug from Kennedy, a group hug with Jackson, his arm around my shoulders and her holding my hands. Jackson's hand on my lower back. Everything felt natural. I forgot how easy they are to be around. I survived high school with their help. I couldn't imagine college without them. *Why did I let them slip away? How did I become so careless? Everything good in my life involves the two of them.*

I feel the bed depress beside me. I cover my eyes with my right forearm and groan. The sunlight filtering through the curtains is too bright.

"Morning," Kennedy's chipper voice greets. "It's almost noon. Time for you to hydrate and eat."

"Ugh," I moan. I vow that, the next time I drink, I'm pouring booze down her throat, too.

"I just woke up Jackson. You two are in bad shape." She giggles.

"Shut up!" I whisper-yell at her.

"Lunch is ready in 15," she whispers. "Don't make me come back in here with pots and pans."

She wouldn't. Wait. She would. I roll to the side of the bed while taking inventory. *Head? Pounding. Eyes? Throbbing. Mouth? Full of cotton. Stomach?* "I will not puke. I will not puke." I repeat my mantra as I slowly pad my way to the kitchen. "I will not puke." I open the step stool. *Damn, that's loud.* "I will not puke." Kennedy giggles, but I ignore her. I'm on a mission. "I will not puke." I open the tiny cabinet above the refrigerator. "I will," I twist the cap, "not puke." I take two long pulls from a new bottle of Jack Daniels.

"I can't believe you," Kennedy chides too loudly. "Aren't you sick enough?"

"Hair of the dog," I whisper. I climb down the step ladder, bottle clutched to my chest. I slide onto a bar stool then lay my head on the island.

"Jackson is in the shower," Kennedy states as she pulls hot rolls from the oven. "He did not win his battle with puking." By the look on her face, one would think she was happy he vomited.

"We finished the open bottle of Jim Beam and half your French Vanilla ice cream at about 3:00 a.m.," I explain.

Kennedy shakes her head as she heads for the deck.

"What are you fixing?" I ask.

"Burgers, chips, rolls, and bacon," she answers. "I thought grease and carbs are what you two would need."

Mentally, I note all four items are not foods she will allow herself to eat.

Jackson interrupts my thoughts. "Hey," he whispers.

I slowly slide the bottle of Jack Daniels towards him. "Hair of the dog."

"I can't," he argues. "I can't keep anything down this morning."

"Duh. Hair of the dog," I chide. "One long or two short. You'll feel better in an hour."

Jackson still shakes his head.

"Between the two of us, who has had more hangovers?"

"You," Jackson moans.

"So, I know best." I unscrew the lid and tip the dark liquid toward his mouth. "One long drink or two short ones. Then we will eat the grease and carbs Kennedy made for us. By two, we will feel better."

"Ah, there he is," Kennedy greets, burgers in hand as the back door slams.

"Shh!" Jackson and I scold.

We quietly fix our plates. I place American cheese on the top half of my roll, KC Masterpiece on the bottom half. I choose a burger then four slices of sizzling bacon to complete the sandwich. I toss a handful of chips onto my plate then choose a barstool.

Kennedy places a bottle of water in front of each of us.

I bite into my bacon cheeseburger. I chew slowly to control my queasy stomach. The warm, salty burger with the soft melted cheese and sweet bar-b-que sauce is delicious. I unknowingly moan in pleasure.

"Easy," Jackson quietly teases. "It's just a burger, not a man."

I ignore their giggles while crunching on some chips. The food is just what our hangovers need.

I keep from moaning as I savor my next bite.

Slowly and in near silence, we eat our lunch. It's not until I finish my last chip that I realize Kennedy is eating half a burger on a bun. She passed on the chips, but knowing she ate a burger and bread makes me smile. She's come a long way since college.

"Why are you smiling?" Kennedy inquires.

I simply shake my head and start clearing the plates. I make eye contact with Jackson. He winks knowingly. It doesn't escape me that Kennedy helps clean the kitchen instead of sneaking off to the bathroom.

Jackson asks what Kennedy has planned for us today.

"I thought we could shop for clothes then groceries." Kennedy looks to me for approval.

I nod.

"Then Jackson can meet us for dinner."

"I have a better idea," Jackson chimes in. "The two of you shop. I will check on the store and get groceries. We can meet back here. Let's invite the neighbors over to meet Taylor."

Kennedy looks questioningly to me.

"I'm game," I state. "I'm going to shower. Give me half an hour."

Kennedy looks at Jackson. "You text the guys; I'll text the girls."

In the seclusion of my room, I check my phone. Seems no one has tried to reach me. I start my Random playlist. Andy Grammer fills the bathroom as I gather my items to shower. Having packed only two outfits, choosing what to wear is quick.

As I shower, I recall our conversations. I often worried Jackson tolerated me for Kennedy's sake. It seems he really does care for me. *Kennedy struck gold with him. Why can't I be so lucky?*

I'm not repelled by Jackson or good guys. My relationships seem to start off promisingly and quickly go south. I tell myself, if I care for the guy, I must be willing to love his faults. I'm blinded by the hope of true love and my soulmate so that, as the faults build, I rationalize each one instead of running. I'm a romantic. I long to find my happily ever after. I've kissed my share of frogs in search of a Prince Charming. I have a severe case of frog lips. Perhaps that's repelling my happily ever after.

After my shower, I groan, remembering what's to come. I dread shopping. I want to spend time with Kennedy, but I am not a shopper. My thoughts drift to tonight's party. I can do this. I attended parties in college. I know how to mingle, and I can carry on a conversation with a stranger. I am out of practice, but these are Kennedy's friends. I will pull up my big girl panties and enjoy this neighborhood party.

Maybe they have a single friend. A neighbor could be a single male. It might be fun to practice being normal around guys. It might be interesting to carry on a conversation. It's been too long since I could look them in the eyes and smile. I was a natural at it before John. It must be like riding a bike, right?

As Kennedy pulls from the driveway, I ask, "How many neighbors will attend tonight?"

She tells me, "We invited three couples."

Couples mean no single guys.

"You will love them all. Isaac and Madison live in the blue house." Kennedy points as she explains. "Tyler and Reagan live over there in the brick home. And James and Martha are in the stone home on the other side of ours." Kennedy turns quickly to me, then her eyes return to the road. "They all know so much about you. We've shared stories over the years."

"Do they know why I am here?" I ask nervously.

Kennedy takes advantage of a red light to take my hand. "Honey, they know we've been friends since grade school, that you've been very busy in Chicago, and that it has been two years since we've been together."

The light changes, and Kennedy concentrates on driving. "We didn't mention anything about your relationship with John ending. It's not our story to share."

I try to ignore the pity in her eyes. I realize she loves me and is only protecting me.

"So, what can I expect tonight?" I wonder.

"We are really just boring married couples. We nibble and drink, gossip and complain." Kennedy parks in a large parking lot. "This is Zona Rosa," she shares. "We will start at Dillard's. There are a lot of shops we can dart into like Chico's, Express, The Buckle, Gap, Loft, Victoria's Secret, and too many more to mention."

"Ken," I tease, "pace yourself. We don't have to do all our shopping today. I'm here all week for Pete's sake."

10

NEIGHBORS FOR DUMMIES

Taylor

My iPhone vibrates in my pocket. It's a text from Jackson.

> JACKSON
> song of the day time
>
> ME
> not fair on phone
>
> U can look up lyrics to cheat

My phone immediately rings. "Hi, Jackson," I greet.
"Song of the Day time," he states.
"Not all of the males grab a gorgeous female..." I start.
"Keep going," he prompts.
"And conceal female from everyone on earth," I continue.

"A little more," he prompts. "It's on the tip of my tongue."

I know that, when I continue, he will guess correctly. "I desire to be the one to stroll in the daylight..." I pause. When he doesn't respond, I finish, "Oh females, want to have entertainment."

"Madonna, 'Girls Just Want to Have Fun,'" Jackson professes.

"Well," I start, "you are only half right. It's not Madonna."

"Then who?" he challenges.

"Cyndi Lauper," I state proudly. "Have fun grocery shopping," I tease.

Jackson hangs up while Kennedy holds open Dillard's door to let me in.

"I was thinking shorts, capris, and shirts first," she starts, "then sandals." She looks at me for agreement.

"Ken, you know I am not a big shopper. Let's take it slow and see how much I can handle."

Two hours later, Kennedy has six bags, and I have four bags as we return to the car. Our shopping ends when I beg Kennedy to have mercy on me and take me home.

As I place my bags on the bed, it further solidifies my preference for online shopping. I am a simple girl.

Murmurs from the kitchen catch my attention.

"All three couples can attend," Jackson states. "I plan to grill chicken and pork chops with a salad, baked beans, and fresh fruit as sides."

"Did you get drinks?" Kennedy inquires.

I open the side-by-side fridge doors to see strawberries, several bottles of wine, and more ice cream. Jackson did good. Listening as I browse, I learn he purchased a variety of beers for the garage refrigerator.

Kennedy informs, "Guests will arrive in an hour."

"I need to shower." I excuse myself.

Before I escape, Kennedy grabs my shoulders and informs me,

"You will want to wear the new black halter top you purchased with khaki capris and wedges."

I inwardly cringe as Jackson smiles at me, knowing I want to wear a T-shirt and shorts with my comfortable Converse.

In my room, I hang my new wardrobe. I place my three pairs of shoes on the closet shelf. Sitting on the bed, I visualize myself in the outfit Kennedy demanded. I fall back onto the bed, feet dangling off the end. High on Kennedy's shopping adrenaline, I loved the halter top when I modeled it for her. The way her face lit up and her words of encouragement forced my purchase. I pull myself from the bed. *Can I really wear it? Skin. Too. Much. Skin.* I liked the way it felt trying on the black halter. I felt free. Liberated. It covers more than a swimsuit, as much as my college cheer uniform, and it's much more fabric than the bikini I packed for this trip.

A turmoil of emotions, I tug open the bedside drawer. I grab the first item I see and flee to the bathroom.

Hot water and steam engulf me. My hands caress my shoulders and arms with the slick bar of soap. I slide my hands from my breasts to my abdomen then south. The soap bubbles slicken my skin. When my hands travel over my upper thighs, causing my nipples to harden, a moan escapes my lips. I release my grasp on the bar of soap as I slide my hand to my center. My thighs spread apart. As my right hand caresses my folds, my left braces on the tile wall. I throw my head back as I circle my clit. The tiniest movements reap big sensations. My excitement builds quickly. I pluck my vibrator from the ledge, and slowly, I slide its length into me. I press the power button three times quickly. A low, guttural moan escapes as I revel in the sensations. Hot water bombards then caresses my skin. Droplets flow with gravity to the apex of my thighs then down to the tile floor. My core contracts into a tightly wound coil waiting to explode. I pinch my puckered nipples, and a moan resonates in the shower stall. I lean back against the cold tile. The butterfly extension teases my clit as the vibrations stimulate my core. I close my eyes tightly as I climb higher and higher.

"Yes!" I exclaim. "Yes! Oh, god, yes!"

My head thrashes from side-to-side, water soaks my body, and my inner walls contract rhythmically. My legs buckle, and I slide down the tile to the floor. I stare as the water plummets to the drain, not seeing.

Moments pass before I float back down from ecstasy. I rescue the bar of soap from the drain. Slowly and shakily, I stand to finish lathering my body and rinse off. As I towel-dry myself, I relish the limpness of my muscles and my tranquil mind. I smile, knowing I needed this release.

"You never disappoint," I inform my pale yellow butterfly vibrator. I place it on the vanity as I proceed to prepare for the party.

I slip on a pair of beige panties before I step, one leg at a time, into my new capris. I reluctantly remove the tags from my black halter top. I *can do this. I can do this,* I recite to myself as I slip it over my shoulders. Looking in the mirror, I like what I see. A strong, pretty woman smiles back at me. I've missed her.

As I apply light makeup and style my hair into loose curls, my confidence begins to fade. Before entering the family room, I slip on a red, three-quarter length sleeve cardigan and opt for my red wedges. I wear my cardigan as a warm blanket, concealing me from the strangers I'm about to meet.

I find Jackson on the deck, chicken and chops sizzling in front of him as I hand him a cold Bud Light.

"Sit for a minute." Jackson glances my way.

I slip onto the patio chair to his left. The slight summer breeze blows my hair.

"How are your finances?" I nearly choke on my beer at his question. "I'm not being nosey. Teacher's salaries aren't much, and Chicago is an expensive city," he explains.

My brain quickly processes my answer. He knows I was recruited by a politician from the inner-city. He knows the package included a small apartment. I inform, "I still pay no rent, and I'm within walking distance of work and stores."

"Okay, but with John not holding down a steady job, how'd you pay expenses? Did he use everything you made?" Jackson resumes his role as the big brother I longed for.

"John didn't know my exact take-home pay. I put a good chunk into a savings account every month without him knowing. I paid utilities and groceries. I made him work enough to cover his drinking and gym expenses." I flash a slight smile at my savviness. "I handed him $500 cash the last day I saw him."

"So," Jackson is not yet convinced, "you have a little saved in case you need it?"

Details. Jackson worries until he knows all the facts. "I saved $500 per month for two years. I worked for two years, and that earned me a $20,000 bonus from the senator. I post my lessons on the *Teachers Pay Teachers* website and earn quite a bit from that, too," I explain.

Jackson relaxes into his chair as he finishes his beer. My big brother is proud. He will not believe the amount I earn online. When he hears about my Mustang, I will have to divulge more financial details to him. For now, I keep it to myself and finish my beer.

I return to the kitchen to remove the plastic then organize the paper plates, utensils, and cups at the end of the island.

Noting I'm alone in the kitchen, I use the step ladder to access the small doors above the refrigerator. I gulp two long pulls from a new bottle of Jim Beam. I sigh as the burn slowly slides down to my belly.

"Easy there," Jackson chides, startling me on my perch. The step ladder shakes as I fight to regain my balance. Sure in my footing, I raise spirit fingers into the air, chanting, "Go, Tigers!"

Jackson shakes his head as he rescues the bottle of Jim from my clutches. His hands secure my waist as I descend the four steps to the safety of the kitchen floor in my wedges.

"Nervous?" Jackson asks knowingly.

I busy myself with rinsing and chopping the lettuce. "So, only three neighborhood couples?" I ask nonchalantly.

He places his left hand in the small of my back as he reaches for the Misty's All-Purpose Seasoning in front of me. "Three couples. Very casual. You will fit right in."

A long sigh escapes my lips as I complete the salad-making task.

"Relax," Jackson encourages. "Kennedy and I will introduce you to everyone, we will eat, and we won't leave you alone."

I button the top button on my cardigan as Kennedy enters, and Jackson returns to the grill on the deck. I busy myself with rinsing fruit before placing it in a colander. Kennedy leans across the island, forearms extended on the granite. I dry my hands and lean towards her.

"Quickly give me the 'Neighbors for Dummies' run down for tonight," I plead.

"Oh, my god," she drawls. "I knew you would overthink this." She plops a wet strawberry into her mouth. "Isaac is a construction guy. His wife, Madison, is a partner in a large advertising firm downtown. Tyler's a doctor; his wife Reagan is a nurse. James runs a restaurant, and Martha stays home."

"Gee, thanks. Now I am ready," I reply with a smile, feeling better about tonight.

11

NEVER HAVE I EVER

Taylor

"Turn on some music," Kennedy prompts.

I link my iPhone to the Bluetooth speaker in the living room. I scroll through my playlists: Running, Reading, Driving, School, Lite, Heavy, 80s, and Random. I select the Random playlist. *Stitches* by Shawn Mendes fills the room. I adjust the volume, so it won't interfere with conversations this evening. Back at the kitchen island, I grab a tumbler and pour two fingers of Jim Beam to calm my nerves. As I finish my drink, I hear Jackson greet guests on the deck.

"Showtime," Kennedy sings as she opens the doors for the guests.

Jackson enters, followed by a slender red-head and a tall, tan, blonde man. He motions to the couple. "This is Red and Isaac." Jackson extends his arm toward me. "And this is Taylor."

The redhead extends her right hand. Her grip is firm and succinct. "I'm Madison. Jackson likes to push my buttons by calling me Red." Her eyes move from Jackson back to mine. "Nice to finally meet you."

"I thought she'd be taller and..." Isaac murmurs to Jackson as his hands signal a buxom bosom in front of him.

"Typical construction Neanderthal," I state, flying two birds in his direction. To escape the asshole, I quickly busy myself asking Madison for her drink preference. Then I excuse myself to my room. I sip some more bourbon before extracting myself from the much too warm red cardigan. The halter top accentuates my chest, making me look like a B-cup. Thought I'd be bigger. From a swift kick to his crotch, the swelling could make him bigger, too. I erase his comment from my mind. He is Madison's problem, not mine. I add 'avoid Isaac' to my mental list for the night before returning to the kitchen. I realize everyone has arrived. Little ones scamper between adult legs, food covers every available surface, and several conversations are occurring simultaneously.

A shoulder bumps into mine. "You must be Taylor." A deep male voice announces. "This is my wife, Martha. I'm James, and somewhere are four little ones."

I choke on my beer. *Four kids? They have four kids? They are our age and already have four kids.*

"Breathe," Jackson prompts as he delivers chicken and chops from the grill. "James, how did you stupefy our dear Taylor so quickly?"

"Dude," James teases. "I just introduced mi familia."

Martha smiles at me knowingly. "It's the four kids, isn't it?" She leans into her husband's chest. "Believe me, there are times the kids scare me, too."

On cue, Kennedy hands a baby girl to Martha, announcing she doesn't smell so good in the diaper vicinity.

"This one is Angelina," Martha informs, walking toward the sofa with diaper bag in hand. "What airport did you fly from? My little brother is a bartender at O'Hare."

I nearly choke on my saliva. *What are the chances?*

"What was the name of the hot bartender you met yesterday?" Kennedy asks, and I nearly die.

Did she have to say 'hot'?

"Jorge is hot," Martha states over her shoulder as she changes the dirty diaper.

"I think I met your brother," I state, my voice cracking a bit.

"Oh, my gosh!" She grins widely, picking up her daughter. "You met him? What was he doing? I mean, I know he was tending bar, but..."

"He gave Taylor his phone number," Kennedy slips in before returning to the kitchen.

I close my eyes, willing the floor to swallow me whole.

"No way!" Martha squeals. "He's been sulking over his wife leaving him. If he gave you his number, then he must be moving on. This is huge. You have to call him. You plan to call him, right?"

Wow! Martha talks fast.

"He caught me removing my engagement ring, and we shared horror stories. He's still wearing his ring. I think he still loves her. We just connected over our stories and talked. That's all." I hope my explanation derails her hopes for the two of us to hook up.

Over this topic of conversation, I return to the kitchen.

As Jackson strides to the counter, I follow in his wake. "What can I do to help?"

"You are the guest of honor." Jackson whispers. He pushes me toward a barstool and prompts me to sit. "The food is ready. Let's eat." He announces loudly.

With no instruction, the guests grab plates and form a buffet line. I patiently wait on my barstool as others float around the kitchen. Gradually, bodies wander toward seats. With the kitchen less crowded, I rise, join the line, and fix my plate. Back on my barstool, I busy myself eating. A glass of dark liquid slides towards my plate. I mutter my thanks to Jackson. He nods as he spoons baked beans toward his mouth.

"So," I begin, "after we eat?"

Jackson scans the room before leaning closer. "We drink, we eat more, we drink more. It's a vicious cycle." He grins. "You can handle this." His arm encases my shoulders. "It's just a party with friends."

Reagan asks Kennedy what we are listening to. Kennedy explains I chose the music. She shares I worked as a DJ in high school and college. I feel all eyes on me.

"I can choose a different playlist," I suggest, pulling my cellphone from my pocket.

A collective 'no' emits from the group. Reagan admits she loves the variety of rock and pop. James likes it contains some 80s and 90s music.

Jackson places his arm around my shoulders. "She has always had eclectic taste. I am just glad she didn't choose a playlist with her screamo bands in it."

"Screamo?" Madison inquires.

My backbone stiffens, and I shake off Jackson's arm before flying the bird near his face. "It's not screamo," I explain entering the living room where most of the group are eating. "I enjoy Five Finger Death Punch, Nine Inch Nails, Slipknot, Seether, Godsmack, Marilyn Manson, and Disturbed." As I scan the room, I find blank stares and fake smiles. "Ever heard of Iron Maiden? Ozzy Osbourne? Or Metallica?" I ask. Now I see recognition in their eyes and nods of agreement. "These are the modern versions of those bands."

"Eclectic," Jackson states. "Told you."

Reagan speaks up for the group. "We like this playlist."

She is begging me not to change it.

I resume my seat at the island to finish eating.

An hour later, with drinks in hand, everyone makes their way to the living room. Martha has two drinks in hand, planning to play catch up as the babysitter just escorted her kids back to their home for the night.

"So back in college," Kennedy starts, "Taylor was the master of all party games."

"Hey!" I chide. "I didn't win all the games."

Kennedy giggles, "I meant she attended many parties and knew all the fun drinking games." Her eyes rest on me. "I think you should choose a game for us to play."

My jaw drops. I know exactly two people in this room. *How do I know what everyone likes, how much they drink, or if they like to have fun? One couple already has four kids-how often could they party?*

Sensing my anxiety, James adds, "Do you know a game where we can ask questions to get to know each other?"

I straighten my back, sigh, then announce, "The game is called, 'I've never'." Over the women's excited clapping, I explain, "I'll start with a few examples before we rotate around the group." I signal around the circle clockwise. "If you have done what I prompt, you drink. If not, you watch." I assess their understanding by meeting their gazes. "As the prompter, I can use things I have or haven't done. I can use intimate details I know about others to force them to drink." I raise my eyebrows to Jackson and Kennedy. "Let's practice before I let everyone have a turn."

"I've never driven a stick shift." I drink and watch as no one else drinks. "Okay, raise your hand if you have driven a stick." Half the group raises hands. "So, you should drink." They do. "The only ones who don't drink are the ones that have never done the item." A collective 'oh,' escapes the group.

"Oh, I forgot, if you are the only one that ever drinks, then you must drain your current drink and grab another one." I am met with wide-eyes from the ladies and approving smiles from the guys.

"Next one, I've never slept with someone in this room." I smile, watching as everyone but Reagan and myself drink.

Tyler asks Reagan why she didn't drink. She responds, "Because I have slept with you."

"So, you drink if you have," Tyler explains. "You don't drink if you haven't."

Madison teases, "I can't be the only one here that was curious to see if Taylor drank or not."

I look at Kennedy, then Jackson. Both smile at the comment.

A lightbulb above James's head blinks on. "So, you chose that one knowing everyone but you would drink?"

I nod. "The object of the game is to get to know each other better and to get others drunk." Scanning the group, I notice they all have more to drink. "Last one, then we'll start taking turns around the room."

"Girls, only this time. I've never kissed another girl." I take a pull of my beer as I notice Kennedy is the only other girl to drink. Jaws drop to the floor. Madison, Reagan, and Martha look to Kennedy for details. I realize I forgot to tell them another detail of the game. "If you drink, you don't have to explain. Drinking and admitting is all that is required. But feel free to share if you want to."

"Wait!" Isaac exclaims. "Did you two make out with each other?" He points to Kennedy and me.

Kennedy locks her lips and throws away the imaginary key. I just shrug.

I motion to Jackson, seated on my left. "Your turn."

Nudging me, he states, "You wasted no time making things more interesting." He addresses the group. "I've never been a college cheerleader."

"Touché," I commend Jackson and take a drink of my beer. "No other collegiate cheerleaders?" I question before chugging my beer. Jackson hands me another Bud Light, then nudges Kennedy on his left.

"I've never done a keg-stand." Kennedy cannot hide her giggles.

"Ganging up on me?" I accuse Kennedy before taking a drink. I am relieved Isaac and James also drink.

As the game continues around the room, on James's turn, James, Martha, Tyler, and I drink for having sex in a public place. Martha gets Madison and Isaac to drink for having sex in a parents' shower. Everyone drinks when Madison claims to never had fantasies of a threesome. I chugged the rest of my beer when Isaac mentions being in an actual threesome. I just shrug when asked for details. James and Martha drink for having sex in his office at the restaurant. Tyler, Jackson, James, Isaac, and I drink for wanting to have a threesome with someone in this room.

As I hand everyone another drink, the guys defend themselves.

"Ladies, ladies," I beckon, "they just admitted they would... not that they did. Besides, all four of you are gorgeous, so take it as a compliment."

Alcohol causes Reagan to verbally scold all of us for drinking on that one before I move the game along. "I've never," I begin, "faked an orgasm." As Kennedy, Madison, Reagan, and I sip, I notice Isaac also drinks.

"Dude!" James scolds. "You've faked an orgasm? Why?"

"No, god, no!" He insists he was just thirsty, so he took a drink.

"Take a sip after each round, not during," I inform the group after the laughter dies down.

The game continues until Kennedy trips on her way to the bathroom.

"Game over," Jackson states. He non-verbally asks my permission to use my restroom.

As I nod my head yes to Jackson, I inform the group, "The winner is the least drunk at the end of the game, so I think Jackson is the winner."

Conversation moves onto Jackson, while I wander to the kitchen to nibble on some desserts.

12

HIDE AND FESTER

Jackson

"Don't," I warn James.
"You will not believe what I saw in there." James points toward Taylor's room.

"James," I plead. "Dude, let's get you home. You've had way too much to drink." I escort him to his wife, trying to change the subject. "Remember last year when you fell off the porch and broke your leg? We don't need a repeat of that."

Martha says goodbye to everyone and joins us on our walk to their home as fireworks light the sky in all directions. I help James into bed, strip him to his boxers, and place water nearby. Martha checks on the kids and pays the babysitter.

"Is there anything else I can help you with, Martha?" I inquire.

"You've done enough. More than he deserves," Martha states. "He will be up vomiting all night and have a killer hangover tomorrow." She sighs. "I will be up at dawn with the kids while he attempts to sleep it off."

I hug her. "Goodnight then." I open the back door to leave but turn to her. "Call or bring the kids over in the morning. We could all hang out while he sleeps."

Smiling, Martha nods.

On my short walk home, I contemplate the embarrassing moment Taylor unknowingly, narrowly avoided. As I used her restroom, I was embarrassed to find she left her vibrator on the vanity. When James exited her room, I knew he had seen the same. He wanted to tell everyone what he saw, and I couldn't allow that. I couldn't let him embarrass her in front of all our friends. I'll discretely suggest she keep them put away.

I enter through the kitchen door, finding all the guests left. Kennedy shuts the front door, turning the deadbolt. Taylor straightens up in the kitchen. Kennedy joins us in the kitchen, suggesting we save the mess for the morning.

"So," I begin, turning toward Taylor. "You let me use your restroom tonight." I pause as Taylor nods in agreement. With a sigh, I continue, "You left a personal item out on the vanity."

Taylor's eyes dart to mine knowingly. Kennedy looks from me to Taylor and back for an explanation.

"James must have seen me exit. I caught him as he came from your bedroom." Alarm is clear on her face. "He is too drunk to remember it by tomorrow."

"That's what he wanted to tell everyone when he came out, isn't it?" Kennedy asks. Turning to Taylor, she questions, "what did you leave out?"

"Only the biggest vibrator I have ever seen!" I exclaim as I throw my arms wide, signaling an exaggerated length.

Kennedy laughs. "And just how many vibrators have you seen?"

Pointing to Taylor, I state, "because of her, two. The one she gave you for your twenty-first birthday and hers tonight."

"Oh, my god," Taylor starts. "So, I left something on my vanity. It's not like it is illegal." Taylor points at me. "It's not like I used it in front of anyone." She points at Kennedy. "If you would ever use the one I bought you, you'd know why it is necessary and not so taboo." She ties the top of the overflowing trash bag then concludes, "It's no big deal."

While Kennedy and I shake our heads, the three of us head to bed.

He wraps my hair around his palm, tugging down until I scream in pain. Before I can escape, he bends me over the back of the sofa, pinning me down with his entire body. I beg John to let me go. I plead with him to calm down. I feel the moisture in his hot breaths on my neck. He whispers his venomous threat, with his lips grazing my ear. "You fucked him, you filthy whore. You spread your legs to show him the cunt you are, didn't you? You've lied to me for months, but now I know. Once a slut, always a slut."

His words cut through my heart. I need to escape. He's too angry. He's hurting my scalp as he fists my hair. His hand on my throat grasps tighter and tighter. Through my tears, I attempt to reason with him. I beg him to let me look him in the eyes. I'm innocent. I need him to see me to understand the truth.

"I heard him bragging to Mica. I heard in great detail how you begged to suck his cock. He said you were a bitch in heat. I've seen the way the two of you look at each other. You think I'm so stupid that you can fuck my best friend, and I not find out? I've known for months." John jerks upright as his phone rings in his back pocket.

This is my chance. I stomp on his right foot as I throw my elbows back into his torso. I turn to run. Two hands squeeze my throat. It's too hard. I can't breathe. I open my mouth to scream. Nothing escapes.

"Taylor!" I'm blinded by a sudden bright light. I swat at the hands on my shoulders and on my arms.

Wait. Four. There are four hands on me.

"Open your eyes. Taylor, it's a dream. Open your eyes, now!" Jackson demands.

I'm in their guest room.
I am safe.
John is not here.
I'm drenched.
It seemed so real.

My fear that John might hurt me still torments me. His words hurt me. His insults, unfounded accusations, and jealousy keep me in a constant state of fear. Although he was never physical, his words hurt as much. Verbal scars hide and fester. They can't be erased. They repeat inside my mind as I look in a mirror, select an outfit, smile at a stranger, or speak to a waiter. John's voice haunts me daily.

Kennedy swipes my hair from my face as she rocks me back and forth. She wants me to tell her about my nightmare. She wants to know why I screamed.

I can't tell them the details. I can't share my fears. *They'll never understand this. They'll never believe he didn't get physical.*

Jackson hands me a glass of water. "Stop prodding," he scolds his wife, as he climbs in bed on my other side. "It's okay. Everything is okay," he whispers as four arms hold me tight.

I'm *too hot.* I try to uncover. I hesitantly open one eye. Kennedy cuddles my left side. Slowly turning my head as I open both eyes, I see Jackson on my right. My head pounds as I take in my surroundings. We're in the guest room.

Blinking, I recall the nightmare, and they came to comfort me. I must have fallen asleep. Being the true friends they are, they stayed with me. I embrace their closeness as I fall back into slumber.

13

NO STRINGS ATTACHED, NO COMPLICATIONS

Taylor

On the Fourth of July, sunlight warms my face, awakening me from my dreams. I roll to my left, noticing a note on my nightstand. Sitting up, I unfold the note.

Had to run to the YMCA until noon. Be ready. We are going out for lunch and shopping all afternoon.

Love,
Kennedy

I glance at my phone on the charger. It's already ten. Slipping from bed, I shuffle to the kitchen. I grab a diet cola and a protein bar for breakfast. Mentally calculate the time I need to shower and be ready by noon for Kennedy, and I climb back into bed while I eat my bar. I scroll through social media and a few emails. My phone vibrates as a new text alert sounds.

> **JORGE**
> r u up?

> **ME**
> am now

> **JORGE**
> sorry go back 2 sleep

> **ME**
> JK

> **JORGE**
> so u were up
> can I call?

I type Y-e-s, then decide to delete it. I scroll through my contacts and FaceTime his phone.

Jorge's face lights up my screen. He is lying on a pillow, his hair a disheveled disaster. "Good morning," he greets with a raspy voice.

"What's up?" I ask.

"Just woke up," Jorge states the obvious. "I can't stop smiling, thinking about you flying back tomorrow. So, I thought I would call you." His dimples frame his quirky smile.

"Jackson and Kennedy have asked me to stay another week," I tease without cracking up.

His smile rapidly disappears, and his eyes close tight. When he realizes I can see him, he quickly recovers.

I can't keep up the ruse. "I am just kidding. Still flying out tomorrow." I can see the relief immediately.

"Any big plans for your last day?" he asks.

I tell him about the note Kennedy left.

"I will be working when you arrive at O'Hare," he hints.

"I plan to stop by to say hi," I tell him.

"That's what I wanted to hear," he confirms. "I better let you get up before Kennedy comes home." He doesn't want to hang up.

I don't either, but how little we know of each other limits our conversation.

Disconnecting, I rest my phone on the side table. I stretch my body out on the bed in a long slow stretch, accompanied by a groan. *Why do some stretches feel so good?* I close my eyes to flashes of Jorge. *He really wants to see me tomorrow, and I really want to see him. He will be at work, so it will be safe enough. Just a quick pop in, maybe a drink or two, then he'll go back to work, and I go on my way. No strings attached, no complications.*

But I could really use his strings. I could really use his dark eyes looking into mine, his long fingers caressing my skin, and his hard muscles pinning me to the wall. Pinning me to the bed.

My hands caress my neck down to my collarbone, then I lightly sweep toward my breastbone. Each hand moves to cupping a breast. I knead them in my palms before my index fingers lightly circle the areolas. After a few rotations, I pinch my nipples. My eyes close, and I imagine Jorge above me. Jorge is working my nipples, my breasts, and he trails light kisses behind my ear then down my neck. One hand slides lower to my navel, then lower still. At my core, he explores my folds. My head writhes, and my body wants. He finds the pinpoint of all my pleasure. His fingers flick the tiny nub. My body squirms as he works all my nerve endings.

Just when I start to fall over the edge, Jorge plunges himself inside me. The fullness, the strength, the motion is too much. I cry out as the orgasm ignites my every cell. Flashes of lightning spark behind my eyelids, and every muscle tightens. I feel as though a million needles puncture my skin at once. The waves of the orgasm flow, my muscles relax, my eyes slowly open, and I pull the vibrator from my core. I lie motionless. I am limp, relaxed, and sated.

I turn my head to the side, finding the clock reads eleven-fifteen. I had better get out of bed and dressed before Kennedy comes barging into my room. I don't move. I close my eyes and savor the sensation of complete relaxation. My cellphone buzzes signaling a text. I slowly rise to a sitting position on the edge of the bed as I reach for it.

KENNEDY
on way be there in 20

I reluctantly stand, gather my vibrator, and enter the bathroom. I rinse it off before spraying it with my toy cleaner. I rinse it once more and set it on the vanity to dry. After a quick shower, I'm almost ready when I hear Kennedy enter from the garage.

Kennedy plops on the foot of the bed to watch as I place the finishing touches on my hair and makeup.

"What's the plan?" I ask.

"We'll head to the Country Club Plaza for lunch and perhaps shopping," she explains.

Not liking her last words, I crinkle my nose at her in the mirror.

She giggles before explaining, "It's a beautiful day for a walk, and the plaza has lots of shops to browse in. I know we can't afford most of the shops, but it's fun to see what they have inside."

I walk towards her with a ta-da motion. She hops up, takes my left hand, and leads me off on our girls' day adventure.

On the drive to the Plaza, Kennedy insisted I have barbecue before I leave. It took little to convince me. We eat lunch at Fiorella's Jack Stack. Kennedy orders a salad, while I dive into a burnt ends platter. Our conversation is light, although I sense Kennedy wants to tell me something. I see a slight hesitation now and then before she starts a new topic of discussion.

"This trip really agrees with you. You were relaxed and glowing when I arrived home today," Kennedy states.

I nearly choke on my food. Sputtering, I gulp some water.

"What?" Kennedy prods. "You are blushing." She taps her red-painted index finger on her cheek.

"You sure you want to know?" When Kennedy nods affirmative, I explain, "I had a FaceTime call with Jorge this morning." Her face lights up as I continue. "I serviced myself after the call."

It takes a minute for Kennedy to process my words. When she understands, she covers her face with both hands and chants, "Oh, my god," over and over.

"Ken," I interrupt. "I am not masturbating right now so you can uncover your eyes." In my periphery, I notice a man at the table adjacent to ours lean a bit closer. Focusing all my attention on Kennedy, I inform her, "You could use a few good orgasms to decompress." As her eyes widen even more and her jaw touches the floor, I explain, "You are stressed, coiled tight from head-to-toe." I motion up and down with my hand. "What could be going on at The YMCA to stress you out this much?"

Kennedy shakes her head.

"Spill it," I order.

Kennedy's eyebrows shoot skyward as she freezes.

"I can tell you want to. It's just me, Ken. You can tell me anything."

"Jackson and I are starting a family," she blurts. After my initial squeal of excitement, she informs me, "We've tried for over a year. I've visited a fertility specialist, and we're weighing other options like adoption or foster care."

My heart breaks, as I know this is difficult for her. Children are her life. She always works with kids. The two of them will be great parents.

"What did the fertility doctor say that has you looking at adoption?" I ask.

"They tested Jackson's sperm, and it's good to go," she sighs before continuing. "They're still running extensive tests on me."

I know her body endured a lot with her eating disorders. She looks older than she is, and she requires extensive dental work as the enamel was damaged with all the acid and bile from vomiting. I'm heartbroken that her disorder will make pregnancy difficult. She's only slightly below her target weight now, but I don't know how she would do putting on twenty pounds during pregnancy.

I need carbs. I suddenly crave a gourmet cupcake from the shop we saw while walking here. My friends are hurting, thus I am hurting. I've always been an emotional eater. I tamp down my craving. I can't suggest stopping at Cupcake À la mode. Kennedy eats better now, but cake and icing are still out. Perhaps if we walk, I can distract myself from the pain and fear in my gut.

"Ready to shop?" I ask Kennedy after we pay the bill.

She smiles at me knowingly; I can't sneak this by her. She knows I'm upset and only want to shop to make her feel better. We window shop for an hour, before I pull her in Rally House, where I purchase Royals gear for Jackson and her, Cardinals gear for me, and a large Busch Stadium print for my wall.

Walking again, I regret the large purchases as I carry them in and out of stores. When I spot a Topsy's Popcorn Shoppe, I nearly squeal with glee. *That will do. I can eat sweets, and Kennedy can nibble lightly, too.*

"Let's buy popcorn and head home," I suggest, raising one bag-filled hand towards the popcorn shop.

We ride home in quiet contemplation. Kennedy's desire to start a family weighs heavily on her, I can tell. I'm not convinced there isn't more to the story. *I wonder if they told her she can't have children. That might lead her to look at foster care and adoption.* My heart is heavy. I grab another handful of popcorn and gaze out the window as the city flashes by.

Kennedy encourages, "Save some popcorn for later. Jackson is fixing pasta for dinner tonight."

I smile at the mention of heavy carbs.

14

A FAVOR OF EPIC PROPORTIONS

Jackson

"There are my girls," Jackson greets, turning from the stovetop, as we enter from the garage weighed down with our purchases. His eyebrows raise at the sight of our large shopping bags. "What is all that?" He motions towards the bags.

"Taylor made all the purchases," Kennedy informs him.

We flop the bags on my bed. I pull out the shirt and hat I bought for Jackson, before I hand the bag with the other Royals gear to Kennedy. He's happy with his loot and assures me it is the correct size.

"What do the other bags contain?" he asks.

I explain my Cardinals purchases, and he shakes his head.

"How can you still be a Cardinals fan?" He teases. "You grew up in Royals land and now live in Cubs territory." At my shrug, he continues, "Stubbornness, that's how."

I set the table while Kennedy makes a salad, and Jackson opens a bottle of wine, bringing me a glass. As I savor my first sip, I witness Kennedy with wine, too.

"The pasta will be ready in ten minutes," Jackson informs, as he checks on the bread in the oven.

I lean against the island as I sip my wine. Jackson hugs his wife as she continues to sip. He takes the wine glass from her grasp to take a large drink. I smile at the intimate gesture, wondering if someday I might have someone special to share my wine with.

Jackson interrupts my thoughts, declaring, "The pasta and bread are ready."

Moving to the table, we fill our plates. I opt for no salad as the pasta and bread are what I really desire. Jackson fills our three wine glasses, then places the nearly empty bottle on the table beside me. As Kennedy nibbles on her salad, I dive into my mountain of pasta.

"Pace yourself," Jackson urges, after a moan of delight escapes my mouth.

"This is so good," I mutter with my mouth full. I dab my garlic bread in the red sauce before taking a bite. I close my eyes as the rich flavor crosses my taste buds.

While we eat, there is little conversation. Jackson immediately refills each wine glass when needed and produces a new bottle of wine as we empty the first.

"You must share this sauce recipe with me," I declare between forkfuls.

"I doubt you'll be able to recreate it with your limited cooking ability," Jackson says, and my friends chortle.

I continue to eat, ignoring their laughter at my expense.

"He could make a batch of sauce and freeze it for me to use when I am in the mood for pasta," Kennedy suggests.

"You might warm it up without fire trucks being called to assist," Jackson comments.

I respond with my middle finger in the air as I sip from my wine.

"I can't believe you finished that pasta plate," Kennedy scoffs.

"I ate too much," I groan. "My stomach is too full."

Warm and comforting, this meal is exactly what I needed, and the multiple glasses of wine are the icing on the cake. As Kennedy and I clear the table, Jackson fills our glasses, moving the bottle with them into the living room for us. I excuse myself to my room to switch into my comfy pajamas, needing the elastic waistband on my full stomach.

Returning, I choose the end of the sofa, curl my legs up under me, and savor a sip of wine. As I stare unseeing around the room, my eyes focus on the wine bottle. It's full. It's the third bottle of wine Jackson opened tonight. I feel warm and full, not tipsy, because the pasta and bread absorbed most of my alcohol. I grab the remote, choose a rom-com to watch, then pull a pillow into my lap.

Jackson and Kennedy return in PJs. He acts disgusted at my choice of movie, but I know he enjoys them as much as we do. As usual, Kennedy chooses the other corner of the sofa and Jackson sits in front of us on the floor. I flash back to the intervention a few nights ago. I finish my glass of wine and pour another. *This is all too familiar.*

We watch in silence for a bit, then conversation flows again. We discuss my plans for the rest of the summer. I suggest maybe I should plan another trip to KC again before schools starts in the fall, and Jackson and Kennedy love the idea. I also invite Kennedy up for a girls' weekend in Chicago.

Jackson challenges my ability to earn good money online, so I whip out my MacBook. I open the *Teachers Pay Teachers* website. My fingers fly over the keys as I log into my account. I scroll through my hundreds of lessons, printables, bulletin boards, and computer-based lessons. I point out some prices are free, ninety-nine cents, and others are twenty-five dollars. Then, I use a search engine to find the article about an educator that made over $100,000 in a year.

"So, you have more than $30,000 in your savings?" Jackson asks, computing my income from what I've shared.

Shaking my head, no, I share, "I went on a shopping spree after John left." I see the fear in his widening eyes, so I hurry to explain, "I only purchased one item on my spree. I paid cash for a car."

Jackson seems glad I bought something responsible.

"It's a Mustang," I proudly state. "It was love at first sight. I couldn't take my eyes off the black convertible." As Jackson shakes his head, concern returning to his face, I continue. "I still have over $25,000 in savings." Boasting, I state, "I'm good at creating lessons that others want."

"You should consider teaching in Missouri. You'd be closer to the two of us, and we could be together more," Kennedy mentions.

"Besides, I worry about you in Chicago alone," Jackson states.

"I live in a secure apartment, and I'm cautious as I walk around the city. I'm a grown woman, for Pete's sake," I remind them.

I've noticed my friends glancing often at each other this evening. *Something's up.* I mute the television as I turn to face my best friends. Their eyes search my face for clues. *Clues to what I don't yet know, but I am going to find out right now.*

"Twice in one day?" I question. "Let me have it. My belly is full, I'm feeling the wine now. I'm as ready for this bomb as I can be."

Kennedy looks to Jackson pleadingly. He grasps her left hand, spinning the wedding ring as he sighs. "You're good," he states. "But it's not twice in one day. It's the same conversation."

Kennedy nods in agreement.

"There's more to the wanting a baby?" I ask.

Kennedy held back at lunch. *What couldn't she tell me?*

"Kennedy can't carry a baby herself." Jackson kisses her cheek before continuing. "We've considered foster care and adopting, but with Kennedy's eating disorder and her shoplifting record, we aren't on the top of anyone's list."

I gasp. I had thought about her health. I hadn't thought about the criminal record she has from shoplifting in college. Although it was petty thefts of laxatives, diuretics, etc. it remains on her record. I look at my friends.

"It seems our only option is surrogacy," Kennedy explains. "We are hoping if we explain my long road through the eating disorder to my current status..." her voice breaks as tears spill onto her cheeks.

Jackson continues for her, "We have reached out to a few local agencies. We've written what I believe is a compelling essay explaining our battles with eating disorders and our current situation." He pauses to kiss Kennedy's hand. "So now it's a waiting game."

"Waiting for what?" I inquire.

"Waiting for a surrogate to choose to meet us, and hopefully, carry our baby," Jackson answers.

I grasp the stem of my wine glass tighter and tighter. "I could do it," I blurt.

Jackson back pedals while Kennedy's hand covers her mouth with a giggle, more tears leap to her cheeks.

"Let me do it. I could carry the baby for you. You know me, I know you. You'd trust me, right?" I look at them for confirmation.

"Wait," Jackson rises from the floor to pace in front of the fireplace. "We were going to discuss this with you tonight. We planned to ask if you might be a surrogate for us."

Kennedy finds her voice again. "When you broke up with John, I had the idea to ask you." She scoots closer to me on the sofa, grabbing my hands. "I approached Jackson two weeks ago. We talked about it a lot. Jackson bought your ticket and here we are."

So, they didn't invite me here to get me over John. I wasn't their poor, broken-hearted, perpetually single friend.

They wanted to spend time with me and ask for a favor.

A monumental favor.

A favor of epic proportions.

"I'll do it," I state more firmly this time. "If it works out, I could be knocked up by October and deliver next summer. I wouldn't have to miss school." I stand and walk toward Jackson. "You'll let me do this for you, right? The two of you have been so good to me. I want to help you with this." I cannot disguise my excitement.

"You don't owe us anything," Jackson demands. "We don't want you to feel guilted into it. This is a big decision. You need to take more time and think about it." He grabs my hands. "Your body will change. You will have to watch what you can or can't eat and drink. You'll look like a pregnant single lady. Society might not look fondly on that. What would you tell your boss, your students?" He places his hands on my shoulders, focusing on my eyes. "You need to take more time to think this over."

"All the time in the world will not change my decision," I assure them. "I'll still want to be your surrogate." I smile resolutely at both of them.

"Take a week before giving your final decision," Jackson implores. "Go home tomorrow, spend some time looking around Chicago, think of your everyday life, realize all the changes that will occur if you go through with this, do some research on surrogacy and pregnancy, then give us your answer."

"One week," I agree. "I will FaceTime you next week to discuss the details."

Kennedy hugs me excitedly, and Jackson joins us.

I'll take a week, but my answer will not change.
This I can do for them.
I will give my best friends the gift of a child.
I will be their surrogate.

PART II
THE DEED

15

WE HAVE A WINNER

Taylor

On Friday, with the closing of the Mustang trunk, my time in Chicago ends. I cram all that I treasure tightly inside. My new life and new opportunities lie at the end of this road trip. My heart beats excitedly as I turn the key; the engine roars to life. I unlatch two locks then press the button allowing the top to open. Sunlight warms my face as the top folds neatly in back. The old-school sounds of Train's, Play That Song escape the speakers.

As the song ends, I fasten my seatbelt before connecting my iPhone to the auxiliary cable. I scroll through my playlists, selecting 'Road Trip'. Aerosmith tickles my ears as I pull from my assigned spot in the lot. Excitement courses through my veins as the over eight hours of highway, traffic, and tunes lie in front of me.

I plotted my route yesterday, choosing to stop in The Quad Cities and Des Moines along my way. My goal is two stops for restroom, gas, and food, allowing me to reach my destination by dinner. Jackson and Kennedy do not know I'm driving down. They expect a call from me tonight. I'm giddy. With Martha's help, this will be a dinner they will never forget.

I wave goodbye at the edge of Chicago and drive towards my new life. Well, at least for a year. After that, I'm not sure where I'll be, but I'm not worried. I am up for this adventure. I look forward to making changes. I desire to better myself. I plan to use this time to focus on me, for soul-searching, and working through my relationship issues. It's a win-win situation. For the next year, I plan to help myself while helping my friends. They chose the right woman for this gigantic favor. I just hope I don't find they have changed their mind upon my arrival. As I navigate toward Kansas City, I leave behind a small apartment and a middle school social studies position I love. I lose myself to my music and the road in front of me.

With one hand on the steering wheel, I carefully place my empty water bottle back in the small blue cooler on the passenger seat. I don't want the light-weight plastic bottle to fly out of my speeding convertible on the interstate. The urge to relieve myself is growing with every passing mile. I shift slightly in my bucket seat. If I don't see a Moline sign soon, I promise myself, I will make an unplanned potty stop. I lift my sunglasses from my eyes and squint to read the approaching sign.

MOLINE 10 MILES

Relief washes from head to toe, I can wait that long.

"Sweet and salty, sweet and salty," I chant as I walk the aisles of the gas station. My road trip food must always be sweet and salty. I snag a bag of cashews and a box of Milk Duds. I pick up two more waters and one more Diet Pepsi for the cooler. I quickly pay the attendant and return to my car.

As I pull back onto I-74/I-80, I choose my 'Heavy' playlist. My speakers sound of Seether, as I accelerate and set my cruise ten miles per hour over the speed limit. I mentally plan my trip. Iowa City to Des Moines will be two hours. I will stop for lunch, then arrive in

Kansas City in three more hours. I should still arrive early enough to beat Jackson and Kennedy home from work.

A smile slides upon my face as I think of Martha helping me hide my Mustang in her garage next door and letting me into their house. She insisted she would help prepare dinner when I arrive then hurry home. Of course, I had to promise to share all the details of the surprise with her the next morning. She doesn't know the real reason I'm surprising Jackson and Kennedy, but she will soon. After dinner tonight, Kennedy will want to share our plan with all her friends. I suppose her friends will become my friends over the next year if everything plays out according to my plan.

Time flies with great music, the wind in my face, and the hot sun everywhere. Soon I am on the outskirts of Des Moines. I didn't plan where to stop for lunch, so I must keep my eyes open and read the exit signs. In Altoona, I can make out the tops of the roller coasters at Adventureland Theme Park. I went there once on a class trip in high school.

A sign ahead states at the next exit I could choose a McDonald's, Jethro's BBQ, Taco Bell... I decide to continue on I-80 for other lunch options. As I drive, I notice a rather large, lonely skyscraper off to the left. Downtown Des Moines is much smaller than Chicago and KC. I wonder if it is the biggest city in Iowa. I'll have to look it up on the internet. A few exits later, I see a logo for Sonic Drive-In. We have a winner. I cannot recall my last visit to a Sonic.

I pull into a slot down from the external bathroom doors. I quickly browse the menu, noting they still offer my favorites. I press the large red intercom button, excitement building in my stomach as I order a chili-cheese dog, large cheese tots, and a large Diet Coke with vanilla. Their vanilla syrup is to die for. While I wait for the carhop to deliver my meal, I dart into the ladies' room.

I opt to eat in the awning's shade before continuing my journey. It's hard to eat and keep paper containers from flying out of a moving convertible. Of course, I ordered too much food; I couldn't resist. Like many things from my previous life, I've missed this fast-food restaurant deeply. I start my meal with a couple cheese tater tots. I wash them down with sips of my vanilla Diet Coke. Next, I open wide for the hotdog on bun covered in hot chili and melted cheese. A moan escapes. I can't help myself. I love food. I rotate between my cheese tots and chili-cheese dog, ensuring I consume equal parts of each before I grow full.

With my meal consumed, I quickly check my phone for any messages prior to the next leg of my trip. I have a Snap from a former student's mom. It seems several of my former students went to the pool today. She recorded a short video of them yelling, 'Hello, Miss Taft!' I am going to miss my middle school kiddos.

My eyes scan other icons on my phone screen. A small red number one states I have an alert on Facebook. Tapping the icon, I find it is a former colleague's birthday. I quickly send a happy birthday wish.

My satiated stomach and I pull back onto the hectic interstate. When I-80 branches off, I'm now on the last leg of my journey, I-35 all the way to KC. I choose my 'Girl Power' playlist. Here's to Never Growing Up awakens my ears. I loudly sing along with Avril Lavigne.

As I cross into Missouri, my Sonic beverage and the following water bottle are ready to escape my body. I tell my desperate bladder, I will stop at the next town. Fortunately, in Bethany, I see Golden Arches, and decide to stop for the restroom. At the last minute, I pull into a Casey's Gas Station across from McDonald's so I can refill the gas tank while I use a restroom. Always safe when I drive, I quickly text Martha before I leave to let her know I am about two hours away. I let her know I am leaving Bethany, MO. I hope she knows where that is.

As I continue to cover mile after mile of rural northern Missouri, my stereo blasts my favorite beats. I startle when two bikers pass me like I'm standing still. I glance at my speedometer. If I am driving ninety miles per hour, how fast must they be going? The growling the tailpipes emit reminds me of riding on Sean Parker's old Harley Davidson our senior year of high school.

16

OPENED MY MIND TO THE WORLD OF VIBRATORS

Taylor

I remember that 18-year-old me arrived at the sandbar with Chris, my guy at the time.

It was a typically warm late summer evening. As the level of beer in the keg lowered, Chris grew louder and mouthier. By eleven, he could barely walk. Chris yelled my name across the bonfire. While slurring his words, he summoned me to bring him a beer.

I hesitantly approached with the beer, and he tightly grabbed my wrist. I struggled to pull away. His strength, though drunk, out powered me. In front of a crowd of over thirty high school and college acquaintances, he loudly demanded I suck his cock right where he sat. When I told him to go fuck himself, he drew back his hand and punched me on the left side of my face. It happened so fast I had no time to protect myself. Drunken mayhem ensued. His buddies escorted him away as he continued yelling profanities at me and struggled to break free.

Several girls swarmed my side, prattling about Chris being a lousy drunk. Many stated I should break up with him. Of course, any one of them would swoop in the minute I did. Chris was an athlete, he was popular, and he was a hot commodity for high school girls. In my mind, he was no longer worth my trouble.

Not interested in their sympathy, I craned my neck around the gaggle of gossip-hungry girls. The first guy I saw was Sean Parker. It appeared he was standing closer to the huddle of girls than the thinned-out herd of guys. Through the flickering flames of the bonfire, our eyes locked. He lifted his masculine chin towards me. I immediately shoved my way through the tipsy girls towards him. As I neared, he mouthed, "Are you okay?"

As soon as I was within arm's length, I tucked my arm in Sean's and asked for a ride home. Without a word, he escorted me from the river bank, through the tree line towards the soybean field where everyone parked. The sounds of the party faded to a whisper. I welcomed the silence.

When he abruptly he stopped, my eyes took in the motorcycle. Crap. I forgot he didn't drive his truck anymore. He handed me his helmet. I grasped the heavy black safety device but could only stare. Slowly, his hands rose to each side of my head. He turned me to the right to examine the damage Chris' fist caused.

"I can't tell in the moonlight how bad it is. I can feel it is bleeding. How bad does it hurt?" Sean's long fingers lightly tapped along my cheek bone then cradled my head.

"Bad enough I need something stronger than beer," I replied with a chuckle to cover the pain his light prodding caused.

"You should wear the helmet to prevent any further damage to your head," Sean suggested. "My aunt is a nurse, and I want to take you to her to see if your cheek needs stitches before driving you home."

Knowing Grandma would be asleep at home and our first-aid supplies were virtually non-existent, I nodded okay to his plan.

I'd ridden dirt bikes and ATVs on the farm. They didn't prepare me for his Harley. Of course, with my short stature, I had to hop to get on it. I tentatively placed my hands on each of his shoulders. Sean grasped my hands, moving them securely to his waist. I squealed when he grasped my knees and pulled me snug to his back.

Sean and I had been friends since the tenth grade. As teachers often chose an alphabetic seating chart, Taft and Parker often sat side-by-side. We each made good grades. He needed to study to keep his grades high, while I found school easy. I rarely read assigned readings or studied before tests. When needed, we paired ourselves together for class projects or study times. Our friendship was strictly platonic.

However, in that position, I found myself plastered pelvis to shoulders against Sean's broad muscled backside, and I saw Sean in a different light. His tall frame was muscular - a fact I had not observed in class. When he started the bike, I felt the vibrations to the deepest part of my core. Shifting the motorcycle, he raised the kickstand, as I clutched my thighs tighter to his. He patted my hands on his abdomen, then yelled, "Hold on tight!"

We made our way from the field, over the bumpy, gravel roads, then onto the smooth highway. I marveled at the power the old Harley unveiled. I understood why Sean went everywhere on his bike. The constant vibration and rumble did wonders for my tumultuous soul. Chris and the punch to the cheek were quickly a distant memory. I felt powerful on this bike. I felt free.

Too soon, we pulled into the driveway of a small blue house near our high school. He steadied my arms as I awkwardly slipped from the Harley. As my feet found purchase on solid ground, I noticed an overwhelming tingling near my core. When Sean slowly and carefully pulled his helmet off my head, I tried to adjust the seam of my shorts away from my over-sensitized clit. He placed his hand on my lower back to escort me to the wrap-around porch, and the throbbing increased with every step. I asked him to hold on. I explained I needed a minute. I'm sure he thought this was because of my bleeding cheek, not my over-stimulated girl parts.

"Why don't I go wake Theresa, and you join me when you're ready?" He asked.

I could only nod in agreement. How was it possible I had this reaction to a motorcycle? I didn't feel it building as we rode. It was as if all the blood in my body flowed straight to my clit upon standing. I slowly took a few more steps, noticing a slow cessation of the sensation. One step at a time, I made my way to the porch, just as Sean reopened the front door.

In the kitchen, his aunt greeted me, smiling. It was apparent Sean had woken her. Her hair was a mess and her nightgown wrinkled. Sean sat me at the tiny wooden table in the small kitchen. I stared at the green placemats adorning the table as Theresa passed him medical supplies from the nearby cabinet. She inspected my cheek, cheekbone, and eye socket with her fingertips. I attempted to apologize for disturbing her between my sharp intakes of breath with the pain. She dabbed lightly at my cut, hoping to inspect it with less blood present. She sent Sean to fetch a cold, wet washcloth from the bathroom. As he disappeared, a smirk slid upon her face before she asked if it was my first ride on a motorcycle. I replied yes. She read my confusion. "It does wonderful things to lady-bits," she added with a wink.

With my hands, I attempted to cover my embarrassment, realizing if she knew Sean must also know, but I winced with pain as I forgot my cheek. Placing her hand upon my wrist, Theresa assured me Sean didn't know. She explained she could see my tiny wiggles to adjust myself. She whispered she had enjoyed the wonders of many a bike ride. I was sure my cheeks were flaming bright crimson, as Sean emerged with a damp cloth in hand. He looked from me to Theresa and back then asked what he missed. Theresa stated I shared the story of my loser boyfriend and how I planned to castrate him if I had a scar. I marveled at her quick thinking. Sean must have shared that night's events with her before I recovered enough from the ride to walk in.

Sean stated I'd have to take a number, as several guys at the party planned to visit with Chris on my behalf. I wasn't sure how I felt about that. Theresa placed two butterfly bandages on my cut cheek, assuring Sean I didn't need stitches or a doctor.

She rose from her chair beside mine. I sensed a hesitation as she looked from Sean to me. "Taylor, I hope you will consider pressing charges. The two of you could call from here. I'd assist you every step of the way." She twisted her hands near her waist and wrinkled her brow. "This is assault, Taylor. You need to press charges. You can prevent other women a lot of pain by reporting this behavior so he can get counseling."

Sean and Theresa's eyes were like hot lasers directed at my face. "I..." My mind was a jumbled mess. "I can't. He was drinking. I was drinking. We are all underage and drinking." I scanned Theresa's face for understanding as I continued. "He never acted like this before. It had to be the alcohol tonight." I wrote off his behavior, hoping this night would disappear.

Reluctantly, she then bid us goodnight and excused herself back to the bedroom. Sean mentioned he crashed at her house often. When I balked at the vodka bottle he offered me, he explained she allowed him to drink as long as he spent the night. He handed me the bottle of vodka, prompting me to drink to ease the pain. I no longer fought and did as he suggested. He refused to drink when I passed it to him, stating he would drive me home soon. I took another long pull before I insisted I had enough. We cleaned up the mess, let ourselves out, then I found myself faced with another motorcycle ride.

Sean slid his long leg over the Harley with graceful ease. I secured his heavy helmet, knowing my motorcycle mount would be less than graceful, and straddled the seat behind him. The vibrations began as he started it up. I clutched his abdomen tightly as I enjoyed the rumbling in my girly parts. In what seemed like mere seconds, Sean, ever the gentleman, walked me to my door and waited as I locked it behind me, before riding the growling Harley into the darkness.

His Harley opened my mind to the world of vibrators. I saved money from my next two paychecks, drove to St. Joseph and purchased my first vibrator. Of course, I forgot to buy batteries. A fact I cursed quietly at, as I lay anxious in my bed that night.

17

I MAY HAVE JUMPED THE GUN HERE

Taylor

The memory fading, I laugh out loud at the fact I'm driving and hearing motorcycles, led my mind to the topic of vibrators. It seems my mind always holds a predisposition for sexual thoughts. Jackson and Kennedy tease me about this often. I'm so glad they returned to my life. No one knows me like they do. They know all my secrets, my heartaches, and the hard knocks life bestowed upon me. The three of us witnessed the sucky parts of life over and over before age twenty-two. Together we have cried, we have fought through, and we have emerged on the other side. My relationships with Chris and John are just colossal speed bumps on our road of life.

If I had pressed assault charges against Chris, would I have continued to choose the men I did? I vow to avoid men for the next year. No dates, no hook-ups - I need time to regroup. I'll use my time with Jackson and Kennedy to work through my issues with the wrong type of men. I nod to myself. I mentally place 'seek a counselor' on the top of Monday's to-do-list. I can do this.

I glance at my iPhone, noting I'll arrive in KC in about an hour.

Excitement washes over me. Arriving in person to deliver my answer will be a great surprise gift to my best friends.

I pull into Martha's driveway, barely before 4:00 p.m. She's standing in the driveway, animatedly motioning me to pull right into her garage. As I exit my Mustang, I stretch overhead, then I touch my toes. Relief encompasses me as I'm done with the driving part of my trip. Martha talks a mile-a-minute. She explains she has invited Jackson and Kennedy over for dinner at 7:00 tonight. She explains she worried they might make other plans for their Friday night. This way they would come home after work and not plan on their own dinner.

As I thank her for all her help, she ushers me into Jackson and Kennedy's home. I place my overnight bag in the guest room and close the door. In the kitchen, I don't immediately see the ingredients I asked Martha to buy for me to prepare a simple dinner. She explains her husband, James, is bringing takeout from their restaurant for our dinner tonight. She didn't want me to worry about preparing a meal after such a long road trip. I thank her generosity while inside I know it is my lack of cooking ability that persuaded her decision. She texts James that we are ready for him to deliver the meal.

As Martha sits comfortably at the island, I ask where her four kids are. She laughs, knowing I thought she left them home alone all this time. Reagan is watching them, and I know this means she couldn't keep the secret from Reagan and James. Note to self, I might not want to tell secrets to Martha in the future. I claim I need to shower to wash the highway off me, hoping Martha will leave. She takes the hint.

I pace a few times from kitchen to living room and back. I attempt to shake out my nerves. My plan unfolds perfectly. We arranged to speak on the phone later tonight to discuss my decision. My arriving in person will be quite a shock for them.

I gave them my answer immediately when they asked me. I repeated my answer many times before I returned to Chicago last week. Jackson insisted I take a week to examine my life and the changes required before I commit. My answer did not wane over the week. I made several lists of items I would give up, need, or face in the upcoming months. I listed negatives and positives. I even spent one evening pretending to talk myself out of it. I'm firm in my decision. I cannot wait to explain this to my two best friends.

At five-thirty, I hear the garage door raise. I shake out my hands while hopping up and down a few times. I might be more excited than they will be. I listen to the sound of one car door closing as another vehicle pulls into the drive. Crap! I didn't think they might arrive home at different times. I want Jackson and Kennedy inside before I surprise them. I scramble into the guest room, peeking through the door frame. Here I can wait until they are both in the house to surprise them.

Kennedy's voice enters the kitchen. "I thought that was you at the stoplight a few cars back."

"I was trying to beat you home for once," Jackson admits.

I breathe a deep sigh of relief that they are both here, as I slowly position myself entirely in sight. I stand in the doorway, an enormous smile on my face, waiting to be noticed. Their conversation continues as they drop keys and bags on the entry countertop. Jackson wraps his arms around Kennedy's waist, pulling her in for a kiss on the cheek. My hand to my mouth, I fight the tears pooling in my eyes at the love between my best friends. The movement of my arm catches Jackson's attention. At first, he startles but quickly recovers.

He stalks slowly but purposefully towards me. The excitement I expected to show on his face is absent. Instead, I see concern, fear, and pain.

"What happened?" Jackson growls. "Did John hurt you?" His hands plant firmly on his hips as he widens his stance mere feet from me.

Kennedy peeks around him. Her face displaying the excitement I hoped to see.

"Jackson," I start. "Everything is great. I drove to Kansas City to surprise the two of you." I step towards my best friends.

Kennedy wraps me in an enthusiastic bear hug, rocking me back-and-forth. "Jackson," she chides. "Snap out of protective macho-man-mode and welcome Taylor, who drove over six hours to see us."

"Eight hours," I correct.

Jackson attempts to hide his apprehension. He slips his long arms around us both.

Raising his nose in the air, he states, "I smell food. You didn't attempt to cook, did you?"

I withdraw from the group hug, and I throw daggers at him through my eyes as I point at him. Then flip him off.

"You ruined my surprise. I drove all the way here, I hid my Mustang, and arranged a nice dinner from Martha's restaurant. I wanted this to be the best surprise ever, and instead of surprise you worry something bad happened."

I see regret on Jackson's face. He does not need to apologize. I won't let him. "You," I point at Jackson, using my stern teacher-voice, "Go upstairs, change your clothes, change your attitude, then march your ass down here before dinner is ruined anymore by you."

Kennedy bursts out laughing as she joins me in motioning Jackson upstairs. We continue laughing as we pull out plates, silverware, and drinks for dinner.

As I turn off the oven, Jackson shouts from the top of the stairs, startling the two of us. "Taylor, you're here!" He descends the stairs while waving his arms from side-to-side pretending he is surprised to see me. "Why are you here? How did you get here? How long are you staying?" His words convey all that I hoped he would say upon seeing me earlier. Entering the kitchen, he swoops me into his arms, spinning us around and around.

"Put me down," I plead. "I'm carsick from my traveling today. I need a meal."

We gather our plates full of food and assemble at the small table in the nook. Still smiling, Jackson pours wine in three glasses.

Before we dig in, I raise my glass. "A toast," I prompt. "To great friends, great surprises," I pin Jackson with a stare, then swing my eyes to Kennedy, "and to becoming your surrogate."

Kennedy bursts into sobs as Jackson places his arm around her and squeezes eyes on me. "The real reason for your surprise?" He questions. I nod as he continues, "You just couldn't tell us over the phone as planned later tonight, could you?"

"Jackson!" Kennedy swats his shoulder. "She'll think she is not welcome here."

I rescue him from Kennedy's scolding.

"I followed Jackson's directions. I made lists, thought of my daily life while carrying their child, and even pretended to argue against my decision," I explain. My eyes take in my best friends, holding each other lovingly as they listen to my every word. "I couldn't imagine myself pregnant and alone in Chicago." Their eyes widen with worry that they misunderstood my previous toast and announcement. I quickly continue, "I thought while I was pregnant with your child, I should live in KC, so you can experience every moment with me."

I look from Kennedy to Jackson, anxiously awaiting their reactions.

Will they want me nearby?

I may have jumped the gun here.

18

OOHY-GOOEY

Taylor

Kennedy leaps from her seat, darts towards me, and hugs me tightly. Her tear-stained cheeks wet my cheek and t-shirt. Jackson drops to his knees on my other side to join the celebration. We hug, then laugh as we all wipe our tears without speaking a word.

I break the silence when I can take it no more. "We need to eat before our food gets cold," I announce.

As he returns to his chair, Jackson mumbles, "Too much oohy-gooey for Taylor."

He knows me too well. It's as if he sees into my inner-most thoughts. I rarely cry. I feel deeply, never wearing my emotions on my sleeves. Displays of affection are not my thing.

Kennedy fans her face, trying to calm her tears. Jackson and I tip our wine glasses towards each other's before taking a sip. For a few minutes, we enjoy our luke-warm Mexican rice and scrumptious chicken enchiladas.

I see the wheels turning as Jackson attempts to eat. Unable to take it any longer, I prompt Jackson, "Just say it."

"Does this mean you plan to teach and move to Kansas City?" Jackson's eyes pierce mine, seeking every detail.

"I plan to take the year off from teaching. I will continue to post my lessons to sell online, and I have some money saved up to cover my expenses," I explain.

Tilting his head to the side, I see Jackson quickly work the numbers.

"I planned to talk about all the details after dinner. We need a planning meeting," I state, noticing Kennedy hasn't drawn the same conclusion regarding money that Jackson has. "I hoped I might stay in your guest room." I look to Kennedy reading she loves the idea, before I turn to Jackson. "If I live here, you can experience every minute of the pregnancy." I pause to sip my last bit of wine. As I continue, Jackson refills my glass. "The two of you can share my food-cravings, my growing pains, my sleepless nights, and even my maternity flatulence."

This draws laughter from the two of them.

I return to my plate of food while they ponder my proposal. Kennedy looks pleadingly at Jackson. His hand caresses her cheek before briefly planting a kiss on her forehead.

"It is a terrific idea," Jackson proclaims as Kennedy claps excitedly. "I'm a bit shocked this wasn't the plan already written in Kennedy's planning notebook."

"I didn't want to intrude upon her daily life any more than necessary during the surrogacy," Kennedy defends.

"Listen," I interrupt. "I'm all in. The in-vitro, the OB visits, the thirty-nine-week gestation, giving up alcohol, the stretch marks, the cravings, the not seeing my toes for a few months, the engorged breasts...all of it."

Jackson shakes his head. Kennedy hangs on my every word. I see she loves the idea of this hands-on involvement in the pregnancy.

I continue to explain, "The thought of emailing and texting pics, along with frequent phone calls about the pregnancy, didn't sit well with me. I don't have a large support system in Chicago. I'm friends with a few teachers from work, but not to the extent of sharing a surrogate pregnancy with them. I'm closest to Senator Adams and Jorge." At the mention of

Jorge's name, their eyes fill with new questions. Questions I choose not to respond to now, so I quickly continue with my explanation. "This is your baby. It should be your pregnancy. You will bond with your baby from day one-not on the day I give birth. I've read many articles written about surrogacy, the journey, the regrets, and the ups-and-downs." I pause to sip more wine, then continue. "You know I am a nerd. I love to read, be informed, and plan for everything. I've been very busy this week."

"Yes, you have," Kennedy confirms, taking my hand from across the table. "I thought your willingness to be my surrogate was the greatest gift you could ever bestow upon me. You've outdone yourself. Living here means..." Tears overtake her.

Jackson wraps his arms around his wife. He whispers in her ear as he tucks her hair behind. Making eye contact with me, he finishes for Kennedy. "Your living here while carrying our child is a wonderful idea. We are truly blessed to be your friends."

"So," I begin, "can I stay here?"

"Of course!" Jackson announces.

"Yes!" Kennedy shouts at the same time.

Needing to move to less emotional topics, I announce, "Song of the day time." Jackson and my old game will quickly lighten the mood. "So, no one said your years would turn out like this," I begin.

"*I'll be there for you* from Friends!" Kennedy blurts loudly.

Jackson simply shakes his head while smiling. "Who sings it?" he asks Kennedy.

She states she has no clue. Jackson states he doesn't know either. At Jackson's surrender, I announce The Rembrandts sing *I'll Be There for You*.

Moments pass before Jackson enlists the assistance of his cell phone. He claims he knows the song he is looking for; he just needs help with the exact lyrics. "And good pals are good pals for all the years," Jackson's deep masculine voice begins.

I recognize the song but need to remember the artist.

"If the Son of God's the Son of God of them."

I sigh in defeat. "I don't remember the artist's name," I admit. Jackson has only stumped me two other times. "I shouldn't have allowed the use of cell phones," I state, defeated. I'm very competitive. I don't like to lose at anything. They know this.

"*Friends are Friends Forever* by Michael W. Smith," Jackson smiles with pride even though he knows his victory is subject to controversy.

After dinner, we move to the family room with a nearly empty bottle and our glasses of wine. Kennedy beams with excitement as she brings her planning notebook with her. Noticing this, I grab my notes from my overnight bag. I fan them to cover the entire coffee-table for their inspection.

Jackson gathers my papers, placing them in one pile on the corner. "We believe you," He states.

"I know you do, but I would like you to review them. I want everything out on the proverbial table." I motion to the coffee-table. "I want to be open. I want the three of us to share our thoughts, hopes, and fears all the way," I inform. "In research, I found this is important for a successful surrogacy."

Kennedy jumps in, handing a new spiral notebook with pen to Jackson, then me. Like a teacher in front of her class, she explains we will use these to plan, to journal our feelings, and to share with our group if we want. She has already adorned the cover with our first names and glued on a picture of a family. I reluctantly note it is a mom, dad, and baby. It's the family they will become when my part of the surrogacy is complete.

19

PICKLE TICKLE

Taylor

Kennedy opens her notebook, flips a few pages, then begins. She states, "These are the notes I made for our phone call we planned for tonight. Since you're here and will live with us, some items may need tweaking. My appointment with Dr. Matthews is on Tuesday. At that time, we'll need to discuss our timeline and Taylor's appointment with Dr. Matthews. All of this will depend on the method the doctor decides works best to harvest her eggs," Kennedy informs.

Jackson, sensing my question, says, "Dr. Matthews is the fertility specialist they referred us to. I already endured my visit to prove my boys are strong swimmers."

To this I laugh, nearly spewing wine everywhere. *Mental note: refrain from sipping wine during our future delicate conversations.* Jackson's cheeks redden with embarrassment. I assume we will have many embarrassing conversations in the months to come.

"Our planning and decisions will begin on Tuesday night," Kennedy continues. She shares the items we will discuss next week. She quickly rattles off a list while looking sternly at Jackson and me.

"We need to find an OB/GYN to use during the entire pregnancy. Diet and foods to avoid during pregnancy need researched. Ways to improve the probability of fertilization need researched." Kennedy pauses to cross items from her list. She looks up, then states, "Our weekly phone call and text planning can now be crossed out."

"Ken," I interrupt. "I love you and am very excited to help." I find the right words. "But you are coming across as a dictator right now. How about you place your notebook on the coffee table, and we all crowd around it to discuss." I hope my words don't hurt her feelings.

Kennedy nods her head and sits on her knees. Jackson and I scan the page. I stifle a giggle as I read her handwriting, with curly-cues and little hearts scattered on the page.

Jackson points to a line regarding his need to practice ejaculating. "You seriously think I need to practice?" He questions, looking at Kennedy.

As Jackson mumbles on, I excuse myself to the kitchen for water while they discuss this uncomfortable topic. Moments pass before I return to the family room, resuming my spot on the floor, as talking seems to have ended.

Kennedy takes my hand. "Honey, we need you involved in all parts of the planning, even the uncomfortable ones."

I simply nod to her. Looking at Jackson, I see he finds this topic very unnecessary.

"Jackson's ejaculation into a cup will not affect my part of the process. So, I wanted him to be comfortable, and I left the room," I explain.

"We are three adults. We all need to know everyone's part of the process," Kennedy argues. She picks up where she left off. Pointing to her next note, she informs, "Books state men have anxiety about ejaculating on demand, so some practice will help."

I pull out my iPhone, open my Kindle App, scroll a few times, find the book I want, then hand my phone to Kennedy. "Here, you read this and bye-bye any anxiety Jackson might have."

Kennedy squeals as my cell phone plummets to the carpet. Jackson grabs up my phone to see what I shared.

"Seriously?" He asks me. "You read this smut?"

I offended him with my suggestion, but soon the hilarity seeps upon his face.

"Excuse me? *Tickle His Pickle* is a very popular book. It sold over a million copies," I inform them. "You know, Kennedy, in my research, I've read wives help husbands with their samples all the time. If you ask me, it'd be kind of hot knowing it would be to create your baby."

I know sex is lacking in their relationship, but Kennedy could keep her clothes on, so she should be able to handle this. *I'll have to chat with her about it this week.*

Sensing the extreme embarrassment emanating from both my friends, I rescue my phone from Jackson's grasp. "Sorry, forget I mentioned it. I just thought it would help."

Without looking up from her notebook, Kennedy states, "All ideas are welcome."

Her hand trembles as she attempts to make note of my idea on her notebook page. We cover a few more items to prepare for a Tuesday planning meeting before Kennedy announces this meeting is over.

Jackson attempts to lighten the mood by suggesting we watch a movie, and Kennedy plops on the sofa.

"I'll be right back," I say, excusing myself to the restroom before selecting a spot on the sofa.

I ponder how difficult future discussions might become. *Fertility, semen, conception…How will we survive them if we are this uncomfortable already?*

Jackson chooses *How to Lose a Guy in 10 Days*. I love this movie; he knows I love this movie. I'm a huge Kate Hudson and Matthew McConaughey fan. I feel the air in the room is too thick to move onto a movie, so I steal the remote from Jackson pressing pause.

"We can't do this." Four eyes dart to me. "We are making a baby. We have to talk about sex, body parts, and fluids. We're adults. We can't clam up and be uncomfortable. I didn't pull out a banana and give a lesson on tickling Jackson's pickle. I simply shared a book that might help our process," I defend.

"I was shocked by the thought, but I see how I might need to help Jackson," Kennedy claims.

Jackson, in denial, states, "No practice is needed. I'll rise to the occasion."

A fit of giggles falls on Kennedy and me at his choice of the word rise. Sensing we're all good, I press play on the remote.

"I promise not to say the lines with the characters in the movie," I chuckle.

My friends know it's a promise I can't keep.

Midway through the movie, Jackson pauses for a bathroom break. I grab a bowl full of pretzel sticks from the kitchen, waiting for his return. Kennedy scoots closer to me on the sofa.

"So Jorge is a close friend now?" She inquires quietly.

"Ken," I look toward the stairs to see if Jackson is in earshot. "It is a long story, with lots of details I plan to share with you, just not tonight with Jackson."

"Every detail?" She asks.

"I will make you blush when I share," I assure.

This seems to appease her. She scoots back to her corner of the sofa as Jackson returns in his PJs.

Not fair. I want to be comfy, too. I tug a pillow to my chest, pouting as we finish the movie.

20

TARGET SUPER POWER

Taylor

I wake to the bright light because of the blinds I forgot to close and the smell of breakfast drifting from the kitchen. I'm not a morning person, but the smells are enticing me from my cozy bed. I quickly pee, wash my face and hands, run a brush through my hair, then pad slowly to a kitchen island barstool.

Kennedy stands dressed for the day at the stove. I smell bacon and see her flip an omelet as I nibble on the fresh fruit in the center of the island.

"Good Morning," I mumble in greeting to Kennedy's back.

"Good Morning," she returns, turning with a smile. She fetches a bowl of yogurt to join the fruit. "Bacon will be ready in a minute. You can make some toast with peanut butter." Kennedy points towards a loaf of bread and peanut butter next to the toaster. She remembers I do not eat eggs.

We eat in silence. I make quick work of my peanut butter toast and five strips of bacon. I place some yogurt in a small bowl, then sprinkle with banana slices and grapes. Kennedy nibbles on an egg white omelet, and a much smaller than mine bowl of fruit with yogurt.

"What do you want to do today?" Kennedy queries. "Jackson will work until noon or so. I usually pop into the YMCA, then run errands."

"I'll tag along," I reply. "Give me twenty minutes to shower; then I'll be good to go."

I quickly shower and choose to wear my white eyelet Converse to match my white eyelet lace tank top. I tuck lip balm, my debit card, and some cash in my shorts pocket before I check my hair in the mirror one more time. Exiting the bedroom, I find Kennedy still getting ready upstairs, so I sit at the kitchen island. I pull out my iPhone and text Jorge.

ME
arrived last night
no problems

JORGE
surprised?

ME
Very surprised
Thanks for the idea.

JORGE
(winking emoji) what you doing today

ME
when Kennedy is ready
running errands
no other plans yet

JORGE
I work 3-midnight

Surrogate Series

> ME
> fun fun
>
> Kennedy ready
>
> chat later
>
> JORGE
> have fun

"Who ya texting?" Kennedy inquires. "You have this wonky grin all over your face," she teases.

When I inform her I texted Jorge, her excitement cannot be contained. Once again, I promise I'll share all the details at lunch today. With some encouragement, she concedes, and we hit the road. Kennedy shares she'll need about thirty minutes at the YMCA. We will run to Target and then Jackson's grocery store before we head home for lunch.

"I think I may purchase a membership while you work." At my words, Kennedy pulls her eyes from the busy street for a second before focusing on the road again. I continue, "I'll need something to do every day during the pregnancy. Besides, I want to stay fit," I explain.

"That's a great idea," Kennedy claims. "I'll set you up on a tour of the Y. I'll finish about the same time you are."

"What are we buying at Target?" I ask.

"They have clear recycle bags I can't purchase at Jackson's store," Kennedy explains.

"Do you have the superpower to walk into a Target store, purchase one item, and leave?" I ask.

After laughter, she admits, "We probably will browse the dollar aisles and a few other departments before steering our cart to the checkout."

"I have a weakness for Target. I enjoy the clothing lines, home accessories and, of course, school supplies," I share. "I've started placing my order online to pick up at the store. This prevents me walking in to buy one item, then walking out with one-hundred dollars less in my pocket," I confess with a shrug.

"We're here." She points out while pulling into her assigned parking spot.

"Hey Kennedy," a cute blonde teenager greets behind the welcome desk.

"Tara, this is my best friend, Taylor. Will you call Matthew to give her a membership tour?" Kennedy takes my right hand in hers, pulling me into the back offices. She shows me her desk, prompting me to sit near her. As her computer wakes, she greets a young man approaching. "Mark, this is my best friend, Taylor. Taylor, Mark works in membership and will show you around."

I examine the blonde gentleman while rising to shake his extended hand. He is roughly six-feet tall, very tan, and very muscular. I wonder to myself if he moonlights as a lifeguard or personal trainer as well. As he guides me to the front, Kennedy picks up her phone. Mark walks me through the entire facility, asking about my current workouts, if I swim, and how long I'll be in KC. He uses my answers to show parts of this YMCA I might enjoy.

Our tour complete, we return to the welcome center. I notice Kennedy talking to a gentleman, while both look at a computer monitor. "There they are." Kennedy waves in our direction. "Matthew, this is Taylor. Taylor, Matthew is our membership director."

Matthew looks up from the monitor to shake my hand. He motions to a line of blue tape on the floor, asking me to stand behind it and smile. Next thing I know, he hands me a membership card and welcomes me to The North Kansas City YMCA.

Kennedy links her arm in mine, hustles me out the door, and escorts me to her car.

"What just happened?" I ask, my thoughts spinning.

"I mentioned to Matthew about your moving in with us and that you will be my surrogate. He allowed you on our family membership because of special circumstances. It's at no extra cost, and it's a perk of working at the YMCA," Kennedy explains.

Our errands nearly complete, we search for an open parking spot at

Jackson's store. It's Saturday; the store is buzzing. We drive up, then down many rows before a spot opens up.

Kennedy grabs a grocery cart from a nearby cart corral, placing her purse in the child seat, and I follow along beside her.

"Is it always this busy?" I inquire.

"On weekends, yes." Kennedy says.

I've become accustomed to the corner grocery store and Walgreen's in Chicago. I forgot how large stores are in the Midwest. Upon entering, Kennedy pulls a paper list from her handbag.

I attempt to contain the giggle that escapes. "Ken," I begin, still giggling. "You know they have free apps on your phone to use for grocery lists?"

I must assist my technology-challenged friend in the upcoming weeks.

We make our way with our cart up-and-down every aisle to buy items on Kennedy's handwritten list. She expertly maneuvers through the other grocery shoppers. I'm out of practice with a shopping cart. In Chicago, I grab a hand basket to shop.

The deep timbre of a male voice grasps my attention. It's Jackson's voice an aisle away. We find him discussing product placement with a vendor. Kennedy simply waves at him and continues shopping. I linger behind. Jackson finishes, then joins me near the crackers. Motioning at the expansive store, I ask Jackson if he really runs the whole thing. He humbly nods. I reach up to pat him on the back and let him know I am impressed. An overhead page alerts Jackson to a phone call, so I quickly wave goodbye. I rejoin Kennedy in the freezer section. I add two boxes of ice-cream to our cart.

"You will need the YMCA membership eating like this," she teases.

Pausing before checking out, Kennedy asks, "What do you crave for lunch?"

"I am up for anything," I explain.

We detour to the store's grille, order to-go from the menu, then proceed to checkout our groceries, before we pickup our lunch. I carry our takeout food to the car. We pull to the drive-up lane so that an employee can load our groceries into the trunk. Our errands complete, we are on our way back home.

Groceries placed in appropriate locations, we sit at the island to enjoy our lunch.

Two bites consumed, Kennedy waits no longer. "So, Jorge..."

I concede I can avoid the topic no more. I share between my bites of burger and fries. Kennedy enjoys her quesadilla and the dramatic story.

21

COCKY MUCH?

Taylor

I begin telling Kennedy my story from the moment I exited the airplane from my visit here last week.

As I walk through the terminal, my thoughts jump from work, to household chores, to phone calls I need to make. I wish I were still in Kansas City, not returning to face my new single status in life. With the ringing of my cell phone, I drop my carry-on to rummage through my handbag. I just turned my iPhone on. *Why is it at the bottom of my purse? Wallet. Gum. Brush. Compact.* Finally, I grab my phone. The screen reveals Grace, John's mother, on the ID. *I should have known.* I went through all the trouble to find my phone in a busy airport and it's someone I don't care to speak to.

I gather up my suitcase and head toward the exit. While walking, loud laughter catches my attention. A group of four frat boys stand in the airport bar and enjoy the flirting of the blonde female bartender.

Bartender! I told Jorge I would stop by his bar on my way home. Since I met his sister while in KC and texted him each day, I can't leave the airport without saying hello.

Entering the bar, I handpick a table for two in the back with a view of the TV. I place my suitcase on an empty chair and plop on another. Within seconds, the blonde female approaches, taking my order. I request my usual Jack and diet cola. She returns behind the bar to the college-age boys, hoping to score. Like puppies in the pet shop window, they vie for her attention. I'm sure each is secretly hoping to hook up with her in the backroom, then brag about their escapades back at the dorm.

I busy myself checking my voicemail, finding two messages. The first is a colleague with gossip to share while grabbing lunch this week. Where is my drink? I glance towards the bartender, still listening to the message. My eyes meet those of a sandy-brown haired college guy at the bar. He smiles flirtingly, nodding my way. I quickly break eye contact in hopes he won't approach me. The next voicemail jars my attention. My ex-fiancé's mother's raspy voice brings me back to reality. Again, she states she has something she needs to give me. Just a quick meeting at my place she pleads. I press end on my cell phone, throwing it in my handbag.

"For the lady." A strong masculine hand places a drink on my table. My eyes follow up the dark-haired, muscular forearm, to bulging biceps hiding in a snug black tee. At last, my eyes meet the sexy smile I encountered a few days earlier in this same location. Thank goodness it's not one of the college guys seated at the bar.

"I see you are home from your visit. It looks like you spent a lot of time in the sun," Jorge states. Quickly, his cheerfulness flees as he notices the tears welling up in my eyes. He slips me a cocktail napkin.

"Thanks." I blot my eyes. It seems I cry every time I'm in his presence. I dab my eyes one more time while fanning my overheated face. I shouldn't let Grace's voicemail have this much power over me.

Jorge eases my suitcase to the floor and sits directly across from me. "Ironic how we can hide away for a while, yet when we return, our problems remain." He reaches across the tiny round table and pats my right hand.

"I should have stayed away longer," I state my tears at bay for the moment.

With his large hand still on mine, Jorge reminds me, "Your problems will not evaporate while you hide. They eventually find you wherever you run." He signals to the blonde to fix another drink.

"Drinking on the clock?" I question.

He chuckles. "I'm off the clock. Would you like to grab a bite to eat?"

Knowing my cabinets are severely lacking in the food department, I cautiously accept his invitation. Once at home, I need to return Grace's call, plan the inevitable meeting, and say my final goodbye to her. I'm in no hurry to find out what she wants. I wonder if she is really setting up a meeting for her son.

Jorge directs our conversation towards his sister and her four kids in KC. It's clear he misses his family. After Jorge finishes a second drink, he gathers my bag and escorts me to the door. With some discussion, we decide to follow each other to a nearby restaurant in separate cars. Gallantly, he walks me to my car in the long-term parking lot.

"I must admit," Jorge's deep voice breaks the silence as we reach my car. "I didn't figure you for a Mustang driver." He smiles approvingly as he inspects my car, brushing his hand along the sleek black interior. He turns to check out the backseat. "And a convertible. You must have a wild side."

I can't contain the chuckle that escapes as he wiggles his eyebrows.

I offer to drive him to his car in the employee lot. With great skill, he folds his six-foot muscular frame into my passenger bucket seat. As he directs me to the lot, his eyes scan all the lights, buttons, and contours appreciatively. He points me to the last car on the right. I gasp in surprise when his vehicle comes into view. It's the holy grail of sports cars in my book, a red 1965 Mustang.

"How?" I gulp. "Where... Uh?" I'm ah-struck. Composing my jealous emotions and dropped jaw, I finally form my thoughts. "Nice car. I'm very, very jealous."

"It seems we have an affinity for cars in common," he states. I pull my eyes from the car to his flattered smile. He exits my car, wearing a proud smile.

He hands me a bar napkin from his pocket. "For your drool," he laughs, pointing to my chin and then his car.

As I follow Jorge's vintage Mustang, my thoughts flow from his car to his hot body and gorgeous face. I am taking Kennedy's advice. I allow myself to enjoy his company. This is just a first date. I can handle a first date. I mean, it has been a while, but I can enjoy myself.

"A table for two," Jorge asks the hostess.

He places his hand firmly on my lower back, escorting me to a booth in the rear of the restaurant. His hand is warm and strong and ignites sparks on my lower back. Along with the electricity, a wave of security and warmth wash over me. A simple touch of his powerful hand upon my back, a touch of friendship or intimacy, makes no difference to me. I like this feeling. It's been years since I've experienced this. I fight the tears welling up in my eyes. I will not cry tonight. So, I pull on my big girl panties and vow I'm going to have fun tonight.

I focus my thoughts back on Jorge as he replies to the server, taking our drink order. "Two," he pauses, looking into my eyes.

I'm sure he sees the tears I attempt to hide. He tilts his head to the right in concern. When he smiles, it seems to reach out and engulf me. My tears evaporate. I feel him lifting me from my sadness.

Returning his attention back to the server, "Two, let me see... Are you a Cubs or White Sox fan?"

"What?" I'm confused about how this relates to our drink order.

The server attempts to hide her annoyance at his delay. She looks at me for my answer.

"Neither. I'm a St. Louis Cardinals fan."

"Two Bud Light draughts, please." As the server leaves, he smiles a cocky grin at me. Answering my questioning eyes, he states, "It's my profession to know what my customers want. You're a Jack and Diet Coke girl. No frills. Tough. If you chose The Cubs or White Sox, I would have ordered a local brew on tap. Since you're a Cardinals fan in a Cubs town, it would seem that you would choose to remain loyal to the Anheuser-Busch family. I chose a light beer because I can tell you work to keep your body firm and lean." His eyes wander up and down my body.

Blushing, I nod to confirm his assumptions. "I drink many beers, but Bud Light is my favorite. You have mad skills," I tease. The smile on his face assures me he already knew this. "Cocky much?"

22

THE VOICEMAIL

Taylor Continues Retelling Her Story

The server returns with our beers, we place our meal orders, and request two more beers. Quickly, we return our attention to each other. He asks about my trip. I tell him more about Jackson and Kennedy. I talk about the long talks, the neighborhood party, and meeting his sister. As the server delivers the bill and clears the table, I realize I talked about myself the entire meal. I'm surprised by the sadness quickly washing over me. *It's time for me to return home. Alone.*

"I don't want to be alone." The words jump out of my mouth before I restrain them. My hands leap to cover my mouth. *This isn't me; I'm not this woman.* I can't even blame it on too many drinks. I don't do one-night stands with strangers.

Placing his hand around my wrist, Jorge pulls my right hand from my face. "My place is nearby." There is no smile on his face as I allow my eyes to meet his. His look is serious. I try to decipher his intentions.

As much as I want to keep the evening going, I need to be in control. "My apartment is fifteen minutes from here." I offer and run my left hand through my hair, keeping my eyes on his. A sly smile slides upon his face. I take it as a yes. "But we need to stop by the store on the way. My fridge is empty." I await confirmation he will follow me home.

A man in my apartment, this is a first. Since the breakup, not even a friend has been in the apartment.

"Which store shall we shop at?" he chuckles as he registers the shock of my actions on my face. I let him know I live around the corner from a store, and he agrees to follow me there.

As I drive, I constantly keep an eye in my rearview mirror, viewing the vintage red dream car with its dreamier driver. He parks behind me on the street. I take a deep breath, trying to calm my nerves. He startles me by knocking on my window. I roll it down as he motions. He states he will run in. I argue that it's my house; I need to go in. I lose the battle as he assures me he can do this alone. I decide I can make do with whatever he buys. Butterflies float in my stomach as I imagine returning to my place with Jorge. My thoughts float to scenes of him in my apartment, my kitchen, my bedroom.

Again, he startles me by knocking on my passenger window this time. I unlock the door. He places two grocery bags on my front seat.

"I will follow you home," he states.

I notice as he returns to his car, he kept a small brown sack with him. *What does it contain?* It's probably something he needs for his house.

I keep a careful eye on him in my mirrors, until distracted by the bags, my eyes wander to the two sacks in my passenger seat. Chips, salsa, half a gallon of two percent milk, shaved ham, sliced cheese, and a loaf of whole grain bread are among the contents. *How long does he think he is staying? We just ate dinner.*

Arriving at my place, I motion him to follow me around back to our private parking lot. Jorge emerges from his car carrying the little brown bag. Without a word, he scoops the grocery bags into his arms and follows me into the stairwell. I fumble, opening the door. This is not how I imagined returning from KC. It's better than being alone. As he kicks the door closed, I hope all of my ghosts run for the closets.

"Make yourself at home; the kitchen is here," I inform as I flip on lights. "I'll be right back." I excuse myself to the restroom.

Jorge puts away the items from the store, tucking the beer and wine into the refrigerator, keeping two bottles of Bud Light out. He makes his way to the living room, carefully taking in my tiny apartment along the way. When I return to find him sitting in the armchair with his feet on the ottoman, beer in hand. I plop into my overstuffed sofa near him and grab the green throw pillow to hug as I reach for a drink of my beer. I wonder where the tiny brown bag is, and what its contents are.

He breaks the silence. "This is a nice place."

"Thanks." I take two large gulps of my beer. "Are you hungry?"

"No," he answers. "I couldn't eat another bite." Patting his stomach, he seems confused by my question.

"Then why did you buy all of that food?" I laugh.

"You were out of town, and I figure you need items for breakfast and lunch. I bought you enough to allow you to take another day before you need to go grocery shopping," Jorge explains.

Wow! Is this guy for real? I'm impressed. I expected him to shop for beer, maybe pretzels. I didn't expect a day's worth of food for me. It doesn't escape me how much I dreaded coming home alone, and how things are looking good so far.

"Can I get you another?" I ask as I return to the kitchen for a beer.

"Yes, please. Do you mind if I turn on music?" He asks while I'm in the kitchen.

Jorge nods his head to the beat of the Linkin Park song from his playlist as I return. I smile approvingly at his choice of rock music. As we return to our previous seats, my cell phone rings. I trot towards the kitchen to check the screen. *It's 10:45, who's calling?*

John Thomas

I freeze in shock. I count to three, taking deep breaths. I decide not to ruin my evening.

"I am not answering it," I inform Jorge, returning to the sofa with my cell in my hand.

I take a long pull of my beer and hold my breath in hopes John hangs up. Moments later, a ping alerts us he left a voicemail.

Jorge recognizes my mood change after viewing the caller ID. "You should listen to the message," he urges. "Otherwise, it will haunt you the entire evening." A sexy smirk slips upon his face. "I'd like to…" He pauses to choose his words.

"Me too," I murmur knowingly. My thoughts falter for a moment. Is it rude to listen to the voicemail in front of him? I'm not sure about the protocol. I select the voicemail and set it on speaker mode. I take a long drink of my beer to prepare for this message.

John's voice slices the air like a razor. "Taylor, I know you are there. (Pause) Taylor, your car is in the lot, and I see your lights on. (Pause) Call me, please. I need to talk to you tonight."

Jorge rises to peek out the window. He looks left and right toward the street below. His hand rubs the back of his neck, just below his hairline. He turns around but remains at the windows.

"I hope you will stay," I begin. "Don't let him ruin this evening." I rise and step toward him. "Help me forget he called," I plead.

Jorge immediately strides toward me. His strong arms envelope me, pulling me tight to his chest and hips. We gaze deeply. As his plump lips are about to greet mine, a violent pounding on my apartment door interrupts our moment. My eyes dart to the door as my hands cover my ears to muffle the noise. Jorge, still embracing me, watches my reaction. My rapid breathing and increasing fear prevent me from speaking.

John's shouts fill my apartment. "You fucking whore. I know you're in there. I saw that fucker in the window, and the lights are on. You're fucking him in my apartment-in my bed. You fucking bitch. You open your legs to every man that looks your way." He pauses his rant to pummel the door with his fists before continuing. "Open the door, cunt; I need to get my stuff. Close your fucking legs long enough to let me grab my stuff." He returns his assault on my door.

I look at Jorge through tears pooling in my eyes. I need to explain. I need to make sure he knows I'm not the woman John claims I am. As I open my lips to speak, he covers them with one finger to silence me. With his other hand, he points to the short hallway and bathroom. As we rush toward the tiny inner room, I don't notice Jorge texting someone. Upon entering the bathroom, his cell phone rings.

Jorge quickly greets the caller, "Jake, I have a situation and need your official assistance." Locking eyes with mine, Jorge asks for my address. He quickly repeats the location to the caller. "Domestic dispute. I'm in Taylor's apartment with her in an interior room. Her ex-boyfriend is at the door threatening her." Jorge listens to Jake. "No, I'll let you go. Just hurry."

23

BREAKS JORGE'S SPELL

Taylor Continues Retelling Her Story

I search Jorge's face for clues as John continues his profane-laced tirade in the hallway. Official assistance? Domestic dispute? I inhale a deep calming breath, but before I can ask Jorge about the call, we hear a neighbor announce to John he has phoned the police. John spews profanities and threats before we hear the neighbor slam his door closed.

Staring into his chocolate eyes, I will Jorge to speak. My erratic breathing seems too loud, and words fail me. I can't explain John's actions. I tuck my trembling hands into my shorts pockets. I need to know who was on his phone. I search their brown depths for a clue.

"Please." I beg, my voice faint and quivering.

Jorge closes the bathroom door before locking it. He pulls me snug to his chest.

"My roommate Jake is on the Chicago PD. He is on duty and headed here now." I suck in a sharp breath. "The man outside your door is not about to calm down and leave until you let him in." Jorge raises my chin to look into my eyes. "I won't let you open that door.

From what you shared and his behavior tonight, it is clear you need to wipe him from your life for good. Jake will help you." His full lips place a delicate kiss on my forehead.

I relish the care and understanding he shares with me.

The two doors between John and us do little to muffle his rant. His profanities repeat as if on a loop. If the repetitive annihilation of fists upon the door doesn't subside, I fear my door will succumb to his violence.

"How soon will the police arrive?" I anxiously inquire, attempting to keep my fear from my voice.

Jorge assures me Jake and his partner will arrive soon. Scanning my tiny restroom, I'm embarrassed. My shower displays multiple shampoo and conditioner bottles joined by my razor, shaving cream, baby oil, and my waterproof vibrator in plain sight. I pray he doesn't spy it. I move to the sink in an attempt to turn his back to the shower. As I splash water on my face, Jorge secures a washcloth from the shelf. He fills it with cool water, wrings it out, swipes my hair over my left shoulder, then carefully places it on my exposed neck. The cool cloth is refreshing.

Our eyes connect in the large mirror. He wraps his free arm around my waist, pulling my back tight against his chest. In our reflection, I realize our height difference. At a mere five feet, Jorge towers above me with his over six-foot stature. My head reaches his pectorals.

I realized long ago I could never change my height. I've adapted, learning many ways to maneuver with the aid of step-ladders, high heels, and countertops to reach as needed. We're an odd pair facing my mirror. I look like a child near his towering male physique.

I quickly spin to face him as the sounds of police personnel loudly address John outside my apartment. Jorge unlocks, then opens the bathroom door. We make our way to the front room. Jorge stares at the apartment door as I look about my tiny apartment. My living room and kitchenette are but one small room. I've never enjoyed my tiny home in Chicago. I attempted to make the most of my time here, and I pretended it was home. All along I felt it would never be home. Chicago was a stepping stone, a beginning, a blip on my life roadmap. Nothing belonging to John remains.

"Taylor," Jorge's voice interrupts my revelation. As I swing my eyes to his, he continues. "Hey, it's okay now. CPD is here." He urges me to sit in the nearby chair. Assessing that I will stay put, he retrieves a water bottle from the kitchen. He places it in my hands, then removes the cap. "Take a sip," he gently urges while prompting my hands toward my mouth with his.

As I sip a small amount of cold water, a stern knock greets my apartment door. "CPD, please open the door," a deep, authoritative male voice demands.

Jorge opens my door. I'm frozen. My many ghosts of my past mistakes hover before me, no longer hiding in the shadows. Tears well within my eyelids as I scan my many mistakes in my twenty-four years. Why must I repeat myself over-and-over? Why can't I learn and move on? In a room of men, how do I find the bad boy every time?

"Taylor, I'm Officer Jake Petree."

I rapidly blink to focus on the officer standing before me.

He looks from me to Jorge, then back. "Taylor?"

Slowly, I stand as anger overtakes me. I launch the water bottle in my hand against the nearby wall. Officer Petree takes a step back. Jorge attempts to approach. I raise my palm toward him to halt.

"Miss Taft," a female officer's voice draws my attention. "John is handcuffed in a cruiser outside. Would you like to press charges?" I realize while sounding cold; she's trying to reassure me I'm now safe.

My eyes dart from Jorge to the two officers. Officer Petree speaks. "He claims he has items in your apartment that you didn't allow him to take with him."

"Bullshit!" I raise my voice. "I packed everything for him. I left them all in the hallway." I raise both arms, signaling the entire apartment. "You are welcome to search the place." I turn to the female officer, who looks very familiar. "What does he claim I still have?" My brain tours the tiny apartment for anything he might claim is his.

Officer Petree states, "He won't name the item, but claims he needs to enter the apartment to retrieve it."

My eyes look from Officer Petree to his partner. "I am sorry, I didn't catch your name."

Stepping toward me, arm extended, she introduces herself as

Officer Blankenship. Immediate recognition dawns. "You're Sarah Blankenship's mother. I'm Miss Taft from the middle school." I greet.

"Yes, mam." She formerly acknowledges. "I attempted to remain professional in hopes of not making you uncomfortable."

"I fear the situation can't be any more uncomfortable." I jest. "My ex is an embarrassment. Everything a teacher should avoid. A drunk, abusive, druggy..."

"Drugs?" Officer Petree interrupts.

I explain, "I found drugs in my apartment upon returning from my Washington D.C. trip." Turning to Officer Blankenship, I assure her, "I do not use drugs and I kicked him out at the first sign of his using them." I'm sealing my fate here. As an educator, if this parent shares drugs were in my home-I would never teach again.

Another male officer enters my apartment through my open door. "Sullivan is transporting the male to headquarters." He looks to Jorge. "Shit, Jorge, what are doing here?" He greets before bro-hugging him. His eyes find me and squint. "Miss Taft, I hope this loser is not bringing trouble to your doorstep." He teases, poking Jorge firmly in the chest.

"Unfortunately, I am the trouble magnet." I admit. "Is Jacob ready for high school this fall?"

"You're still Jacob's favorite teacher. He claims he is ready for high school. However, as parents, we're not," Officer Staton informs me.

"He's a good boy," I assure smiling fondly. "Smart-alecky, but when he channels his energy, a good kid."

"It's his channeling I worry about," Officer Blankenship complains. "He's already been grounded three times this summer. I fear one day even my reach as an officer won't save him from the trouble he finds."

I shake my head, smiling knowingly. Jorge's hand securely molds to my lower back. He smiles at me. I tilt my head, trying to decipher his actions.

Officer Petree asks the two of us to excuse them for a moment. The three officers exit to the hallway. I hear murmurs but can't understand their words. I look to Jorge for help.

"Jake is a good cop. Trust he will help you," Jorge pleads, bending his knees to lower so we are eye-to-eye. His hand grasps the back of my neck before pulling me into his powerful chest. His hands gently glide up and down my back, calming my racing heart, my unsteady breaths, and my soul. The sound of a throat clearing interrupts.

Jorge raises my chin to assess my emotional status. His dark eyes search mine. With another sound of a throat clearing, Jorge states without breaking eye contact, "Jake, you're killing me."

Male laughter breaks Jorge's spell on me. I pull back and turn toward the officers adorning my apartment once again.

"Jorge, may I speak to you for a moment..." Jake inquires. Looking at me, he states. "Alone?"

24

SALT, TEQUILA, AND LIME

Taylor Continues Retelling Her Story

I wave them off as I head to the kitchen for another water. Jorge approaches as I finish a long refreshing drink from the bottle.

"Can they search your apartment?" Acknowledging the question forming upon my lips, he continues, "They want to search for drugs that John may have hidden here. They believe he may have a stash and that is why he is so frantic about entering the apartment." Placing a finger upon my lips to silence me, he finishes, "They will not hold you responsible if they find drugs. They only want to remove them to keep you safe."

I can't speak. The mere mention that drugs might hide in my presence upsets me. I witness the destruction they reek on the students and their families every day at school. Congenital disabilities, learning disabilities, homelessness, foster care, and addiction to drugs affect many of my middle school students. The thought of such a vile substance in my apartment cripples me. I simply nod in agreement to the search, prior to my world spinning as hot needles crawl up my spine.

A mist of cold water sprinkles my face. I struggle to open my eyelids. Voices murmur; I can't comprehend. I attempt to focus on one thing. One thing might allow me to regain consciousness. Blurry haze consumes my vision. I flutter my eyelids as I reach for…

"Taylor," Jorge's voice pierces my heavy fog. "Hey, there you are," he greets as I focus and smile at his concerned face near mine. "Easy," he prompts as I attempt to sit up. "Take it slow. You fainted."

Leaning on the lower cabinet door, I pull my legs toward my chest before I secure my arms around them. I'm on the kitchen floor. Jorge and Officer Blankenship squat nearby.

As I sip from the water bottle Jorge forces to my lips, the female officer states I didn't hit my head because Jorge's cat-like reflexes cushioned my fall.

"How is Sarah?" I ask my student's mother.

"Sarah is fine. Let's focus on you right now." She places a hand to Jorge's forearm, drawing the water bottle away. "Have you fainted before?"

As I slowly shake my head no, she continues to ask another question each time I answer. "Any new medications?" No. "Any family history of fainting or seizures?" No. "Might you be pregnant?"

"I can't be pregnant, unless by immaculate conception. I'm fine. I flew home today. I ate supper, had a few beers; then my night spun out of control as my dumb-ass ex-fiancé decided to drop by." *Pregnant. That's hilarious. I haven't had sex for a year, so it's not possible. However, I plan to become pregnant for Jackson and Kennedy. I will become pregnant without having sex.* The irony isn't lost on me.

Jorge helps me stand as the officer hovers nearby.

"Emily," I state suddenly. "Emily Blankenship. Do you mind if I address you as Emily and not Officer Blankenship?"

Jorge believes I've lost my mind. He doesn't understand I know her as a parent of my student Sarah. Though she makes every attempt to be professional, I'll only see her as the mother at school functions without her uniform and sidearm.

"You may call me Emily." She answers.

"May I call you Emily?" Jorge asks with exaggerated pouty lips and fluttering eyelids.

"You," she begins, poking him on the tip of his nose. "Must still call me Officer Blankenship while I am in uniform."

Jake motions for his partner to accompany him to my bedroom.

Officer Staton approaches me. "We found two stashes."

I cover my mouth after a cry escapes. "We have called in the canine unit. We hope to find every ounce, so you may rest assured you are safe."

"Can I take Taylor to my place?" Jorge asks.

Officer Staton discusses this with the other officers.

Jorge's roommate Jake returns. Looking at me, he states, "The officers will be in my apartment for a couple more hours." Looking at Jorge, he suggests, "She should stay elsewhere tonight."

I blurt, "I'll take a drug test. You can use a sample of my hair." I pull a few strands out for him. "I don't use drugs. I've never used drugs."

"We believe you. John displays unmistakable signs of drug use tonight. He was high at your door, threatening you. You need to prove nothing to us." Jake pats Jorge's shoulder. "Take her to our place. She's been through enough tonight." Looking at me, he continues. "Tomorrow, you need to come to the station to file a report and a restraining order."

I ride to Jorge's in a haze. I don't see the neighborhoods pass by my car window. I don't see the road before me. I see nothing. Nothing but the rock-bottom my life has fallen to. I've reached a new low. I invited John to live with me. I allowed him constant verbal abuse. I allowed his drunken binges to dictate my life. His drug use has now penetrated my acquaintances. *Why did I allow him to hurt me?*

Can I ever find happiness? Can I allow myself to find someone worthy of my love? Kennedy has Jackson; can I ever find what she had? Am I capable? Or will I continue to torture myself by seeking out those who will hurt me?

Jorge turns off the ignition, then turns towards me. Hoping to salvage what little night remains, I persuade the ghosts of my past to run toward the shadows.

"We're here," he states as he opens the driver's door.

Exiting, I realize I rode in my dream car without enjoying a single moment. Jorge entwines his hand with mine. We're in a parking garage. An elevator ride carries us toward the apartment he shares with Jake.

"Make yourself at home," Jorge prompts. He turns on a few lights, illuminating the space. The apartment is much larger than mine. I stand in a large open living room, kitchen, and dining room area. This space alone is bigger than my entire apartment.

"A bathroom is the second door on the left down the hall," Jorge announces. I quickly glance toward the long, dark hallway. I do not notice him approach behind me.

"Beer?" He asks, extending his arm around me with a cold bottle of Bud Light. "Come join me on the sofa."

I accept the proffered beer and settle into the over-stuffed sofa. I remove my Converse, dropping them to the floor and pull my legs under me. When Jorge turns on a random movie, I stare at the TV unseeing. My beer turns warm before I consume half of it, as I leave it on the coffee table in front of me.

Jorge's empty bottle joins mine when he lowers himself before me. My eyes survey his slightly-wavy black hair, his coffee-colored eyes, his stern caramel jaw, and broad shoulders. Everything about this strong, masculine man softens my mood.

"What can I do?" He pleads. "How can I help you tonight?"

"Help me forget my mistake. Help me accept it and move on," I beg.

Jorge retrieves a bottle of tequila from the kitchen with a salt shaker and a bowl of sliced limes. I chuckle at his mode of erasing my past.

"I've only been with Rosalynn." His words slice through the thick air. "We moved to Chicago so she could join a dance troop here." Taking a seat at the other end of the sofa facing me, he continues speaking. "After six-months, she received an invitation to audition in New York. I wouldn't let her miss the opportunity. I insisted she audition, knowing she had an excellent chance to make it." He runs his fingers through his hair. His eyes sparkle while speaking of Rosalynn. "She was called back a week later, accepted into the company, and I haven't seen her since." Jorge shares his story to take my mind off my own troubles.

"How long has it been?" I question.

"It's been one year, seven months, and ten days," he explains. "She filed for divorce after six months. I didn't want the divorce, but I love Rosalynn enough to let her go. We still talk and text occasionally. I still wear my ring because I love and miss her with every breath."

Jorge licks, then sprinkles salt upon the arch of his left hand between thumb and forefinger. He sucks the salt upon his hand, takes a long pull of tequila from the bottle, then sucks a lime wedge. Removing the wedge, he motions for my turn.

"I met John at a frat party. Jackson played on the baseball team with him and introduced us." I secure a loose strand of hair behind my ear. "I have demons from my childhood. Alcohol and parties allow me to forget. In college, I took every opportunity to escape. Some would say I was out of control." I deeply sigh while playing with the hem of my t-shirt. "I kept my grades up, my spot on the cheerleading squad, and my scholarships. I focused when I needed; I escaped when I could. Jackson and Kennedy took care of me when I really let go." I smile fondly.

"After the party, we hung out. We never really dated, and he rarely took me out in public." I wrap my arms tighter around myself. "His controlling behavior began immediately. His verbal and emotional abuse started soon after." I glance up through my lashes to Jorge. "I let him manipulate me, shrink me, and define me." I swallow hard before continuing. "I suspected he cheated on me for a couple of years. I could never speak of it-he would have…"

"Did he," Jorge interrupts. "Did he physically hurt you?"

25

MY NICE-GUY-RADAR IS FAULTY

Taylor

I meet Jorge's eyes. In them I see his worry John physically abused me.

"No, I feared he might, but he never crossed that line." I reach for his hand, grasping it between my two, and I continue, "I returned from a trip to Washington D.C. with my students. I found women in bed with him. The apartment was a disaster. Drugs, used condoms, and trash were everywhere. That's when I threw him out and changed the locks." Jorge squeezes my hands. "We were over the minute I moved us to Chicago. He found work in a bar. He partied too much. He stayed out, sometimes overnight. We were two roommates, nothing more. It wasn't a healthy relationship. I did what I had to, to protect myself. I should have found the strength to end it years ago. I just couldn't bear the thought of being alone."

"But you were alone," Jorge points out. "You cut ties with friends; you never went out, you worked, and cowered at home alone."

Ouch! The truth hurts.

"I thought he was finally out of my life." I whisper.

"He is now." Jorge replies sternly. "He will go to jail if you press charges. With a restraining order, he won't come near you again." Jorge motions to the bottle on the sofa table. I follow his previous actions in consuming salt, tequila, and lime.

"On to the next topic," Jorge leads.

Without thinking, I blurt, "Jackson and Kennedy asked me to be their surrogate. I accepted, and now I'm going to prepare to carry their baby."

I watch as surprise, concern, and something else crosses Jorge's gorgeous face.

"That's a mighty big favor," he states the obvious.

I explain what their friendship means to me, the struggles Kennedy has overcome, and my strong desire to help them with this.

"It's a selfless act, a great testament to your friendship, and your true character," Jorge admits.

I brush it off. I'm not agreeing to be a surrogate for my personal gain. My friends deserve a baby. I can give one to them.

Jorge licks my hand before his own; then he sprinkles salt on us both. One after the other, we lick the salt, we take a shot of tequila, and we suck a lime.

"When is this surrogacy is to take place? And have you worked out all the logistics?" Jorge asks.

"I immediately said yes, but Jackson insisted I take a week to consider it. Then I am supposed to call to announce I still want to be their surrogate on Friday," I explain. "We will start planning, then."

"Well, I hope you will allow me to help you as your belly expands. I can carry groceries up the stairs, move heavy items, and run to the store for the foods you're craving," Jorge offers. "As you know, my sister has four kids. I was nearby for the first two, so I'm familiar with the mood swings and food cravings."

"We will see," I reply.

Suddenly, I realize I have no other friends in Chicago to assist me. My work friends are not really close friends. I won't have a local support system during the surrogacy. Jackson and Kennedy will do their best via phone and internet to stay in touch, but I'm truly alone.

"Have any snacks?" I ask, my stomach growling. Glancing at my phone, I see it's just after midnight.

Jorge laughs as he pulls me from the sofa to join him in the kitchen. He offers chips and queso, sandwiches, or crackers and cheese. I wrinkle my nose.

"Have any sweets?" I inquire hopefully.

Reaching above the refrigerator, he reveals a cabinet stacked full of Oreos, cupcakes, store-bakery cookies, powdered donuts, and ice cream toppings. He moves a few items to reveal even more sweet snacks behind.

Needing a better view, with no step-ladder in sight, I easily hop to sit on the counter, then turn as I stand next to the fridge to inspect the loot. With marshmallows, chocolate, and graham crackers in hand, I turn to dismount and find Jorge with cell phone raised, recording me. I flip him the bird before gracefully climbing down.

Jorge pushes a few buttons before tucking his phone in his back pocket. "We don't have a fire-pit." He nods towards my chosen sweets on the counter.

"I can make s'mores in the microwave," I announce as I prepare the ingredients. "Where'd you send the video?"

Through a devilish smile, he admits, "I texted Jake and Martha. They won't make it public."

"Need I remind you I recently met your sister and all her friends?" I assemble four stacks of s'mores, then turn to face him. "It'll be on social media by noon tomorrow."

Jorge nods in agreement, then shrugs his shoulders. Pointing to the four raw s'mores, he asks, "Do you plan to share?"

Teasingly, I shrug my shoulders before placing the s'mores in the microwave.

After consuming our s'mores, Jorge suggests we grab a couple of waters and continue our conversation while lying down. My heart leaps into my throat at the thought of the direction our evening together would take laying down in his bedroom.

Jorge seems like a nice guy, but I know my nice-guy-radar is faulty. His roommate is a cop, but that doesn't make him a nice guy by association. He demonstrated many moments of compassion toward me in multiple situations.

Meeting his sister led me to believe he is just as he seems. Again, I'm not to be trusted in my judgement.

"Hey," Jorge's deep voice beckons me. "No pressure. I'm exhausted. I just thought we could lie down and talk." His large hand ran through his dark hair. "We've got all night." He swallows hard. "I'll sleep on the sofa. We'll just talk."

I can only nod before I rise from the sofa. My bravado from earlier tonight no longer emboldens me. I link my hand in his, hoping I absorb some of his strength as he leads the way.

His bedroom is very masculine. I find a black dresser and headboard with a small brown folding chair near the closet. There are no wall-hangings and no knick-knacks. He quickly grabs a pair of jeans and socks from the floor, then places them in a nearby hamper.

Frozen in place at the door, my brain plays through several scenarios. The bed is a flashing neon light advertising sex.

Wham-Bam-Thank-you-Mam.

I don't want a one-night-stand with Jorge.

I could be myself with him. If this was a first date and I slept with him, would I lose him?

I'm drawn to him. I feel a connection. My heart tells me he needs to be in my life. My head tells me we connect.

I've been burned too many times. I can't trust my instincts.

"Will you drive me to a hotel?" I request. My shaky voice transmits the fear building in me.

He freezes. Shaking his head to regain control, he rapidly approaches. His arms extend and hands grip my shoulders. "I promise to remain a gentleman." He motions towards the bed. "Above the covers, on the pillows, we will talk." His eyes convey his sincerity. "I promise to sleep on the sofa."

I sweep my hair over my left shoulder as I ponder his statements, his intentions, and his good-guy appearance.

Is it a façade? I don't think it is.

I exhale. Focusing on my surroundings, I find Jorge is on the bed. I carefully lower myself on the mattress, anchoring my head on two pillows.

Smiling at my concession, Jorge begins, "What were you like in high school?"

26

A MORNING WOOD!

Taylor Continues Retelling Her Story

I squint, assessing the seriousness of his question. "I lived with my grandmother on a farm in rural Missouri," I begin. "My mom was in-and-out of my life from the age of four. I realized my education was my only way to escape my trailer-trash life. Cheerleading and straight A's allowed me to attend college."

"I don't see you as a goody-goody, snobby cheerleader," he states.

"I wasn't. I made the grades with little effort, and cheerleading opened more scholarship money for me. Don't get me wrong, I was good at it, but I lived three very different lives." I pause, not believing I'm about to share this. I find Jorge too easy to talk to. "In school, I focused. I contributed. As a cheerleader, I was loud, energetic, and creative." I sit up and sip from my water bottle.

"And the third Taylor, what was she like?" Jorge prompts me to continue.

Placing my head back on the pillow, I explain, "I partied. A lot. Weeknights and weekends. Alcohol turns off my anxiety, my worries, and my cares. It allows me to find peace, if only for a while." I take a deep breath.

I've never shared this with anyone. "I'm not an alcoholic. I don't crave or need it. I enjoy the serenity it brings. I longed for the acceptance at the parties. I didn't have to be perfect. I didn't have to perform. I, I..." My eyes dart left and right, searching for my words. "I'm not saying alcohol allowed the real me to surface. I was hiding. Hiding from feelings, expectations, and real-life. I don't need alcohol to have fun. I've always been capable of causing a scene, embarrassing others, and letting go. But inside, I question everything. I worry about everything. On the outside, I'm displaying 'Here I am. Don't like it? Then Fuck You!' While on the inside I worry, fret, and contemplate the reactions to my every action." I blink a few times. I can't believe I'm spilling my guts.

"I see you as the life of the party. You're magnetic. People are drawn to you." Jorge's statement throws me. I fit in easily with others. However, trusting others enough to become friends isn't easy for me. Jorge adjusts his pillows before continuing. "I imagine guys flock to you."

I flip to my back, breaking our stare. "The wrong type of guys..." I reply. "The kind that wander around behind my back, punch a girl when drunk, call her horrible names in public or in private, are controlling, and verbally abusive." I turn my head for a moment to gage his reaction.

"That streak of terrible relationships has now ended." His empathetic eyes convey his sincerity. "Jackson and Kennedy are back in your life." He smiles while tucking my hair behind my ear. "I'm making it my mission to see you never choose a bad boy again."

This topic causes too much pain. The actions of John tonight are too fresh. I need to choose a different topic. I roll to face Jorge once again. "Will you get back with Rosalynn, or are you ready to move on?" As I replay my words, I realize it sounded as if I plan to make a move on him. "I mean..."

Placing a single finger over my lips, he silences me. "Jake will help wrap up this John mess. With your friends back in your life and the surrogacy lasting nine months, you'll have plenty of time to regroup before your next relationship."

He pauses momentarily. "As for Rosalynn, I hope we'll find our way back to each other. She admitted she has dated a few men while in New York, but nothing felt right. Those are her words." He fights a smile.

"What?" I pry.

"Confession… promise you won't judge me?" I sense he is torn. I need to know what has him so conflicted at this moment.

He motions towards the small brown sack on the nightstand. I realize it is the same small sack from the store earlier. "I purchased some condoms, hoping to enjoy them with you tonight." His eyes search for my reaction. "It's just…"

It's my turn to silence him with my finger to his lips. "Tonight's been amazing. I mean, other than my ex-fiancé showing up and the police involvement. I feel safe with you. I can easily open up to you. But neither of us are ready to hook-up." I hope the feeling is mutual. "It's easy to see you are still madly in love with Rosalynn, and I should give up men for a while."

Rescuing me from my rambling, Jorge states, "We will make great friends."

I nod. *I can use another friend.*

"Should I go?" I question hesitantly.

Before I understand his movements, Jorge rolls me over, pulls me closer, and tucks my back to his front. "I need a friend tonight."

His words engulf me.

I'm not sure how long we talk while cuddling. I couldn't bear the thought of spending the night alone, and he's been alone for too long. I fall asleep in his strong, muscular arms.

The next morning, I wake sharing a bed with Jorge. While I'm snug under the covers. Jorge remains on top. My eyes sweep over his face, bare chest, strong abs, to his tented boxers.

Oh my gosh! A morning wood!

My giggle wakes the sleeping Jorge.

Rubbing his sleepy eyes, he greets me with his dazzling smile. His hand scratches his chest briefly before adjusting himself. "Sorry," he says as he slides a pillow to cover his midsection.

"It can't be helped," I reply. I attempt to move my thoughts elsewhere, unsuccessfully. My curiosity gets the best of me. "How do you usually deal with…that…condition?"

Jorge chuckles nervously. He asks, "Are you serious?"

I nod.

"It just goes away after a few minutes," he explains.

I'm not satisfied with that answer.

"You never take advantage of the situation to, um… masturbate?" My words clearly shock Jorge. "I mean a year with Rosalynn gone, you must be a master at self-pleasuring by now. Not to judge. I mean… I'm a master, too."

Smiling ear-to-ear, Jorge inquires, "So, if you woke each day with a stiffy, you'd pleasure yourself daily?"

"If I didn't have a partner in bed, yes, I would take advantage of the situation," I explain. *My filter is clearly still asleep.* "I'm very familiar with a wide variety of toys in my nightstand," I explain. I sense Jorge trying to decipher the truth of my statements. "I have a very healthy libido. I'm not a one-night-stand kind of girl. So, I must be creative on my own."

"So, these toys…" Jorge curiously prompts.

"I'd show ya, but I'd have to kill ya," I tease.

Jorge understands I don't plan to describe my toys.

In a moment of bravery, I tug the pillow covering his groin. Seems the passage of time hasn't solved his situation.

"Your topic of conversation is to blame," Jorge claims.

"I'll leave the room so you can rub one out," I state.

He quickly clutches my wrist, preventing my exit.

"Um… Jorge, I can't remain just a friend if I help you," I remind him of our mutually agreed upon status.

"I want to play a game," Jorge nervously blurts. "I have a competition in mind."

Intrigued, I motion for him to continue explaining.

"First one done wins."

Perverted minds must think alike.

"Two questions," I respond. "Win what?" I smile sheepishly. "Done doing what?" I purse my lips towards Jorge.

"You know very well what I mean by done, and the winner gets to choose the prize. Anything goes."

This has just become very interesting.

Internally, I quickly debate this game.

Friends.

We are friends.

We want to remain friends.

I need him as a friend. I need someone in Chicago I can contact when I need to talk.

He is very hard, his muscles are tight, and he needs a release.

Would we remain friends if we watched each other?

I assess my body. Because of our recent topic of conversation, I'm a bit aroused but nowhere near enough to compete.

"You have a head start, and I have no toys with me to assist," I contemplate out loud.

Jorge steeples his hands while wearing an ornery smirk. "Are you afraid you'll lose?" he asks.

"I only want a fair battle," I reply.

"I'll allow you a three-minute head start," he states.

"I believe I should get a five-minute head start," I haggle.

Jorge agrees.

I lay out the ground rules. "We have to remain on the bed, above the covers, no talking, no distracting or interfering."

In agreement, Jorge sets the timer on his cell phone for five minutes. We each lie on our side of the bed with his phone between us.

"Once we start, there is no going back," I state.

When I question if Jorge plans to compete. He doesn't speak. He simply smiles, then starts the timer with a flourish. I remove my t-shirt and shorts to begin.

I end my story there.

"No way!" Kennedy interrupts. "The two of you had a masturbation competition while sharing a bed?" Her bright red cheeks express her embarrassment. "No sex, just masturbation?"

I assure her we completed the competition, just as described. Jorge quickly won after the five-minute alarm signaled he should begin. I struggled to light my own fire until Jorge finished. The vulnerability and power of his orgasm proved a powerful aphrodisiac. I learned I depend too much on my machines to pleasure myself.

Kennedy shakes her head in disbelief. "The two of you didn't have sex, don't plan to sleep together, and now you are good friends." Still shaking her head, Kennedy states, "You never cease to amaze me."

27

BUSTED

Taylor

I rise from bed to an empty house. I glance at my phone to see it's 9:15 a.m. It's earlier than expected. I tidy up in my bathroom before fixing my toast. On the kitchen island, I find the list Kennedy and I created yesterday. I plan to make my friends' lives easier while I live here. I plan to clean, shop, and run errands. Jackson claims he has no items for me to help with. Kennedy asks for my help with research on fertility, surrogacy, and a few phone calls.

I start my to do list with a phone call.

"Thank you for calling The Blue Agency. How may I assist you?" A friendly, female voice greets.

"I have questions regarding my coverage," I respond. I lightly cross off item number two on my list. Pretending to be Kennedy, I give details so the agent may pull up the policy under Jackson's name through his employer. I ask if fertility treatments are covered and make a note on my list.

"Is a surrogate covered?" I ask.

At my question, the insurance woman asks me many questions.

"Am I (Kennedy) to be the surrogate for another couple? Is my (Kennedy's) surrogate on the same employer's insurance already? Will eggs be harvested or donated? Will sperm be donated? Will in-vitro be performed?"

I do my best to answer each question.

She explains, "Your policy doesn't cover a surrogate pregnancy for us (Jackson and Kennedy). Harvesting my (Kennedy's) eggs and all medications would be covered. At the point of egg and sperm donation and in-vitro fertilization, these and all further items would not be covered by the policy."

I thank her for her help, then disconnect as I scribble more details into my notes from the call.

I pour myself a large glass of iced-tea. I sprinkle True Lemon into my glass and stir. My mind swims with this new knowledge. I open my laptop to research costs of in-vitro fertilization procedures. I find surrogate pregnancy insurance policies available as an addition to current health insurance. I print these and ten more pages of information to share.

Frustrated by the daunting surrogacy decisions ahead of us, I empty my half-full tea glass in the sink. I pull out the step stool to reach the small cabinet doors above the refrigerator. I grab the first bottle I find and pour two-fingers of Captain Morgan into my glass. I toss it back, savoring the burn. I pour two-fingers more, filling the rest of the glass with cold Diet Pepsi.

If I hadn't resigned, my insurance would cover my pregnancy. I only have insurance now until the end of July. Jackson's policy won't cover me either. I know they cannot afford multiple in-vitro treatments. They won't be able to pay cash for my OB appointments or delivery. *By resigning, I may have ruined my chance to give Jackson and Kennedy a baby.*

How will I share this information tonight?

I decide a long bubble bath might help me relax and hopefully devise a new plan. I carry my laptop and drink into my bathroom.

The fluffy bubbles and hot water lull me to daydream. Instead of finding a new plan, I imagine myself eight months pregnant. Kennedy is decorating the nursery, while Jackson attempts to assemble a crib.

My friends deserve to be parents. I must do everything I can to help them with this.

I'm so enthralled in my thoughts and daydreams; I don't hear the garage door or the kitchen door. I jump from my relaxed reclined position as Kennedy knocks on the open bedroom door.

"Taylor, you in here?" She calls.

I pull my knees to my chest and wrap my arms around them tight. "Yes," I answer.

Kennedy peeks into my bathroom while remaining in the doorway. "I'm only home for a minute. Two girls called in, and I can't find replacements for them. I'm gonna have to work in childcare until eight tonight." Kennedy's tired eyes and slumped shoulders let me know she is much too tired to work until eight. "I'm just changing out of my skirt, grabbing a bite to eat, and heading back." She pulls the hair tie from her ponytail, releasing her blonde hair to fall around her shoulders. "I could use a bubble bath." She states, walking toward her bedroom.

I extricate myself from the warmth of the tub, making a mental note to have a hot bubble bath ready for her tonight. I wrap a robe around me quickly before padding to the kitchen. I pull fruit, yogurt, turkey, lettuce, and the other items Kennedy might like from the fridge. I place a plastic container with a lid and a box of plastic bags nearby. I pull a reusable grocery bag from the pantry and place two bottles of water in this bag.

Kennedy rapidly descends the stairs.

"What can I fix you for dinner?" I ask.

She squeezes in next to me, placing items in the plastic container and bag.

"Thanks. I'm sorry I'm leaving you alone," she states as she closes the garage door.

As I replace the food in the refrigerator, I realize I will need to wait for Tuesday night to share the results of my research today. This gives me twenty-four hours to brainstorm a new plan.

At seven, I note Jackson hasn't arrived home from work yet. I send a quick text

> **ME**
> plan to be home for dinner?
> or should I eat without you?

Forty-five minutes later, I have yet to hear from him. I begin to text again when my phone vibrates.

> **JORGE**
> how was research?

> **ME**
> thought you working 2nite

> **JORGE**
> on break

> **ME**
> Ken had 2 work 2nite
> Jackson still @ work

> **JORGE**
> house 2 self
> time 2 party

> **ME**
> partying hard
> Lifetime Movies, popcorn, & peanut butter ice cream

> **JORGE**
> party animal

> **ME**
> right?

> **JORGE**
> called Rosalynn like you advised

Surrogate Series

ME
and?

JORGE
you were right

she wants a visit

ME
planning?

JORGE
talk 2 boss tomorrow

will if new schedule allows

ME
yay!

JORGE
told her about you...us

ME
everything?

JORGE
yes

ME
and?

JORGE
can I call tomorrow?

2 much 2 text now

ME
yes hint? all good?

JORGE
(thumbs up emoji)

back 2 work GTG

ME
call before 4

> JORGE
> (thumbs up emoji)

I stare at my iPhone for a bit, hoping new texts will arrive. I lay it down. Something must have come up at work for Jackson.

Popcorn and ice cream for dinner. Hell yeah!

In between Lifetime Movies, I grab the notebook Kennedy gave me. I decide I'll journal about today and tomorrow. I open to the first page, write today's date on the heading line, and write. I write about the research, my findings, my fears…I list things I might do while Jackson and Kennedy are at work to pass the time. I'm half watching the movie, half randomly listing things to do when Jackson pulls into the driveway. After quickly stashing the notebook in my room, I'm carrying my popcorn and ice cream to the kitchen when Jackson enters.

"Busted," he claims as I freeze mid-step. "That looks healthy," he states, motioning to my arms.

28

NEED TO UP THEIR INSURANCE COVERAGE

Taylor

"I popped the popcorn to nibble on while watching the first movie. I moved to the ice-cream after seven, when I couldn't reach you by text," I explain.

Jackson apologizes, stating, "There was a crisis at the store. I stayed until everything improved, instead of heading home to call and email the store every few minutes."

His white shirt is filthy. I see finger trails from rubbing his dirty hands on the rib area. I assume the blue ovals are detergent or liquid soap. He has a torn left knee in his black slacks. His dress shoes are dusty and scuffed. *Whatever it was, it must have been a very messy crisis.*

"you should go change while I prepare you some dinner," I encourage.

"I can fix my own sandwich," he states.

"I have nothing else to do," I inform.

He drags himself up the stairs as I remain in the kitchen. While butter melts on the griddle, I assemble a ham and cheese sandwich. When the butter hisses, I place the bread in the pan. I quickly grab a fork to assist with flipping the sandwich. I remain standing at the stove watching the sandwich, for fear I might burn it. Jackson returns as I nestle the grilled sandwich on a plate. Sliding the plate across the bar, I toss a bag of chips and place a jar of pickles nearby.

Jackson cuts the bread diagonally. He marvels at the oozing cheese. He attempts a bite, finding it much too hot for his mouth. A handful of chips in hand, he inquires about how I spent my first day.

"It was eerily quiet today," I announce, before I share details of my morning workout at the YMCA, my afternoon of online research and phone calls, and the evening of Lifetime Movies. I purposefully share very little about the research, not wanting to tell him how I've let them down. I place the focus on Jackson by asking about the crisis at the store.

Jackson insists it isn't interesting. He finishes his meal, then cleans up the mess. "What will you do with all of your free time?" He questions. "I'd go crazy alone with nothing to do all day."

"I used Kennedy's journal to start a list of possible ideas for my free time," I share. When he raises his eyebrow, I list a few examples. "Workout, read, enroll in a cooking class, or art class…"

Of course, Jackson teases me about needing the cooking class. "I'll need to contact the cooking school so they might up their insurance coverage before you learn to cook."

Making light of his teasing, I ask, "What time will Kennedy be home if she closes the Kids' Zone at eight?"

He tells me she will be home by 8:15-8:20. I glance at the clock, noting it's already ten after eight. I explain my plan before ascending the steps to draw Kennedy a bubble bath. I start the hot water, then scour the main bath for bubbles. Finding none, I jog to my bathroom for my bottle of bubble bath. I also snag my two candles and the lighter. *My girl needs to relax.* She has a fertility doctor appointment tomorrow morning. Anxious would be an understatement.

I ensure the water temperature is just right by dipping my wrist under the surface. I turn off the faucet, light two candles, lay a fresh towel near the tub, flick off the light, then descend the steps to await Kennedy's return from work.

Jackson is watching a DVR of ESPN *Sports Center* from earlier today. I join him on the sofa. Moments pass before Kennedy arrives. She breezes in as if she had not just completed a twelve-hour day on her feet. I notice she places nearly untouched food near the sink from her packed supper. I hope she ate something else and didn't skip a meal. Jackson pauses *Sports Center* before informing her a hot bath awaits her upstairs.

Kennedy kisses my cheek, and then Jackson's before retiring for the night. Jackson returns to the show. At its end, Jackson bids me a good night and tells me he will see me for dinner tomorrow night. I debate staying in the living room or retiring to my room. I decide to grab a drink and snacks to keep me company in my room for the rest of the night.

The next morning, I opt to work out after lunch, so I might visit with Kennedy after her ten o'clock fertility appointment. I dust, clean, vacuum, and sweep, starting upstairs and finishing in the kitchen. As I have thought of Jackson's sandwich non-stop since last night, I fix a grilled ham and cheese for my lunch. I grab my workout bag and make my way to the YMCA.

Kennedy is not at her desk when I finish, so I peek in the Kid's Zone without success. I ask Pamela at the Welcome Desk if Kennedy is available. She states Kennedy called after her appointment, stating she would not be back this afternoon. I decide she drove home to be with me, thank Pamela for her help, and scurry to my car.

Kennedy's car is not in the garage when I arrive home. I pull my cell phone from my workout bag, but I have no texts or missed calls. I decide to hop in the shower before she gets back.

After my quick shower, I text Kennedy.

ME
what ya doin?

I stare impatiently at my screen. Moments pass, but nothing. I dial Kennedy's cell phone; it goes straight to her voicemail. I leave a message explaining I worked out late, stopped by to see her, and was told she wouldn't be back. I state I am back home, anxiously waiting to hear from her about the appointment.

To pass the time, I log onto my Teacher's Pay Teachers web page to check sales. I wonder if I will ever stop being surprised by my online sales. Surely at some point I will expect it. Now I'm still thrilled when I check on it. I mentally predict my deposit total for July while logging into my bank to check my account balances. My checking hovers at $1000. I try to maintain this balance. I feel it is enough for a shopping spree, emergency repairs, or to cover my general expenses. My savings account balance is $12,000. My Mustang purchase nearly wiped me out. With my online sales, my savings will grow the end of July.

I could suggest using some of these funds to assist with the in-vitro fertilization we need to get pregnant. I could use my savings to purchase the additional surrogate insurance to assist with the pregnancy expenses. It would wipe me out. I would have nothing left to assist with any out-of-pocket expenses. If I didn't become pregnant on the first attempt, I would have nothing to assist with paying for more in-vitro appointments.

I'm not sure if Kennedy and Jackson have money in savings. I know Jackson is a new store manager making the minimum salary. Kennedy can't make over thirty-thousand dollars at the YMCA. *How will they pay to create this family? So many questions, so few answers.* I decide to journal my thoughts to share tonight at our informational planning dinner.

Promptly at 5:15, Kennedy arrives home as planned. I choose not to interrogate her on her whereabouts this afternoon.

She breezes by me. "On my way to change before we prepare dinner," she states.

Jackson pulls into the driveway at six. He hoovers around the kitchen nibbling and chatting about his workday before he excuses himself to shower and change.

With dinner nearly ready, Kennedy asks us to grab our notebooks.

Jackson and I fetch our notebooks and pens. The four of us meet back at the table.

Worried about Kennedy's reaction to my research news, I suggest we say grace before dining. Jackson volunteers to lead us in prayer. I think he senses I know our plans have detoured already. He knows I'm trying everything to assist the three of us with this surrogacy. Our eyes dart at each other and away before Kennedy catches us silently communicating our worry.

Kennedy encourages us to eat; our conversation is light as dinner begins.

I decide to break the ice. "Ken, how was the doctor's appointment?" I smile encouragingly as I place my hand on hers.

Jackson places his hand on her free hand.

Kennedy clears her throat. "Let's eat now and talk as soon as we are done. That way we enjoy the warm food, and don't talk with our mouths full."

I glance Jackson's direction, noting his eyes convey his worry. I slightly nod, signaling something is up. We quickly clean our plates, eager to hear Kennedy's news.

I begin our planning as I open my notebook, explaining I journaled two days in a row. I read my list of items I might do to pass my free time while they work. Jackson admits he journaled some last night before bed. He doesn't read straight from the page, but admits he is nervous about the in-vitro process and hopes it happens sooner, rather than later. He turns to a blank page in order to take notes tonight.

Kennedy sighs deeply. "Today's appointment didn't go as we hoped." She looks to Jackson. "We can't use my eggs," she blurts, bursting into sobs.

29

TURKEY BASTER METHOD

Taylor

Jackson and I search for words to say.
What?
Why?
How?
What now?

Are the only words I can come up with. Jackson stands from his chair, wrapping his wife in an embrace. I feel as I am trespassing witnessing this tender moment.

"So, we find another way," I suggest. "We make a new plan. We're not giving up—this is just a speed bump." I fight the urge to pace and the urge to hit or throw something. I cannot let her give up. "Ken," I carefully address her. "Do you have anything in your notebook for this scenario?"

I witness my words registering on Kennedy's face. She pulls away from Jackson, her hands darting for her baby planning notebook. Jackson mouths 'thank you' over her shoulder.

Kennedy frantically flips page after page, seeking the exact list. She turns more than ten pages in her notebook before finding the information she wants. "Ah-ha!" She shouts, tossing the open notebook in the center of the table. 'Egg Donor' heads the page in large bold writing.

"I'll do it!" I exclaim. "I'll be your egg donor."

Jackson tries to pull the reins back to logically discuss prior to moving forward. Kennedy engulfs me in an over-animated bear hug, thanking me over and over.

"Ken," Jackson begins, but pauses. "Ken, let's step back and discuss all options."

He is hesitant, even though he wants nothing more than to give his wife everything. Despite his desire to be a dad, he must be a voice of reason for every step in their process.

Kennedy returns to her seat. Her eyes quickly meet Jackson's as she nods in agreement. However, she resembles a child watching the second-hand on the classroom clock as the recess bell draws near.

"I actually had some issues come up while doing my phone calls and research yesterday," I state. "If you allow me to be your egg donor, it actually saves a lot of money. Money for the donor and money on a second in-vitro procedure." All eyes on me, I excuse myself to grab my printouts. "Your insurance doesn't cover surrogacy, egg donors, or in-vitro," I inform Jackson and Kennedy. I quickly continue toward a brighter side. "If I am your egg donor, it costs you nothing. I mean, my eggs could bring top-dollar on the market with my intelligence and skills," I tease. "And I saw a method while conducting my surrogacy research..." I open my iPad, scrambling to find it. I continue as I browse. "We can improvise and skip the in-vitro costs, too. Here it is." I turn the tablet towards them. "We can create this baby here at home, just the three of us, and save over fifty-thousand dollars," I announce.

"I've read about this," Kennedy confides, flipping her notebook to a page titled 'The Turkey Baster Method.'

One convinced, one to go. I focus on Jackson. Ever skeptical, Jackson furrows his brow while reading the webpage. "Now," I continue my sharing of my research. "There are supplemental policies you can purchase to cover a surrogate pregnancy. They seem pretty expensive." I swallow hard, preparing to share my confession. "If I hadn't resigned from teaching, my insurance would cover my appointments." I sigh and run my fingers through my hair. "I'm sorry. I didn't think far enough ahead. I should have kept my job. I would've had to stay in Chicago and update you via phone and text, but it would have saved you money." I rise and stand nervously behind my chair. My hands wringing at the spindles. "I could try to find a position here, but insurance will not kick in for at least sixty days," I lament.

"Show me the surrogacy insurance information," Jackson requests. "We have some savings. Maybe it'll cover it."

"I have a healthy savings account we could use, too," I share.

"No!" Jackson emphatically states. "This is our baby. We will pay for it. You're already sacrificing so much for us." Jackson's voice loses its harshness. Softly, he continues, "We can find a way. Surely the three of us can figure this out." He smiles my way.

I simply nod.

"Let's walk through this from the top. Kennedy, tell us about your fertility appointment today," he asks.

"My Chronic Kidney Disease, coupled with the havoc the eating disorders wreaked on my body, makes it too risky for me to attempt a pregnancy. My ovaries aren't producing eggs, so harvesting my eggs isn't a possibility," Kennedy shares.

My heavy heart feels it might explode in my tight chest. Kennedy couldn't know her actions in her late teens would have lifelong consequences. I've witnessed every step in her journey to overcome the anorexia and bulimia. She shoplifted food, diuretics, and laxatives. She punished her body by withholding nutrients. She binged and hid food wrappers in her trunk. Her five-foot-seven body wasted away to eighty pounds. I assisted Jackson in admitting her into the hospital; I took part in the counseling sessions. She worked hard to become the person she is today. Now, Kennedy maintains a healthy weight. She still pays attention to calories and her daily intake, but in a healthier manner. She allows herself to nibble an occasional dessert and consume an alcoholic beverage. It's heartbreaking that all her work won't allow her to overcome her past and have a biological child of her own.

I hope this news won't trigger a relapse. I hope she will allow me to provide her with a baby of her own. I pray she's strong enough to find another way to become a mother.

I long to be that way.

"I want the two of you to listen to my words, then discuss them together," I begin, my tone firm. "I would be honored to be your egg donor. I want to donate my eggs. I'm already your surrogate. I'm a natural choice for your egg donor. I'm healthy, I'm athletic, and I realize I'm short, but with Jackson's height, perhaps my shortness won't be a factor." I smile at my two best friends. "Allowing me to be your egg donor and surrogate while living here saves you tens of thousands of dollars. We can attempt fertilization at home a couple months before resorting to pay for in-vitro," I plead my case. *I hope they see the sound reasoning for choosing me.* "Sleep on it. Make a pros and cons list. Discuss as much as you would like. I'm going nowhere. I'll support you no matter how you choose to start your family."

Kennedy turns to face Jackson, while he maintains eye contact with me a few moments more, before facing his wife. No words are spoken as a silent conversation flows between the couple.

"We'd be honored for you to be both our egg donor and surrogate," Jackson states, smiling widely. "We already consider you family. Our baby would just make it official."

Kennedy focuses on a page in her notebook.

"Ken," concern saturates my voice. "What do you think?"

Without hesitation, Kennedy echoes Jackson's words. While she updates her notebook, I smile at Jackson. Kennedy crosses out page after page, before turning to the front of the notebook again. Finding what she seeks, she hesitates. I sense her worry as she balks at this next topic. "I would like the three of us to have individual and group counseling sessions." Looking at me, she explains, "I love Dr. Wilson. She recommends an individual appointment every other week then a group appointment on the alternating weeks."

Confused, I ask for clarification as I open the July calendar on my phone.

"Individually, we have appointments on Thursday, July Fourteenth," she states. "Then as a group we meet on Thursday, July Twenty-First. An individual session every other week. A group appointment every other week. Dr. Wilson claims this will help us cope with our unconventional creation of our family." Looking to me, Kennedy suggests, "You might discuss the connection to the baby in utero and then what it will be like giving up the baby at birth. We will all have fears and concerns. She will be a resource to guide us on our journey."

I've only seen a shrink in the group sessions for Kennedy's eating disorders years ago. Although I understand I have many issues therapy could assist me with, weekly visits seem pretty intense. I'm not opposed to the thought of counseling. Kennedy seems excited by the routine of these appointments, so I choose to embrace them.

Voicing my concerns, Jackson asks, "Do we really need weekly visits for nine months?" He looks between Kennedy and me. "Will the surrogacy cause that many issues?"

Kennedy turns the page in her notebook. As she reads, she points to each line on the paper. "Topics might include infertility, stress, helplessness, trouble conceiving, financial burdens, allowing another to carry my baby, any pregnancy complications, strains on our friendship or marriage, patience, personal issues for each of us, etc."

Wow! Dr. Wilson and Kennedy thought of it all. I want to work through my personal relationship issues, and I'm sure my childhood and lack of parents might need to be discussed. I make a personal vow to keep an open mind as I attend my sessions.

"Insurance will cover Jackson and my sessions, and Dr. Wilson offered to see Taylor pro bono throughout the duration of our surrogacy," Kennedy announces. "It seems the doctor has a soft spot for the journey infertile couples experience as they attempt to become parents."

I'm unsure how I feel about attending free sessions. Perhaps I will address this on my first visit.

Kennedy flips toward the center of her planning notebook. I read the heading 'Turkey Baster Method'. As Kennedy and I discuss our findings on the modified turkey-baster-method online, Jackson's eyes widen, and all color drains from his face.

Sensing his growing discomfort, I suggest, "Maybe we should table our discussion and conduct further research."

30

DID I JUST AGREE TO COMMIT INSURANCE FRAUD?

Taylor

An hour later, I'm on social media in my room. Kennedy as she lurks just outside my bedroom door.

"Hey," I greet.

"Can I come in?" She asks.

"Of course," I reply.

She joins me at the head of the bed, sitting with our backs against the headboard.

"What are you doing?" she asks, peeking at my screen.

I show her my Pinterest Boards and new pins I just discovered. As I explain, I find her too distracted to truly see the addiction that is Pinterest.

"Spill the beans," I tell her.

"I have yet another favor to ask of you," she nearly whispers.

I search Kennedy's face for any clues. She's not sad or mad, stressed maybe.

She continues, "I hate to even ask. You already agreed to be our surrogate and egg donor. I fear we're taking advantage of you."

I place my left arm across her shoulders to pull her in a for a side-hug. "I'm here for you. You are my best friend. You know I would do anything for you." I close my MacBook, placing it beside me on a pillow. I release Kennedy and turn to face her with my full attention.

"I've run the numbers a few times." Kennedy's face scrunches. "Depending on the number of appointments and fertility drugs it takes to become pregnant, we might not be able to cover the labor and delivery costs at the hospital."

"I have a savings account we can use to cover some medical costs," I remind her.

"Jackson will never allow that," she reminds me.

"I have an idea. A plan that will save tons of money. Enough money to allow us all the procedures needed." As Kennedy pauses to place a strand of hair behind my ear, the suspense kills me.

"Ken, ask already," I demand.

"What if we used my name for the appointments and you use my insurance card?" Before I can speak, she places two fingers across my lips. "Martha gave me the name of a great baby doctor for you to use. Since my insurance will cover my pregnancy, I thought maybe you could use my card. You will be pregnant with my baby, so my insurance should assist us with the costs." Her slight smile seeks my acceptance. "I know it's a huge favor. I know we have asked a lot already. Taylor, I want to be a mother so bad it hurts. When I see babies at the YMCA or the store, I clutch my belly as tears well in my eyes. I long to cradle a baby in my arms, smell the baby scent on its bald head, rock a baby while feeding him a bottle, and lose sleep, frantically checking the nursery to ensure it's okay. I need to be a mother, and Jackson deserves to be a father. Can you imagine Jackson teaching his son football, basketball, baseball, and golf? I wouldn't ask this of you if I had another option. Financially, we will be so much better off two years from now. We are just catching back up. Jackson is a store director now; we won't have to move unless we choose to. His earnings will double in the next five years. I've only been at the YMCA nine months. Everything is going our way, except starting our family. We're so close. I can almost feel the baby kicking in your belly. In my mind, this seems very simple. You carry my insurance card with you. When you fill out paperwork, you use my name and birthdate. The medical history will be your own. No one will know. It'll save us lots of money." Kennedy's eyes scan back and forth across my face for answers.

I refrain from answering. *I need to process this; I need to think it over.* This additional request clutters my brain.

"Can I browse your Pinterest stuff while you think it over?" Kennedy pretends to be interested.

I open my laptop and quickly show how she types in the search area, then browses results. I stare unseeing at the screen.

I want to give my friends the baby they deserve. I know they will rock at parenting. And I believe it's unfair insurance doesn't cover alternate methods on the road to parenthood. Infertility is hard enough on couples without the added financial burdens. The screening process for foster parents and adoption further alienates some couples. Drug addicts and displaced people can become parents easily, while a couple like Jackson and Kennedy remain unlikely candidates because she shoplifted during her battle with eating disorders. They're not felons, addicts, or working in illegal businesses, but they flag them as high risk in the foster care and adoption processes.

Fertility doesn't make you a perfect parent; putting family first makes great parents. They have so much love to share, and they'll love a child unconditionally.

I think I know my answer.

"Ken, I'll do it." Hearing my own words, panic causes my heart to flutter rapidly.

I'll just be ensuring their healthcare insurance covers their pregnancy care. I'll need to research the implications of my decision and future actions.

"Really?" Kennedy replies, her voice rising an octave. "You'll do this for me? You're doing so much for me; I hope someday I can repay the favors."

I assumed Kennedy would cry and hug me. Instead, she throws a 'Thank You, Taylor' over her shoulder as she exits my room. I chalk it up to stress. I startle when she pops her head back in to inform me she made me an appointment at an OB/GYN for Friday morning. In a flash, she is gone.

I marvel at the speed she moved from a stressed-needy friend to an appointment scheduling, want-to-be-mom with a plan. My head spins. I turn to my ever-trusty internet for information. *Did I just agree to commit insurance fraud?*

Kennedy
At Dr. Wilson's Office, July 14th, 11 a.m.

"Welcome back," Dr. Wilson greets as I grasp my favorite throw pillow and get comfortable in my usual chair. "Water?" She asks.

I reply no, she sits, and we begin. After the usual how have I been, any eating issues, and how my work at the YMCA is, we really begin.

"Please explain where you are on your surrogacy journey," she prompts.

"I'm so excited Taylor decided to live with us during the pregnancy. I'll get to feel my baby move, watch it grow inside her, and experience most of the pregnancy day-to-day this way. It threw me when she offered, but now I am even more excited about the baby." I share.

Dr. Wilson asks, "In the past, you shared your baby planning notebook in our sessions. Are your plans moving along smoothly?"

"We are progressing nicely," I inform. "Taylor is visiting the OB/GYN tomorrow and we'll start."

She sees right through me. Looking at her notes, she asks, "How did your appointment Tuesday with the fertility specialist go?"

At my hesitation, she only folds her hands in her lap and patiently waits.

I draw in a long breath before I begin. "Because of my eating disorders and my CKD, my ovaries aren't working properly. So, we altered my plans to now seek an egg donor. It kills me I can't use my own eggs for our baby, but the second-best eggs would be Taylor's. She has been like a sister to me since elementary school. She's always been in our lives and will always be in our lives. If her appointment goes as planned tomorrow, we can start trying to have a baby in a month." I inhale quickly and continue, "To save money, instead of in-vitro we are going to try artificial insemination at home."

The doctor's eyebrows arch, so I hurry to explain. "Jackson and Taylor will not have sex to create our baby." Although that would be easier and faster, I think to myself. I continue to explain the modified turkey-baster-method we found online.

Before my time is up, we discuss my thoughts on becoming a mother, how a pregnant woman gaining weight in my home might trigger some of my eating issues, and my feelings about another woman living in my home with me and my husband.

As I exit, *I wonder if Taylor will share the details of her appointment with me. I figure Jackson won't. I hope they both trust Dr. Wilson as much as I do.*

"Jackson will be in later to take care of my bill," I remind the receptionist.

31

ALREADY RATTED US OUT

Taylor
At Dr. Wilson's Office, 2:30 p.m.

"Dr. Wilson will see you now," the middle-aged, red-haired receptionist interrupts my perusal of a random waiting room magazine. Abandoning the tattered tabloid, I rise to enter the interior office of Dr. Wilson, Kennedy's beloved therapist.

I remind myself to keep an open mind. *I need to work through my issues with men, and I need to discuss issues with the surrogacy that I can't share with Kennedy or Jackson.* Nervously, I will myself to place one foot in front of the other.

I find Dr. Wilson seated behind an imposing, dark-wooden desk. She rises, adjusts her pencil skirt, and walks towards me, extending her right hand.

"Taylor," she greets with a firm handshake. "I'm Dr. Wilson." She motions for me to take a seat. "You can call me Greta."

I believe she is already testing me. There are three chairs in the seating area to choose from. One, I think, is hers, sits next to a round table with a lamp. Another bright red, over-stuffed chair takes up space directly across from her chair. The third chair is beige with a red, blue, and black plaid pattern. *Red or plaid, red or plaid; I'm not sure what it says about me.* I choose the plaid chair. I immediately find it stiff, causing my short legs to remain parallel to the floor. I rise, crossing over to the red chair. The over-stuffed cushions mold to my body. As I am short, my feet do not reach the tan area rug below, but my legs are not forced straight out in this chair.

"Make yourself comfortable," Dr. Greta Wilson states as she opens a notebook and chooses a pen from her side table.

It is a test; I knew it.

Crap! This is going to suck! Not wanting my legs to fall asleep, I fold them beside me. It may be rude to put my Converse-covered feet in her chair, however, without an ottoman, it's a necessity for me.

"Let's begin," Dr. Wilson prompts. "Tell me about yourself." She giggles, then apologizes, claiming it isn't professional.

My eyes bug out. I'm sure I look as scared as her words make me. *How should I describe myself? What will my words tell her about me?*

"Breathe Taylor," she commands. "I'm not testing you. I need to know who you are, what you do, where you've been. All I know is that you are a friend of Kennedy's, you've agreed to live with her, and agreed to carry their baby." She pauses while turning a page in her notepad. "I can begin by asking several general questions if you prefer."

I share, "I am an educator. I teach middle school mathematics and social studies. I am taking time off to become a surrogate. I've been friends with Kennedy since second grade and Jackson since our freshman year of high school. I love technology, music, reading, sports, and fast cars." My rambling foils my attempt to hide my discomfort.

In response to Dr. Wilson asking my initial thoughts when asked to be surrogate, I explain, "I had no hesitation in saying yes. I'd do anything for them. They would do anything for me."

When she asks how my thoughts on surrogacy have changed since then, I allow the question to simmer a bit. My response flows from my lips easily. "I'm afraid it may take months to get pregnant. I'm also afraid I might have a miscarriage. I'm afraid my surrogacy may cost more than they can afford. I'm afraid we might get caught."

"Let's explore that fear." Dr. Wilson leans forward, briefly making eye contact before she continues taking notes. "What might you get caught doing?"

My body freezes, my breath escapes me. *I fucked up. We haven't committed fraud yet, and I have already ratted us out. How many ways can I screw this up for Kennedy? I lost my insurance and now I can't keep a secret.*

"Taylor, our session is private. We abide by doctor-patient confidentiality. Anything we discuss remains between us," she urges.

I reluctantly explain, "I resigned from my job in Chicago to move in with Kennedy and Jackson. Thus, I no longer have my own health insurance." Dr. Wilson takes fewer notes as she listens to my answer. "Jackson's healthcare cannot cover me as their surrogate. It will cover the baby after I give birth, but not before. In-vitro, OB visits, medications, tests, and procedures during the pregnancy will be very expensive. We investigated a surrogacy healthcare policy, finding it expensive, too."

I glance her way, finding Dr. Wilson no longer writing. Her ink pen and notebook lie on the side table. One hand lightly covers her lips, the other clutches the arm of the chair. I have Dr. Greta Wilson's full attention.

I continue explaining, "Kennedy proposed I visit the OB/GYN using her name and her medical insurance. I fully understand this insurance fraud is illegal. It's just so unfair that they want a baby but can't afford the expensive procedures to get one. They pay for health insurance; it should cover them. So, I agreed to commit this crime. The crime of forcing their health insurance to cover their pregnancy, instead of denying them because Kennedy can't carry the baby traditionally." I note Dr. Wilson sits transfixed by my explanation. "What do you think? Should I have not offered to move forward? Should I have insisted they fall deep into debt to create this baby?"

Rising from her chair, Dr. Wilson crosses the office. Behind her desk, she pours two glasses of water with ice. As she returns, she answers my questions. "I cannot tell you what to do. I cannot force you to choose one way or another. I'm here to guide you through your life, your choices, and interpret why you feel and act as you do." Now sitting, she sips her water prior to placing it on the table. "How sure are you about continuing this surrogacy while committing insurance fraud?"

"I will worry about getting caught, but I already worry about a healthy, full-term pregnancy." I sigh. "I have not been asked for a photo ID when attending a medical appointment in the past. I assume the chances of my getting caught will be slim." I look to the doctor for affirmation but see none.

Pulling out her notebook, she asks me to explain my relationship with Kennedy and Jackson individually. She asks if I will miss teaching. She inquires about my plans for the months after the baby arrives. She encourages me to describe my relationship with the baby, as well as Kennedy and Jackson, two years after the birth.

At the end of our session, I'm exhausted. I feel I need a nap. Dr. Wilson explains true therapy takes a lot out of patients. She encourages me to journal between our sessions, and she suggests I make a list or highlight a few items to discuss at our next appointment.

At reception, I prepare to pay for today's appointment and schedule my next, but I'm told the account has already been taken care of. *Crap!* I forgot to discuss the whole pro bono offer for my sessions. I make a mental note to write about this in my journal for our next session.

Jackson
At Dr. Wilson's Office, 4:00 p.m.

"Jackson, welcome," Dr. Wilson greets me at her open office door. "Take a seat. Would you like water?"

I decline. I quickly glance at the three chairs. *Is this a test? What will my chair choice divulge to Dr. Wilson? I consider the red chair and the plaid chair. I assume red will say I'm bold. As it sits directly across from her chair, it might state I am up for any challenge. Red it is.*

My first test complete, I lean forward, placing my arms on my legs, and take in her office. It's exactly as I imagined. The wall shelves are lined with books and photos. Her diploma is framed on the wall of honor near her desk. The blinds allow some light in however, outsiders cannot see us. The only item missing is the couch.

We begin the session with me telling her about myself. When asked about trying to have a baby and how I feel about the surrogacy, I reply honestly. "Kennedy lives for children. She has provided child care in some way, shape, or form since middle school. As we married and continued to work on resolving her eating disorders, the topic of children came up. We agreed we should wait until all doctors and counselors agreed her disorders were under control. Kennedy worked so hard for so long. It just broke my heart when she found out she couldn't carry our baby herself. She amazed me by pulling out a notebook and coming up with new plans."

"Jackson," Dr. Wilson stops me. "I know about Kennedy. I need to know your feelings." She sets aside her ink pen and notebook, directing her full attention on me.

"I'm excited to have a baby," I share.

Next, the doctor inquires my thoughts about Taylor carrying our baby and staying with us. I explain, "Taylor is the perfect surrogate for us. She's like family. We can trust her. She blew my mind when she asked to move-in during the pregnancy. This wasn't because I didn't want her with us. I didn't expect her to put her career on hold to help us. It feels like old times. We were a threesome and were always together. Taylor even lived with my parents to finish high school, after her grandmother passed away."

As for Taylor carrying my child, I state, "I have no reservations."

The doctor explains, "It's normal for men to develop feelings toward the mother of their child."

"Kennedy will still be the mother," I argue.

"During pregnancy, you might have confusing feelings towards your surrogate," Dr. Wilson explains.

"I already love Taylor like a sister, so feelings should be no issue," I explain.

We move to discuss my part in the conception process. *I don't understand why so many feel they need to discuss my ejaculation. I just need to masturbate in a jar; it's not that hard.*

"At the time of ovulation, the pressure to produce sperm on demand might become stressful," she shares and suggests, "As the time for ovulation draws near, discuss all parts of the process with Kennedy and even Taylor. An open dialog with all involved will ease the tension."

I'm not surprised when Dr. Wilson suggests I keep a journal to share items at our next appointment. Kennedy has journaled addictively as part of her work with Dr. Wilson for over a year now.

I thank Dr. Wilson and pay for Kennedy and my visits today before returning to work.

32

HAND-HELD SHOWER MODE

Taylor

After my therapy appointment, I decide not to attempt cooking dinner myself. I drive to Jackson's store to purchase a rotisserie chicken and some prepared sides from the kitchen. The cook laughs when I ask for detailed instructions on keeping it warm until dinner. I type his instructions on my Notes App on my iPhone. I don't want to screw this dinner up.

Kennedy arrives home first at five-fifteen. I explain my dinner plans while she changes into shorts. We decide to take a walk while we await Jackson's arrival. As we stroll around the block, our conversation steers clear of our counseling sessions. Jackson pulls into the garage before we make it to the driveway. I'm surprised he is home before six. Kennedy isn't. They must have discussed being home at a decent time tonight.

Kennedy assists pulling food from the warm oven while Jackson changes into casual clothes. Upon his return, the table is set, and drinks are ready. The room is too quiet as we eat. The tender chicken melts in my mouth. The seasoned mashed potatoes and green beans compliment it well.

Unable to take the quiet listening to Jackson's jaw pop with every chew, I start the conversation. "I liked Dr. Wilson today. It wasn't as uncomfortable as I envisioned." Kennedy smiles while Jackson freezes with a loaded fork midway from plate to mouth. I continue, "I think I need to share a few things we talked about."

"That's great, but know you don't have to share anything you don't want to. That's what she is for." Kennedy glances at Jackson, then back to me. "She's available to discuss items you can't share with us."

I sip my water. "We talked about how I worry it will take months to get pregnant, or that I might have a miscarriage."

Jackson reaches for my hand, and Kennedy mirrors his action. Both friends squeeze my hands atop the table. "Honey, you worry too much," Kennedy soothes. "We know complications may arise. It doesn't do any good worrying when everything seems to be okay."

Jackson chimes in, "We can plan all we want; some things we cannot control. It's best we don't worry before we need to."

That is it; all the conversation is over. They do not share from their sessions, and I attempt to let it go.

With my upcoming OB/GYN appointment, I wake the next morning very anxious, so I drive to the YMCA for a workout. Forty minutes of laps in the swimming pool does not calm my nerves, so I decide to work on some weights. I punish my muscles for another thirty minutes before I call it quits. Once home, I prepare to shower. I have an hour and a half until my appointment.

I open the shower door, adjust the water temperature, then close the door again. I turn on my 'Girl Power' playlist, lay my cell phone on the vanity, then slide off my sweaty workout clothes. I test the water temp on my left wrist. Lukewarm, just how I like it; I climb into the glass shower enclosure, pulling the door closed behind me. I allow the warm stream of water to blanket my front from head-to-toe. I slowly turn, my hands rest on the glass wall as the spray pummels my shoulders to lower back. The gentle massage feels divine. I stand and run my fingers through my hair. Stalling in a few tangles. I face the shower spray, knowing my conditioner will remedy my tangles.

I lather my hair with my shampoo. The fruity scent tickles my nostrils. It's the reason I chose this shampoo. I apply soap with my loofa. The bubbles slicken my shoulders, my arms, and my abdomen. I raise my hand, soaping my breasts. I drop the loofa to the tile floor. I pump a quarter-size puddle of soap into my palm. With my back to the spray, I slowly lather each breast with a hand. The soapy bubbles cover my warm, wet skin. I lighten my touch; each nipple hardens. *This is what I need.* This will relax my nerves for a while.

I select the hand-held shower mode from the knobs on the tile wall and lift it from its cradle. Turning the nozzle to pulse, the spray spatters in a rhythmic cycle. I lean my back against one of the three glass walls and widen my stance. Loving the anticipation, I slowly aim the spray on my shoulders, my breast, then my abdomen. Finally, I allow the spray to hit the apex of my thighs. My knees immediately bend ever so slightly at the intense sensation. The pulsation quickly escalates my desire. My abdomen tightens, my insides coil tightly, and I feel I'm on the edge of a cliff. I'm teetering. I rotate the hand-held nozzle in slow clockwise circles. The third rotation releases my coiled spring, and I fall over the edge. My toes curl into the tile floor as water puddles around them before escaping to the drain. As my core pulses, I slide down the wall to the tile below. My arms and legs go limp. I'm gasping for air as my legs to fall wide open. I'm relaxed. I allow the water to massage my limp muscles.

As my breath steadies, I raise the hand-held nozzle, so water soaks my hair. Using my free hand, I run my shaky fingers against my scalp to ensure my shampoo rinses free. Slowly rising to my feet, I'm careful not to slip on the wet wall or floor as I switch back to shower head mode. I apply conditioner and lather my body with my loofa before turning the temperature to a slightly cooler temp to rinse my hair and body.

As I wrap my hair in a towel and pat myself dry, I marvel at my relaxed state. Prior to my shower, anxiety tightened my every muscle. My brain ran a hundred miles a minute. Now I'm sated, my muscles are loose, and my mind is calm. When thinking of the OB/GYN, now it's no big deal.

I slowly prepare for my appointment. I choose a simple non-distinct outfit, light makeup, and loose hair. It's my usual style. As I'm about to commit fraud, I don't want to be too memorable. *Calm, casual, I need to just be myself using Kennedy's name.*

Looking in my mirror, I chat myself up. *Jackson and Kennedy deserve a baby. It is not fair their health insurance won't cover expenses if Kennedy doesn't carry the baby. Just because a woman can't carry a baby doesn't mean insurance shouldn't cover a pregnancy. Kennedy shouldn't be punished financially for infertility. She is punished enough mentally. I can do this. I can be Kennedy Hayes. I can give them a baby.* I nod to myself, then leave my bathroom.

At the physician's office, I check-in at the registration desk. The receptionist types 'Kennedy Hayes' into her computer. She announces the information I submitted online is complete; she only needs my insurance card. I open my small wristlet to produce the needed card. She quickly copies it front and back, before returning it.

I settle in an open chair in a corner. A smile creeps upon my face as I realize in upcoming months, I will be pregnant, attending these appointments with the excited anticipation like the couples I am observing. Patients are called back frequently as others exit. My daydreams of upcoming months allow my wait to pass quickly.

"Kennedy Hayes," a nurse calls while holding the door open.

I rise, following her in the narrow hallway. I observe multiple nurses scurrying in the hallways from room to room.

"Let's get your weight," the nurse states, motioning to the scale.

I step upon the base. The digital display reads one-hundred twelve point five pounds. *That's up, but I always weigh heavier at a physician's office.* As the nurse escorts me to my room, I realize I had my wristlet and Converse with me while on the scale. I am sure they added to the weight difference between home and this office. I'm not obsessed with my weight. I'm only five-feet-tall. I know my appropriate weight range is one-hundred five to one-hundred nineteen pounds for my frame and age. A trainer at the YMCA shared this information on my first visit to the weight room on a slow day. *I am right where I need to be.*

I sit on the crinkly paper covering the exam table as the nurse signs into her tablet. She takes my blood pressure and pulse, then enters my vitals into my digital file. When she inquires about the date of my last menstrual period, I explain I seldom have them. I believe it was last summer.

"What's the reason for today's visit?" She asks.

I take a deep breath before I lie. "My husband, Jackson, and I have been actively attempting to get pregnant for over a year now. We desperately hope to start a family. I'm here to see if there might be something wrong with me."

While I talk, she lays out the devices necessary for a pelvic exam. I better get used to it, I remind myself pregnancy requires frequent exams. She instructs how to the use of the robe. Patting my hand on my thigh, she cautions, "You shouldn't jump to conclusions. There might be nothing wrong. We see this scenario often."

As she enters more information into the tablet, my mind worries that if I don't have periods, I probably can't get pregnant. Wrapped in my own thoughts, I fail to notice her beside me, so she squeezes my hand.

"We will help you get pregnant one way or another." Her smile is genuine. "No period doesn't mean you are not ovulating. Let's wait to see what the doctor thinks." She pats my knee before excusing herself. "The doctor will be with you shortly."

33

ARE YOU DECENT?

Taylor

As I disrobe, I remind myself I'm giving my friends the gift of a baby, so I can endure this necessary ugly gown. I overlap the front two flaps before I assume my seat on the crisp white paper. Some woman needs to invent a cheap but softer covering for the exam tables. *Do I know any women in engineering or science?*

Waiting in a patient room is the worst. I'm sure my blood pressure is rising with every passing minute. As my feet dangle, I nervously kick them forward and back. This causes the annoying paper to crinkle. I can't take it. I hop down, slowly pacing the three steps back and forth from the door to the exam table. I choose to sit myself in the lone chair near the table. I pull my legs up yoga-style with me in the chair, so my feet won't fall asleep while dangling. *If only I were tall enough to reach the floor, my life would be simpler.*

I take a few deep breaths to recenter myself. *I am a young, healthy woman. All will be okay. I will get pregnant. Jackson and Kennedy will be parents.*

A rap at the door signals the doctor's entry. "Good morning, I am

Dr. Harrison." He extends his right hand to shake mine. He scans my chart on his tablet. "I see you and your husband are attempting to become pregnant. A year now…" He looks up from the tablet, placing it on the counter. As he washes his hands, he asks me to tell him about my irregular periods.

"Irregular is an understatement," I explain. "I have one period every two years or so."

Drying his hands, he asks for the duration of my periods. As he throws his paper towels into the trash, I answer usually two or three days. Continuing to answer more questions, I explain my periods are very light, sometimes more like spotting. I started my period at age sixteen, and yes, it has always been light and random.

Dr. Harrison adds notes to my digital file. After he listens to my heart with his stethoscope, he asks if I have previous medical records he might request.

Crap! Lie. I need a reasonable lie to cover this. I quickly state they have only seen me at the local Planned Parenthood Clinic and I have had yearly Pap smears with no issues.

He peeks his head into the hall, asking his nurse, Elizabeth, to reenter.

"Lie back," he instructs. I do as told, and he begins the exam. First, he examines my breasts. His fingertips press in as he circles each breast. After examining underarms and each breast, we move to the pelvic exam. He prompts me to move down the table and place my feet in the metal stirrups. I escape to my happy place. For the rest of the exam, I am riding top down in my Mustang with my favorite music crooning from the speakers and miles of highway before me.

The two excuse themselves for me to dress before they return. Dr. Harrison speaks immediately upon his reentering. "I'd like to start by stimulating a period," he begins, hands folded over his femininely crossed legs.

I hate when men cross legs like a lady in a skirt. I hate skirts.

His words draw me back to the matter at hand. "You suffer from secondary amenorrhea. I propose a progesterone shot today. You will have a period in five to ten days. It is healthier if you shed your lining at least twice per year."

I gulp. *I have a condition called secondary amenorrhea. Can I get pregnant? Deep breaths. Deep breaths.* I internally chant.

"Kennedy. Kennedy," Dr. Harrison prompts for my attention.

I temporarily forgot at these appointments I am not Taylor; I'm Kennedy.

"It is pretty common and, in most cases, does not interfere with conceiving." He uncrosses his long legs, leaning forward. "I am prescribing a course of Clomid tablets. Start these three days after your period ends. Clomid stimulates egg production. You will take the Clomid for five days. You should ovulate seven-ten days after the final tablet. Ovulation kits exist, or you may begin simply taking your temperature each morning. When it rises a bit, you're probably ovulating. The more scientific approach uses a basal thermometer to track your ovulation. We will repeat this therapy for three consecutive months. At that time, we will look at more aggressive tests and therapies moving forward." He collects his tablet and stands. "Any questions?"

Rather than speaking, I simply shake my head that I have no questions. My brain swims with its new information.

"I recommend monthly appointments as we are trying to conceive. Your next appointment should be thirty days from the day your period ends. So, you will have to call in to schedule. My nurse, Elizabeth, will return shortly," He informs then exits.

When the nurse returns, she hands me a bundle of stapled papers. "I've printed out Dr. Harrison's notes and instructions from today's visit. I've also included information about the shot and the medication. The last page is your Clomid prescription for your pharmacy." As she speaks, she is preparing my progesterone injection, cotton balls, and a bandage. Turning to me, she says, "The injection must be given in your backside."

I rise, lowering my shorts and panties a bit. She cleans the area with ice-cold rubbing alcohol.

"You will feel a stick then slight burning," she says, shot in hand. She pinches some skin before stating, "now."

I endure the needle stick. As the liquid is injected, I feel the slight burn spread like she mentioned. The nurse covers my injection site with the bandage. I pull up my underwear and shorts before she hands me my information packet and escorts me back to the front desk.

I am told I will receive a bill once the insurance pays, given a business card to contact for future appointments, and it is over. I have successfully committed the crime of insurance fraud on my road to be a surrogate.

I stop by Jackson's store on my way home from the appointment. I pick up items to make my version of a sloppy joe. Once home, I brown the ground beef, then place it in a slow cooker with KC Masterpiece Barbecue Sauce.

I place my notes from my appointment on my nightstand to read later. I decide to unwind with a soak in a bath. As I fill my tub with warm water and bubbles, I download the next book in *The Rock Chick Series* to my iPad to enjoy as I relax.

First one foot, then the other, disappear below the white, foamy bubbles. A moan of pleasure escapes as my entire body submerges up to my neck. I dry my hand on my nearby towel before grasping my tablet to read. With my drink, my Kindle App, and the warmth of the tub, I lose myself to the city of Denver once again.

I squeal when Jackson's hand enters the bathroom, knocking three times. "I'm sorry." He quickly stammers, withdrawing his hand to my bedroom. "I called for you several times, but you didn't answer," he explains. "I'll meet you in the kitchen."

"Jackson, wait," I holler after him. "Come in here, please."

"Are you decent?" He hesitantly asks.

"Yes," I reply. "Everything is covered." Slowly he peeks around the door frame. He doesn't enter but remains standing in the door.

"You beat Kennedy home tonight?" I ask.

"Please refrain from moving," he requests.

I snicker before continuing, "Why are you home so early?"

"My meeting ended at four," he explains. "Rather than return to the store, I came on home. Your appointment and our plans consumed my thoughts. I didn't want to wait until seven to hear the news," he explains.

"I cannot tell you without Kennedy; it wouldn't be fair," I remind him.

"Please, just a hint to know if there will be yet another road block in our pregnancy journey," he urges.

"I'm in a tub, relaxing with a great book instead of researching on the internet. I promise that is the only hint I will share until Kennedy is here." I motion him out the door.

He pulls my door closed behind him. *I really need to start closing and locking it.* I exit my tub and dress in a comfortable pajama short set. I opt for comfort this evening, knowing I am in for the night.

I find Jackson leaning on the island, phone in hand.

Upon my entry, "I'm sorry for interrupting your bath," he apologizes.

I glance at a clock before stating, "I'd been in over forty minutes. A good book can make time fly."

He's checking work email on his phone. Even when he's home, he's working. The man works too many hours at the store and while at home. With only one day off per week, he never allows himself to step away. *He needs a long vacation.*

When he tucks the phone in his shorts pocket, his eyes take in my pajamas. A crooked smile adorns his face.

As I pass a beer his way, I explain, "I opted for comfort."

I grasp the step ladder before walking towards the refrigerator. Jackson blocks my path.

"You should just ask for me to reach you an item from the liquor cabinet," he states.

"I'm not here to be…" I begin, but Jackson interrupts.

"You are *not* a burden; asking for help is *not* a sign of weakness." As he talks, he places his hand on each bottle, moving from bottle to bottle as I shake my head no. "You're helping us. Please allow us to help you, too."

He lowers the bottle of Captain Morgan to the counter. Then he places both hands on my shoulders. "You are no longer alone. Kennedy and I are here for you. We will never let you pull away again." His muscular arms draw me in to a tight embrace. "We love you. We always have and always will love you."

34

A ROLL OF COOKIE DOUGH

Taylor

At that moment, Kennedy enters from the garage. Observing our embrace, she reads the situation as a bad outcome from my appointment. She leans against the closed door with tears filling her eyes.

Jackson escorts me toward his wife. "Bad day at the Y?" He asks the crying Kennedy.

She cannot speak, so she only shakes her head left to right.

"Then why are you in tears?" I inquire.

Kennedy explains the scene she witnessed upon entering. Her mind worried all day about my appointment.

"Okay, you two," I extend my index finger at both of them. "I'm going to have too many appointments for you to react this way each time." I pull down plates and fetch silverware as I continue. "Fix a plate and I will give you all the details from my appointment." I promise.

"You can spare me some of the details," Jackson states as if I would discuss my pelvic and breast exam with him at the dinner table.

We settle in our usual table spots. I allow a few bites before I share my results. I start with the big detail they have waited to hear all day.

"We are officially trying to get pregnant for the next thirty days." My announcement causes Kennedy to leave her seat and hug me. As I sweep her blonde locks from my face, I witness Jackson wiping a tear from his eye. I promptly look away. He will not want me to watch him in a moment of perceived weakness.

I encourage Kennedy back to her seat. We eat a bit before I continue. I explain the shot, five to ten days to start my period, begin our calendar following its cessation, take my Clomid three days later, then using the thermometer to track ovulation. I pause for a bite and a drink.

Kennedy gleefully announces, "We are really going to do this!" She cannot contain her excitement. "We could get pregnant this month."

I beg her to slow down. It can still take months to become pregnant. Although the doctor seemed positive, there are many factors at play. We need to follow our plan, continue to research, and do everything we can to encourage pregnancy while remaining patient. Stress doesn't help.

Kennedy brings her notebook to the table as I finish my meal.

Jackson fills another bun with my loose meat mixture and returns to our table. "This is surprisingly good," he teases.

On a new page of her notebook, Kennedy asks me to repeat our directions so she may write them down. When I mention the printout, she hops up to grab it.

"She will never sleep tonight," Jackson mutters with his mouth full.

I nod in agreement.

As we finish eating, Kennedy transcribes step-by-step each part of our plan for the next thirty days.

On Saturday morning, once again, I roll over, placing a pillow over my face to block out the morning light filtering in my blinds. As I reposition, I notice my panties are wet. I wiggle a bit to readjust. *They aren't damp; they are soaked.* I sit up, throwing my legs over the edge of the bed. I slowly slide my feet towards the bathroom, my body following reluctantly. Yawning, I remove my underwear with my eyes closed and watering. I look down, noticing red on the tile floor. *I'm bleeding.* The wetness is blood. In my groggy state, I stand from the stool, turning on the shower. It's too early to get worked up over anything, and it's much too early on a Saturday to be up in the shower. *I better be able to fall back to sleep or this day will suck big time.*

When my shower is complete, I pull my tampons from under the sink. I fill the sink with soapy water, placing my panties in to soak. Then I make my way to the cozy bed, calling for my return. As I prepare to slip back under the covers, I notice a large red spot in the center of the white sheet. *Great.* I pull off all the bedding to find both sheets stained. I make my way to the laundry room, stain treat each spot, place bleach in the washer, then start the load. I turn off the end-of-cycle-alert. Task done, I snag a quilt from the sofa before I tuck myself back into bed, pillow covering my eyes.

I wake with abdominal cramps. *Perfect. This day is cursed.* I make my way into the restroom, searching everywhere for some Pamprin or Midol. Finding none, I slip into the kitchen to search.

Kennedy enters from the laundry room. "Rough night?" She asks, pulling orange juice from the fridge. "I put your sheets in the dryer."

"Did the two stains come out?" I ask.

"I didn't see anything," she responds.

"I started my period," I explain.

It is at this moment, more alert than earlier, I realize the doctor said the shot would take five to ten days to start my period, not twenty-four hours.

"Do you think I should call the doctor's office since my period started immediately?" I ask.

"It's a Saturday, so you could call the ask-a-nurse line," she states.

"I will after caffeine and breakfast," I promise. "Do you have any cramp medicine?"

She disappears to her bedroom. Upon returning, two Midol are dropped into my palm. I thank her quickly before downing the pills with a Diet Pepsi chaser.

"I need a nap," I grumble.

Kennedy giggles before heading out the door to work for an hour or two. I retrieve the business card from my room, along with my printouts. I scan each sheet of the printout to see if it contains the answer I need. Finding none, I grasp my phone to call ask-a-nurse.

"Yes, my name is…" I pause, remembering my assumed identity. "Kennedy Hayes. I had an appointment with Dr. Harrison yesterday. I received a progesterone injection and was told my period would start in five to ten days." I take a quick breath, then continue. "My period started this morning. Is that okay, or…"

The nurse jumps in, asking me to allow her a moment to pull up the information. I hear her fingers tapping on her keyboard. She informs each woman's body reacts differently. On rare occasions, this can happen. She encourages me to call back in if any complications arise. I thank her for her time and disconnect, feeling like an idiot for calling in.

I choose to lie in bed until the meds kicks in. I curl on my side with a pillow clutched to my abdomen, and thankfully, I slip back to sleep.

Kennedy sits on the side of my bed, calling my name to wake me.

I roll towards her mumbling, "I need more sleep."

"It's almost noon," she states. "You need to wake, eat, and take more pills if needed for the cramps." She places a new box of Midol on my nightstand and doesn't leave until I promise I will get up and not fall back to sleep.

I spend my day with a heat pad on my abdomen, curled up on the sofa, attempting to manage the pain with Midol every four hours. Kennedy encourages me to push fluids and nibble on food often as she flies from room-to-room cleaning. When asked what I want for dinner, I reply pasta, pizza, or anything loaded with carbs.

I squeeze in another nap late in the afternoon. I wake as Jackson arrives home from work. He carries two grocery bags in with him. Kennedy announces she has exactly what I need. *I wonder what that could be.* I need the pain to stop. I have never experienced a heavy flow and painful cramps. *Guess Mother Nature is making up for all the lucky years of no periods I experienced.*

Kennedy carries a plate and spoon my direction. As the plate lowers, I spot a roll of refrigerator chocolate chip cookie dough sliced open for me. *She remembered.* Kennedy winks as she hands me the plate.

"You shouldn't eat too much. I'm fixing pasta for dinner with garlic bread," Jackson announces.

I thank Kennedy again for knowing just what I need.

35

BLEED IT OUT

Taylor

"What the..." I bolt upright, awakened from sleep by *The Imperial March* from *Star Wars*. Nervously, I scan the room. I'm in my room at Kennedy's. My new blackout curtains keep the room perfectly cool and dark. *Why is my cell phone alarm set for...* I pick up my iPhone to see it is 6:00.

"Too early," I growl to the walls of my new home. As I replace my phone on the bedside table to retreat into slumber, I notice a print out.

Oh yeah, today I start logging my temperature. I sat my alarm for six, so I could take it daily before Jackson wakes up for work. This way, when I'm ovulating, I can text him and he will still be at work on time. Barring any stage fright on his part at the collecting of his super-swimming sperm.

I place the thermometer under my tongue. My eyes cross as I try to watch the digital readout climb. Instead of enduring the eyestrain, I focus on the ceiling while concentrating on the reason for this 6:00 a.m. interruption to my peaceful sleep. *Becoming a surrogate - giving Jackson* and Kennedy a healthy baby - *waking up, taking my temp, then falling back to sleep - totally worth it.*

The beeping stick alerts me I can now log my temperature on my new chart. I place 97.9 in the slot for 7/20. After I log day one's temperature, I contemplate rising for the day. I quickly squash that thought, and I curl back into my pillows; sleep is what I really want.

At nine, I slowly slide from sleep to alertness. Sitting up, I spy a note from Kennedy on my temp chart.

Thank you for waking up early to do this for me. I can never express what this means to me. Enjoy your day. See ya tonight.

Love,
Ken

Sliding my feet along the hardwood, I slowly enter the bathroom. I wash my face, brush my teeth, pull my hair into a ponytail, then use the restroom. Seated on the stool, I yawn, then remember I need to log my mucus discharge daily, too. I glance at my panties. No signs of discharge. *This will be simple to log.*

While eating breakfast, I remove our calendar from the fridge door. I circle today's date, then write 'cycle day#1' in today's box - as my period ended yesterday afternoon. I write the cycle day on each day for the next thirty days. I write "Clomid #1" on the 22nd and continue through "Clomid #5". Moving to August 3rd-5th I pencil 'ovulation?' for each day. I am a little scared seeing these three days during which we might attempt my fertilization twice a day. Surrogacy becomes more and more real with each passing day.

Noting my cycle day number thirty falls on August 18th, I grab my phone to call Dr. Harrison's office for my next appointment. The first opening is Monday, August 22nd at eleven-forty-five in the morning. I write this appointment on our calendar before returning it to the refrigerator door. I notice today is the 20th - my payday. I open my banking app to check my balance. *Yep.* My last teacher paycheck arrived. Part of me wants to splurge today, go shopping, buy myself or Jackson and Kennedy something special. The other part of me knows it's more prudent to move the funds into my savings. I may be out to work for 12 to 24 months. *Splurging is out.* I tap a few buttons and my funds safely reside in my savings account for a rainy day.

---

*D*arth Vader stalks onto the YMCA swimming pool deck. I freeze mid-stroke near the shallow end of the pool. Other swimmers do not see him. They continue their laps without the knowledge danger lurks near. I frantically tread water. How can they not hear The Star Wars Song? I'm the only member that can hear and see him.

Wait?

I roll to my left side, shutting my alarm off on my cell phone. I place the thermometer under my tongue as I close my eyes. Moments later, I log my temperature after the beep-97.6 on 7/21. I pull my eye mask down; sleep returns quickly.

Later, a text alert sounds on my phone. I hop up from my comfy reading nest on the sofa to snag my iPhone from its charger on the nightstand.

KENNEDY
Appt in 1 hr

ME
I'll be there

KENNEDY
C ya soon

I close my Kindle App on my iPad then carry it to charge in my room. I hop in the shower, then prepare for today's group counseling session.

With my journal in hand, I enter the lobby. Kennedy checks in at the reception desk, then turns to wave my way. We choose two adjoining chairs to wait in. Jackson arrives minutes later.

Soon, Dr. Wilson welcomes the three of us in her now open door. Walking in, I immediately notice another chair added to the office. I'm unsure how a group session works. *Do we talk about each other? Do we have to share secrets I hoped to discuss in a private session?*

Jackson and Kennedy take chairs next to each other, so I slowly lower myself into the remaining seat on the other side of Jackson. I tuck my journal between the cushion and arm of the chair and fold my hands in my lap, awaiting instruction. I notice Jackson and Kennedy seem at ease.

"The purpose of our group session will be to discuss items from our individual session that affect the group and topics that I feel need to be discussed together," Dr. Wilson explains.

"First, let's discuss the surrogacy process so far and what the next steps are," Dr. Wilson states. "Kennedy, please begin."

Kennedy explains the results of my OB/GYN appointment last Friday, me starting my period, and me now logging my temperature and mucus discharge each morning.

Dr. Wilson asks me to share my feelings following the appointment.

"I feel very excited following the appointment. We have a green light to try.

I explain. "But now I'm scared to death. My period started one day later instead of 5-10 days, as explained. The ask-a-nurse eased my worries, but I'm still scared to death. My period started over a week early. This means my ovulation may be earlier, and I may become pregnant earlier. I realize it's rare to get pregnant in the first month of trying, but it could happen."

She asks me if I am having second thoughts.

While looking at Jackson and Kennedy, I vow, "That I haven't changed my mind. It's just I thought I would have a few weeks to wrap my head around the process and the possibility of becoming pregnant. I'm a little panicked thinking I will ovulate in two weeks."

Jackson takes my hand in his and squeezes before slowly rubbing his thumb over my knuckles. Dr. Wilson suggests my nerves are to be expected. She asks Kennedy and Jackson if they were aware of my panic. They simply shake their heads. Dr. Wilson instructs Jackson and Kennedy to be more attuned to my feelings. Turning to me, she asks if she may scan my journal. I hesitantly pass it to her.

While she quickly scans the final entries, I chance a glance at my friends. They smile at me. I feel bad for hiding my fears, but I'm trying to prevent them from stressing any more than they already are.

Dr. Wilson passes my journal back. She does not comment on my writings.

"The three of you should strive for openly sharing your feelings - the good and the fears." Dr. Wilson looks directly at each of us for a few moments. "The three of you will work as a couple normally does. Caring, love, and trust are important. In order for this surrogacy to benefit all of you, each person must commit to sharing openly and honestly with all members of the group." She sips her water before continuing. "Think of a married couple that becomes pregnant. The two share their joys and fears every step of the way to the birth. The three of you are a non-traditional family unit." Pointing at Jackson and Kennedy, she says, "Although you are a couple, during this pregnancy you need to allow Taylor in." Pointing to me, she adds, "Taylor, you need to trust this couple loves you enough to see the vulnerable side you attempt to hide from the world. You are a strong, independent, young woman - that doesn't mean you can't be afraid. Sharing your feelings with those you love and trust is the true meaning of friendship and family."

For the rest of the time, she encourages us to share times from our entire lives where we felt fear or panic. We share openly. Many of Kennedy's fears were already known to me. Jackson's fear during Kennedy's eating disorders before and during her hospitalization was no surprise. I shared a few times. I couldn't allow myself to share some. *They will stay buried. I cannot admit to them—the worst times of my life. Some fears do not need to be shared.*

I spend my drive home wrapping my fears in chains with concrete cinder blocks attached and bury them deep in the pit of my stomach. I pull into a Quick Trip Gas Station about halfway home to purchase a Diet Pepsi. Back in my car, I lower the convertible top while sipping from the pop bottle, I secure my hair with the tie from my gearshift, and I pull my Cardinals ball cap from under my seat. Placing it upon my head, I pull the end of my ponytail through. I select my 'Heavy' playlist, then merge back into traffic.

I sing along to my favorite metal songs. The wind in my face as I speed along I-435. I drive past my exit. *I need more time.* My highway-therapy soothes my soul. I decide to extend my cruising for a few more miles before I exit to turn back toward Kennedy's house. Linkin Park's *Bleed It Out* escapes from the speakers. As I belt out the lyrics, I realize it describes today's therapy sessions. This will be my song of the day when I get home.

A song or two later, my playlist pauses as I have an incoming call. I connect and Kennedy's voice greets me via the speakers.

"Are you lost?" she asks.

I realize the two of them probably tracked my location with the information I shared with them recently when I shared my location indefinitely in the text apps on our iPhones. I'm not sure Kennedy can use it on her own, but assume Jackson remembered how to use it.

I quickly explain, "I needed a drive. I am turning around and heading home now."

"Why?" Kennedy asks for more information.

It is too difficult to hear on speaker phone when the top is down and I'm driving over seventy miles per hour. I will leave my explanation for when I am home.

As I pull into the driveway, I notice Jackson walking towards the house from a block away. *Seems he needed a walk to clear his head. I'm glad I'm not the only one affected by today's session.*

36

AFTER TWO MARTINIS AND A SHOT OF VODKA

Taylor

My scream punctures the silence of the dark house; I sit up, gasping for breath. My hands feel around my neck repetitively.

My bedroom light flicks on as Jackson darts to my side. He climbs in bed right next to me. His muscular arms wrap around me tightly. "It was a dream, only a nightmare," he whispers into my hair while rocking me back and forth. "Just breath-in and out, in and out."

Kennedy appears moments later, climbing in on the other side of me. Tears fall from my eyes and down my cheeks.

When will this end?

Out of my life for three months now, John still torments me. He was violent when mad, always verbally and emotionally abusive, but he was never physical. *In my nightmares, he escalates to the next level.*

I do not know what time it is. We fall to the pillows, no one speaks. Jackson holding me, the three of us fall back asleep.

At 6:00, my alarm cuts into the silence. Today The Beastie Boys alert me it is time to be a model patient. As Jackson and Kennedy try to make sense of the noise, I reach across Jackson to silence the alarm. I slip the thermometer under my tongue, then lie back on my pillow. As I wait for the impending beep, I feel Jackson and Kennedy's eyes upon me.

"So, this is how you do it each morning," Kennedy teases.

I simply nod my head. At the beep, Jackson sits up, pen in hand to record my temperature. I show him the digital display, and he records it. As he reads the next entry for today, he nervously looks at me. I explain I usually fall back to sleep now and make that observation hours later. I see the relief sweep over his face. *The thought of my vaginal discharge had to horrify him.*

"Thank you both," I say. "I'm sorry I woke you last night."

"You can't help it," Jackson says. "You cannot control your dreams."

"I hope you'll discuss them with Dr. Wilson to work through your fears," Kennedy states.

"You said he never..." I cut Jackson off before he puts my dream into words in the light of day. *I might not be able to bury it deep again if he does.*

"He never became physical," I promise. *I don't want to discuss John with them again. I'm trying to move on.* "I'll fix breakfast while the two of you prepare for work. It's the least I can do for staying with me last night," I declare.

Before opening the refrigerator door, I see today is cycle day number three and I'm to take my first Clomid pill. I grab a Diet Pepsi and swallow my pill. Returning to the fridge, I cross out "Clomid #1" to show I took it.

I cut some fruit, set out yogurt, and brew a cup of coffee for Jackson. I fill his travel mug and place it by his favorite protein bar on the kitchen island. I fix myself a bowl of Honey Nut Cheerios and sit at the island while they dress for the day. The sunlight through the patio door catches my eye; I never get out of bed this early. *Maybe I should go for a walk before it heats into the nineties today.*

"I'll be home early so we can get ready for ladies' night," Kennedy informs.

Crap! I forgot that is tonight. Reagan planned a night to celebrate the impending surrogacy and welcome me to KC. I try to smile excitedly for Kennedy's sake. *As we prepare to conceive, my drinking will end, so I should enjoy one last night of fun.*

That night, Tyler pulls to the front door of the club. Everyone thanks him as we exit the SUV. He tells his wife, Reagan, to call when we are ready for a ride home. We all wave and cheer as he pulls away.

"Let ladies' night begin!" Martha shouts as we slide past the bouncer holding the door open for us to enter. Reagan leads the way to a hostess stand, speaks to the hostess, then motions for us to follow. They escort us into a private roped-off section labeled VIP.

It seems Reagan called ahead for a private table and VIP bottle service for our ladies' night. I don't even want to guess what this will cost her. I'm just excited to enjoy our evening out.

Reagan orders a round of appletinis for our group, along with some party mix, pretzels, and tortilla chips.

"Question," I alert my group of lovely ladies of my pending query. "Do any of you wax?"

Martha shares a hilarious and painful story of attempting to wax her legs at home. Reagan offers to share her hairstylist, that also waxes her eyebrows at the salon. Madison states pain is not her idea of fun, so she shaves in the shower.

Laughing, I proceed. "I am looking for a Brazilian wax." Wide eyes circle our private table. "I had a fabulous lady in Chicago. She talked the entire time to distract me, and she worked fast." I sip my appletini before continuing, "I was in and out of her care in under fifteen minutes."

My new friends continue to stare my way in disbelief.

"Have any of you ever trimmed your bikini area?" I ask.

For swimsuit season, many confess they have shaved a bit.

"A bikini wax and Brazilian are relatively painless, the maintenance is virtually nothing, and I fell in love after one visit," I explain. "I started out with a bikini wax for two visits, then decided the Brazilian was for me. Once you go hairless, you never go back," I share.

Near the end of their first appletini, questions flow, and I answer honestly.

I will need to research spas on my own. I cannot wait another week. I'm already a week overdue, and I feel like a yeti. I open my calendar app, creating a reminder to research and call spas tomorrow.

At the delivery of our second round of appletinis, Reagan orders a bottle of Grey Goose Vodka. I know for this group, martinis are like boobs. *Two is enough, three are too many. A bottle of vodka ensures they are stumbling out of here tonight.* I smile to myself. *This will be fun to watch.*

I sip my appletini even though it's not my drink of choice. *Not even close. It's too sweet. I like beer, whiskey, bourbon, shots; but on girls' night I must drink like the girls.*

These ladies deserve a fun night out. I make it my mission to entertain them.

"Question," I announce. "What is your favorite part of a man?" All eyes on me, I continue, "the sexiest part?"

Kennedy shares, "I'm drawn to eyes."

Murmurs from all the ladies about Jackson's brown eyes abound. *As my best friend, I know his eyes are brown and caring, but after listening to these women, I need to look closer at them.*

Madison passes.

"The penis," Martha blurts.

"I call bullshit stating they aren't sexy," Reagan argues. "We enjoy them, we need them, but sexy they are not."

Others agree.

"Powerful thighs make me hot," Martha amends.

"I...Well, I must admit there are sexy cocks out there," I protest. "When they groom them and..." I demonstrate length with my hands. "I've even seen one tilt to the right that was magnificent."

Again, all eyes bug out in my direction. *When will I learn? Why do I even open my mouth? This is not a group of adventurous, worldly ladies. I need to keep most of my thoughts to myself.*

I realize this topic is working us into a frenzy. They'll go home to their men for release. I will crawl into my bed alone. *This sucks.*

"I'm a sucker for chiseled abs and obliques that form," she signals with her hands beneath her naval. "A V-shape beginning wide on the hips and narrowing when joining a smattering of hair, forming a happy trail."

Ladies ooh and ahh at this visualization. All agree this is hot.

My turn. I should have gone first. Now I'll sound stupid.

"I am drawn to forearms," I confess. At their shock, I continue. "Yes, forearms. I think an exposed forearm, muscular and strong, is sexy. I like to run my fingers over the contours and hair from elbow to wrist. It is the body part I lean on in public and clutch desperately in the bedroom."

I am surprised by their response.

"I've never thought about it, but yeah," Kennedy agrees.

I watch as they inspect their forearms. They agree they have never considered it, but they are drawn to that area too. In times of weakness, they grasp it. In times of sadness, they cuddle it. *Seems my favorite body part isn't lame after all.*

Later, I line five shot glasses up, filling them with vodka. I slide a glass to each of my new friends.

"A toast," I announce. "To friends, family, husbands, and hot, sweaty sex."

When their giggles subside, we raise our glasses, then slam them down. Well, I slam mine, as does Reagan. Others sip, sputter, and fan their open mouths in pain. *At this rate, we will waste half a bottle of vodka tonight.*

"Question," I state. The ladies laugh at my party game. They know I am trying to keep the conversation interesting. "Ever have sex in a public place?" *After two martinis and a shot of vodka, this should be interesting.*

"I had hot sex in the hospital utility closet," Reagan confesses. "And doctors' quarters."

"We've christened the office at the restaurant and my in-law's bathroom at a family function," Martha brags.

Kennedy confesses a story of sex in Jackson's room before a frat house party.

"We've parked a couple of nights in parking lots and public parks for car sex," Madison claims.

My turn. Eyes anxiously turn to me. I see they expect craziness from me, so I pretend to struggle to recall any public sex.

37

THE PERFECT GUY

Taylor

Kennedy jumps in for me, "Taylor had sex on the balcony at the frat house."
Crap! I forgot about that.
"Details," Reagan demands.
"I...uh...I forgot about that one," I sputter. "It was dark. The party spilled out onto the front lawn. I stood against the railing with a hot Division-One quarterback behind me. You know, the classic tall, blonde, muscles for miles, and hands..." I pause while I fondly recall those magical hands. "To an onlooker, we were watching the party below. Kennedy insisted on dressing me that night. We wore similar skirts with matching shirts. He had the back of my skirt lifted with his pants undone. He didn't want anyone to know. I thought it was sweet that he couldn't wait another minute to have me, but didn't want to brag to the guys." I lick my lips, the club evaporating around me. I'm transported back in time. "It was slow torture. I remember wanting to press myself back into him. He was so good. No good does not do him justice. He knew what he was doing. He was sensual in his words and

touch. He nibbled, sucked, and licked from neck to ears. He whispered. He moaned..." I pause my story.

Why did I let him go? Oh ya, he lied about not having a girlfriend. Lying sack of shit. Next!

I scramble to think of another so I can forget how much it hurt to learn from Jackson my quarterback had a girlfriend - a very serious girlfriend.

"I had bathroom sex in a club in college," I blurt.

Crap! Now they will think I'm a slut.

Reagan claps her hands near her face in excitement. Madison urges me to spill the details.

"I had flirted with a guy in my Western Civilizations Class. I hated that class; it was Monday, Wednesday, Friday at 8:00 a.m. Carson's flirting with me made it bearable. It started with a disagreement over Dante's writing on the circles of hell. I pegged him as a jock, history major, aspiring to be a future coach. His intelligence startled me. It turned me on. We debated in class so often the teacher prompted our discussions before calling on others. We bumped into each other a couple of times on campus, but that night at the club was the first time we weren't in a rush." I bite my lower lip as images flood my mind.

Kennedy butts in, "She had been dancing for an hour. Jackson and I were about to leave when he pointed out Carson staring at Taylor dancing. We watched as he stared for an entire song. He grabbed two beers from a server, before strutting to the edge of the dance floor."

She smiles at me, reveling in her retelling. "Carson waved the beer at Taylor, and she moved in his direction."

She makes me sound like I'd do anything for a beer.

"He stated I looked parched." I take over my story. "I told him I don't accept drinks from guys at bars. He crossed his heart and swore on his mom's life, stating he was a momma's boy, that he slipped nothing into my beer. He took a long pull from both bottles to prove it. I decided to trust him." I shrug, smiling widely. "I was hot and very thirsty. We walked to an open area at the bar along the wall. We talked for an hour. He offered to walk me home. I informed him I was here with Kennedy and Jackson. I couldn't ditch them. He leaned in, breathed in my scent near my ear before whispering, 'he needed me'. I pulled back, looking into his eyes. I searched for answers. I liked him. For weeks, my attraction to him grew. I mean, I put on makeup and fixed my hair three days a week for an eight o'clock class, because of him."

The ladies hang on my every word.

"Our debates were foreplay leading up to this. This moment when looking into his eyes, I wanted him as much as he needed me. He recognized my want. He took me by the hand, pulling me to my feet, and lead me to the women's bathroom. He didn't check inside, he just opened the door, pulled me in, then locked us in. We were all hands and lips, removing clothes while exploring each other. We had sex right there on the women's room sink. It was hot. The most daring encounter I have ever had." I can't wipe the smile off my face.

"But," Madison interrupts. "If you liked him, why have a one-night stand?"

"It wasn't a one-night stand," I reply. "We were hot and heavy for two months before I learned he was hooked on pain meds from a baseball knee injury his freshman year. I tried to get him help. He refused. He denied he had an issue. I gave him an ultimatum, and he chose the pills over me, so I ended it." I shrug. "I know I'm better off without him, but I really think we could have gone the distance."

Of all the losers I've fallen for, he might have been the literal one for me. I've often wondered if I had escorted him to rehab if we might have made it.

I hesitantly glance toward Reagan and Martha, worried about what they must think of me. Instead of judging me, they smile.

"You've had some amazing lovers and can tell quite the story," Martha says, fanning her face.

"I'm so worked up I might jump Tyler on the ride home," Reagan claims.

We all beg her to show some restraint for our sakes until we're dropped off safely.

I create and distribute another round of vodka shots to the group. Then prompt for someone to come up with the next question.

"What are you looking for in a man?" Madison quickly asks. "I mean, I know it's the opposite of my husband, Isaac, but I would like to know what that is."

My first interactions with Isaac infuriated me, as he didn't hold his tongue. He made comments on the day I met him that ensured we might never get along.

"This is tough," I admit. "I know better what I don't want. I know that from experience. I have the keen ability to seek the guys that look great on the surface but are deadbeats or bad boys underneath. I kind of judge a book by its cover. I dream of an intelligent guy. Not a Brainiac nerd, but someone to keep me on my toes, to challenge me."

Reagan holds up one finger as if keeping a list for me.

"I hope he's sensual and domineering in the bedroom, while a best friend everywhere else. I want a guy that thinks of me as often as I think of him. I want him to struggle to keep his hands and mouth off me in public. I want someone with a libido as strong as mine. I want a soulmate. I don't want him to be abusive, a smoker, a drug-addict, a gym rat, or a cheater. I want his entire world to begin and end with me. I want him to go out on guys' night, so I can go out with the girls. I want him to enjoy his job, want a family, and enjoy talking until three in the morning."

"Okay," Kennedy interrupts. "Uncle, we surrender." She squeezes my hand. "Honey, Mr. Perfect does not exist," she slurs.

Martha joins in, slurring even more than Kennedy, "My brother is all that and more."

Reagan shrieks, "That's right. Jorge is the perfect man for you. And you have already had sex with him."

Madison spews her drink at this knowledge. My eyes dart to Kennedy.

What did she share with them?

For what seems like the hundredth time, I explain. "Jorge and I are friends - nothing more and we did NOT have intercourse."

"You said you are looking for a best friend outside the bedroom," Reagan reminds me.

I sigh heavily to convey my exasperation of this topic. "He loves his wife."

"Ex-wife," Reagan interjects.

"He is getting back with his wife. We are friends." I state. I can tell by their faces that they will not give up the hope that I'll find my way back to Jorge, or he finds his way to me.

"I don't need a man right now. I am trying to get pregnant. A man would just complicate that." I stop as the entire group of ladies bursts out laughing. "What?"

"Um," Kennedy attempts to talk through her laughter and intoxication.

Reagan assists her. "Turn around, hurry."

I do so.

"That hunk was approaching you when you spouted loudly that 'you don't need a man, you are trying to get pregnant, and a man will just complicate that.' It's a wonder he is not running away."

A well-built, well-dressed, dark-haired male slowly walks towards the bar. His head is shaking, and his friends are taunting him as he returns empty-handed.

We giggle and chat about what he probably said to his group of guys when he returned. *I'm sure he thought I was a psycho trying to trap a guy by getting pregnant.*

38

THE DEED

Taylor

I do my best to have dinner ready every night for Jackson and Kennedy. For dinner tonight, I choose to keep it simple. I placed three chicken breasts in the slow cooker at noon with a can of Rotel and a can of enchilada sauce. An hour before we eat, I shred the chicken easily with two forks. I open a bag of shredded lettuce, rinse it in the sink, then place in a bowl in the refrigerator. I open shredded Mexican cheese, placing it into another bowl. I move the salsa, sour cream, and guacamole beside the bowls, hoping not to forget to set them out as well.

I open my iPad and Pinterest to find the recipe I saved earlier today. I mix the ingredients following steps one through eight. Finally, I add the fruit I soaked in peach brandy all day, before pouring my glass to ensure it is consumable. *Holy buckets! It's so good.* I would love to add more alcohol, but Kennedy will drink it with a fruitier taste.

My preparations complete, I snag my sangria and iPad, deciding to read in the family room while I wait. My thoughts with *The Rock Chicks* in Denver, I do not hear when the rising garage door announces Kennedy's arrival.

"Hellooo," she sings from the kitchen island. "Taylor, wake up."

I startle at her words. I close my Kindle App. *The Rock Chicks and The Hot Bunch* will keep Denver safe until I return before bed tonight.

"Good book?" Kennedy greets as I approach the island. "Never mind, I don't want to know. I still cringe at the sight of the pickle jar from the last book you shared."

I playfully swat her shoulder before asking when Jackson might be home. As if on cue, the garage door lifts. We giggle.

"What's so funny?" Jackson asks upon entering the kitchen.

"Taylor just asked me when I thought you would be home, then we heard you open the garage door," Kennedy explains.

"Ask and you shall receive," Jackson announces as he climbs the stairs to the main suite.

"Conceited much?" I joke, causing more giggles.

Giggles are good. I'm dreading our 'Convo-Dinner' tonight. My ovulation and insemination are our topic. *Awkward*.

Kennedy and I line the meal items upon the kitchen island buffet-style. I prepare a glass of sangria for Kennedy and Jackson before I refill mine.

Upon her first sip, Kennedy's eyes light up. "That is delicious," she announces.

"I know, right?" I reply. "It's a very simple recipe. I dumped it all in and chilled. The hardest part is slicing the fruit and soaking it in brandy ahead of time," I inform. Placing my forearm across my brow, I claim, "It's a rough life, but somebody's gotta do it."

Another fit of giggles overtakes us as Jackson reemerges. He says nothing of our laughter as he sips from his own glass. We fix our plates, then take our places at the table. We enjoy my simple dinner as much as my sangria. *Not bad for my sub-par cooking ability*.

"Let's chat during dinner, so we can relax after," I suggest.

Kennedy hops up for her planning notebook. I stifle another giggle. As she returns, she announces tonight's conversation covers ovulation and insemination.

"Stop," demands Jackson. "We agreed to refer to it as 'The Deed.'

No more using words like ejaculation or insemination. We say, 'The Deed.'"

"Yes," amends Kennedy. "We need to prepare for the days approaching and 'The Deed.'"

I excuse myself, fetch my calendar and a bag from my room, as I return, I announce, "Ovulation should occur the week of August 1st. If my calculations are correct, it should be Wednesday and Thursday."

Kennedy turns the notebook page; I see 'Insemination' written in red marker at the top. My eyes dart to Jackson's. His eyes widen as he browses the page, and the color drains from his face. Uncomfortable doesn't begin to describe him. I sense fear. Fear putting into words our actions on ovulation day.

I decide to hop to his rescue. "I will continue to take my temp each morning at six," I state. "When it peaks, I will text Jackson." I hold up my iPhone. "If a few minutes pass with no reply, I will call, so the ringing phone will wake the two of you. I will hang up before you answer. I think it is best if we avoid awkward conversation during 'The Deed.'" I signal air-quotes with my fingers. "Upon a simple return text, we will begin 'The Deed,'" Again I mimic with air-quotes. Setting my bag in the center of the table. I select The Star Wars Theme on my phone. As the music theatrically escalates, I pull a small, wide-mouthed Mason jar from the bag. "Jackson will fill this." I slide the jar to him. "While he does 'The Deed,' I will prepare in my room."

I pause the music. Next, I pull two baby wipe containers from my bag. I pass one to Jackson. I pull out a small pillow, a syringe, and a vibrator to empty my bag. Four eyes widen at the vibrator lying on the center of the table.

Sensing their unease, I quickly continue. "Kennedy will carry your jar down to my room."

"I will keep it close to my body for warmth," Kennedy states.

"Simply knock on my door and hand me the jar without talking," I remind her.

She nods her understanding.

"I will lock my door, then turn on relaxing music." I point to my phone. "I will use the syringe." I lift it. "To place as much sperm as possible near my cervix. Then prop myself with pillows to lie still for an hour." I point to the pillow.

"And violá!" I extend my arms, signaling the end of the magic. "'The Deed' is done."

Kennedy skims her notes, her finger following along with her eyes. "A few items to point out," she declares.

I cringe. I worry she will go into detail and make Jackson more uncomfortable.

Kennedy starts, "We need the start to finish of 'The Deed' to be as quick as possible." She slides her notebook my way, pointing at the next item.

I read her note. I pick up the vibrator. Waving it in front, but not too near her face. I state, "Hello, I know. I'm prepared." I lay down the simple blue device. "I just tried to keep things as comfortable as possible in my explanation of the process."

Jackson mouths, "Thank you" my way. Kennedy closes her notebook before raising her glass. Jackson and I raise ours to meet hers.

"To best friends, to great food, and to babies," she toasts.

As we sip our sangria, I note my unfinished plate has cooled. I suggest we clear our tools from the table, prepare fresh, hot food, then return to eat. I'm suddenly starving. I quickly return my tools to the bag and place it on the floor near my chair.

Preparing our plates, Jackson moves our conversation to safer ground. He asks "Where did you find the recipe for this delicious Mexican meal?"

"My Pinterest Boards are loaded with simple meals I plan to attempt. Many claim to be fool-proof but that remains to be seen," I tease.

"I could endure a few ruined meals if you create one like this from time-to-time," Jackson states.

"Be nice," Kennedy pleads.

I refill three sangria glasses as we return to our seats and enjoy our meal.

"I grabbed a flyer for the take-and-bake meal prep classes at your store," I tell Jackson. "It will give me something to do while the two of you work. Plus, we will have some new meals to try."

"The Freezer Club," Jackson corrects. "That is perfect for you." Jackson explains to Kennedy about the meal prep using the store's party room. We will use its kitchen to prepare up to ten freezer bag meals to take home. Each has simple baking instructions.

"What do you think?" I ask Kennedy.

"Ten meals in my freezer to prepare without an enormous mess sounds too good to be true," she replies.

"Good, I will attend the next one and see how it goes," I confirm.

39

PAGING DR. WILSON

Taylor
At Dr. Wilson's Office

I enter Dr. Wilson's office and assume my usual chair. I immediately open my journal before placing it on my lap. The doctor leaves her desk with a legal pad in hand to join me.

"Good morning, Taylor," she begins.

I return her greeting, more nervous about this appointment than I was at my first. I promised myself to work on my relationship issues while in Kansas City. It is go-time, and I don't know how to start.

Dr. Wilson opens by inquiring about my thoughts about the group session.

"You were correct. I need to open up to Jackson and Kennedy and ask for help occasionally," I respond.

Sensing my closed demeanor, instead of asking more questions, she motions for me to hand her my journal. I watch closely as she reads the list of goals I hoped to work on in counseling. She smiles at me before asking if she may read my journaling during the week. I allow her, knowing I only journaled once. This will probably disappoint her.

"Your goals for our sessions," Dr. Wilson begins. "I need to copy those so we may address them over the upcoming months." As she copies my list to her notepad, she prompts me to describe my childhood.

I begin with my earliest memory. "My mother left me alone to play in my room often. Once, when I was about four, she left for three days. I played in my room as long as I could. I tried to find food in the kitchen when she didn't return. I found a cracker in the empty cabinets and ketchup in the refrigerator. Nothing else. I was so hungry I left the house planning to walk to the grocery store. It was a couple of blocks away. To a four-year-old, it seemed far. The store clerk and manager ask where my parents were. When I stated I didn't know where my mommy went, they called the police. Long story short, I started living with my sixty-five-year-old grandmother. My mom came and went from my life. She hid from the law and was an addict. She would pop in for a safe place to hide, to rest, and to sponge money off Grandma before disappearing again." I lift my eyes to meet hers.

Dr. Wilson questions about what my life with Grandma was like.

"She was old," I explain. "She worked the three to eleven shifts at a nursing home to put food on our table. We lived in an old farmhouse she rented cheap. The landlord refused to make repairs. We made do with what little we had. To save money, I stopped going to a sitter at eight. I spent my lonely nights reading my library books and completing extra assignments for fun while at a table at the nursing home until it was time to go home. Grandma hurt her knee at work my sophomore year. She had surgery, went on disability, and couldn't return to work. Money became even tighter. I started using her car and babysitting to earn money. Grandma passed away my senior year. I wasn't eighteen yet, but Jackson's parents petitioned the courts to allow me to live with them."

"Did your grandma attend school functions?" she asks.

"Her work hours didn't allow her to attend," I explain. "I became self-sufficient. I arranged rides with friends when needed. I spent weeknights at the nursing home until eleven. I realized my grades and cheerleading were my key to scholarships for college, and my way out of my small town."

"Did you play with peers or attend birthday parties of classmates?" Dr. Wilson inquires.

"I played with others at recess. I occasionally spent the night at Kennedy's house. When I started driving, I began hanging with friends outside of school. My social calendar filled up quickly in high school," I explain.

"Are you still in contact with my mother?" she asks.

"My mom quit visiting my seventh-grade year," I share. "Grandma assumed she moved out of state. I believed she over-dosed or was killed by a john she used to score drugs."

Dr. Wilson makes several notes in her notebook about this topic.

Our session drawing near its end, I am prompted to share I had no serious relationships. I dated some guys for a few months. I just never found Mr. Right.

Dr. Wilson states we will discuss Mr. Right and my Mr. Wrongs at our next session.

"May I ask a question?" I blurt.

"Of course," Dr. Wilson replies.

"Why are you offering my sessions pro bono?"

She squirms a bit in her seat. I hear her intake of breath to center herself. "I understand infertility. My partner and I tried to conceive for five years. We endured hormone shots, multiple in-vitro procedures, along with the stress and strains it placed on our relationship."

As I attempt to interject, Dr. Wilson raises her hand to stop me. "We adopted a beautiful baby girl seven months ago." An enormous smile upon her face, she explains. "I know the exorbitant expense trying to conceive brings. I understand much of the journey the three of you are embarking upon. I want to help by making my part less taxing. This is my gift to The Hayes Family and you."

I cannot argue with that. I don't want to offend her for trying to give back to others enduring what she endured. I will gladly allow the pro bono sessions. Somehow my 'thank you' seems lacking. But thank you is all I can say.

She encourages me to journal *daily* about my feelings, my past, and the surrogacy, before sending me on my way.

On Friday, I agree to babysit James and Martha's four kids tonight, so they can enjoy some adult time. As I prepare to load my iPad in my shoulder bag, I decide I need to leave a gift behind for Kennedy. I log into my Kindle app and open the *Tickle His Pickle* book. I sneak upstairs and place it on the end of their bed. I hope one or even both of them read it. *They need it.* As my ovulation window draws nearer, they need to be ready to perform their part. I really want Kennedy to help Jackson with this. I pray all the time that Kennedy can openly trust Jackson and enjoy sex. I slip back downstairs before announcing I am on my way to Martha's.

Hours later with the children tucked snuggly in bed, I journal while a reality show plays on TV.

Journal Entry-Title: Boys
Let me start by listing the boys/men that lasted more than a month in my life in order from my first. (Chris, Eli, Gerald, Max, and John) Now let me analyze each.
The night that ended my relationship senior year with Chris, he drunkenly demanded a sex act from me in a public place. When I refused, he punched me in the face. Although someone mentioned it at the time, I didn't want to believe it was an assault. I was young, trusting, and naïve. I wanted so badly to believe that Chris only did what he did because of the alcohol. Looking back now with my many failed relationships to refer to, it was assault. He assaulted me publicly, and I allowed it. I didn't fight back by talking to the police. I allowed him to belittle me and hurt me. Could this be the catalyst for my future failed relationships? Did my lack of action set the precedent for my future male interactions? (Dr. Wilson, help me here!)
Although many guys sought my affections, I avoided relationships until fall my freshman year at MU. I met Eli at orientation. He called me late at night, once or twice a week. We hooked up. Kennedy said I was just his booty-call. When I confronted him, I learned I was indeed the girl he called when his steady girlfriend wasn't available. I let him

use me. I didn't ask him to go where I wanted or do what I wanted. It thrilled me he was interested in me and dropped everything for him. I allowed him to walk all over me—I was a doormat. Regrettably, I even continued the farce of a relationship for three weeks after I knew he had a girlfriend. Why am I so desperate to not be alone? Will I do anything to not be alone? (Dr. Wilson, input please)

My relationship with Max barely lasted a month. After a few dates, his temper become more prevalent. He flew off the handle often and his actions scared me. I hid from him on campus and social media for over a week, before I sent him an email to break up. I then hid in the library and my dorm room for several weeks after avoiding any possible retaliation.

Carson is the guy I worry was 'The One.' We hit it off intellectually, publicly, and sexually. His constant need for pain killers from an athletic injury became our undoing. When I offered to get him help, we unraveled. He didn't feel he abused his meds. The need for multiple doctors and scripts didn't seem an issue for him. In the end, he needed the effects of the pain meds more than he needed me. I know I was right. I know he had a substance abuse problem. He was a great guy with so much going for him. I wish I had been enough for him. I wish his love for me had been the only high he needed. I avoided relationships for over a year with this heartbreak.

I was at an all-time low when John entered my life. Kennedy was struggling with her eating—Jackson stressed over her. I felt more alone than ever. Looking back now, perhaps this is why I allowed John's behaviors so soon in the relationship. I was desperate. I overlooked many signs—many warning signs. I kept my head in the clouds to avoid the reality quickly becoming my life. If I could have changed a few things, John and I were happy. I altered my schedule, my hobbies, my clothes, and my friends—this helped to avoid fights. With John in my rear-view mirror now, I can say I wasn't happy. Each change chipped away at my happiness. I allowed myself to believe it made our relationship better. In reality, it didn't. For every item I gave up, a new issue arose. I gave and gave with nothing in return. I was still lonely. I spent many a night alone at home while John went out. I thought I was compromising to better our relationship. In reality, I *was being manipulated and used. I am a strong person. If high school Taylor saw my relationship with John, she would have kicked my ass. Does my reflection on this relationship prove I am cured? Am I over his damaging hold on me? By allowing myself to fall under his dominance, will I always be weak to abusive guys? Am I no longer the strong, goal-orientated women I once was? Am I broken? Can I be fixed? (Paging Dr. Wilson)*

I tuck the journal into my bag and relax, watching local news until James and Martha return.

40

SET THREE TIMERS

Taylor

The impending ovulation day quickly approaching, I opt for a special dinner. My tablet is open on the counter, I follow each recipe exactly. I have my phone timer, the microwave timer, and the oven timer set, ensuring I don't forget any part of this meal. Filets warm in the oven, the slow cooker contains loaded potatoes with bacon and cheese, and a saucepan of green beans with bacon simmers atop the stove.

The microwave timer signals my cheesecake chilling is complete. I pull it from the refrigerator, and I take my time decorating the top with strawberry slices, blueberries, and kiwi slices.

My phone timer alerts me to turn down the oven until we eat. I reduce the green beans to low, then end the oven timer. Now I need Jackson and Kennedy to arrive before the filets dry out. I decide to text both.

> ME
> I prepared special dinner

This might encourage them to hurry home. It is now 6:45. Kennedy is usually home by 5:30 and Jackson is between 6 and 7. I thought I planned this meal perfectly. *Seems I forgot to ensure everyone would arrive on time.*

Moments later, I hear the garage door. I scurry to the front window to see Kennedy pull into the garage, with Jackson following. I rush back to the kitchen, turning everything off. The two enter the kitchen laughing. Kennedy holds a shopping bag in her right hand. I recognize the bag. It is from my absolute favorite store. The familiar white, rectangular shopping bag hides a large, heavy box.

"Wow," I greet. "I introduced you to a few apps and now you leap to a big tech item."

Kennedy extends her right hand with the bag to me. I grab and quickly peek inside. *An iPad Pro! Holy crap! Way too much for her limited knowledge and use.* I flush green with envy. I extend the object of my desire back to its novice owner.

"No silly," Kennedy looks to Jackson, giggling. "It's yours."

She continues speaking, but I hear nothing. Excitement overtakes me. *My two devices combined into one means no more switching back and forth or emailing and air dropping items to myself.*

"Hey," Jackson grasps my shoulder, shaking me gently. "What do you think?"

"I, umm..." I desperately attempt to calm and pull myself together. "I'm sorry..."

Kennedy laughs, realizing I didn't listen to her explanation. She repeats herself. I force my brain to listen this time. They bought me a gift to thank me for all I have given up helping them start a family. They have witnessed my researching the iPad Pro online of an evening. Now I can sell my iPad and MacBook, but Kennedy mentions she might like to learn how to use and keep my iPad.

I throw myself into their arms, my Apple bag grasped firmly in my hand. Kennedy shakes with glee as we embrace. Moments pass before Jackson announces the end of the group hug.

"What is that enticing aroma?" He brings me back to the present by mentioning the meal I've worked hard on.

"Crap!" I shout. "You two change quick. I will set the table." I rush to remove the beef filets while yelling thank you as they climb the stairs.

The three of us settle at the table. Jackson raises an eyebrow as he examines the meal I place before him.

"I need to learn all about these Pinterest Boards of yours," Kennedy says.

"I will teach you Pinterest and so much more on you iPad," I explain. "Thank you again for the gift. It's too much, but I love it. Jackson, would you like my MacBook?"

"I already work too much at home with my cell phone. I don't need another reason to work," he grumbles.

He slices his filet, noting the warm, pink, juicy middle. "You've really outdone yourself this time," he announces.

I rat myself out, explaining my excessive use of multiple timers to keep all of my attention on the meal prep.

First bite on his tongue, Jackson's face expresses his genuine enjoyment of my meal. Kennedy excuses herself. She returns with three glasses of red wine. A delicious compliment to the meal. Jackson and I enjoy the loaded potatoes and green beans with our steak. Kennedy avoids the potatoes. I figured as much, thus I prepared a side she would allow herself, the green beans.

Near the end of the meal, as my wine level dwindles, Kennedy promptly refills it. When I carry my cheesecake and dessert plates to the table, she refills both Jackson and my wine glasses.

It pleases me that Kennedy consumes a very tiny sliver of cheesecake I serve her. I enjoy witnessing her allow herself to enjoy foods. She has come a long way from the days she used food as a punishment. Although she eats carefully, red meats, carbs, and desserts, she consumes in moderation now.

"Let's leave the dishes for later," she suggests, rising from the table, glass in hand. We follow her to the living room, all claiming our favorite spots. It's my turn to choose a movie. I select *Pitch Perfect*, knowing Jackson pretends to hate it. Forty minutes into the movie, I use the pause button, allowing for a bathroom break.

I return, noting Kennedy again refilled our wine glasses. I mentally calculate the wine I've consumed over how many hours. I cannot afford a hangover in case tomorrow is my ovulation day. I'm very aware of my limits. I can allow only one more glass. I press play to restart the movie and we settle in once again.

Hours later, the urge to pee wakes me. I glance at my cell phone, finding it to be after three. I sit up, swinging my legs to the edge of the bed. My head swims and throbs. I slowly rise while keeping a hand on my nightstand to steady myself. My stomach rolls as I walk slowly toward my bathroom. *I drank too much wine.*

Preparing to sit, I reach to lower my underwear, finding none. *Odd. I have not allowed myself to sleep nude in Kennedy and Jackson's home.* I lower myself to the toilet, noting my thigh muscles are sore. *I must have pushed myself too hard at the YMCA.* As I relieve myself, I note I am tender. Wiping further shows this tenderness. My mind swims.

I slowly return to the bedroom. I pull on a pair of panties before I climb back into bed, taking it easy to keep from falling or vomiting. As I quickly pull the sheet over me, my vibrator bonks me on the head. *Ouch! Why is this out?* I move it from my right hand to my left. As I replace it in the top nightstand drawer, I realize it is too light. It doesn't have any batteries in it. *How could I be this out of it? I only had 1,2,3...4- four glasses of wine over four hours with food. It never affects me this way. I must have had some fun before I fell asleep.* I make a mental note to read the wine label and alcohol content from last night. I'm usually very good at keeping tabs on my consumption.

41

THE DEED IS DONE

Taylor

"Wake me up before..." I turn my Wham alarm off. Today, I decide to wash my face and use the restroom prior to my temperature. As I wash my face in the mirror, I feel butterflies in my tummy. *I might be ovulating today.*

I assume the peeing position on the toilet, I'm reminded of my tenderness discovered during the night. Moving through the soreness, I check my underwear as I conduct my morning business. I rub my index finger over the creamy white discharge on my cotton panties. I pinch my finger and thumb together, then apart as the internet stated. The consistency is sticky and stringy. *Shit! This is a sign I might be ovulating. Oh crap! Oh crap! I'm not ready for this. I'm not ready for this.*

I quickly log my mucus observation, then place the thermometer under my tongue. I'm too nervous to I sit on the bed, I pace to the bathroom, to the door, and back with my aching thighs. I am afraid to look after the beep. If it is up, I will have to text Jackson, letting him know it is time to ejaculate into a cup and hand it to me. *Talk about awkward. I mean, we discussed this many times. It's a process we must* complete to become pregnant. And I want to be pregnant. I want to carry their baby. I want to give my best friends this gift.

Shit! I stare at a blank display. My mental pep talk took too long. *Wait, there is a memory recall.* I breathe a sigh of relief before I tap the recall button. My temp this morning is 99.2. *Definitely not my normal 97-98 range.* I log my temperature. With hands trembling, I pick up my cell phone to text.

> ME
> temp up
>
> time to do the deed

I tap the back of my phone nervously. If he doesn't reply, I will have to call or knock on their door. I don't want to see him during this.

> ME
> Jackson u there?
>
> JACKSON
> I'm up hold your horses
>
> can only cum so fast

I stare dumb-founded at the screen. *Did he really just send me that?*

> JACKSON
> JK
>
> Kennedy will deliver the package soon

The package? Crap! Kennedy will hand-deliver her husband's sperm to me. In minutes, I will introduce Jackson's sperm inside me. *Holy Crap!*

I fan my face and decide I need to prepare. *Where is my list?* I rummage through my nightstand drawer. *Ah-ha! Close the blinds—check. Soft music—check. Syringe and wet wipes—check.* I glance around the room, then return to the list. *Vibrator…*I pull my toy drawer open. *Which of these bad boys gets the honor?* I move a red one and a purple one to the side before deciding on the yellow butterfly vibrator. I quickly place batteries inside and secure the cap. My list complete, I sit nervously on the edge of the bed. I pull a stapled print out from my drawer. I quickly review the highlighted tips. I have all the necessary utensils. *Oh, pillows to prop myself up.* I pull the decorative pillows from the corner chair, tossing them back onto my bed.

I glance at my cellphone as the sounds of my 'Lite' Playlist fill the room. Ten minutes have passed since I texted Jackson. *I can't wait another ten minutes. I'm about to explode.* I secure the lock on my door, then slip under the sheet on my bed. With one tap, my yellow vibrator hums to life, and I place the vibrations directly on my clit. Still a bit swollen from last night, instantly my body jumps to attention. Realizing time is of the essence, I tap the button two more times. Instead of humming, now it emits a low steady purr. I slide the tip into my entrance. My insides are sore. *What in the world did I do last night?* In then out, in then out. All the way in, I freeze. My abdomen tightens, my aching thighs strain, my toes point. *Yes!* I lightly caress my fingertips over my collarbone, my breast, my lips as I coil tight, my body reaching for the precipice. I'm climbing, climbing. *Yes! Yes!* I'm standing on the edge, coiled too tight. *I. Am. Going. To. Explode!* My legs twitch with spasms; my calves cramp. Like a goldfish out of water, I gasp for breath. A delicious wave of release sweeps from head to toe. I flex my feet forward, then back to relax the cramps in my calves, as I slide my vibrator from my core and tap it off. I lay content in my post-orgasmic bliss.

A hesitant knock on my door snaps my thoughts back to the task at hand. I spring from my bed to unlock it. Kennedy stands with two hands hugging the jar containing Jackson's sperm. I extend my right hand.

"Would you like me to help or need anything from me?" Kennedy asks.

I shake my head, stating, "I have it all under control."

As she transfers the glass, she places her two hands over mine. Her eyes convey the excitement, the fear, and the magnitude of this process. I simply nod, then close the door. I return to my bed. Slipping under the sheet, I place the jar between my thighs to keep the sperm at body temperature as we researched. *I can do this. I can do this.*

I pick up the syringe from the side table and stare at the small plastic device. I go over the procedure in my mind. *Place the syringe in the sperm, pull the plunger back, try to suction up all the sperm I can, place the syringe inside me, slowly release the sperm into my vagina near the cervix, relax, and 'The Deed' is done.* I press the excess air from the syringe as I pull the jar from between my thighs. I tip it to the side, using the syringe to withdraw every last drop. "This is not Jackson's sperm. This is not Jackson's sperm," I chant. I place the glass on the table before kicking my legs free from the sheet. *I can do this.* I slowly insert the syringe. It's much smaller than my vibrators; it slides easily in my slickness. My walls are still swollen and sensitive from my recent orgasm. I try to place the tip as close to my cervix as possible before slowly pressing the plunger. Continuing to press, I realize sperm has entered my fertile body. I could be pregnant in a matter of hours. I pull the syringe from my body, standing it in the glass on the nightstand.

With a wet wipe, I clean my hands. I prop my hips and legs up, as stated in our research, with the pillows. Following all our discussed plans to a tee, I place my vibrator once more on my clit. I start on a low vibration. My bud, still swollen, tingles immediately. As I up the vibration setting, I slowly rock the vibrator up and down over my clit. My sensitive skin hums with desire as I increase the vibrator to high speed. I rock my hips, frantic for friction, and my orgasm blindsides me. My abs contract, causing my torso to rise and fall as if in seizures. I turn off the vibrator just before it tumbles to the sheets. I lie motionless and close my eyes, allowing the music to penetrate. I sing along to *Lips of*

An Angel by Hinder. I focus on the lyrics, avoiding my racing heart and mounting fear of what might take place inside my body right now. As I croon with Pink to *Give Me A Reason*, a light rap beckons from outside my door.

Jackson's voice rips my thoughts into the present situation. "Taylor…" I faintly hear the rustle of his dress slacks as he nervously shifts weight from one foot to the other.

I'm frozen stiff.

"Um…" he clears his shaky voice. "I'm heading to work." Jackson sighs nervously. "If, um, you need anything from me, um, text." I hear the retreat of his dress shoes on the hardwood floor.

I stare unseeing at the ceiling.

What might I need? Did he mean more sperm?
Did he mean we should try insemination this afternoon?
Why did he knock?

Our plan was for Jackson and Kennedy to go to work as usual. I would lie still for an hour or so, then go about my day as normal. We planned to try insemination morning and after dinner for two days while ovulating. We discussed how awkward this situation might be and we decided minimal interaction during 'The Deed' would be best. This is why I texted him instead of waking him up myself. This is why Kennedy would carry the semen to me, then leave. He deviated from the plan. Now I feel all kinds of awkward, confused, and pissed off.

Kennedy arrives moments before Jackson. Like a good girl, I placed the lasagna from the freezer into the oven as directed by Kennedy's afternoon text. Currently, we have twenty minutes until we need to place the garlic bread in the oven. Jackson changes his clothes, while Kennedy busies herself in the kitchen, and I stand awkwardly at the island.

As Jackson descends the steps, he claims, "The delicious lasagna scent ascends the stairs and is very strong."

I cling to his words as they crack through the awkward silence.

He looks from me to Kennedy, then back. "Everything okay down here?" He motions between the two of us.

I simply nod. Kennedy raises her eyes to me.

Before I can decipher the emotions present, Jackson declares, "Family meeting, everyone to the table."

42

TREAT IT LIKE A FART

Taylor

Reluctantly, I join him at the table.
"What is up?" He asks.
I shake my head back and forth.
"Song of the day time," he announces.
Shit! He doesn't play fair. I'm feeling all kinds of awkward and confused, and now I have to sum it up in a song. Closing my eyes, I attempt to focus. I can't find the perfect song. I grasp the first lyrics I can. Instead of summarizing, I recite a line of lyrics from the end of *Total Eclipse of the Heart*. "Once upon a time..."
As I continue the line lyrics, Jackson shakes his head.
I continue the lyrics, "But now..."
Kennedy chimes in, "Sounds emo to me."
Nothing from Jackson, so I finish the song.
"Bonnie Tyler, *Total Eclipse of the Heart*." Jackson proclaims proudly.
"I thought if you stated the title in the lyrics, it didn't count as getting it right," Kennedy bursts Jackson's bubble.
I sense Jackson is going to ask me to explain how those lyrics make

me feel today. I awaken from my awkward numbness and take control. "Okay, so we did 'The Deed' this morning. It wasn't as smooth as it could be, but we can fix it."

"What went wrong?" Kennedy asks, concern etched on her entire face.

I quickly set her mind at ease by explaining, "Everything occurred and I could be with child at this very moment."

This elicits a gasp of excitement from her.

"I found two things we need to improve on," I state.

Jackson lowers his eyes to the tablecloth. Kennedy finds her planning notebook and returns to the table. *Seriously? Enough with the flipping notebook already. I'm too stressed. I'm glad I kept my thoughts to myself.*

"Jackson knocking on my door as he left sent me spiraling for over an hour," I mention.

He lifts his eyes to mine in question.

I continue by explaining, "Our plan was for the two of them to leave with no contact. His words made me worry. Made me question his meaning. I did not know what he meant by texting him if I needed anything more."

Jackson just shrugs.

I move on. "The mood as you returned from work tonight was extremely uncomfortable. No one spoke to each other. It was as if Dumbo The Elephant was in the room with us."

Kennedy attempts to summarize. "So, awkwardness is really what went wrong today."

"I felt so detached and helpless," Jackson confesses, averting his eyes. "I feel like I need to do more. Taylor, you are doing everything. You monitor your temp for weeks. You are injecting the sperm. You are following suggestions to encourage implantation. You will carry the baby for nine months. I simply," he pauses. "Jack off."

Kennedy grasps his hand across the table for support.

"Yeah, Jackson, I get that," I acknowledge his desire to assist. "No offense, but it's awkward enough placing my best friend's husband's sperm in my vagina with a syringe. I really don't want you around when I do it."

A heavy silence again plagues the kitchen.

"So, we are going to treat 'The Deed' as we would a fart," I state.

Kennedy snorts with laughter, while Jackson shakes his head at me.

"I'm serious, people. We know everyone farts. We know it can be a bit messy or unpleasant. But we don't talk about it, and we go on as if it didn't just happen."

"It'll take some getting used to," Jackson says.

Kennedy agrees.

"We only have a two-day window, so getting used to it may be a month or two down the road," I remind them.

"You could just get pregnant this month, and the awkwardness would disappear," Kennedy mentions.

"Stress isn't conducive to conceiving, so placing more pressure on Taylor isn't necessary," Jackson chastises.

"I was thinking..." Jackson reluctantly admits. "Maybe we could perform 'The Deed' before dinner, so we can hang out and be normal the rest of the night and it not be a cloud hanging over us all."

Kennedy glances at me for my thoughts. Her over-excitedness at this process and its outcome are clear upon her face.

"Okay, Jackson," I tease. "If you need to rub one out before you eat lasagna, I will take one for the team and let you."

I can't tell if my teasing lightened the mood or pissed Jackson off.

He quickly rises but calls back to Kennedy before he reaches the stairs. "Ken, will the lasagna be okay if we do this now?"

"I'll place the bread in the oven later, so all is good," she replies.

"I guess I need to go assume the position," I joke to Kennedy.

"He'll snap out of it," Kennedy comforts, grasping my elbow. "He puts a lot of pressure on himself. He'll blame his sperm if you don't get pregnant in a month or two. He has never been a patient man, you know that."

I nod. "See ya in a bit." I wave, leaving for my bedroom.

I ready all the utensils for my part. I decide against the vibrator and suggested orgasm, as the two of them will probably be in the living room or kitchen just outside my door for my part. I slip off my shorts and underwear, placing them on the corner chair. I open my door a crack and slip under the sheet. I turn on my 'Heavy' playlist, deciding

I need to mean business on this attempt. I'm singing Fake It with Seether when Kennedy peeks her head in.

"Ready?" she questions without entering.

"Come on in and please close the door on your way out," I prompt.

She does so with no words. I again warm the glass between my thighs as I mentally prepare.

I toss a brief prayer to God to help the three of us as we start this family. I ask that He guide and protect us as He awards us at His will.

Next, I fill the syringe as best I can, insert, then release the sperm inside me. I lay motionless for ten minutes as I enjoy my rock music. As Buckcherry's *Crazy Bitch* ends, I rise and clean up. Kennedy will probably be upset I didn't lie still for an hour. She will just have to deal. Her head might explode if she knew I didn't orgasm to promote insemination this attempt. I am starving and the aroma of lasagna is not helping.

I rinse the items in my bathroom sink, wash my hands, then fix my hair before exiting my room. Jackson pulls garlic bread from the oven, as Kennedy places plates and utensils by the large pan of lasagna on the island.

"Perfect timing," I declare.

Two sets of eyes meet mine. I vow to nip any awkwardness in the bud right away.

"Are we eating at the table or in front of the TV?" I ask.

Jackson places a large piece of lasagna on my plate, suggesting we watch TV while we eat tonight. Kennedy places two pieces of garlic bread on my plate, as she hands me a fork. I sit at the bar and eat while they fix their plates. I can't help it. I'm starving.

43

HIGHWAY THERAPY

Taylor

Promptly at 6:00, 'Work It' by Missy Elliott wakes me. I silence my alarm before texting Jackson.

> ME
> I'm awake

> JACKSON
> Me too Kennedy will be down soon

I nervously retrieve my utensils from the towel on the vanity where I dried them last night. I toss the extra pillows on the bed, select my vibrator for the day from my drawer, crack the door, and climb under the covers.

Kennedy peeks her head in several minutes later, and I motion for her to come on in. Her tender smile conveys all I need to know. I tuck the jar of sperm between my thighs. I again mentally walk myself through the entire process. I withdraw the sperm, use the syringe, and complete 'The Deed.'

My morning orgasm relaxes me such that I fall instantly back to sleep until later my ringing phone wakes me. Looking at the display screen, I see it's nine-thirty, and Jorge is calling. It's about time he called me. I connect the call. Before I can speak, he says hi.

As we talk, I glance around the bed, noticing I didn't clean up before I fell back to sleep. The syringe and sperm cup, a caked-on mess, grace the side table, and my vibrator lies between my legs on the sheet. I'm vigilant about keeping my toys clean. I use a gentle soap, then rewash with my special adult toy cleaner. Today, I will need to clean everything twice.

Jorge raises his voice on the phone to win my attention. "Where are your thoughts?"

"I could be pregnant at this very moment. My body feels no different, but I could be with child," I explain.

"Your agreeing to be your friends' surrogate is the greatest gift you could ever give. I'm afraid I'll never achieve anything as great," he warmly says.

I move our conversation to his progress in winning Rosalynn back.

"I enjoyed my recent visit with her. We speak on the phone almost daily, and I think we're moving in the right direction," he proclaims.

Because of a knock at his apartment door, he lets me go. I decide it's time to get up and clean up. Before I hop into the shower, I send him a text.

> ME
> have a good day

That afternoon, Dr. Wilson welcomes the three of us into her office. As I sit, I open my journal to the items I would like to talk about if she calls on me. Again, this week, Kennedy and Jackson did not bring theirs. *I'm such a nerd following the doctor's directions.* I quickly close my journal and secure it behind my back.

Dr. Wilson begins by asking Kennedy for an update on our progress in surrogacy. "Ovulation began two days ago. We have completed three attempts at fertilization at home," Kennedy explains.

Dr. Wilson asks Jackson how his part in the process makes him feel.

"My part went much smoother than predicted," Jackson reports.

His grin directed toward Kennedy stirs many questions in me; I'll ask her about this later.

The doctor asks Jackson to share his feelings.

"I'm eager to see if Taylor's pregnant or if we will try again next month. At first, I felt detached by the unconventionality of this process, but feel that all three of us worked together. We discussed missteps openly after the first time, and things went much smoother because of our conversations before the next attempt," he admits.

"I enjoyed the morning the three of us woke up to the alarm and witnessed Taylor taking my temp," Kennedy shares.

The doctor immediately picks up on the fact the three of us slept together. Dr. Wilson asks Kennedy if the relationship between the three of us has transitioned into a romantic one. The confused Kennedy does not answer.

"Taylor experienced another nightmare, waking everyone up. While calming her, we all fell asleep," Jackson explains.

The doctor jumps to me to discuss my nightmare.

"It was nothing," I claim.

She reminds me that Jackson used the words 'another nightmare'. This indicates more than one. Sensing my hesitation, she makes a note and moves on. I'm sure we will delve into it at my next appointment.

Knowing tonight is our last attempt to become pregnant this month, Dr. Wilson asks what we do next.

Kennedy excitedly announces, "We wait. We wait to see if Taylor starts her period. We wait to see if Dr. Harrison has us repeat the process for another month."

As the three of us rise at the end of the session, Dr. Wilson requests I remain for a moment. Jackson leaves, and Kennedy squeezes my arm in support before joining him.

My eyes closed tight, I see a flash of two naked bodies entwined on the sofa. Kennedy, with her hand on my shoulder, urges me to kiss Jackson. I'm hesitant. Her other hand on Jackson's neck, she pushes us towards each other. Again, she instructs us to kiss. Our lips connect. Jackson's plump lower lip dances over mine.

Frozen, I will my lungs to seek the air they desperately need. I open my eyes. I attempt to shake away the flash; I'm shocked by the horrible scene. *It never happened. It can never happen. I don't want it to happen.* I'm still in Dr. Wilson's office, Kennedy is no longer beside me, and my temporary daydream and reaction have thankfully gone unnoticed by her.

When the door closes, Dr. Wilson wastes no time. "I noticed you sat beside Jackson last session, but sat on the opposite side of Kennedy today." I can see the concern on her face. "Has something happened between Jackson and you to upset you?"

"No," I immediately reply.

"I noticed you hid your notebook during the session." She points to my journal in my hand. "Is there anything you'd like to share?"

Reluctantly, I open my journal. "I made notes for our next session to talk about my nightmares." I take a steadying breath. "I've started having flashes, sort of like glimpses at a memory, but it's not a memory."

"In these flashes, what do you see?"

"It's silly," I explain.

"This is a safe place to share and work through anything," Dr. Wilson reminds me.

"I have flashes of Jackson with me," I explain.

She asks me to explain what I mean by 'with me'.

"We are in bed. Together." Tears fill my eyes at putting these feelings into words. "We are intimate, and Kennedy is there," I quickly continue. "They aren't fantasies. I. Do. Not. Fantasize. About my best friend's husband. I don't." My tears are now rivers down my cheeks. "They upset me. I can't control them. I can't explain why or when they happen. Sometimes Kennedy will say something or do something and boom. I freeze, these images invading my brain."

"Moments ago, when Kennedy squeezed your arm, you froze." She licks her lips. "Was that due to my asking you to stay or…"

How does she know? Am I that transparent? My face is on fire, and I cannot control my tears.

Dr. Wilson places a tissue box in my lap without a word. She waits. I realize she wants me to answer. All I can do is nod my head up and down.

She places her notepad and pen on the side table and tosses a decorative pillow at my feet. I wipe my eyes. When I open them, she is kneeling in front of me in her tight pencil skirt. She takes each hand in hers and asks me what I saw and felt when Kennedy grasp my arm moments ago.

"I saw Jackson on top of me. He was inside me. Kennedy had one hand on him and one on me, directing us. Urging us." I gasp in a breath. Speaking between my hiccup-sobs, I continue, "I want to scream. I want to hit, and I feel like I could puke."

Dr. Wilson embraces me. We rock to-and-fro several moments. My crying calms and my breathing eases.

Pulling away, she inquires, "Do you feel Kennedy bosses Jackson and you in trying to conceive?"

I quickly answer, "No. Her planning notebook is annoying, but she isn't domineering."

She explains, "You've shared how John was domineering and abusive. Are I afraid all relationships will become this way?"

Again, I state no. "You ask about changes in my relationship with Jackson. Nothing happened between us. The two of them held me after a nightmare. We watch TV together, and we tease each other. I just feel guilty about the flashes. What if they are really fantasies? What if I am lusting after my best friend's husband? I try to keep my distance. I don't want to encourage anymore flashes," I explain.

After she states feelings towards the father of my child will be normal, she encourages me to write down what happened to trigger them, where and when they occur, and the content of each flash between now and my appointment next Thursday. I nod my agreement. She states these flashes do not sound like fantasies. They may be my fears about the surrogacy process taking another form.

Dr. Wilson hands me another business card. "Please call my cell number at any time to talk. Day or night, about anything."

She does not release the card until I acknowledge my understanding. She attempts to rise from her knees as gracefully as possible in her long, snug skirt. "Now, I have no more appointments. You are welcome to stay in here or out in the lobby as long as you need. I'll just be finishing some notes then heading out. My receptionist will be here for another hour. I'd like for you to drink some water and regroup before you attempt to drive yourself home."

I simply nod and accept the proffered water. Remaining in my chair, I wipe my eyes and blow my nose. The cold water is a welcome addition to my raw, dry throat. I allow myself ten minutes. I say thank you and goodbye.

I lower my convertible top and crank the tunes before I leave the parking lot this time. By the time I'm home, I've gained control again. Highway-therapy calms my turmoil yet again.

44

DREAM FAMILY

Taylor

Looking at the clock on my iPad, I cringe when I see it is six. *Where did this day go?* I uploaded a ton of new lessons to sell before reading a few chapters in my current book. Since I have nothing planned for dinner tonight, I guess we will need to order a pizza. Kennedy is usually home by now; Jackson should be home soon. I return my iPad to its charger for the evening, then search the fridge for any dinner options.

At the sound of the garage door opening, I'm excited my alone time is ending. Jackson emerges from the garage. He freezes awkwardly at the door, scouring the house for signs of Kennedy. When I explain she hasn't texted and isn't home yet, he quickly excuses himself to change from work clothes. *Am I imagining it, or is he as hesitant to be around me as I am with him?*

With a few minutes to spare, I scan my email on my phone.

Junk.

Junk.

Spam.

To read later.

What is this one? The sender is Middle Tennessee Pomskies. I completely forgot I looked into purchasing a dog in April. Alone in Chicago, I thought a puppy would be a good idea.

I read through the entire email. Then I read it again. I passed the first round of screening and may now continue the process of adding my name to the waiting list.

I can't believe how much my life has changed since April. Instead of my own apartment in Chicago, I now live indefinitely with Jackson and Kennedy. I felt so alone when I took to the web for a pet. Now I'm surrounded by friends and creating a baby.

I became obsessed with Pomsky photos across all social media, so I liked and followed a couple of breeders on Facebook. I became intrigued with The Middle Tennessee Pomsky breeders. They treat the purchase as an adoption process. Their attention to details and screening process shows the love they have for each puppy.

Before I place a five-hundred-dollar deposit to secure my spot on the long waiting list, I need to discuss this with Jackson and Kennedy. Both grew up with pets. They love dogs. Thinking about it now, I'm surprised they don't own a dog. Jackson's family owned two Siberian Huskies. I fell in love with them while living there. My queen bed felt like a twin as both large dogs slept nightly with me. They are the reason Pomskies interest me.

I need to find the perfect situation to bring up the topic of a puppy. A broad smile climbs upon my face as I imagine a puppy scampering around the house. No more lonely weekdays or lonelier nights. Puppy cuddles and licks will definitely brighten my days. We could practice our parenting skills on a puppy.

Focus. Focus. Focus. It is time to talk to Jackson about dinner. I push playful puppy plans to the back of my mind.

Tucked in bed, I pull out my notebook and pen from my nightstand.

HALEY RHOADES

. . .

Journal Entry-Title: The Ultimate Goal Has Always Been Family
My earliest stories and diary entries were fantasies about my future family. I longed to feel the love and acceptance of a mother and a father growing up. I often imagined conversations with a father I never knew and a mother the polar opposite of my own. My imagined parents greeted me after work, excited to hear about my school day and friends. We enjoyed dinner together each night at the table. We played games or watched a movie together. They tucked me in with a kiss and story each night.

As I grew, I planned for my own future family. We were not perfect, but we loved one another. My future husband supported my career, he couldn't keep his hands off me, and peppered me with gifts for no reason. We had four kids, and our home was a lived-in mess. My kids, surrounded by our unconditional love, took risks and excelled.

I chose education as my career to surround myself with children. I wanted to share my love with them to help them through their imperfect lives. I wanted to be the bright spot for children with a childhood like mine. I hoped I could help kids realize their potential and ability to strive for the life they wanted.

My lack of success in love worries me. I hope to one day find a love like Jackson and Kennedy's. An unconditional love, a love through the good times and the bad. Will I ever fall in love—real love? Not the love that I overlook faults because I'm so desperate not to be alone? Will I ever marry? Will I get a chance to be a mom?

I realize with this surrogacy, I will be a mom of sorts. I will be a mother to Jackson and Kennedy's baby for nine months. Once the baby is born, my maternal role will shift to that of an aunt. As I prepare for this surrogacy, I long even more for my opportunity at motherhood. I'm not old yet, but with dating to find the right guy, then dating the guy long enough before an engagement, then marriage for a while prior to starting our family—I am a good five to ten years from a family. This upsets me. I'm tired of waiting. I'm tired of being alone. I want to start my family ASAP.

45

A POSITIVE PREGNANCY TEST

Taylor
At Dr. Wilson's Office, Thursday, 10:00 a.m.

Today's session with Dr. Wilson, starts with my explaining what I mean by bad boys. I list the cheaters, the liars, the drunks, and the drug abusers I fell for. I share they were like shiny pennies for a week or two before showing their true tarnished side. We discuss whether I try to change these men or fix them and discuss these failed relationships in detail before tabling this discussion for another session.

Next, she asks about my nightmares.

"I didn't experience any nightmares for the last two weeks," I answer honestly.

Dr. Wilson's forehead scrunches while scrutinizing my honesty.

"I've had troublesome daydreams instead," I explain. "I feel blurry or drunk in the flashes. After each one, I immediately experience guilt for these thoughts. I feel like I'm hurting Kennedy, but I know I'm not. I don't want to act upon them. I over-think my interactions with Jackson and his reactions to me. Our once comfortable friendship seems strained. I long for the days I could relax and be myself with Kennedy and Jackson."

Dr. Wilson encourages me to plan activities-like we used to and allow myself to enjoy them. Glancing at my journal, the doctor asks why I worry I have issues with my libido.

"I'm more like a guy than a girl. I'm very sexual and worry this with the flashes means I'm lusting for Jackson," I share.

The discussion deepens:

Does Jackson turn me on? -NO.

Do I think of Jackson when aroused? -NO.

Do I long for or plan alone time with Jackson? -NO.

When I masturbate do I see Jackson? -NO.

She assures me I am not lusting for Jackson, stating the flashes are due to the three of us working together in a non-traditional method to create a baby. My mind shows flashes of the three of us in more traditional methods. The doctor assures me many women experience active libidos. She asks me to describe my sexual encounters for the past six months. She states my masturbation is healthier than seeking multiple partners. Women aren't publicized as having high sexual appetites or frequently masturbating...that doesn't mean it is not natural. Women are sexual beings just as men are. Multiple partners increase my chances of STD's, while suppressing feelings can cause more issues. I am told my current behaviors are a healthy way to relieve stress and pleasure myself until I find the elusive Mr. Right to share myself with.

Moving to the next topic of today's session, Dr. Wilson asks how the surrogacy is progressing and if anything new has entered my life.

"I'm nervous that I might already be pregnant," I share. "I'm not afraid, just anxious, worried, and hopeful. I'm finding I'm not a patient person." I explain, "We performed 'The Deed' last week during my ovulation window, and we are now simply waiting for the outcome. Then we'll know if we start over for next month."

Dr. Wilson asks why I have not taken a home pregnancy test.

"I'm scared to death," I confess. "If I take it and I'm not pregnant, I will have to tell Kennedy." I sigh. "I don't look forward to disappointing her. If it takes several months, I'll disappoint her over and over. I'm in no hurry to witness her heartbreak."

"Let's focus on this," Dr. Wilson instructs. "The three of you discussed the likelihood of conception taking several months." She continues, "In our group sessions, we covered expectations and possible outcomes."

I simply nod my agreement.

"Do you want to know as soon as possible if you are pregnant?"

Her question intrigues me.

"I'm not sure," I respond honestly. "I believe we won't become pregnant our first attempt. I can see myself purchasing pregnancy tests in future months. I'll become more excited each time we try to conceive." I flick a piece of lint from the arm of my chair. "I'm in no hurry to learn we need to perform 'The Deed' another month. It's not that I'll be disappointed. It's my fears of Kennedy's reaction that prevents me from taking a test." I look directly at the doctor. "We can't start the process over until August 22nd. A negative test now will only give us eleven days to mourn the fact we're not successful. It won't speed up our next attempt. It won't give us hope for next month."

Dr. Wilson appreciates my honesty. "Kennedy is stronger than you give her credit for." She scribbles notes on her tablet. "Rest assured we cover all possible scenarios at each of the three individual sessions. It's my hope I'm preparing everyone for the long journey to conception." Placing her notes aside she continues, "Taylor, let's imagine you are pregnant. Imagine an embryo is growing inside your womb at this very moment. Close your eyes please. There is a used pregnancy test on your bathroom vanity. Your timer signals it is time to read your results. You look at the symbol. The test reveals you are pregnant. What happens now?"

I slowly open my eyes. A wide smile embellishes my face. "My first thought is how can I get creative to reveal the pregnancy to Jackson and Kennedy." I place my hand upon my belly.

"Taylor," Dr. Wilson demands my attention. "How do you feel knowing you are pregnant?"

I search my thoughts. "I'm proud. I'm proud that my body is fertile and accepted Jackson's sperm so quickly." Absent mindedly my hand caresses my belly. "I'm excited to read my pregnancy books. I need to make a list..."

Dr. Wilson smiles broadly. She interrupts our scene, acknowledging I do not appear to fear pregnancy. She stresses I should live each day with the thought I might be pregnant affecting my decisions. Changing my eating and drinking habits now will have a positive impact when I am pregnant. She encourages me to spend equal time considering both outcomes. It's just as important to prepare for pregnancy as it is for a not pregnant result.

I understand her concerns. If I focus all my energy toward keeping Kennedy's expectations in-check, I forget to consider I could become pregnant in the first month.

Dr. Wilson inquires about my day-to-day life outside the surrogacy.

"I received an email from a dog-breeder I registered with before I visited Kennedy and Jackson. I've passed round one of their screening process. If I'm still interested, I can start the final steps to purchase a Pomsky. I open a photo on my phone to show how adorable the breed is. After I kicked John out, I decided to purchase a dog to keep me company in Chicago. So much has changed since then, and I now temporarily live in KC. As much as I long for a pet, it is just not a great time," I share.

"You should discuss this with Jackson and Kennedy. If you planned for a puppy, chose a breed, and still long for a companion you should see how they feel. A puppy might ease some tensions during our surrogacy journey. You still spend most of your days alone...a puppy could keep you company," Dr. Wilson encourages.

I confess, "I'll consider sharing."

As our session ends, Dr. Wilson asks me to journal my thoughts, fears, and concerns for both possible pregnancy outcomes.

46

KENNEDY "DIRECTS" THEM

Jackson
At Dr. Wilson's Office, Thursday, 4:00 p.m.

I quickly assume my seat anxious for my appointment to begin so it can end. I stand my journal between the seat cushion and the chair arm, hoping she doesn't see that I brought it. I inwardly cringe at the reaction of Dr. Wilson if sees my meager attempts at placing my thoughts on paper.

I refuse the water when offered and Dr. Wilson begins our session. "Let's discuss ovulation and your thoughts on the in-home insemination process."

I cannot contain the groan that escapes.

Dr. Wilson prompts, "Last week, we discussed the first three attempts of fertilization, do you have any concerns for next month."

I realize I cannot avoid her our entire session and decide to participate. "After our first awkward attempt at 'The Deed' I think we perfected our process in the second and third attempt. Taylor's nature is uncomplicated." I smile. "She makes everything easy drama-free, and..." I search for the right word to summarize the sum of all that is

Taylor. "She allows those near her to relax and just be." I shrug as I didn't find the right words.

"Taylor helps make the uncomfortable process easier for Kennedy and you?" The doctor questions.

"After the first evening's dinner discussion," I begin. "We made light of the tasks. With Taylor's prompting, we started joking about it some," I explain. "We are blessed to have Taylor as a friend all these years, and even more blessed she offered to be our surrogate." My smile broadens as I think of the many blessings Taylor bestows upon us. "She really helped me during Kennedy's battle with eating disorders and her hospitalization. I wouldn't have made it through without her to lean on." I chuckle to myself. "How that woman juggles everything she does and never shows signs of stress, I can't comprehend. She is always positive, resourceful, and giving…"

Without warning, my eyes stare unfocused at the side table and lamp. I fight the bile rising my esophagus. I close my eyes tightly to fend off the coming vision. I'm transported to my house with Kennedy and Taylor.

"You mentioned in our first session, Taylor is like a little sister." Dr. Wilson's words draw me to the present. "As her role as surrogate living in your spare bedroom has evolved, what are your current feelings towards Taylor?"

My face contorts at her prying questions. I knew the doctor would continue to ask if feelings she mentioned in our first group session might arise for Taylor. My struggles journaling this week were due to my fantasies like the one I just experienced.

"Jackson, this is a safe place, I am her to assist you. Share with me. I see the pain on your face. Let it out, so we might work through it."

"I'm not this man," I blurt. "I love Kennedy. We've been through so much. I can't imagine a future without her in it." I swallow hard before I continue. "I'm monogamous. I don't cheat. I don't wander."

Dr. Wilson interrupts. "Jackson, what happened to test your loyalty?"

I quickly explain, "Nothing happened. I've had these…" I sigh as I wring my hands in my lap. "I… I'm not sure what they are. I always assumed fantasies occurred in private alone times. But I can't seem to control mine." My eyes look anywhere but at Dr. Wilson. "I can't prevent them. I can't turn them off; they pop into my mind at the worst times. I mean, what is wrong with me?"

"These fantasies," she begins. "Describe them to me."

"I'm above Taylor." I shudder at my memory. "We're on the sofa; the lights are on." I shake my head then look to the door. "Kennedy's there. I mean she is fully clothed, watching, and I don't know…" I sigh. "It's like she's in charge of Taylor and me. Everything is spotty, blurry, and very confusing." I prepare myself for her inquisition. *I hate that she correctly predicted I might have these feelings for Taylor. I don't like being a weak cliché. I detest it's the typical guy fantasy of a three-some.*

Silent moments pass; I return my gaze to Dr. Wilson. She flips through her notebook scanning for something. Still searching she asks, "You stated you are not alone when you see these images, where and when do they occur?"

I explain, "Sometimes I'm in the kitchen as the three of us fix our dinner plates. Other times, we are watching TV. One time, Kennedy and I were saying our good-byes to Taylor after breakfast before work. I assumed fantasies happened in the shower or the bedroom."

"When they occur how do you feel? What do you do?" Dr. Wilson further pries.

"I freeze." Recalling these fantasies gives me the creeps. I feel sleazy. "The current scene becomes invisible as the fantasy intrudes upon my vision. I sweat head-to-toe. My head feels fuzzy. It's as if the scene fades in and out. It jumps. It's choppy and confusing."

"How do you feel in the fantasy?"

"My body is not connected to my brain. I don't feel in control. I feel my body's connection to Taylor, but my brain isn't processing it. I'm fighting it." A chill crawls up my spine. "They are short flashes. I'm left feeling guilty and sleazy. My feet feel like lead as I excuse myself to regroup in private."

"You claim you are not in control. Who is in control?" Dr. Wilson scribbles frantic notes as I explain.

"I'm on top of Taylor and I appear to be in charge," I begin. "But I feel drunk, as if I am just going through the motions. Taylor is blurry, too. I strain to gain some control, but Kennedy's words are the only things I understand." My right hand attempts to massage the knots forming in my neck.

"These words, are the endearments, suggestions, or…"

"Commands," I interrupt. "Kennedy is in control. Her hand is on my shoulder and Taylor's neck. She is in charge." This realization perplexes me.

Dr. Wilson instructs me to journal each time I have these images. She suggests I document the situation and scene that sparks the fantasy, the fantasy itself in detail, as well as, my feelings and reactions after it. As I cringe, she explains further. We need to better understand when and why you have these flashes. The triggers are vital to controlling the images.

I concede to journaling more intently this week, because I need to squash these urges.

Dr. Wilson assures me fantasies are common. She restates fathers often develop feelings towards surrogates. It's natural to care for the mother of my child. She promises we will continue to address these issues in the weeks to come.

The thought of weeks of fantasies and the guilt causes a large, heavy pit to consume my stomach. I desire a quick fix. I attempted avoidance—that didn't work. Taylor is a fixture in our daily lives. *It's not fair to punish her for my sleazy thoughts.*

"Jackson," Dr. Wilson draws my attention. "Your current family unit and living situation are not traditional. It is expected for all three of you to struggle to adapt to these unconventional roles. It's important to communicate openly with each other and when you can't, then with me. Our individual and group sessions are a conduit to explore and develop bonds during the surrogacy journey. Be patient, be open, and journal."

With that our session ends. As I exit, with journal in hand, I feel more confused than when I arrived. However, she promises we will work through my issues. A small ray of hope implants itself in my chest.

I choose to drive home, instead of returning to the store. My thoughts turn to the girls and their counseling sessions today. Dr. Wilson often mentions everyone's feelings.

I wonder what they struggle with? What issues haunt Kennedy and Taylor?

Should I open a discussion tonight?

Maybe they need my help.

I tend to work too many hours. I should work less on my phone at night.

I pledge to make an effort to be present each evening and limit my smart phone usage.

Dr. Wilson
In Her Office, Thursday, 5 p.m.

Concerned after today's session, I make a note of Taylor and Jackson's similar descriptions of intercourse while Kennedy "directs" them. I highlight the fact they both mention confusion, blurriness, and feeling out of it. I make a note to work with Jackson and Taylor in the future, while also broaching the subject with Kennedy. Perhaps these flashes and fantasies are not imagined.

47

BUSTED

Taylor

Jackson arrives home prior to Kennedy again.
"Kennedy will be at Madison's house for most of the night," he informs. "Madison and Isaac are experiencing problems. Isaac left for a few days, so Madison asked Kennedy to come talk it over and keep her company tonight. What shall we do for dinner?" He asks.

I simply shrug.

"We can pick up some fast food. The kind of food that Kennedy will never consume," Jackson suggests.

We discuss a few options before I choose Sonic Drive-In, and Jackson agrees. We pile in my Mustang, lower the top, and cruise to the nearest Sonic, where we eat in the car parked at the curb. *What is it about the simple burger and tater tots that tastes so delicious? Try as I might, I can never prepare a meal as yummy as this at home.*

"Why don't you own a dog?" I blurt as Jackson pulls the car back into traffic.

"I haven't given it much thought," Jackson replies. "We both love dogs, just not sure we have time for a pet. I work long hours, and Kennedy doesn't have a set schedule. What prompted you to ask?"

I remind him they both grew up with dogs as pets. I work up my courage to explain my real reason for inquiring. "I looked into purchasing a puppy in April when I was alone in Chicago."

"I would have felt better if you owned a dog there. Do you know what type of dog you wanted?"

I explain my selection process and my reaching out to Pomsky breeders. At a stoplight, I show him a couple pictures on my phone.

"They look so much like my parents' dogs, Denali and Isis," he claims.

I remind him I met his parents' dogs as I see sadness crawl upon his face. I'm sure he misses the dogs and his parents. Do distract him, I tell him about the application process and the email I received today.

"You should pay your deposit and place your name on the waiting list," Jackson states.

I'm shocked. I planned to drop hints over the course of a week, point out dogs around the neighborhood or on TV. I thought I would have to beg for a dog or give up my dream. I'm lost in my dog thoughts for the remainder of the drive.

Jackson grabs my hand before I exit the car. "A dog is a great idea. We love dogs. A puppy running around the house would be so much fun."

I try to decipher his honest feelings. It seems he really would like a dog. I hope he realizes it would be my dog, and I would take it with me when I move out after the baby is born, but maybe they would get a dog of their own at that time. I mentally add 'contact Pomsky breeder' to tomorrow's list of items to do.

Later that evening, while Jackson takes care of business in the master bathroom, I take a look at my email.

"What's that?" Jackson questions fear upon his face.

Quickly I try to find the words to explain with minimal pain for Jackson. "I email your parents a few times a week." I close my iPad and direct my attention to Jackson still standing behind me and the sofa. "We never lost touch after high school graduation." His eyes search mine as I continue. "Remember they teased that I was your adopted sister?" I attempt to smile, but it's forced. "I needed them, and they were there for me. They still are. I would not have survived high school or college without them. They were the parents I never had."

"How much do they know?" Jackson demands. "Did you tell them you live here? Did you tell them about the surrogacy?" Jackson's pained eyes remained locked to mine as he seats himself on the end of the sofa.

"I would never!" I inform. "I talk about my life, my problems, and my decisions. They give advice without being overbearing." Jackson's words hurt. *I can't believe he thought I would be a spy for his parents.*

"I'm sorry," Jackson starts. "I was shocked. I know you wouldn't..."

I interrupt, "I would tell them when I heard from the two of you. But I never shared details." I want to ease the pain from his face. "Yes, they know I moved to KC. Yes, they know I see you often. I have shared nothing more, I promise."

I take in his sadness. I know being estranged from his parents all these years hurts him. His family was very close. "They are healthy and good. Nicole is too. They miss you."

Jackson swallows hard. "I miss them, too." His runs his fingers through his hair. "I had to choose Kennedy. I never thought they would hold out this long."

I reach for his hand. Together we squeeze tight.

"I'm glad you kept in touch with them. Don't mind me. It shocked me that is all. Finish your email." He rises and starts towards the kitchen. "I'll fetch us popcorn and maybe we shouldn't mention this to Kennedy."

"Hey, wait a minute," I request. "The problem is now that I live closer, they want to see me. I figure I better plan a visit before I'm pregnant. I might not be able to keep our secret when I gain a baby bump." I search his eyes for understanding. He simply nods before fetching our snack.

I don't return to my iPad and email, and I make a mental note to email from the privacy of my room from now on.

Days later, Kennedy hugs me, then kisses Jackson on the cheek as she pulls plates from the cabinet. At her kiss to his cheek, I'm transported to a moment on the living room sofa. *Jackson is in a plank-position above me. His eyes seem as unfocused as my head feels. Kennedy whispers in his ear. She pecks him on the cheek. Slowly, he fills me. I want to scream "no". I need to scream "stop", but my brain and body are no longer connected.* Warm tears trickle down my face.

I'm transported to my present location in the kitchen as I wipe the arrant tears. Jackson stares frozen at my eyes, before disgust creeps upon his face. When he turns and darts upstairs, I look to Kennedy.

She shakes off the situation. "I wonder what got into him?"

Her lack of empathy and reaction to this moment enrages me. *Something is wrong. I froze and cried. Jackson froze then darted from the room. No words were spoken, but something is definitely wrong. Yet she goes about her day as if she didn't witness any of it. How can she be so obtuse? How can she not react to the two people she loves struggling in a moment?*

I excuse myself to my bedroom and pull my journal from my bedside table. I quickly make note of the scene, the last actions before I experienced the flash, what I saw behind my closed eyes, and our reactions following it. I rest my head on a pillow, close my eyes, and attempt to find my happy place.

Too soon, Kennedy announces dinner is ready as she peeks in my room. Conversations at the table flow normally. Kennedy informs Jackson and I we are invited to go to the lake with Tyler & Reagan this weekend. When Jackson promises he will attempt to take Saturday off, Kennedy looks to me.

"Of course, I have nothing preventing me from going," I respond dead-pan. "But is there room on the boat for all of us? I could stay here, so it doesn't get crowded. You two should still go. You could use a mini-vacation."

Kennedy explains the trip details as shared by Reagan. In two vehicles, we caravan down Friday afternoon. While the men place the boat in the lake, the women will buy groceries for the condominium. We all meet for dinner Friday night. Saturday, we take the boat out, ski, tube, and swim. After a late lunch those that want may stay at the pool or the dock, others will head back out on the boat. We will eat a late dinner and party in the condo. Sunday, we can boat until two, then load up for the drive back to Kansas City.

Summer is almost over, and a trip to the lake could be a great way to end the summer. I won't be able to ski, tube, dive, ice-skate, sled-ride, and many other high-risk activities when I become pregnant. A part of me would enjoy a weekend at the lake; while another part of me wants Jackson and Kennedy to enjoy time away from me. *Like in high school and college, I'm a third-wheel again.*

"We should wait until I check my calendar at the store before we commit," Jackson states.

Kennedy reminds him his calendar is on his cell phone. He promises to check it after dinner.

48

OVER. DONE WITH. GONE

Taylor

I'm weeding the front flower beds when a text alert rings from my phone in my back pocket. My gloved hands are much too dirty to read it. I continue to rake the mulch and pull pesky weeds by the root. I wipe sweat from my brow with the sleeve of my T-shirt. Just a couple more feet of flower bed left before I can return to the cool air-conditioning inside.

With the last weed in hand, my cell alerts I have another text. I gather the bag of weeds, remove my gloves, and enter the garage. The bag of weeds I place in the garbage can and the gloves I return to the shelf. In the kitchen, I wash my hands and forearms and dry them before extracting my phone from my back pocket.

KENNEDY
Well?
Aunt Flo?

> Where are you? Period start?

S*eriously? What happened to no added pressure?* I remind myself she's excited. Kennedy knows my periods are never predictable. I knew it wouldn't start on the exact day the calendar predicted. My body never follows a twenty-eight-day or thirty-day cycle.

> ME
> No
>
> I don't have periods remember

I strip out of my filthy clothes in the laundry room before padding my way to my shower. Because of the heat, I turn the shower on a cooler setting than usual. I pull out a towel and fresh razor. With my hands on the shower door, another text alert rings, then yet another.

> KENNEDY
> text if you spot or start
> please
>
> ME
> duh
>
> showering now bye

On Wednesday, I peek my head in the door to Kennedy's office, on my way to the weight room.

"Hey," Kennedy greets. "Any visitors?"

I look around the offices to see if anyone is in earshot.

"You'll be the first person to know if I ever start my period. We can't get our hopes up. I don't have periods. This doesn't mean I'm pregnant," I inform in a whisper. "It may take several months before I'm pregnant."

The gleam in her eyes proves she isn't listening to my words. I fear she's setting herself up for a huge letdown. Maybe I should talk to Jackson and Dr. Wilson about this.

"After you work out, let's grab lunch," Kennedy suggests hopefully.

"I will be sweaty, but okay." I remind.

We grab a light lunch at a deli a few blocks from the YMCA. I opt for a sandwich and baked chips. Kennedy chooses a salad with dressing on the side. We sit at a corner table by the front window. I feel the heat just outside the glass. While we eat, we discuss options for tonight's dinner. Kennedy asks me to stop by Jackson's store to pick up something for him to grill.

"Would it be too early to buy a pregnancy test?" Kennedy asks.

I study her face for any sign she is joking and see none.

"Ken," I scramble to select the words to convey I'm serious, while sparing her feelings. "I won't be pregnant the first month we try. We need to prepare to continue 'The Deed' for two or three more months."

She smiles as a red blush creeps from her neck onto her cheeks.

"What?" I ask, worried she has already purchased a pregnancy test.

She purposefully places another large bite of salad into her mouth, shaking her head that she doesn't want to share.

"Spill it," I demand.

Finishing her current mouthful then washing it down with water, Kennedy stalls prior to sharing, "Jackson will be excited if it takes several months to get pregnant." Her eyes focus on her hand fiddling with her silverware. "He kinda," she pauses nervously, "he kinda likes…"

"Ken, what? Just say it," I plead.

"I read your *Tickle His Pickle* Book."

I didn't think it possible her face could be any redder.

"Well, I kinda helped him, you know, with my hands." Kennedy covers her face with her hands.

"Oh, my god! Ken, I am so proud of you." She needs to know this is normal for married couples and nothing to be ashamed of. "Of course, he liked it. You know he'd like some other things too." *I will not push her.* "Did you like it? I mean, were you okay with it?"

"It felt powerful," she confesses. "I never knew my touch could cause such a reaction."

"You have unlimited power over your husband, if you choose to use it," I assure. Jokingly, I state, "I have other books she should read."

"Uh-huh." Kennedy shakes her head vigorously left-to-right. "No more of your filthy books." Suddenly, her face scrunches and her smile evaporates. "Why did you buy the book in the first place?"

I quickly take in our surroundings. The two tables near us remain empty. Keeping my voice low, I lean toward her to answer. "I didn't buy it for a fun reason." I struggle to find words to explain. "John worked at the bar. He would come home late and usually drunk." I have already shared so many of my troubles with John to Kennedy and Dr. Wilson. Somehow, this should become easy. I sip my iced tea before continuing. "He is loud when he's drunk and horny. I didn't want him when he was like that. So, I learned some techniques to speed his release without me getting too involved. He'd pass out not remembering the next morning." *There I shared. Now, I feel horrible.* I just admitted performing hand-jobs to avoid sex with my live-in fiancé. *How weak do I seem?* A smart woman would break up with him. I allowed him to continue his verbal and mental abuse, while I performed hand-jobs to avoid having sex with him. My eyes averted, I stare at the table and not at my best friend. I don't want to see her judging me. I don't want to see her pity, but I can't avoid it.

"Hey," Kennedy lowers her face to my line of sight. Her gentle smile coaxes me to engage. "You did what you had to do to survive. I can't fault you for that. I hate that you, who loves sex, had to perform these acts and not enjoy them. You seem okay now. You're working on this with Dr. Wilson, right?"

I nod yes.

"Then, boom! We close the door on that topic."

Over. Done with. Gone. Just like that, our conversation moves to happier topics.

49

I HAVE BOOBS AND I DON'T PEE STANDING UP

Taylor

On Thursday, Dr. Wilson asks me to share items from this week. I open my notebook slowly. Jackson and Kennedy watch, waiting to see what I report.

Taking a deep breath, I share. "I have one item I wish to discuss as a group." I look at Dr. Wilson as I remind her, "I suffer from secondary amenorrhea, so I don't have regular periods. Kennedy texts and asks me daily if my period starts. Even though I remind her often that I don't have periods, she continues. She even asks if I should buy a pregnancy test. I don't want to disappoint Kennedy, but the absence of my period is normal. It's not necessarily a sign that I may be pregnant."

Dr. Wilson sympathizes with the added stress this causes me. Directing her attention to Kennedy, she asks, "Kennedy, how does hearing Taylor's words make you feel?"

"I remain optimistic that Taylor could be pregnant," Kennedy states, smiling. "I understand the lack of period doesn't mean we're pregnant. I only text and ask because if she started her period, we would know it's time to plan for next month. I'm not trying to stress her out."

Looking directly at me, Kennedy apologizes. I rise and hug her.

"I understand. I just don't want you to get your heart broken in our first month," I state.

We discuss this weekend's trip to the lake, the dynamics of the relationship between the three of us, and our upcoming physician's appointment on Monday. She prepares us for a pregnant and not pregnant outcome. We discuss each outcome and reactions. Before ending the session, Dr. Wilson asks each of us to make a list of items to consider or change for our next month as we attempt pregnancy again.

Later that evening, we move around the kitchen preparing for dinner.

"What's this?" Kennedy asks, pointing to the printed, color photo on the refrigerator door.

"It's a Pomsky," Jackson informs as he places a platter of grilled pork chops on the counter.

Not satisfied with Jackson's reply, Kennedy continues. "Why is an adorable Pomsky gracing my fridge?"

Jackson explains, "Taylor is attempting to buy a puppy. In fact, she made a deposit to remain on a waiting list." His eyes dart to mine, checking for an update on the waiting status.

Kennedy turns my direction. "You're buying a dog?" When I nod, she asks, "What is a Pomsky?"

"It's a mix of Siberian Husky and Pomeranian," I explain. "I should be able to choose a puppy in the next litter or two. I researched the breed months ago." I excuse myself from the table, fetch my iPad, and open the Middle Tennessee Pomsky website for her to view.

Kennedy cannot contain her excitement. I knew they both loved dogs. When she smiles, I assume she imagines a puppy padding around the kitchen, attempting to climb the stairs, and chasing leaves in the backyard this fall.

Jackson must work on Friday, so the three of us plan to drive ourselves down later, then connect with the group. My Mustang's gas tank is full, so is the trunk. Kennedy and I nibble on pretzels as we anxiously await Jackson's arrival home from the store. When the garage door lifts, Kennedy hops up and down, clapping excitedly. She dances around while singing, "We are going to the lake. We are going to the lake."

Jackson shakes his head at her antics when entering the kitchen. She begs him to hurry and change, so we can hit the road. In their seven years together, he knows her excitement cannot be contained. He places a peck on her forehead prior to ascending the stairs to the main bedroom.

Glancing at her phone, Kennedy states, "Reagan says the caravan stopped for a flat tire on the boat trailer. We may arrive at the same time."

"Let's hit the road and catch up with them," Jackson urges.

In the driveway, Jackson reaches for the Mustang's driver's side door.

"Jackson," I begin. "Can I drive, so I don't get carsick on the hills?"

Holding the door open, he motions for me to climb in. "Shotgun!" he shouts, jogging around the hood.

Kennedy climbs into the backseat prior to Jackson taking the passenger seat and shutting the door. I smile at my passengers before, turning the ignition. *Heathens* by Twenty-One Pilots blares from the speakers. I quickly turn the volume down, noting the display reads 98.9 The Rock.

"Co-pilot is in charge of the tunes," I inform Jackson.

His face lights up with this knowledge. I mentally wave goodbye to my rock station, knowing Jackson's music preferences don't include modern rock bands. I secure my iPhone in the mount on the air vent, letting Jackson know he can use my playlists if we lose the radio reception along the way.

We pull from the driveway, beginning the three-hour journey to the Lake of the Ozarks. Jackson settles the radio on a station playing Justin Bieber's *Love Yourself*, and our road trip begins.

On the other side of Jefferson City, Jackson points out a red SUV towing a boat. As we approach, we see it's Tyler and Reagan's Navigator with James, Martha, Isaac, and Madison inside. I honk repetitively as we pass, and Jackson and Kennedy wave excitedly. Soon Kennedy's cell phone pings, signaling a text. She reads aloud, "We get to lead the way, and they will attempt to keep up with us the rest of the way."

"You should slow a little so they can keep up," Jackson states.

I reluctantly slow and reset the cruise control to eight miles over the speed limit.

"It will not kill you," Jackson teases. "You're still speeding."

I can't help it; I enjoy driving fast. It's not for an adrenaline rush, as much as it is a stress reliever. Slow traffic causes me to become stiff and uptight. I detest it. Fast flowing traffic and speed free me. It's a release. Yes, eight miles per hour over the speed limit is speeding. It's slower than my usual highway speed, but I can handle it.

An hour later, I hesitantly pull into Parkview Bay. I'm not sure of our unit number, so I choose an open parking spot in the middle of the lot. Tyler pulls the red Navigator along the outer edge of the lot. We exit our vehicles, meeting near the clubhouse entrance. I hang back a bit as excited conversations launch. Isaac, James, Tyler, and Jackson discuss my Mustang, the drive, and an animated tale of the flat tire adventure. Madison and Kennedy discuss items they packed, while Reagan and Martha plan to check in, unload, then grocery shop.

"Taylor," Isaac calls. As I approach the men, he continues. "Why didn't you opt for the GT?"

I flashback to the boob comment he made upon meeting me weeks earlier. *I must play nice.* He's a friend of Jackson and Kennedy's. Standing with the group of guys, I respond, "I'm not flashy. I don't need my car to be an extension of my penis. But if I did, it wouldn't be just a GT. I would choose the Shelby GT350."

I notice Isaac looks stunned, Jackson smiles knowingly, while Tyler and James stare in shock.

Forgetting I'm trying to be polite, I continue, "Yes, Isaac, I know my cars. I'm not some dim-witted bimbo trying to catch a man with a flashy car." I pause quickly for a breath. "I know what a Gimlet is. I can change my own tires and oil, I know the difference between a V-6 and a V-8, I watch the NFL and MLB drafts, I follow sports, I drink whiskey, I drink beer, and although I have boobs and I don't pee standing up—my brain still functions." Looking at Jackson, I plead, "Keep him away from me this weekend. He is a misogynistic asshole, and unless you wanna ride home with him…"

Jackson wraps his arms around me while escorting me far away from the group. My head spins and my stomach feels full of monarch butterflies.

"Breathe," he prompts. "Easy. He asked a simple question. Nothing more. You flew into a tirade over nothing." We stop, and he caresses my shoulders. "I realize Isaac can be a dick, but you…" He runs a hand through his hair, trying to find his words. "You need to relax. I know he pushes your buttons. If you ignore him, he'll stop. Remember, we're on vacation. It's time to relax, swim, eat, and drink."

I nod in agreement. Jackson escorts me to the girls' group, standing by my side in support. Kennedy joins us.

"Everything okay?" she whispers into my ear.

I simply nod.

As a group we decide Reagan and Tyler will go check-in. Once checked in the girls will soon go grocery shopping. Isaac walks off to explore. Kennedy and Madison pull away to a private conversation. James approaches Jackson.

"Taylor, we're putting you in charge of securing drinks for the guys on your trip to the store. Can you do that for us?" he asks.

"I won't you down," I promise.

After unloading vehicles into the condo, the men take off to place the boat into the water.

"What vehicle are we driving to the store?" I ask.

"Can we take Taylor's car?" Reagan asks.

"It only seats four," I state.

"We should take the Navigator," Kennedy suggests.

Containing my urge to laugh, I remind her. "The guys need it to unload the boat."

After some discussion, Kennedy and Madison offer to stay behind while the rest of us shop. I grab my keys, then drive Reagan and Martha ten minutes to the nearest grocery store. It's the same company as Jackson's store. I'm amazed how this store resembles his. I push a cart of my own.

"I'll get the alcohol, then find you in the grocery aisles," I inform the ladies.

I buy bottles of whiskey and rum for the guys, then a bottle of flavored vodka the ladies. I place three types of beer in my cart, then select a variety of wine. I finish with some sugary sweet mixers for the women, then set out to find Reagan and Martha.

50

LIKE SOLAR FLARES FROM THE SUN, HOT

Taylor

My cell phone buzzes as I approach the girls near the meat case. I look at my text.

> JORGE
> at the lake yet?

> ME
> shopping with your sis

> JORGE
> careful she's used to feeding toddlers

> ME
> I'm in charge of alcohol

> JORGE
> smart choice

> ME
> what you up to?

> **JORGE**
> working
>
> on break

> **ME**
> weekend's gonna suck

> **JORGE**
> hair down have some fun

"Tell him I say hi," Martha says, bumping my shoulder, startling me.

My eyes dart from my phone to meet two very prying sets of eyes. I attempt to brush it off as nothing important.

"Don't put your phone away," Reagan pleads.

"We won't pry," Martha states. "Jorge needs you."

I stare at Martha in fear. Jorge and I are friends, nothing more. We are honest with each other. We keep in touch, but we have moved on. He's attempting to win Rosalynn back, and I'm helping my friends have a baby. My phone vibrates repeatedly in my back pocket, as Reagan and Martha excuse themselves to allow me to continue our conversation.

> **JORGE**
> you need fun before you get knocked up

> **ME**
> Martha says hi

> **JORGE**
> LOL
>
> I called her yesterday

> **ME**
> trying to set us up

Surrogate Series

> JORGE
> whatever, I've told Martha everything
> knows where we stand

> ME
> I don't think so

> JORGE
> doesn't want me alone
> protective big sis

> ME
> may be a long weekend

> JORGE
> wear sunscreen

> ME
> tell Rosalynn hi

I hesitantly push my cart behind the girls. Occasionally, I place items in my cart for me or the guys. I separate from them at the registers to pay for these items myself.

"I want to pay," Reagan insists.

"Renting the condo is enough. I can help with food and drinks," I state.

"Everyone chipped in for groceries," Martha argues.

"I didn't, so I'll pay for my cart. I don't enjoy owing money to others. I'm not a freeloader and never will be," I state.

The topic of Jorge re-emerges on the ride back to the condo.

"Jorge and I are close friends, nothing more. He is reuniting with Rosalynn," I inform her.

"He told me you had sex," Martha responds.

Reagan gasps in surprise. "You slept with Jorge?" She looks from Martha to me in the driver's seat. "Oh. My. Goodness. You slept with Martha's hot brother?"

Martha playfully swats at Reagan's shoulder from the backseat.

"We met, and we didn't have sex. You must have heard him wrong. We decided we were better as friends, end of story," I state, keeping eyes on the road.

"Bullshit!" Reagan taunts. "I've seen Jorge. He is hot. Like solar flares from the sun, hot. No one decides to friend him. And masturbating side-by-side is sex, honey."

"We are friends. Nothing more," I explain.

I breathe a sigh of relief as the condo comes into view. Reagan texts for help in carrying the groceries. The guys are chatting in the parking lot by the SUV, so they arrive first. I pop the trunk as they approach. I discreetly pull a bottle of Dramamine from my console. Then I grab a couple of bags from the back seat. I hear acknowledgements and appreciation from the men as they inventory the beverages I purchased. Kennedy and Madison join us just in time to grab the last two bags of ice.

We tuck the groceries away and fill the coolers with beverages and ice. Once we consume dinner and load the dishwasher, Reagan states we are playing a game. Deemed the game queen, all eyes fall on me. I decide a lake vacation requires excessive drinking for my friends.

"The name of the game is sippy-tippy. We need two teams and a plastic cup for each of us," I explain.

"Girls against the guys," Reagan shouts.

With no objections, we divide. As there is an odd number, Kennedy offers to sit out the first round and rotate in the next.

"I'm the only single in the condo. I will sit out," I explain.

The men agree, so they line the cups up in front of each of them on their sides of the table.

"When you start, you go in order down the line on each side, chug the beverage in your glass, turn the empty cup over, then try to tip the cup over so that it stands upright before the next person goes. First team done wins," I share.

"Now, we need to decide on one drink everyone will chug," I say.

Guys immediately state beer, girls name a few different beverages.

"We gulped down the rum punch the ladies prepared. Let's play with that," I suggest.

Winking at the guys, they agree with me. We fill each glass one-fourth of the way full. I explain the rules one more time and show by chugging the contents of my glass, placing it upside down on the edge of the table, then on my first attempt flipping it to land upright. I explain, most will have to replace the cup and attempt multiple times before it lands correctly. The next person cannot start early. Everything is ready, we prepare to begin.

I announce, "On your mark, get set, go!"

Martha chugs faster than Isaac and places her cup upside down on the table before he finishes drinking. She flips the cup upright on her first attempt, and Reagan starts her part of the game. Isaac takes three flips before his cup lands upright. The men are behind by two women by the time Isaac completes his first part of the task. The women win, easily.

After the many beers the men have consumed, rum will not sit well. I learned in Jr. High, "Beer before liquor never sicker, liquor before beer in the clear." I love the pain this game will inflict on Isaac most of all.

I fill three red Solo Cups one-quarter full on the ladies' team before running out of rum punch and excuse myself to the kitchen to prepare more, while the guys taunt the women. I mix this batch of drinks with twice the rum as the last. It is party time. Upon my return, we fill the rest of the glasses.

The guys huddle to plan for this round, while we ladies smile, knowing they will win again.

This round begins. I chug fast and flip my red cup upright immediately. Martha again chugs fast and flips her red cup on the first attempt. Isaac doesn't fare as well; he's still trying after two of us finish. The girls win by a smaller margin this time.

After consultation in a huddle, the women suggest we rearrange the lines to shake things up a bit. Sippy-tippy continues for three more rounds, with the boys winning only once. They admit defeat as they wobble on their feet. The ladies lay their victory on thick. The guys return to drinking beer, unaware of the turmoil brewing deep within their stomachs.

I excuse myself and quickly make my way to the upstairs bathroom. I splash water on my face. As I towel dry, I peek at my reflection in the mirror. I'm flush. Pale. I still feel a bit motion-sick. It must be from the long drive from KC. I always battle car-sickness, but only occasionally when I drive. I quickly down another Dramamine before exiting the restroom. Peeking inside the nearly empty plastic tube, I realize I need to purchase more before the ride home.

In the hallway, I'm face-to-face with Jackson. "What's up?" He questions concern on his face.

"I'm motion-sick, so I grabbed the Dramamine," I explain.

I wave the bottle for his inspection, sensing he doubts my explanation. I brush past him to find a water bottle in the kitchen.

"Maybe it's the alcohol," Jackson slurs, following me.

"I didn't drink earlier, and I consumed a tiny amount of alcohol during the game," I share. "It's motion sickness. I've felt it all afternoon and evening."

Jackson simply nods, before turning, then staggering to leave the kitchen.

"Jackson," I interrupt his retreat. "Maybe you should drink some water for a while."

"I'm fine," he states, or at least that is what I think he says as he walks away.

How can he be concerned about me, but so out of it he doesn't know he needs to hydrate and stop drinking alcohol? Lack of partying, that's how.

I return to the group of extremely inebriated friends. As they walk, talk, and slur, I laugh at myself. They are a fun group of lightweights, enjoying a weekend of no-holds-barred-drinking. I use my phone to video and take still photos of the hilarity for replay tomorrow, while I enjoy my bottle of water that goes unnoticed by the group.

51

WHAT ARE YOU READING?

Taylor

Saturday morning, I sit up slowly from my air mattress. Rising from its edge, I sway on my feet. I steady myself, hands on the wall. Carefully, I slowly stride down the hall to the restroom, where I brush my teeth, wash my face, and brush my hair. Still feeling dizzy, I attempt blowing my nose, then yawning to pop my ears. I try the remedies that usually give me relief with no success.

I lightly pad my way downstairs to the kitchen. I place two slices of bread into the toaster, while I find butter, jelly, fruit, yogurt, and a Diet Pepsi. Sitting at the breakfast bar, I nibble on my breakfast while I scan my social media accounts. Deep in thought, I do not hear Kennedy approach. I jump when she touches my shoulder.

"Sorry," she apologizes. "Anything interesting on Instagram?"

I shut my phone, placing it on the counter next to me. The toast filled me up, so I slide my fruit and yogurt Kennedy's way.

"I heard a noise in Reagan's room and Jackson is also up," Kennedy tells me. "Won't be long until we are boating on the lake." Her excitement is contagious. "It'll be crowded, but we can all go out this morning."

Swallowing my last bite of toast, I excuse myself to go get fun-in-the-sun ready. I exchange high-fives with Reagan as we pass on the stairs. She is already in her bikini and black knitted cover-up.

As I rummage through my suitcase, Jackson approaches. "How did you sleep on the air mattress?" He walks over and sits on the mattress to check it out for himself.

"I slept all night without waking up," I respond.

Finding my one-piece suit, cover-up, and flip-flops, I excuse myself to the hallway bathroom. I chose a one-piece because I plan on tubing, and I don't want to worry about my bikini top or bottoms sliding off. I secure my locks into a high ponytail and apply my moisturizer for some extra SPF protection.

Jackson stands, leaning over the railing, watching breakfast preparations when I return my PJ's to my suitcase.

"Feel better?" he inquires.

"I do," I reply. "I'm ready for sunshine, water, and beer. Get your butt in gear so we can get to the boat."

He raises both hands, palms towards me in defense.

"How's the hangover?" I do not need him to answer. I know he is in pain. He's pale in the face. "Go get some food and plenty of liquids."

"Okay, bossy," he teases. "I'll eat fast."

It's now I notice he has on a t-shirt and swim trunks. He's almost ready to go as he descends the stairs.

I grab my cell phone from the bookshelves before I follow. I settle into a comfy chair in the living room, open my iPhone, tap my Kindle App, and continue reading my current book. On my flight back to Chicago a few weeks ago, I downloaded a book by Kristen Ashley. I immediately fell in love with her writing. I'm now on the fifth book in her series.

"Earth to Taylor." Reagan attempts to gain my attention. As Reagan repeats her words, Kennedy waves a hand between me and my phone. This catches my full attention. I close the book on Denver, Colorado, and rise from the chair.

"Posted!" Martha shouts from across the sofa. "Our first vacation post is Taylor reading sideways in the chair."

I ask to see her post, and she shares her phone. I lay sideways with my head on one arm, my legs across the other arm of the chair. I have two fingers on my lower lip while I read. I know exactly which steamy part I read at the moment it was taken. I pass her phone back.

"You are blushing," Reagan accuses. "What are you reading?"

To change the subject from me, I open my photos on my phone and pass it to Reagan. "I took several incriminating pics and videos last night. Be careful, or I will start posting, too," I warn.

The group huddles around my phone, astonished by the moments I captured.

"Why weren't you taking part last night?" James asks.

"She took Dramamine for my car-sickness, so she couldn't drink too much," Jackson states.

I snatch my phone back.

"We will play nice," Reagan promises. "No posts without approvals of all those in the pic, okay?"

Everyone murmurs agreement.

I let Martha know her Instagram post is okay as we move through the door toward the dock. The men carry our coolers, while the women carry our sunscreen, towels, and snacks.

Tyler and James take turns driving the boat. In a quiet cove, they pause, allowing us to bob up and down on the waves.

I approach Tyler. "May I be the first to tube?"

He agrees.

"You're the lone driver while I am off the boat," I demand.

He quickly agrees, realizing how deep my distrust for Isaac lies.

I dive from the rear of the boat into the cool lake water. I tread water a bit before requesting a life-jacket. I climb upon the tube, prior to slipping my arms into and securing the life-jacket. Then, I signal I'm ready to the boat.

Tyler eases the engine forward, and the boat moves in wide circles within the cove. Eventually, Tyler steers the boat from the cove with me in tow. The lake is busy, as everyone attempts to enjoy every ounce of summer available. Tyler scans the vicinity, carefully directing the boat away from others, while allowing me to enjoy bouncing over their wakes. I bob and bounce until my arms turn to jelly. I carefully remove one hand from the grip to signal to the boat I'm finished. It takes a couple of waves before they relay my signal to Tyler. The boat slows as Jackson and James pull me closer. I slide into the lake and swim the best I can with the cumbersome life vest on. At the boat, my arms tremble as I attempt to climb aboard. Jackson and James pull me up.

"That was awesome!" I share. "My arms are jelly. I'll be so sore tomorrow."

"That's what she said," Isaac shouts.

I do my best to roll my eyes and ignore him. I extricate my limbs from the life vest, then wrap in the beach towel handed to me. Without a word, Isaac dives from the front of the boat into the lake. He swims straight to the tube, refusing a life jacket. I decide if his wife doesn't insist on a vest, then I don't care either. I arrange my towel under me, so that I might dry in the hot sun as we maneuver around the lake. Once dry, I'll slip into my cover-up before applying more sunscreen.

After Isaac's turn, Martha dawns a vest for her ride. The traffic on the lake doubled since we arrived. Two large wakes cause Martha to fall from the tube, but she held tight to the rope handle. As we shout for Isaac to stop the boat, Martha flails, dragging behind the boat. She yells for the men to stop their attempt to pull her in. We anxiously watch as she seems to struggle to remain upright. Finally, Isaac listens to all of us and stops the boat.

Moments pass before she dog-paddles toward the boat. Once pulled aboard, she announces her bikini bottoms came off. She states they were past her knees before she caught them.

"This is why I wore a one-piece," I state to the girls, as everyone laughs.

Glancing at his watch, Tyler announces it's time to dock for lunch. We secure all lose belongings for the long, windy ride to the condo. Although the fresh air helps, I find the rocking of the boat over the waves and wakes brings back my motion-sickness. I haven't been on a boat since high school with Jackson's family. I forgot how sick they make me. I must buy more Dramamine.

Tyler expertly steers the boat into our dock, and the guys secure it. I quickly exit the boat first, needing the stability of land. I hang on the dock when I realize I have no key to the condo. The gang takes their time climbing from the boat.

"Reagan, may I have the key, so I can run on up?" I ask.

She pulls it from her beach bag for me.

I unlock the door, laying the key on the entry table. I climb the stairs two at a time in my quest for pharmaceutical relief to my queasiness. I carry the Dramamine into the bathroom. I place the pill on my tongue, using my hand to cup water from the faucet to wash it down. My reflection in the mirror is sun-kissed and windblown. I let my hair down, running my fingers through my tangles. I leave the bathroom in search of my brush. As I clutch my makeup bag for my return to the bathroom, the others enter the condo. I ignore them, as I desperately need to take care of my hair.

Three light knocks to the open bathroom door draw my attention from the mirror to Kennedy, standing in the doorway.

"Are you okay?" she asks.

"I'm seasick," I answer.

I pull my Dramamine bottle from my cover-up pocket to show her I am trying to control it.

"I hope it kicks in quickly, so you might enjoy the trip," she states, hugging me.

We exit the bathroom and join the group, preparing lunch.

I catch a look between Jackson and Kennedy. She signals that I'm okay. I wave at him, hoping to reassure him. Jackson's constant acknowledgement of my disappearances and queasiness unsettles me. In the past three weeks, our relationship felt strained. He seemed distant. I wrote it off as work and baby stress, coupled with my over-analyzing his interactions to me.

My flashes, daydreams, or fears, whatever they are, have me on high alert. Here at the lake, he seems very in tune to my every movement and need. He probably just wants me to feel comfortable around his friends. He knows I'm the only single person in the group of married couples, and I feel like an outsider. I know he worries about

my constant need for Dramamine, but my motion-sickness is nothing new.
He knows that.

52

I'VE NEVER SLEPT WITH MARTHA'S BROTHER

Taylor

Too many people move about the kitchen, so I select a seat at the table until it's my turn to fix a plate. Jackson and James join me.

"Is the lake too busy now for skiing today? Should we do it first thing tomorrow morning?" James asks.

"There are plenty of coves to ski in if the center of the lake is too crowded," Jackson states. "We go home tomorrow, so we need to ski this afternoon and again in the morning."

"Can you show me how you slalom?" James asks.

"I'll show you on the dock, then ski first this afternoon to demonstrate," Jackson promises.

As we take turns fixing our plates, I choose small portions and nibble slowly to calm my stomach. I feel Jackson's watchful eyes on me throughout the meal. I avoid looking his way. Kennedy and Jackson are overprotective. *They seem to forget I'm an adult, and I can take care of my motion sickness on my own.* I rise, plate in hand, walking to the kitchen for more cheese and crackers. I grab a bottle of ginger ale from the refrigerator, then return to my seat. I slowly sip the cold, bubbly beverage. Occasionally, I nibble a cracker, and my stomach slowly relaxes.

As we replace the food into cabinets, plastic containers, and the refrigerator, we discuss plans for this afternoon.

"I plan to check out the three swim pools," I mention, needing to remain on shore.

"I'll stay with you," Kennedy offers.

Reagan and Marie express a desire to ski.

Madison approaches Kennedy, asking, "May I join you at the pool?"

As the afternoon sun fades, I take another Dramamine with a bottle of water on the pool deck. I glance at my phone, noting we have sunned at the pool for more than three hours. Kennedy and Madison are fair-complected. Although we religiously applied sunscreen every hour, I know they need to find shade.

"We need to return to the condo to shower and relax before the other six return," I suggest, and they agree to my plan.

At six, Reagan enters, announcing their return. Jackson's sunburned his face, and so are all the guys' faces and shoulders. Shame on Reagan and Martha for not forcing sunscreen on them. The skiers are tired and hot as they disperse to their individual bathrooms to shower before dinner. Kennedy and Madison start the grill, pepper the steaks, prepare a salad, baked beans, baked potatoes, and desserts. I watch, not wanting to ruin any part of the meal.

Tyler arrives first. He carries the steaks to the grill and returns for butter, tongs, and the thermometer. Kennedy removes the potatoes from the microwave. We quickly place butter, salt, and pepper on them before wrapping in aluminum foil. Madison carries them to the grill for Tyler. When she returns, she grabs a beer, then delivers it, too. Kennedy pulls five wine glasses down and a bottle of red wine from the wine fridge.

"I'm still taking Dramamine, so I won't be drinking wine," I quickly explain.

She frowns my way, but quickly recovers as Madison returns. We place plates, silverware, and napkins on the island. I fix five ice water glasses and place them at the end of the island. Kennedy and Madison stir the beans as I pull condiments from the fridge.

With everything ready, we relax in the living room until Tyler finishes the steaks. As the men materialize one-by-one, they grab a beer and join Tyler at the grill. Reagan and Martha carry wine glasses in to join us. I look up from my book occasionally to join the conversation. Reagan asks what I am currently reading. We compare books on our Goodreads To-Be-Read Shelves. I add a few to mine, as Reagan adds to hers.

After dinner, the guys decide to play poker at the table.

Reagan wraps her arm around my shoulders. "Let's play the game you taught us over the Fourth of July. It would be fun with just us ladies. Right?" She squeezes my shoulders with an expectant smile on her face.

I nod, and Reagan gathers the women into the sitting area. We relax onto the two sofas and chairs arranged perfectly for conversations. Before I explain the game again, Reagan ensures everyone has a drink and a large pitcher of rum punch is nearby for refills.

"Taylor will go over the rules again before I start the game," Reagan announces.

I remind the group, "You drink if you have done the item the person claims they haven't. Let's practice before Reagan starts. I've never..." I pause for effect. "Waterskied." I watch as Reagan and Martha drink. "Raise your hand if you have waterskied." I need to check for understanding. Only Reagan and Martha raise their hands. Good. They remember how to play. "Do you remember what happens if you are the only person who has done something?"

Several announce in unison 'chug your drink'. I motion for Reagan to start our game.

"I've never slept with Martha's brother," Reagan prompts.

I'm shocked. This is a direct strike to me. I take the tiniest sip from my cup before I stare daggers at Reagan. I will get even. As I am the only one for this one, I must now drink the entire contents of my red cup. "Just a reminder, we *did not* have sex." A few ladies murmur. "We didn't have intercourse." I raise my voice.

I quickly chug my drink, refill it with the nearby pitcher, then excuse myself to the kitchen for a bottle of water. I will need to hydrate if I continue playing this game while on Dramamine. As I pass the poker table, Isaac informs me, "We can hear every word and also see everyone who drinks." His laugh unnerves me.

Great. No secrets here.

Back in my seat, I sip water as the game continues. Fortunately for me, I pretend to sip from my cup and never need to chug again. I make it my mission to make everyone else drink instead.

As we play topics include: I've never…had a baby, been married, lived in KC, owned a house, had sex at a neighbor's house, faked an orgasm, and joined the mile-high-club among many other topics.

On my turn, I get even with Reagan. I state, "I've never had sex with Tyler."

Of course, she is the only one to have sex with her husband. She chugged like a champion.

Kennedy giggles. The alcohol lifting her inhibitions. "My turn," she claims. All eyes swing to her side of our group. "I've never had an orgasm during sex." The alcohol doesn't keep a blush from creeping up her pale neck and face.

Everyone drinks but Kennedy and me. I feel six eyes piercing my flesh. Martha, Reagan, and Madison share their disbelief.

"I have orgasms many times a week, but never with a man," I explain.

"Well, you had one in the presence of my brother," Martha slurs.

Giggles and lewd comments about the very attractive Jorge fill the air.

"It was masturbation. Jorge didn't elicit an orgasm from me," I inform the intoxicated group. "I've never had an orgasm while having sex with anyone," I reiterate.

"Bullshit!" Kennedy challenges. "I know you had one. I was there when you had one with…" Fear washes over her expression as she tries to cover her tracks.

It's as if she thinks she was exposing some deep, dark secret of mine. I know I have never had one with a guy. As hard as I tried, no one could affect me that way. I assume it is the amount of alcohol she has consumed in the last nine hours that causes her to think she knows something. As I keep an eye on her for the next five minutes, she avoids all eye contact with me. When I lean toward her and bump her shoulder, she pulls away as if I burn her. I didn't get mad at her statement. I didn't say a word; she simply recoiled. She struggles to react to others in the group, too. *Something is up.* It can't be the drinks. *Something upset her.*

53

DRAMAMINE

Taylor

On Sunday our last day at the lake, I awake queasy as I have been since we left home. I slowly sit up, swing my legs over the side of the air mattress, then make my way to the hallway bathroom. I splash water on my face, while avoiding my reflection in the mirror. How has anyone not mentioned my flush face and neck this weekend? I take a Dramamine with a quick sip of water from the sink. I place the tiny bottle in my pocket, so I can take another if needed.

"Good morning," I greet Kennedy in the hallway. I block her path toward the stairs. "Are we okay?" Her eyes widen, her smile seems forced. "Last night, what was that about?" *I need information; I want information. She is not escaping until I understand.*

"I'm not sure what you are talking about. Last night is a bit of a blur." Kennedy speaks, but her eyes don't convey the same emotion as her words. "I drank all day. I have a killer headache today. Don't you?"

"I didn't drink much yesterday, due to the meds," I remind her.

"What did I do last night? And why do you think we might not be okay today?" She asks.

I shrug it off. I'm sure she is very aware of the exact moment I'm asking about. I allow her to brush it off. I don't want to spend our last day here on edge. I want her to enjoy the last day of her getaway weekend. With work and baby stress, she needs this fun time with friends. I'm probably over-reacting, yet again. *Maybe the baby stress is getting to me, too.*

I pad quietly to the kitchen and pull-out items to make a big breakfast. We should use the groceries, so we don't have to pack them home. I pull up a recipe for French toast on my phone and quickly snap a picture so that I can refer to it again. I whip up the mixture, prepare the griddle and bread. I pull fresh fruit from the refrigerator, placing it on the counter along with butter, syrup, and juice. I place the syrup in the microwave for a minute to heat before the griddle is hot enough to cook. I quickly place plates, utensils, and glasses on the counter, then dip the first slices of bread and place them on the sizzling griddle.

I refer to my recipe often to ensure I'm cooking correctly. As the first four slices of bread are removed from the heat, Reagan and James appear in the kitchen. They claim the smell woke them up. As I start more toast on the griddle, we hear bumps upstairs, signaling more will arrive soon.

"I love the French toast," Reagan informs.

Maybe I'm starting to get the hang of this cooking thing. I nervously peek often at the toast to ensure I don't burn it. One by one the others join us in the kitchen, and I pass platefuls of hot French toast to everyone.

"Let me take over at the griddle, while you eat," Reagan insists.

I pass the tongs to her, then fix my plate. I choose one slice of toast, butter, and a tiny bit of hot syrup. I don't trust my stomach.

"Still not feeling well?" Reagan asks, the nurse in her always present.

"I'm afraid motion-sickness is a staple in my life. Boats and waves are much worse than car rides," I explain.

Satisfied, Reagan motions for me to attend to my plate.

We join the group and their conversation planning for the day. The men and Reagan are taking the boat out until one. The rest of us plan to lay by the pool and on the dock. We will eat by two, pack up, and hit the road. A sadness creeps over our group as we think of returning to KC and for most, work tomorrow.

While the others soak up the late-summer sun, I choose to read in the shade of an umbrella near the pool. I finish one book and start the next in the series before it is time to head to the condo. It takes no time at all for me to pack my bag. I lounge on the sofa, reading while waiting for the couples to pack.

Kennedy interrupts, "You and your reading." She teases.

"You would love Kirsten Ashley's books," I assure her.

"I'm much too busy to read," she claims.

I proceed to read two paragraphs out loud to her. She leans in to read along with me. *I knew she would be hooked.*

Jackson peeks his head in between ours, startling us. "Such filth!" he teases. "How can you read that porn."

"Old man you need your eyes checked. There is not a sex scene on this page," I inform.

Jackson laughs, "But it does have sex scenes, doesn't it?"

I simply shake my head at him as I close my Kindle App. Looking around, I see everyone stands with multiple bags ready to load the vehicles.

"It's raining," Martha announces.

The guys offer to pull up the SUV and load it for their wives.

"You can pull the Mustang up, Kennedy and I will carry our bags out to meet him," I inform Jackson. "A little rain won't make us melt."

"Does that mean we can drive home with the top down," he asks.

While I love his enthusiasm, I inform him, "Thunderstorms will greet us as we approach KC so the top stays up."

I decide to sleep in the back, allowing Jackson to drive and Kennedy to sit up front. I pop two Dramamine as Kennedy and I carry the bags from the condo. I feel like I wasted a great trip to the lake by popping Dramamine non-stop. *I hope I didn't dampen the fun for everyone else.*

The vehicles loaded with bags, coolers, and humans we set our course for home. I fall asleep quickly; it's a good thing. The hills and curves and my motion sickness don't mix.

54

DESSERTS ARE TO EAT

Taylor

Just like any other day, I wake on Monday to a quiet house. I enjoy a light breakfast, complete cleaning tasks, then shower and prepare for my 11:45 doctor's appointment. With an hour before I need to leave, I print off a new calendar for the refrigerator and a temperature tracking calendar for my room. Then, I save the old calendars in my top dresser drawer.

I opt to stand as I wait for the doctor to enter my exam room. Already weighed, left a urine sample, and had my vitals recorded by a nurse, this should be a quick visit. We just need a new script of Clomid and to follow the same steps as the month before.

Soon, the doctor enters, tablet in hand. He greets me. "How have you been feeling?" he asks.

"We followed all the steps, and we think we're ready to repeat them again this month," I answer.

He lays the tablet on the counter, looks me in the eye, and states, "That won't be necessary."

I'm confused. I rack my brain for our conversation from the last visit. I'm sure we discussed following this plan for a couple of months. "But..." I begin.

"Kennedy, you are pregnant," Dr. Harrison interrupts.

All the air vanishes from the exam room, and heat washes over me from head-to-toe. I fan my face, trying to calm my uneasy stomach. Quickly, I hop from the exam table, bend over the trash can, and puke.

"I see morning sickness has arrived," Dr. Harrison teases.

When my stomach is empty, I rinse my mouth in the tiny sink.

"I've been carsick from Friday on our trip to the lake," I explain.

"It's most likely morning sickness. Movement, smells, and tastes can aggravate morning sickness," he states.

The entire visit passes in a blur. I leave the office with a card, announcing my next appointment and many congratulations from the office staff.

I sit in my idling car, a few minutes blasting the air conditioner on my face. *What do I do now?* Closing my eyes, I rest my forehead on the steering wheel. *Shit! Shit! Shit! Only I could be so lucky to never have periods but get pregnant the first month I try.* I lift my head. As I focus on the silver Mustang emblem on the center of my steering wheel, I take several deep breaths in and out. Next, I open my shopping list app. I add pregnancy test, baby book, gift bags, and tissue paper. Closing the app, I decide I'm driving to Target and pull from the lot, determined.

I select a pink gift bag for Kennedy and a blue for Jackson with white tissue paper. Next, I place two pregnancy tests in my cart. I scan the book section while reminding myself I'm not looking for my next romance novel. I quickly spot the *What to Expect When You're Expecting* book for Kennedy. Nearby, I see a book perfect for Jackson. I lay the *Dude You're Gonna Be a Dad!* Book in my cart and dart to the check stands.

On my drive home, I plot several ways to announce our news. Before dinner, after dinner, as soon as they walk in the door, with dessert, placing the bags on their bed, Kennedy's in her closet, Jackson's on the grill...pulling in the garage, I still have no plan.

I assemble the gift bags on the kitchen island, and I grab two quart-size plastic bags to place them on my bathroom counter with the two pregnancy tests.

I prepare a large glass of ice water to ensure I need to pee soon. With water nearby, comfy on the sofa, I open my iPad and Safari to research pregnancy and the first trimester. When my glass is empty, I promptly prepare another. Looking through the cabinets, fridge, and freezer, I decide I need to go get groceries for dinner.

Wait. I've got it. I will order a pizza, so Jackson and Kennedy will think I need comfort food because of my doctor's appointment. It will throw them off the scent of the real outcome of today's appointment.

Later, Jackson and Kennedy follow each other down the street and into the driveway. I knew they planned to be home early tonight. As they enter the kitchen, Jackson announces a pizza delivery car pulled up out front. I gather my money and greet the pizza dude at the door. Hearing Jackson and Kennedy murmuring in the kitchen, I know they're reading into my decision to order the pizza. *I can't wait to surprise them.*

As I carry the pizza to the kitchen, Jackson announces he only needs a moment to change from his work clothes. Kennedy and I lay out everything we need to eat dinner before Jackson returns. We enjoy our meal with small talk. Jackson and Kennedy avoid discussing my appointment. After two pieces of pizza, I excuse myself.

When I return, I announce it's time for dessert. I place the gift bags near each of them.

"Desserts are to eat. These look like presents," Jackson says.

"So, open them already," I prompt.

First, they pull out the books. Thanking me, they assume that's the end.

"Please, look inside your bags again," I urge.

Kennedy peeks past the tissue paper to the bottom of the bag. She screams while hopping up and down. Confused, Jackson continues to feel for the bottom of his bag while watching his wife scream and cry. Hesitantly, his hand emerges, holding the plastic bag. He turns from Kennedy to me, then looks at his hand. He turns the pregnancy test repeatedly.

"It's a pregnancy test, silly," Kennedy yells. "We are pregnant!"

Jackson's brow furrows. He swings his eyes to mine. So quiet I almost don't hear, he whispers, "Are you pregnant?"

"We're having a baby!" I cheer. "We did it! 'The Deed' is done."

I correctly predicted Kennedy's reaction, but Jackson's reaction baffles me. He's frozen. I mean frozen as in stiff as a board. His dark brown eyes are the size of Oreos. I've seen the man tear up twice. Once, when Kennedy's illness became so prevalent, we could no longer ignore it. The other time, when his parents wrote off Kennedy for stealing one-thousand dollars from them and when she proceeded to lie about it, they forced him to choose between her and them. I watch tears fall from his eyes, flow south on his cheeks, before they plummet to the table below. He doesn't attempt to hide them or wipe them away. He sits paralyzed with the positive pregnancy test in hand. He stares at the used pee-stick and weeps.

I pry my body from Kennedy's embrace and slowly approach Jackson. I place my hand on his, removing the stick. With my other hand, I wipe the rivers of tears from his cheeks. I place both hands on the sides of his face and turn him towards me before he breaks from his trance. He doesn't hug me. He doesn't embrace his wife. He simply asks, "May I?" and extends a hand tentatively towards my abdomen.

I freak a little on the inside. I've seen many television shows and movies in which strangers touch the pregnant bellies of women. I'm not an oohey-goohey, touchy-feely girl. The thought of strangers touching my stomach freaks me out. I quickly force myself to take some deep breaths. *This is Jackson, he is one of my best friends, and I am carrying his child.* I simply nod, and he splays his long, strong fingers and palm over my stomach.

At his touch, the reality of my current condition hits me like a lead balloon. *I'm pregnant. A living embryo grows inside me. I carry a baby for my two best friends that is half-Jackson and half-me.*

The next thing I know, I find myself seated near the table with a cold, wet washcloth on the back of my neck. Kennedy fans my face with a magazine, while Jackson prompts me to sip from a bottle of water.

"What?" I ask, my head foggy. I take in my surroundings as they become clearer. "Why?" I look from Kennedy to Jackson for answers.

"You almost fainted," Jackson says. "Your body wobbled, and your face went white."

I sip from Jackson's water bottle, then push it away. I swat the magazine to the table from Kennedy's hand. "I'm okay." I stare at Kennedy, then Jackson, before I continue. "I wasn't motion sick all weekend. It was morning sickness. Today, it progressed to vomiting and hot flashes," I inform. "Dr. Harrison stated it's common. I have a pamphlet to read to help me work through the nausea." I pull the cloth from my neck and wipe my brow. "I'm okay now. I think it was just the adrenaline from my big announcement. I looked forward to telling the two of you all afternoon. The anticipation and nerves finally caught up with me."

Kennedy relaxes into a nearby chair, but Jackson doesn't look as convinced. "I didn't sleep well last night. I was dreading the doctor's appointment today and breaking the news that we needed to try for another month to get pregnant."

Jackson offers three saltine crackers and the bottle of water, not taking no for an answer. I place my hand over his, holding the saltines.

"Everything is fine. I should have napped this afternoon," I admit.

"Nibble, drink, and let's move to the sofa for a bit before you turn in for the night." Jackson's tone leaves no wiggle room.

I take the proffered crackers and water. "I will not spend the next nine months being coddled," I inform my protective friends. "Pregnant women have worked in fields up to the day they delivered. I won't take it easy. I won't allow the two of you to order me around. I am not a child." With that, I turn and stomp over to the sofa.

Just because I give in to this one demand, doesn't mean I will in the future.

When I recover, I explain, "I bought myself a copy of the same book that I gifted Kennedy. I read a little this afternoon. It contains information that all three of us need to read. I researched online for some triggers of morning sickness and remedies. There are a lot of treatments others claimed that worked for them. The consensus seems to be trial-and-error for a remedy that works best for me."

I yawn for the umpteenth time since dinner.

"You should turn in for the night. You're extremely tired," Jackson prompts.

I don't refuse.

PART III
THE CONFESSION

PART III

THE CONFESSION

55

OVERPROTECTIVE MUCH?

Taylor

Kennedy raps on my door before entering to place saltines and a glass of tepid water on my nightstand.

Jackson peeks his head in, reminding me, "Text either of us if you need anything while we're at work today."

I decide I'll need to nip this over-protective hovering in the butt tonight.

Kennedy texts me four times prior to noon. Jackson texts three times before 4:00. I'm happy they're excited to be pregnant, but I can see why so many women and couples wait until the second trimester to announce a pregnancy.

Surrogacy Journal Entry-Tuesday, August 23rd

I am officially off the sauce. Of course, that means no more alcohol, but I'm referring to quitting Diet Pepsi cold turkey. No caffeine sucks big time. I realize it's what is best for the baby and healthier for me, too. My new pregnancy diet feels like a metal chastity belt. Speaking of chastity belt, I am officially knocked up and won't be having sex for the next 44 weeks. Pregnant for 38 weeks, then at least 6 weeks postpartum—yes, I researched how long I would have to refrain from sexual intercourse when I agreed to become their surrogate. If I add to that the year I have already survived without sex, it will be a total of 96 weeks without a man. That is nearly 2 years with no sex. Guess I now have sex on the brain. Note to self, I might want to edit this surrogate journal before I hand it over to Jackson and Kennedy at the end of the pregnancy. I don't want their future child reading about my sexual tantrum later in life.

My goal on this, my first full day with the knowledge I'm carrying Jackson's and Kennedy's baby, is to read through the first month of my pregnancy book. Make a list of dietary guidelines, a list of morning sickness triggers and possible remedies, and to rest more than I did yesterday.

As I have many hours of free time each day while Jackson and Kennedy work, I read ahead and highlighting items in my pregnancy book. My rationale is that if I read it now and read it as I approach that point in my pregnancy, I might be better prepared. I use an orange and a green highlighter as I read. The orange is important information and tips to ease pregnancy. The green highlighter I reserve for interesting facts.

With my orange highlighter, I shade possible triggers and possible ways to ease my morning sickness. I find references to the size of the baby each week during pregnancy compared to objects. These, I highlight in green.

Next, I set a reminder on my cell phone calendar to purchase and photograph the items to show visually the size of the baby for the three of us. In my grocery app, I list the items I need to gather. I figure if I take pictures of all these and print them now, I can tuck them in the pages of the book to pull out and hang on the refrigerator when appropriate.

Taylor
At Dr. Wilson's Office, Thursday, August 25th

I actually look forward to my appointment with Dr. Wilson today. I assume my favorite chair, pull my feet up under myself, and smile as Dr. Wilson seats herself across from me.

Before she's ready with notepad and pen, I begin, "I'm pregnant!" I wiggle excitedly in my seat. "We are officially pregnant! I am officially a surrogate!"

Dr. Wilson beams. I assumed from our previous conversations about her battle with infertility that she vested herself in our journey. I love her excitement at our news.

"I can see that you are very excited by this diagnosis. At the moment, the physician stated you were pregnant, what was your initial thought?" she inquires.

"At first I was confused, then in shock," I explain. "I didn't believe that 'The Deed' really worked in the first month we attempted to become pregnant. I found a creative way to announce the news to Jackson and Kennedy that night after dinner. I was an emotional wreck all afternoon waiting to share the news and hoping I chose the right way to do so."

"As seventy-two hours have passed now, how do you feel? What fears do you have?" Dr. Wilson inquires, with pen poised ready to transcribe. She looks at me for my response.

"I already have morning sickness," I frown. "I thought I was carsick all weekend on our trip to the Lake of the Ozarks." I chuckle, remembering the weekend. "I popped Dramamine all weekend for my dizziness and queasiness." I scan her features for concern about my intake of the medication while pregnant. "I'm afraid the Dramamine might harm the baby. I'm afraid I already messed up the task Jackson and Kennedy entrusted to me." With no reaction, I continue to address her prompts. "I vomit several times a day now. Instead of morning sickness, I have all-day sickness. I read about the first and second month of pregnancy in my book and researched online. I posted a dietary restriction list on the refrigerator and started a list of morning sickness triggers with remedies. I try each remedy twice and document to assess which remedies work best for me."

Dr. Wilson attempts to reign in the smile, creeping upon her face at my obsession with lists and research. "How does changing your diet make you feel?"

"I was aware of most of the dietary constraints when I agreed to be the surrogate. So, it's no surprise. I did not prepare for quitting the caffeine cold-turkey." I look to the doctor and see her sympathetic smile. "I don't fear my new diet, and I don't fear the morning sickness. I will continue to read and reread each month of my pregnancy book and research online. I plan to prepare and stay informed as the pregnancy changes arise."

"Multiple bouts of morning sickness each day will exhaust you as your body changes rapidly. Because of the vomiting, you need to rest more to keep up your strength." Dr. Wilson reiterates, "You have an increased need for fluids to prevent dehydration that will further strain your body." She scans her notebook. "Please share items from your journaling this week."

I open my journal to my list of items I wanted to address today. I skim over a few we already talked about. "Jackson and Kennedy are hovering," I begin. "They text and call frequently from work, and they wait on me hand-and-foot at night. I explained that I'm not unable to care for myself; I'm not on bedrest. But they continue to be overprotective."

"You mention you voiced the need for them to ease off," she starts. "How did they react to your statement? Did they change their behaviors?"

"They did better for a few hours, then returned to their hovering," I admit. "I encouraged both to read about the first and second month of pregnancy. I showed my lists and remedies. I plan to try for nausea. I plan to continue by proving my strength and ability to return to the life I had prior to finding out I was pregnant."

"You must continue to discuss your need for independence with them," Dr. Wilson states. "Ask for help when you need it but let them know you will ask if you want help. An open dialog will ease their nerves. Remember, they feel detached, more so than they would in a traditional pregnancy. Sharing your feelings, nausea, dizziness, and fatigue will allow them to help when needed. Demonstrating, as well as, discussing your need for independence, will allow them to pull back on the hovering." She takes a sip from her water. "I suggest you refrain from replying to texts immediately, so they will gradually learn this behavior is not welcome. You should reply before too much time passes, so they do not worry. I want you to keep a list of their overprotective behaviors to discuss in our next group session."

Dr. Wilson places her notepad and pen on her side table near the lamp. She leans forward slightly, placing her folded hands in her lap. "Let's discuss your dream flashes."

Dread encases my middle. Though not plagued in the last seventy-two hours, the flashes continued this week. I turn in my journal to my section with my documentation of the triggers, locations, visions, and reactions to my flashes. "I had a couple last week and while we were at the lake."

"Might I look at your notes?" She cautiously inquires, her arm extended.

I pass her my journal. Although, I'm more comfortable sharing my flashes and my journal with her, I'm not more comfortable with the flashes. They seem to strengthen and are much clearer now.

"I understand why you state you feel guilty for each flash involving an interaction between Jackson and you. I notice many occur after Kennedy touches your forearm or shoulder. Why do you think this is so?" She looks at me for answers.

I ponder her statement and question. I did not make the connection between Kennedy touching me and the flashes. "Nothing has occurred between Kennedy and me. We're friends, nothing more. She doesn't hurt me; they are casual touches between friends."

Kennedy and I kissed in college, but never again. In my flashes, Kennedy and I are not intimate. It is Jackson with me in my flashes; I'm cheating with her husband while she watches.

"In descriptions of your flashes, you mention Kennedy grasping your shoulder, the back of your neck, and encouraging the two of you," Dr. Wilson continues. "Perhaps her casual touches remind you of her actions in the flashes. These could be the triggers."

"Why am I seeing intercourse between Jackson and me when Kennedy touches me?" *I don't understand.* "Why do I have flashes of my best friend's husband? Why were they fuzzy before, but clearer now? And why can't I prevent them?" My breaths are quick and shallow. I feel light-headed and queasy. *Not now.* I don't want to vomit in Dr. Wilson's office.

56

SEE SLUGS

Taylor

"Taylor, look at me," she sternly directs, taking each of my hands in hers. "Deep breaths in-and-out through your nose. In-and-out slowly. Good. In-and-out. Perfect." She releases my hands and excuses herself to fetch me water with a cold cloth from her private bathroom. "You are frustrated, and the hormones aren't helping." She pats my knee before returning to her seat. "I left the door open." she motions to the restroom. "Feel free to use it anytime during our sessions." The doctor jots quickly on her notepad. "We've made progress. Today, we found the triggers. We are closer to understanding these flashes." Her smile seems forced. Looking at my journal, she continues, "Kennedy seems unaware of your reaction to the flashes when they occur."

It's a statement and a question. I simply nod.

"Twice you wrote, Jackson noticed your discomfort. When you return to the common areas, does he approach you?" *It seems the good doctor is reading my notes thoroughly now.*

"He disappears for fifteen to thirty minutes," I divulge. "When he returns, he avoids my gaze, and he is silent for long periods of time." I close my eyes tightly. "It's like he knows I'm thinking of him inappropriately. I don't speak out loud, I don't share my flashes, but it's as if he can read my mind and is disgusted with me."

While continuing her notes on my session, Dr. Wilson promises, "Jackson cannot know the content of your flashes. Perhaps he is reacting to the signals your body displays. You state your eyes close, you freeze, and tears form." Done with her note taking, her eyes meet mine. "Perhaps Jackson is aware you are not sharing something. Maybe he fears you have flashbacks of John. In previous sessions, you stated he worried John was physical with his abuse. Maybe Jackson hurts because he senses you are hurting and not being open about it."

This explanation seems plausible.

"What can I do differently?" Frustrated, I rise to pace near the window. "I can't know when a flash will pop into my mind, and I can't tell him the contents of my flashes. How can I shield him from this?"

"It is not your job to shield him. We need to focus on the flashes, the triggers, and find a strategy to assist you in healing." Dr. Wilson spins toward me in her high-back chair.

I cease my pacing. "I can't tell either of them what I see." I attempt to massage the tense muscles in the back of my neck. "They would not understand. I don't even understand." I massage deeper as I hypothesize. "Maybe the flashes will stop now that I'm pregnant."

"Do you believe the flashes show another method by which you might try to get pregnant?" She scribbles more notes on her pad. "Perhaps the stress of attempting non-traditional methods to conceive caused your subconscious to envision a more traditional method."

I ponder her words. "I wouldn't describe intercourse with my best friend's husband while she instructs us as a 'more traditional method'." I take my seat once again.

"Have any new feelings developed toward Kennedy or Jackson now that you are officially their surrogate?"

"I didn't magically grow closer to either friend in the past three days," I state. "I have not developed romantic feelings towards Jackson, or Kennedy."

"I suggest you continue to journal the flashes." Dr. Wilson wraps up our session. "I hope all three of you can keep communication open. Share your fears, your feelings, and your concerns. Open dialog is vital. Let's continue to document, continue to work as a team, and continue to discuss the flashes in our sessions. We made progress today in discovering similarities in the triggers and parts of the visions. It's a process. We continue peeling away the layers each visit and find a solution."

"In the future, let's meet once per month individually and once as a group," Dr. Wilson proposes. "Our sessions will now shift to concerns during the pregnancy and the end of the surrogacy. If needed, you may call for another appointment."

"Let's plan a party," Kennedy blurts as Jackson emerges from the deck, and we place the final dinner dishes in the dishwasher. "We should have a potluck, invite everyone, and announce we're pregnant."

Kennedy cannot contain excitement about the pregnancy. Yesterday she mentioned she almost told Matthew at work. Three days barely pass, and she is ready for everyone to hear her news.

I panic, looking toward Jackson for support. Jackson and I, excited like Kennedy, realize waiting to share our news might be for the best. The pregnancy books and internet state no perfect announcing window exists. Complications arise at any stage of the pregnancy, but many suggest waiting until the end of the first trimester.

"I don't know, Ken," I carefully explain. "I don't know of any health concerns or family history that might suggest complications, but I'm still nervous." I attempt a smile as I look again toward Jackson for assistance.

"Can I tell only our closest friends?" Kennedy suggests. "Nothing will go wrong; the hard part is over. We are pregnant. Now it's time to celebrate and prepare. Our friends deserve to celebrate with us."

Jackson enters the conversation. "Ken, if God forbid, Taylor miscarries, the need to tell each friend will be hard." He brushes his hand across my shoulders as he moves towards Kennedy.

"There will be no miscarriage. The two of you worry way too much." Kennedy is intent on her mission to become a mother. She sees a baby, needs a baby, and will not give up without a baby. While I love her fortitude, I fear she doesn't look at reality. In setting goals, she should plan for the best, look at all possibilities, and prepare.

"If I were pregnant, telling the two of you wouldn't wait three months. I would need my best friends to know, to talk to, to plan with..." I am not allowed to finish my statement.

"That is exactly why I want to share with Reagan, Martha, and Madison," Kennedy interjects. "I need their help, their advice, and their support."

Jackson runs his hands through his hair. His eyes on the floor, he opens his mouth, but I jump in. "I didn't think of it that way," I admit. Jackson directs his furrowed brow toward me. Kennedy tilts her head and smiles. "I assumed I would be all that you would need. However, since this isn't a typical pregnancy, you might need to talk to your friends and not your surrogate." I sip my water quickly. "I can see now that there might be times when you want to talk and not want me to worry, stress, or hear your concerns. I want us to be open. I want communication between all three of us, but just as we share items with Dr. Wilson that we can't with each other, you might need your friends, too." Taking Kennedy's hand, I decide. "Let's do this. Let's invite your friends over and share our awesome news. Let's widen our circle of support."

"Really?" Jackson asks, unbelieving.

Kennedy wraps me in an embrace while rocking me from side to side. This motion upsets my volatile stomach. My hand darts to my mouth as I tug away and sprint to the nearest bathroom. I barely lift the lid before I'm sick. I wretch and heave. Breathing between eruptions is difficult. My legs tire; I sink to my knees and struggle to prevent my hair from falling in my face.

Suddenly, my hair moves to the nape of my neck. I can't turn to see who came to my rescue. I must focus on a quick breath before the next eruption occurs. A cold cloth finds my right hand. I flinch as another cool, wet cloth lies on my neck. It soothes, and the chill helps. Several long moments pass, I wipe my mouth. Then fold the other cloth and slowly dab my overheated brow and cheeks.

"Better?" Jackson's deep masculine whisper queries. He flips the cool cloth over on my neck.

"Um," attempting to speak, I cough instead. I gingerly clear my throat and slowly rise to sit on the edge of the bathtub. I continue dabbing the cool cloth over my face. The chill feels refreshing on my tempered skin.

Motioning for my cloth, Jackson holds it under the water and returns it to my hand without speaking. He flushes the toilet and closes the lid.

"I think I'm okay now," I rasp, my throat raw.

"That was brutal," Jackson announces, prior to chuckling. "It sounded like a scene from *The Exorcist*."

I brace the wet cloth against my lips to stifle a giggle.

"I was worried I would see slugs hit the toilet water or a demon crack through your spine," he continues.

"Stop," I plead.

I rise to rinse my face and hands in the sink behind Jackson. He watches with rapt attention as I wet my toothbrush, then rinse my teeth and tongue. I've learned toothpaste upsets me sometimes. I read online to use water sometimes and toothpaste as I can tolerate it. I look at my reflection in the mirror. I have tiny bruise dots surrounding both eyes. *I will need to research these online.* I try to hide my worry about the dots decorating the edges of my eyes.

"No need to hover." I turn, motioning for Jackson to lead the way from the tiny restroom. "I spend too much time in bathrooms nowadays. Let's get out of here," I tease.

Kennedy is on the sofa, watching TV. She turns to wave as I walk to the kitchen. Jackson follows me. I appreciate his concern. "Thanks for helping with my hair and the wet cloths." I touch his forearm. "It helped."

"I feel so helpless. *We* are the reason you are sick all the time." Jackson's guilt surprises me. "I read in the book that there are things we can do to make your morning sickness a little more bearable."

It's not lost on me, he said we and not just he. *There is no room in the bathroom for the three of us while I am sick.* I doubt Kennedy would venture in because she spent many years vomiting after eating. *I wonder if my morning sickness could trigger her eating disorder. Will hearing me vomit upset her?* I pull out my phone, open the Notes App, and make a memo to speak to Dr. Wilson about this.

"I would tie your hair back with a tie if I knew how," Jackson confesses.

"I should probably place hair clips and ties on the back of each stool. Thanks for the idea." I smile, and Jackson returns a genuine smile.

Before bed, I type "dot+bruise+around eyes+after vomiting" into my internet browser. I find several online health sites call this a petechial hemorrhage. Seems my trouble breathing while puking causes them. They are mild compared to the petechial hemorrhages victims of suffocation display. I make a mental note to relax more when sick, so I might breathe better.

57

OLYMPIC SWIMMERS

Taylor

Friday afternoon, I make my way one more time through the entire house before tonight's party. Kennedy and Jackson did most of the heavy cleaning on Thursday evening. They insisted I only dust, unload the dishwasher and take it easy. My fatigue makes it hard for me to argue with them. Today, I spray air freshener, straighten vanities, and prep the kitchen for company. The activity taking its toll, I cuddle up on the sofa for a movie and a nap. I need energy well past my ten o'clock bedtime. Turning in early is my new-norm. As I stare unseeing at the television, I realize my exhaustion is much higher than I expected. I set an alarm on my phone to ensure I wake early enough to get dolled up for the guests. Normally, I don't worry about impressing anyone, however, tonight I am at the center of the party. All eyes will be on pregnant Taylor and her non-existent baby bump.

I startle at the cellphone alarm over two hours later. Once silenced, I slowly rise to a seated position. Morning sickness taught me to move slow. I shuffle my way towards the kitchen, pour a small glass of ginger ale, and grab a handful of crackers. Seated at the island, I nibble and sip while browsing my social media apps. I jump when my phone vibrates with a text.

> **KENNEDY**
> Leaving in 20 need anything?

> **ME**
> No

> **KENNEDY**
> K home soon (smiling emoji)

Although I dread this get-together, I can fake my way through it for Kennedy. It's difficult to relinquish so much of the becoming a mother process to someone else. My goal in this surrogacy is to involve Jackson and Kennedy as much as I can. I want them to have many pregnancy memories, like normal couples do. For her, I can smile, chat, and listen to pregnancy stories for a few hours. The thought of copious amounts of food actually sounds delicious.

My eyes and thoughts in my social media, I do not hear the garage door signaling Kennedy's arrival. At the door to the kitchen opening, I emerge from my phone and scurry to assist her with her bounty of plastic grocery bags.

"What is all of this?" I inquire, attempting to peek into the bags I carry. I find paper plates, utensils, red plastic cups, and a cake.

"I shopped during my lunch today, so Jackson doesn't need to after work," Kennedy explains. "It's difficult for him to leave the store. The thought of him attempting to shop while leaving worried me he would be late tonight." While speaking, she organizes the paper products at the end of the island. "I hope he arrives before the guests. I want the three of us together when we announce."

I gingerly slip the cake in its clear container from the bag to the island. Spinning it around, I read the decorative baby blue and pale pink frosting. "We Are Pregnant!"

Kennedy beams when I look her way. "I thought I would keep this in the pantry until everyone arrives. I plan to slide it next to the other desserts and wait for the first guest to see it." She shrugs. "I couldn't think of anything more creative for our announcement. But Pinterest boards are full of gender reveal announcement ideas. You warned me; I'm now officially addicted to Pinterest. I must attempt to keep from opening it while at work. Last week, I needed an idea for the bulletin board near the child care door. I opened Pinterest on my work PC. An hour later, I pinned over ten bulletin board ideas plus recipes, nursery decorating ideas, and even lists of baby names."

"That is why I only allow myself on Pinterest while I am on a treadmill," I remind her. "Time flies. It's very easy to spend an hour walking while pinning."

"I should do that," Kennedy confesses. "I don't think I have your willpower to only do it on a treadmill. I'm weak; I sneak a peek while in the restroom all the time."

As I laugh at her confession, the garage door signals Jackson's arrival. I'm thankful he isn't late tonight. I need him as my buffer.

At 6:30, all our neighbors arrive. Wives carry the food to the kitchen and organize the buffet line. Husbands line their coolers near the patio door before congregating in the living room, where conversations flow, catching everyone up on the week.

Seated at the island, I'm near the women, but listen to the men's conversation. I'm more comfortable discussing sports and cars than handbags, shoes, and clothes found on sale.

Jackson excuses himself from his friends. He mouths, "Ready?" as he passes me on his way to Kennedy. I simply nod. Kennedy signals for Jackson to retrieve the cake. She continues the conversation with Madison. Jackson places the cake near the cookies and dessert bars, then assumes the seat next to me.

He nudges my arm, then clears his throat before asking, "We gonna eat tonight or tomorrow?" The ladies giggle and swat at him.

"It's time to eat," Kennedy informs. "You men to get in here and fix a plate before the famished Jackson eats it all." She gestures, her extended arm for a line to begin at the paper products.

Madison, followed by Reagan, secures a plate, and begins selecting food from the slow cookers. Martha demands Kennedy and I line up with her. I try to hang back as Madison, plate full, skips the desserts this trip through the line. Jackson shakes his head, smiling. His eyes are bright with excitement.

"I knew it!" Reagan shouts, placing her full plate on the counter and making a bee-line towards me. "I knew it! I knew it!" She points both index fingers towards me.

"Knew what?" James and Martha ask, while looking at everyone in the room. Reagan shakes her head, stating, "You will know soon enough."

As my spot in the line moves toward the food, the aroma of barbecue sauce teases my nostrils. Surprisingly, my stomach doesn't revolt. Perhaps I will get to eat a meal and keep it down. At my turn to take a plate, I excuse myself, claiming I need to wash my hands prior to eating. Jackson stifles a laugh at my smooth avoidance of food until the crowd reacts to our news.

"You the man!" James announces to Jackson. "Those must be some Olympic swimmers." As James stands, pointing to the cake, the rest of the bunch crowd in and read.

Kennedy tucks into Jackson's side to prepare for their reaction to her news.

"So, this isn't an 'avoid a boring Friday night at home' potluck?" Martha both states and asks.

"We wanted everyone here to celebrate our good news this week," Kennedy beams. "We found out on Monday."

Ever the nurse and doctor, Reagan tells everyone becoming pregnant on the first in-vitro attempt is unheard of.

"Superhero sperm," James claims, patting Jackson on the back.

Madison and Martha swarm Kennedy

Reagan moves towards me. "You were experiencing morning sickness at the lake. I knew it then. My senses were tingling. I'm so excited," she says, barely above a whisper.

Jackson raises his voice to draw everyone's attention, ceasing the three different conversations. "Let's fix our plates, then the three of us will share how we found out Monday and answer questions once, instead of over and over."

I mouth "Thank you," to Jackson for this.

Everyone seated and eating, Kennedy begins. "Taylor returned to the doctor on Monday. We believed she wouldn't get pregnant on our first attempt, so we were ready to begin the process over for another month." She sips her water before continuing. "Jackson and I didn't attend the appointment, because it was a routine visit." Kennedy prompts me to continue the story.

"You can imagine my shock when Dr. Harrison stated I was pregnant. We were prepared for many months of trying to conceive." I pause for a breath. "When I left the office and the shock let up a bit, I knew I needed a plan to creatively announce the news to Jackson and Kennedy. I bought gift bags, parenting books, and peed on two pregnancy tests. I gave them the gifts after dinner."

"It was much more exciting than that," Kennedy proclaims. "She had a pink bag for me and a blue for Jackson. She used colored tissue paper to conceal the contents. We reached into our bag and pulled out the book first. We thought that was the entire gift. My book was *What to Expect When You're Expecting* and Jackson's was *Dude, You're Gonna Be a Dad!*" She shoots a smile my way. "Taylor prompted us to look deeper into our bags again. We pulled out a clear plastic sack with the positive pregnancy test. It was the best way to tell us the news. We were so surprised."

"I've never been so excited to see a stick that was peed on in my life," Jackson teases.

For the rest of the evening, we dodge the questions or requests for details of our in-vitro process. We plan to keep 'The Deed' to ourselves. Friends don't need to know how we performed our own insemination at home.

58

AN ORANGE SEED

Taylor

On the last Monday of August, I reset the oven timer for ten minutes. The taco-bake looks amazing. I start to close my recipe on the iPad but decide Kennedy might like to see the Pinterest pin. I place it on the island near the barstools and glance around the kitchen. *I have plates, salad, utensils, water glasses, guacamole, and tortilla chips all ready. I just need my two friends to arrive home soon.*

Ask and I shall receive. I hear the garage door rising. I use my phone to lower the volume on the speakers. I leave Spotify playing in the background as Jackson enters while texting from the garage.

"Have you heard from Kennedy?" He asks, and I shake my head. "I'm texting to ask why I beat her home tonight."

"I haven't chatted with her. Dinner will be ready in ten minutes," I reply.

He excuses himself. "I need to change my work clothes."

"Kennedy is with Madison and won't be joining us for dinner tonight," he announces when he returns.

"Seriously?" I shout. "Seriously!" I rant. "I'm home every afternoon. I prepare dinner every weeknight." I let out a low growl. "I can't believe she can't give me the courtesy of a text that she won't be here."

I'm not sure if I see astonishment or fear on Jackson's face. He stands frozen near the refrigerator. "Taylor, I'm sorry. We appreciate your dinners. It allows the three of us more time to relax each night together. What did you fix? Will it keep for leftovers?"

I toss my empty plastic water bottle with more force than necessary into the recycle bin. "That's not the issue." I don't attempt to hide my irate tone. "I could enjoy fast food tonight if I knew she wasn't coming home. You think I want taco-bake. Hell no, I don't want taco-bake. I want to eat at Sonic Drive-in or Steak 'n Shake or enjoy pizza." I grab handfuls of my hair. "But can I? No, I can't. I have to eat the taco-bake I found online and made."

Raising his hands in front of his chest, Jackson hesitantly takes one step towards me.

"Don't you dare," I warn. "Don't defend her. Don't try to make this better. I refuse to put my dinner in the fridge. We will eat the fucking taco-bake. Crap!" I walk around him toward my bedroom. "I need to pee." As I close my bathroom door I yell, "please pull the pan out when the timer beeps."

As I wash my hands, I splash some water on my face. I pat it dry, catching a glimpse in the mirror.

What just happened? Did I really go all bitch at Jackson?
Fuck.

Three light knocks to my open bedroom door coax me from the bathroom.

"I pulled out the pan. It looks delicious. Should I…"

"I am so sorry. You did not deserve my tirade," I interrupt him.

"It's the hormones." Jackson wraps me in a hug, tucking my cheek against his chest. "Your hormones are going crazy. It was only a matter of time before the hormonal roller-coaster we read about made its debut." His hands rub up and down my back as he speaks calmly.

This feels too good.
I need to escape his arms.

"Let's try this taco-bake before it cools," I prompt. "I've craved guacamole all day, and for once, my stomach seems to be a team player tonight." I lean back and look up. "I'm in the mood for Mexican, and I need to eat it when I don't feel like I might lose it."

"After you," Jackson motions, arm extended to my bedroom door and the kitchen beyond.

Dinner is everything I hoped it would be. Jackson tiptoes around me during our dinner conversation, and my hormones seem to even out.

So far, no nausea.

After dinner, Jackson suggests we go for a walk. I know this is something he read to encourage the pregnant mother in the expecting book. I lace on my walking shoes and grab a bottle of water. We walk at a slow pace, discussing landscaping we like, cute houses, pet a few dogs, and converse with adults and children we meet.

"Thanks for this," I say as I lightly touch Jackson's forearm before quickly pulling my arm back. "I need to do this a couple of times a day."

"You do a lot every day. You work out, run errands, work online, and fix dinner," Jackson informs. "You need to rest more. Let's plan your walks for evenings when you aren't too tired."

I nod, removing my shoes and placing them in my bedroom. I place my empty water bottle in the recycle bin before filling my large, reusable bottle for the night. I ponder the granny smith apple in the crisper. As delicious as apples are, the acid tears my throat when they don't stay down. I opt for some pretzel sticks as my evening snack. Maybe tomorrow I'll find a time to eat the apple, I don't want to push my stomach any more this evening.

I find for the hour right after I vomit, I'm able to keep food down. I slowly nibble and sip during these times to provide nutrients for the baby. I no longer dread vomiting. I see it as a task that I might feel better after completing. I relax more when I get sick; this seems to make it less traumatic.

Later, I sit in the sofa's corner, a blanket covering my legs. I'm reading the section about the second month of my expecting book while watching The Royals host The Yankees with Jackson. "Uh-oh," I gasp jokingly at the next commercial.

Jackson's head turns from the TV my way. "What?"

"I have had no heartburn," I state matter-of-factly.

"So?" Jackson prods.

"Read this," I attempt to pass my book his way.

"You read it to me," he rebuffs.

"It says mothers that experience heartburn during pregnancy have babies with full heads of hair. I've had no heartburn, so your baby will be bald." I shrug, fighting a smile.

Jackson shakes his head at me. "As long as it's healthy, it can be bald at birth."

I didn't even get a rise out of him. No fun. His attention returns to the game.

"Royals won, time to go to bed." Jackson wakes me later.

I groan sleepily as I slowly rise from the cozy nest of throw pillows in the sofa's corner. "Kennedy home yet?"

"Not yet," Jackson sighs. "Need anything before I head upstairs?"

I shake my head, wave goodnight, then collapse on my bed.

Mid-morning, a calendar alert on my phone reminds me to post this week's baby size photo and take photos of my abdomen. I open my book and remove the week-five picture of our baby's size. The tiny orange seed is lying near an orange slice and a quarter to compare its tiny size. I place the picture in the magnetic frame I purchased on the refrigerator. In red permanent marker it reads "This Week Our Baby is This Big" around the frame. I hope Jackson and Kennedy like this visualization of our growing little one.

Next, I grab the rustic chalkboard and the chalkboard markers I purchased after I found this cute idea on Pinterest. I carefully write on the board before I set my iPad to record and lean it at the dresser mirror recording me. I turn sideways while holding the chalkboard out from my stomach. This will show my growing belly each week. Each week of pregnancy is creatively documented on the board. I lay the board on my bed for a moment and remove my snug white t-shirt.

Standing in my navy sports bra with low-waist black shorts, I pose once again sideways with the board.

I plan to isolate a still-frame of each pose every week. At the end of the pregnancy, I will print these in an album for Jackson and Kennedy documenting their pregnancy. As they aren't very tech savvy, I don't worry about hiding the photos on my iPad. I back the pictures up on iCloud, so I will have access to them anywhere I want. I erase the chalkboard and hide it in my dresser drawer for next week.

59

PORCELAIN GOD

Taylor

At 2:00 in the morning, I lay on my bathroom floor with my head leaning on the chilly edge of the tub. Yesterday, I spent more time over the bathroom stool than usual. It became bad enough, I moved the ginger ale, water bottle, and crackers onto my dresser so I could attempt to nibble without leaving my bedroom area. I found walking caused dizziness, which led to nausea, and thus another visit to the bathroom. In my weakened state, I napped most of the day in my bed.

Tonight, I attempt to sleep, but most of my night, I find myself on the bathroom floor. I'm not fighting it anymore. The cool tub feels good on my cheek and neck. I grab the towel off a nearby rack to use as a blanket. My stomach quiet for the moment, I close my eyes, hoping for sleep to rescue me. My headache grows worse with each passing hour.

I wake when I hear movement on the stairs and then in the kitchen.

"Hey," I attempt to yell. My dry mouth, cotton tongue, and raw throat make talking difficult. "Help!" I beckon louder. I adjust to a more upright position. "Help! Kennedy! Jackson! Help!"

My head feels ready to crack in half. I place my hand on the toilet bowl, attempting to stand. My weak limbs cannot complete this task. I pick up the half empty water bottle and shakily launch it from the bathroom into my bedroom. I hope the sound will draw the attention of the person in the kitchen.

"Help!" I croakily yell one more time.

My eyes fall shut, and my head pounds.

"Tay…" Jackson's voice trails off when he spies me lying on the floor, unable to move.

He places his palm on my brow to assess my body temperature.

I try to keep my eyes open. *I need to tell him what I need*. I open my mouth, unable to communicate this to him. He swoops me into his arms. *I hope this motion doesn't cause more vomiting.* I am gently placed on my pillow and he tucks covers around me.

"I will be right back," Jackson promises. He grabs the trash can from the bathroom. Placing it near my head. "Puke in this if you need to before I come back," he instructs.

With a weak thumbs-up, I signal my understanding.

Moments pass as I lie, eyes closed, focusing on my breathing. The overhead bedroom light alerts me to Jackson as he enters, scoops me along with my blankets into his arms and carries me toward his car.

"Kennedy, grab the trashcan, a washcloth, and a bottle of water for the car ride," he instructs.

I don't want a car ride.

Why a car ride?

I need to sleep. I want to sleep in my bed.

As the car backs from the driveway, I hear a cellphone voice give driving directions.

"Where?" my croaky whisper questions.

"We are on our way to the E.R.," Kennedy informs me, wiping my forehead and cheeks with the cold, damp cloth.

"No," I protest. "Want… sleep."

"Honey, you can sleep soon," Kennedy promises. "We need a doctor to see how sick you are. This is not morning sickness."

I must fall asleep, I wake to much too bright florescent lights and incessant beeping. I turn my pounding head away from the overhead lights, toward the beeping. I struggle to focus. I can make out a machine.

"Hey," Jackson greets, moving into my line of sight. "We're at the hospital. You're in the E.R. They have you on IV fluids because you are dehydrated." He pats my ice-cold arm. "You need anything?"

I nod, then regret it. My head throbs. "Too cold," I rasp.

Jackson presses a button on my beside. Soon a nurse appears.

"She's awake and cold," Jackson informs the nurse.

She disappears for a moment. I attempt a smile to let Jackson know I'm okay. The nurse returns with a warmed blanket. Instantly, I'm engulfed in a toasty cocoon.

"Better?" she asks, looking at my vitals on a loud machine.

Again, I nod yes.

My head.

"Head hurts," I croak.

She pats my arm through the blanket. "The doctor will be back in a moment to check your progress," she informs and fiddles with the nearly empty bag of clear fluid hanging near the head of my bed. "I'll be back with another bag," she excuses herself.

"Ken?" I ask, noticing she's missing.

Jackson slides a chair near my arm. "She's asleep on the blankets we wrapped you in." He lifts his chin toward the corner.

I chuckle.

Ouch. My head. Why can't I avoid causing more pain?

A solemn look slides over Jackson's tired face. "You had me worried. Lying on the bathroom floor, wrapped in a towel, you were so pale. I thought I heard a sound in your room, so I peeked in. You weren't in bed, so I chanced a glance into your bathroom." As his right hand rubs my arm under the blanket, his left gently runs through my hair. "I couldn't get you here fast enough. I would never forgive myself if something happened to you."

"Hey," I interrupt. "I'm okay." I smile, and he smiles back. "Just a severe case of morning sickness today," I explain. "Your baby is fine."

"I was more worried about you," he whispers.

A doctor enters, prompting Jackson to move his chair across the room. The nurse returns, hustling to hang a fresh IV bag. Another nurse enters with my chart in hand and hands it to the doctor. The female doctor flips a few sheets of paper before looking from Jackson to me. "You gave them quite a scare tonight." I appreciate her attempt to lighten the mood, but we're too anxious. "We drew some blood and started an IV. You are dehydrated. The fluids will have you feeling better soon." She looks at the chart again, sliding her finger down the page. "Your hormone levels are high. This causes your nausea. How many weeks are you?"

Jackson speaks before I can. "We just passed four weeks."

"I see Dr. Harrison is your OB Doctor. I will send him the blood work from tonight. I'm sure he will follow up with you."

"How worried should we be about the hormone levels and dehydration?" Jackson inquires.

I look his way. He is attempting to be strong for me, but I see his fear.

"We will push one more bag of fluids. Kennedy should feel better by then." The doctor turns back to me. "We will discharge you at that time. Try to drink as much liquid as you can. Maybe try ice chips when your stomach is at its worst. Popsicles sometimes work." She hands the chart to the nearby nurse. "Your hormone levels are nothing to worry about. Except for the dehydration, both mom and baby seem healthy. Following up with Dr. Harrison will only be a precaution."

The doctor moves from my bedside towards Jackson. "Rest and fluids for the next two days. The more she's sick, the more she should attempt to drink. Dehydration happens sometimes. It doesn't mean there is a problem. It just means momma has been too sick. With more rest, fluids, no stress, both mom and baby will be up and in action before you know it." She pats his shoulder. "A mother's body is truly ingenious. It knows which functions are vital for the baby and which ones to shut down if it needs to. The baby is safe. Kennedy will feel better soon. You did good, Dad, bringing them in tonight." With that, she leaves.

The nurse presses a button on the machine. "This second bag of fluids will flow faster. I'll bring you another warm blanket." She turns toward Jackson. "She may need another warm blanket soon because the liquids make her cold."

In a flash, she returns carrying a small plastic cup of ice chips and a warm blanket.

"So, Kennedy," Jackson begins. "Do you feel a little better?"

I freeze.

The doctor called me Kennedy. Jackson called me Kennedy. This means Kennedy told him of the last favor she asked of me.

"Are you mad at me?" I ask.

"No," Jackson moves his chair back to my side and places both hands on my arm under the covers. "I'm upset with my wife. She should not have put you in that position. After everything you are doing for us, this is just too much to ask. I had to go along with it tonight. It was an emergency, and they needed to access your records."

"Don't be mad at her," I plead. "She only wants to prevent at the added stress the expense this pregnancy will cause."

"Enough," he gently urges. "We don't need to discuss this tonight. My only concern is getting you full of fluids so you can sleep in a bed and speak out loud." A small chuckle escapes.

The doctor's assurances are sinking in. Jackson believes we are safe.

"I'm sorry. I try to nibble and sip every time I'm sick. Today, I just couldn't. I was always in the bathroom; I couldn't leave my bedroom."

60

I'VE BEEN PROBED

Taylor

After my ten minutes of worshiping the porcelain throne, I brush my teeth, shower, and dress for today's obstetrics appointment. Choosing an outfit is simple. I only have one pair of shorts with an elastic waistband.

I really need to shop for some new clothes.

I am not ready for the maternity attire; I just need to purchase a size or two larger now or all elastic waists. Although I can see and feel my baby bump, it's not apparent to others. It's my goal to keep it this way as long as I can. The thought of my baby-bump drawing strangers to touch my belly already causes anxiety. I am not ready for that.

I tug on my comfy navy linen shorts with the gently scalloped hem. I pair it with a simple navy and pale blue striped V-neck t-shirt. I opt for a ponytail and very light make-up. Comfy and casual will help calm my nerves for today's appointment.

As I slide my navy slip-on Converse upon my feet, a text from Jackson pings on my phone.

Surrogate Series

> **JACKSON**
> if change your mind
> can meet you at appt

> **ME**
> Thank you
> blood work & lectures on pushing fluids during morning sickness

> **JACKSON**
> my phone in my pocket all day
> no meetings I'm available

> **ME**
> (thumbs up emoji)

I appreciate his support, however, there will be plenty of appointments for him to attend with me. This is not a regularly scheduled appointment, so it will not be an exciting one. There's no need for him to leave work today.

After I check in with the receptionist, I take the first vacant chair along the wall. Instead of the tattered magazines, today I choose to read on my iPad. I make a mental note to stay alert in the office and not lose myself in my story, as I usually do. I don't want to miss when the nurse calls my name.

As the nurse escorts me down the hallway, we pause at the scale. My weight has dropped five pounds. I know this is because of the morning sickness. I eat many times a day and drink plenty of water. I remind myself my informational books state weight loss is normal. The nurse deposits me in my room; I sit on the exam table. She hands me a crisp white sheet.

"Please undress from the waist down, then drape the sheet over your lap on the table," she instructs, before stepping in the hallway for a few moments.

A quick rap on the door signals her return. Dr. Harrison emerges, too.

"I hear we had a bit of a rough night." Washing his hands, he continues sharing the information he read from my emergency room visit. "Has the nausea improved?" he asks.

"I'm still vomiting a lot," I explain. "I have no energy and often feel light-headed. I nibble and attempt to sip water after each time I get sick. I'm not as bad as I was, but it has not improved."

"I see your hormone levels are quite high," he observes on the chart. "This causes the morning sickness." He steps partially in the hallway, signaling someone to join us.

Can my little exam room hold a fourth person?

A scrub-wearing tech pushes a large computer-looking device to my bedside.

"Lie back and place your feet in the stirrups," Dr. Harrison instructs. "This is an ultrasound machine."

Crap!

I lied to Jackson and Kennedy. I assumed nothing important would occur at today's visit. They will miss the first ultrasound.

I suck.

How will they ever forgive me for this?

I am the world's worst surrogate.

Sensing my nerves, the nurse pats my shoulder. "No worries, dear."

"I told the baby's father this would be a boring visit," I share. "He wanted to come, and I made him stay at work. I figured a blood or urine test and information on dealing with my morning sickness was all we'd cover. He'll never forgive me."

How will I even tell Jackson I had an ultrasound?

"He will forget all about it when he sees the printed photo of his baby," the nurse soothes. "There will be plenty of time to attend future appointments. He will be here when you hear the heartbeat for the first time and the ultrasound to determine the sex of the baby."

I force a smile at her words, my nerves growing instead of waning. I attempt to calm myself with long slow breaths in-and-out.

"Kennedy, this will be a trans-vaginal ultrasound." The technician holds a long plastic wand for me to see. "As it is early in the pregnancy, we have a much better chance to see the fetus with this method."

Great.

Nope, not a boring visit.

Just my luck, I get an internal probe at my extra obstetric appointment.

I try to focus on the dark monitor screen with its gray static areas. *How will we see a baby in this mess?* I've seen the ultrasound pictures of a kidney bean-shaped baby, but I can't see anything like that on this screen.

The tech moves the curser on the display and clicks from one point to another a few times. He turns to Dr. Harrison and points to areas of interest. There is no conversation in the room, as I feel the wand move and turn inside me. I see the screen adjust as the viewing area changes. Dr. Harrison signals for the nurse to look at the areas the tech is pointing out.

I need someone to speak.

I need to know if I should worry about the areas they point to repeatedly.

If all three of them focus on the monitor, it can't be good, can it?

Unable to take any more, I open my mouth just as the tech withdraws the wand, stating we are all done.

What?

I lie stunned. The technician and ultrasound machine exit followed closely by Dr. Harrison.

"You may dress now. Please crack the door when you're ready," my nurse instructs.

Seriously?

The three of them leave my room without telling me what all the commotion on the screen is about?

It can't be good news. They are probably discussing my delicate situation right now in the hallway.

I quickly pull on my shorts and shoes, open the door, and resume my seat on the exam table.

Breathe. Just breathe.

I feel light-headed. I close my eyes and concentrate on my breathing. I open my eyes when the door closes behind Dr. Harrison. He sits on the stool and wheels close to me.

"Well, Mrs. Hayes, we now know the cause of your elevated hormone levels."

I try to read into his wide smile and pleasant tone. He extends his hand with the printed ultrasound picture. There are two red circles around two tiny shadows.

"You are having twins," he proclaims.

Having twins...I lie back on the table, close my eyes, and fan my face with the tiny paper he handed me.

"Elizabeth," I hear Dr. Harrison call into the hallway.

I feel a wet paper towel applied to my forehead. I do not open my eyes. I continue to focus on my breathing.

"I'm placing a small basin in your hand in case you need to get sick," Nurse Elizabeth says.

"Kennedy," Dr. Harrison starts. "Did you hear what I said about the babies?"

With eyes closed, I move the cold towel to each of my cheeks before I speak. "I heard you," I answer.

"Would you like saltines?" Nurse Elizabeth inquires.

"I'm okay. I will not vomit," I explain. "I just need a minute to process...everything." I open my eyes, immediately shielding them from the overhead lights with my forearm. I slowly sit up while moving the wet rag to the back of my neck.

"So, twins. What does that mean?" I chuckle hollowly. "I know it's two babies. Do I need to find a specialist? Will I need bedrest? Will my morning sickness get worse? Now that we know I am carrying twins, what do we do?"

Dr. Harrison rolls his stool closer towards me. "I have delivered many multiples. It is your decision, but I would like to continue as your physician. Our monthly OB visits will now be every two or three weeks. I would like to see you two weeks from today, as your morning sickness is severe. I need to monitor you closely." He pats my hand. "You are healthy, and the babies are healthy. Carrying multiples means we will monitor closely the entire pregnancy. As for bedrest, I don't foresee the need currently. You should rest often. If you are tired, you rest. Continue to read your pregnancy books, research support groups for parents of multiples, and push fluids to avoid dehydration because of morning sickness."

"Do you have questions?" he asks.

When I don't, he reminds me, "Please schedule an appointment for two weeks."

He exits with a wave.

Nurse Elizabeth confirms the email on my chart is correct. "We'll be sending you a sample schedule of OB visits for twins. It will let you know what to expect each visit and contains information concerning a twins-pregnancy." She hands me two more copies of the ultrasound photos. "Congratulations." She smiles and directs me from the room back to the lobby.

At the desk, I schedule my next appointment in two weeks. I have no balance due, and again I'm congratulated on my twins. As I make my way to my car, I continually glance at the pictures of the twins. I place my hand on my belly.

Two babies, not one. I now have two babies to grow and protect for eight months.

Sitting in my driver's seat, I ponder how to share this news with Jackson and Kennedy. Nothing comes to mind apart from placing the ultrasound photos on the fridge door.

An hour later, I sit at the kitchen island searching the internet for ideas. As I can't reach out to Martha, Reagan, or Madison for advice, since they can't know before Jackson and Kennedy, I decide to call Jorge. Maybe he can advise me.

ME
R U busy?

JORGE
@ work what's up?

ME
nvm

> **JORGE**
> @ break call soon

> **ME**
> K

I sip my ginger ale, nibble my pretzel sticks, and wait for Jorge's call. Moments pass before a FaceTime call from him comes through.

"Hi," I greet, smiling.

He didn't need to FaceTime.

He's in an office at the bar. I see the stacks of paperwork on the shelves behind him.

"How are you feeling today?" He asks.

Since Martha told him I made a trip to the E.R., he texts or calls daily to check on me.

He is so sweet.

"I'm actually nibbling right now, so feeling okay." I sip my ginger ale before continuing. "I saw Dr. Harrison today for my follow up on the E.R. visit. He stated my hormone levels are high."

Concern clouds Jorge's face. "What can you do about that?"

"There is nothing we can do. But I need some advice. We thought today would just be about the morning sickness, so I went alone. The doctor did an ultrasound. So... Jackson and Kennedy missed their first ultrasound."

"That sucks," Jorge agrees.

"It gets worse; I'm pregnant with twins." I stare at Jorge's shocked face upon my screen. "How do I break the news to them tonight that they missed the ultrasound, and they're having twins? I mean, I have ultrasound pictures to show them."

With Jorge's help, we decide I should keep it simple. I will apologize that they missed the ultrasound but tell them I have a picture for each of them. I'll let them look, waiting to see if they figure out the red circles. If they ask for help to find the baby, then I will show them the twins. Too soon, Jorge's break is over, and I'm alone waiting for my friends to come home tonight.

I quickly shoot a text to each of them. I am glad Jorge reminded me to do this, as I forgot about all the commotion.

ME

appt good

feeling good

JACKSON

(thumbs up emoji)

Tired, I lay on the sofa, waiting for Kennedy's response. My eyes grow heavy. I close them for a minute but take a two-hour nap.

61

SURROGATE FAIL

Taylor

Whispers.
I hear whispers.
The soft murmurs pull me from my slumber. Opening my eyes, I find Jackson and Kennedy in the kitchen. They notice my movements.

"Stay," Jackson encourages. "Stay on the sofa. We will come to you."

I shift slightly to sit up.
My stomach feels okay.
I should eat.

I attempt to rise, but Jackson raises his palms between us. "Stay put and use your words to ask for help," he instructs.

"I should nibble and drink," I confess. "Would you mind bringing me some pretzels and water or ginger ale?"

Eager to hear about today's visit, they quickly bring me snacks and a drink. Kennedy kneels on the floor in front of me while Jackson sits beside me on the sofa. I chomp on a few pretzel sticks, needing my mouth occupied while I figure out what to do next.

When I sip the ginger ale, Kennedy breaks, "You're killing us. We need details."

Jackson nods in agreement.

"I need to pee, then I'll spill all the details," I lie. I need to retrieve the pics from my dresser. When I return, they are back in the kitchen, so I take a seat at the table. "I'm supposed to rest when I feel tired, eat when I can, and drink as much as I can all day." I pause. This is the information they expected. "Come sit by me, please," I request.

Concern floods their faces.

"I need to apologize. The doctor ordered an ultrasound today." I hurry to explain before they can speak, "I'm so sorry. Everything I read stated this was too early for them to do an ultrasound."

"It's not your fault," Jackson states. "We should have been there for you today. Even if we thought he'd just talk to you. We should have been there."

"I do have ultrasound pictures for you." I slide one copy of the picture to each of them. "The doctor states we're all healthy." I let my words penetrate while they stare in wonder at the photos.

"I need you to show me what we're looking at here," Kennedy announces, marveling at the printout.

I use two fingers on each photo to point at the two red circles. "These are the babies."

Long moments pass. They stare at their tiny blobs, unable to comprehend. I can't wait any longer. "He circled around the babies." I pause again. Nothing. "Do you see two red circles?"

When they nod yes without taking eyes off their pictures, I continue. "We are having twins. That is why my hormone levels are higher than usual. It may also be why I've been so sick."

"Twins?" Jackson chokes. "As in two babies? These are the two babies inside you right now?" He lays the picture down and looks at me.

Kennedy clutches the photo to her chest, tears welling in her eyes.

"Yes, congratulations! You're having twins!" I cheer.

Unfortunately, at this moment my stomach takes a turn for the worse. I run to my bathroom with my hand over my mouth. *This is not the perfect ending for the big announcement I planned.*

Taylor
At Dr. Wilson's Office, Thursday, Sept. 8th

"Would it be okay if I choose our first topic for today's session?" I ask before I assume my chair in Dr. Wilson's office.

She nods, smiling and walking towards her chair. I settle into my chair, tucking my legs beside me.

"I'm having twins!" I announce into the quiet office, fear clear in my shaky voice. "I am a big wimp. Huge. Enormous. I can't handle pain. I can't pull bandages off because they hurt too much." I quickly swallow. "How am I going to endure delivering two babies?" I sigh. "I couldn't just have one baby. No, I had to have twins. Twice the pain. What am I going to do?" I ring my shaking hands in my lap.

Finished taking her notes, Dr. Wilson places her notepad on the side table and leans towards me. "We discussed your aversion to pain in past sessions. It is important that the three of you decide on a birthing plan and discuss it with your obstetrician. There are options for pain medications during labor."

I find no comfort in her words. "Everyone tells me I will forget the pain the moment the babies are in my arms, but they aren't my babies. I may not have the same motherly connection that allows me to forget. Besides, this doesn't erase the fact I will be in pain for hours. The worst pain of my life."

"Taylor, close your eyes for me," she instructs firmly. "I want you to envision your answers, but do not speak them out loud."

Now she whispers, "Why did you agree to be a surrogate?" Dr. Wilson pauses for a moment. "How did you feel when you heard you were pregnant?" There's a longer pause this time before she continues. "How did you feel when Jackson and Kennedy found out you were pregnant?" As she pauses, I hear the rustling of her notepad. "Now open your eyes. Do you regret offering to be their surrogate?"

With tears in my eyes, I shake my head as I cannot speak.

I don't regret my volunteering to help my friends. I would do it again if I needed to.

"It's important that you journal about the reasons you chose to be a surrogate, your feelings when announcing your pregnancy, and your visions of Jackson and Kennedy meeting the twins," Dr. Wilson encourages.

"You should still journal about your fears, but communicate these with Jackson, Kennedy, and your doctor along the way. In order for you to prepare for the delivery, you should be informed and open with all involved," she states. "Is there another topic from your notebook?"

I've stewed over contacting Jackson's parents all week. I can't take it anymore. I need advice to make my decision.

"Well, you know Jackson is estranged from his parents because of Kennedy." I begin by explaining, "Gerald and Elizabeth are outstanding. Jackson was very close to his parents and his sister growing up." I pause, twisting my fingers in my lap while organizing my thoughts. "I've remained in contact with them since high school. I would like to contact them and set up a meeting with Jackson. They need to mend fences." I sigh deeply, then smile. "They'll be awesome grandparents. I don't want them to miss out on any more of their son's life."

"Have you discussed this with Jackson or Kennedy?" Dr. Wilson asks.

"No, I am struggling with a few things. First, should I encourage this reunion? Then, do I surprise Jackson with it or talk to him about it ahead of time?" I lift my eyes from my lap towards the doctor. "I email or talk on the phone every week with Elizabeth. I haven't shared our current living or surrogacy situations. I'm hiding it all. They've asked to drive to KC and meet for lunch. It's something I would do if I weren't pregnant, so I feel I should do it. Jackson knows I'm in contact with his mom and dad. He found me emailing them a while back. He never brought it up again. But I give him an update when I hear from them." I pause for a few moments. When she doesn't speak, I continue. "I know you won't tell me what I should do. I just need input from another person. What do I need to consider? What do I need to be prepared for? If I do this, what would be the best way to arrange it?" I know I will not get all the answers I seek. It's not how therapy works.

"First, if you want to eat with them, do it before you start showing. If you plan to keep the surrogacy from them," she advises.

We discuss the idea of reuniting Jackson with his parents for the rest of my session. I'm now certain I will speak to Jackson about his parents. It's for the best.

As is often the case, my session time flies by.

62

A PREGNANT CHEERLEADER

Taylor

After my morning trip to the porcelain throne and breakfast on Monday, I close this week's reminder. I remove the photo of the head of a nail from the refrigerator and replace it with the week seven photo of a blueberry. *Our little ones are getting bigger and bigger.* My hand absent-mindedly rubs my belly.

As I pose for my two baby belly photos, I notice my stomach. It's not much. No one would notice, but I do. I read that because of my petite stature, I notice changes sooner than some pregnant women do. I won't share with Jackson and Kennedy that I'm already fattening up. I'm not ready for my abdomen to be the primary focus of everyone around me.

While eating my lunch on a barstool, I notice the waistband on my only elastic shorts is no longer comfortable. I decide I can't wait until Saturday to shop with Kennedy as we planned. My waist expands and so should my wardrobe. I grab my cell phone.

ME

feeling good, need shorts, think I'll shop today

KENNEDY

go for it

catch a movie Saturday instead of shopping

ME

would Jackson join us for dinner and movie?

KENNEDY

great idea let's ask him tonight

I grab a water bottle and a plastic snack bag of crackers for my shopping adventure. I don't plan to shop for more than an hour or two, but my stomach is not predictable. As I lower the convertible top on my Mustang, I type Zona Rosa into my map app. I place my phone in its dashboard holder and start the app. I lower the volume on my stereo so I still enjoy my music and can hear the directions from my phone. The fresh air as I drive invigorates my perpetually tired body.

I park near Dillard's. Before exiting the car, I place my water and crackers in my oversized handbag that also contains an airsick bag. Preparation is key. Although I feel fine now, I quickly learned it changes from moment to moment.

I browse several sections in Dillard's before continuing my walking and shopping at Old Navy, Victoria's Secret, and Marshall's. As I prepare to walk back toward my car, I take inventory of my many bags and today's purchases. I found two tops at Dillard's along with two loose dresses for fall. I bought five shorts, two t-shirts, and two adorable pairs of leggings at Old Navy. All with forgiving, elastic waistbands. At Vicki's, I purchase two pajama sets and a t-shirt style night gown. It's hard to resist the sales on panties and bras, so I purchased a couple of each in a size bigger than my usual size. *I must be prepared to grow everywhere during this pregnancy.*

After dinner, I find myself in my bathroom. Unfortunately, my burger and french fries aren't staying down this evening. As I assume my position sitting on the side of the bathtub, while hunched over the stool, I feel the bile rise. I almost made it five days without an evening episode. I keep track of small milestones in my battle with my morning sickness. As my stomach purges my most recent meal, I see Jackson's sock-covered feet before I feel the cool, damp cloth on the back of my neck. The sound of the running faucet does little to distract me from my loud retching.

Several moments pass before the dry heaves subside, signaling the end of this unpleasant episode. I'm not sure when Jackson finally excused himself from the torture chamber that is my bathroom. I'm sure it is not pleasant to listen to and watch this aspect of my pregnancy. As I sit a moment on the tub to ensure I won't be darting right back in here, I spy my adult-toy cleaner spray bottle on my bathroom counter beside my vibrator.

Crap! Crap! Crap!

How uncomfortable must Jackson be?

This is awkward.

I rinse my mouth twice with water and run a toothbrush over every nook and cranny. I put away the toy cleaner under the sink and carry my vibrator back to the drawer of my bedside table. Leaning on the side of the bed, I prepare myself to face Jackson. I cringe, noticing my large, plug-in, body massager still on my nightstand near the lamp.

Just my luck.

I'm sure Jackson saw it, too.

Crap!

I bet he thinks a sex-addict is carrying his unborn children.

Returning to the kitchen, I fetch a bottle of water and some pretzel sticks. Through my lashes, I glance at Jackson, trying to get a feel for his reaction. As cool water caresses my scratchy throat, he approaches.

"I will not mention it. It's not my place," Jackson's deep voice murmurs. I prepare to explain as he continues. "I've read the books. I know about the increased hormones. Let's just not discuss it."

I'm glad to avoid discussing my vibrators, their use, and my overactive sex-drive over the last couple weeks. I'm impressed he knows this is a common symptom of pregnancy. Still, it looks bad to have multiple vibrators out in plain sight.

He doesn't need to see that.

He doesn't want to think of me that way, and I don't want him to.

On Friday, I try out a new yoga class at the YMCA. I like the water aerobics class but crave some variety in my workouts. I approach the class, hoping it's easy enough for a beginner.

"Welcome," the instructor greets. "I see we have unfamiliar faces in attendance today. Go at your own pace. I'll show alternative poses for different skill levels, so you choose the level you feel most comfortable with."

I breathe as instructed while bending my body in each pose. It's relaxing. I feel my muscles stretching and enjoy it. I vow to myself I'll attend three times a week, when I feel good enough in the morning.

I stop to chat with Kennedy on my way out, but her desk is vacant. I jot a quick note on her desk to say "hi" and head home.

I draw in a long, calming breath as I pull into the parking lot. I spy Elizabeth and Gerald standing on the sidewalk near the restaurant entrance of The Smokehouse Barbecue. As I open my door, exiting the driver's seat, they approach. Before I shut my door, I'm immediately engulfed in hugs. Elizabeth cries tears of joy at our long over-due visit.

"You look good. You've gained weight," Elizabeth blurts.

"Elizabeth!" Gerald reprimands his wife.

I laugh at her observation, hoping she doesn't learn why I'm gaining weight. Our meal and conversation flow effortlessly. Before I know it, our messy barbecue plates disappear, and Gerald snags the check.

"Jackson and Kennedy are well," I blurt. I know they want to know; they're too afraid to ask. *I must start a dialog on both sides to bring about this truce.*

"That is great to hear," Gerald pronounces. "Please pass along our love the next time you see them."

"I'm actually living with them at the moment," I confess.

I don't elaborate on my reason for residing with their son and Kennedy.

"I am working through a few things, and they are helping me land on my feet," I simply state.

Gerald and Elizabeth ask a few questions about their son, none about Kennedy, then change the subject. *They don't want to put me in the middle. They care about their Jackson and miss him.* When I say my goodbyes, I'm further invested in my plan to reunite this family than when I arrived.

"We're hosting a Halloween costume party," I announce at dinner Saturday.

Jackson and Kennedy chuckle at me.

"I don't do costumes," Jackson declares cockily.

"I don't care. I'm carrying your twins, so you will reward me with a costume party." I stand firm in my assumption we are having this party. "I'm thinking we should plan for two Saturdays before Halloween. We'll invite your friends. Anyone else?"

Silence.

That's not an answer.

"Should I dress as a pregnant cheerleader?" I ask. "Or Harley Quinn? Or an oven with a bun where my baby bump is?" I look at the two of them. "No comment? This is a rough crowd," I tease.

63

I'M INCOMPLETE

Taylor

On Sunday, we prepare tailgating foods to watch The Chiefs football game. By mid-day, my breasts ache something fierce. I enter my bathroom, remove my bra, then replace it with the next size up that I purchased on my shopping trip. The fact, I move from my slightly too large size 34A bra to a snug 34B concerns me. Of course, I have read many places that breast size increases during pregnancy as they prepare to produce milk for the baby after giving birth.

I knew this day would come, so why am I so uncomfortable?

Standing in my bra and panties in front of my mirror, I observe the changes my body already undertook in my first weeks of pregnancy. My abdomen grows, my hips round, and my breasts swell. Before I redress, I decide to take advantage of being in the bathroom before I return to the living room.

While washing my hands, I notice my upper arms scrunch my breasts over the sink. These boobs are out of control. Walking through my bedroom, I observe my profile walking in the mirror on the dresser. I'm top-heavy. Turning this way and that, I feel like Dolly Parton.

How do other women live their entire lives with large breasts?

I return to the living room, very self-conscious of my body. I clutch a throw pillow to my chest as we watch The Steelers demolish The Chiefs 43-14.

"That sucked," I state.

"Let's go for a walk," Jackson requests. "We'll knock on Madison's door and invite Kennedy to join us."

Much later that evening while watching TV, I excuse myself to pee, yet again. As I return, I hear whispering in the living room. I take my seat on the sofa, finding Jackson and Kennedy smiling at me.

"What?" I chide.

Both shake their heads, avoiding the rather large elephant, or should I say boobs, in the room. I fetch a bottle of water and make a production of walking around the entire living room before taking my seat. They still smile.

"I realize they are humongous. Trust me, I know my boobs enter the room minutes before the rest of me now. I can't help it, so stop looking at me that way." I point my finger at each of them. "Don't be judgey. They are so swollen and sore. I had to go up a bra size."

Jackson struggles in his attempt to not smile or laughing.

Kennedy swats his shoulder. "Taylor, they are not humongous."

"Oh, please," I argue. "I'm lucky I don't topple over. I'm so top heavy."

Through her laughter, Kennedy informs me, "You are only average now. Your tiny titties have been below average your entire life." Jackson laughs out loud, and Kennedy continues, "You were half an A size. You wore the bras most middle school girls use as training bras. I remember your complaints when a bra you liked at Victoria's Secret didn't come in an A. That won't be a problem anymore."

"I am sure you will get used to them," Jackson adds on his way to the kitchen for a drink.

Really?

I can't believe a guy gives me advice about becoming comfortable in my body. Weird factor over load.

I need to change the subject.

"I'm starting a blog on my surrogate adventure."

Jackson peeks in from the kitchen, and Kennedy turns her entire body to face me.

"I played around with the idea of writing a book for a few weeks now. I may still attempt it, but for now I will blog every day or two about the good, the bad, and the funny in my life."

"I've heard you can get paid to write a blog," Kennedy inserts.

"I did some research on that aspect. I plan to write regularly, recruit some followers, and then branch into the advertising and income part," I explain.

Jackson and Kennedy like this idea. Through our continued discussion, they offer topic ideas, social media connections, and ask many questions. My insides warm with delight as I decide tomorrow I open my new blog.

My vibrating phone draws my attention from creating online lesson plans. Glancing over, I see it's from Kennedy.

KENNEDY
going to Madison's after work

ME
everything ok?

KENNEDY
called upset, needs to talk

ME
K, let me know if I can help

Surrogate Series

> **KENNEDY**
> don't wait up

My *Friday just got better.* This means Jackson and I can enjoy anything we want to eat. I hope all is well with Madison, but I can't hide my excitement for dinner tonight. I text Jackson so we can plan.

> **ME**
> Ken @ Madison's tonight, we get fast food
>
> what do you crave?

I know he won't check his cell on his desk until after five tonight. He will text that I get to choose where we eat. My mind dances as all the possibilities come to mind. I decide to make a list. I open the notes app on my iPad. I title this list "Fast Food Fun Nights" and begin listing the local fast-food joints. When I stall in my brainstorming, I feel a sense of accomplishment. I'll be able to remove a restaurant when we eat there.

Wait. I won't remove it; I'll simply move it to the bottom of the list to enjoy again later. I've got this. Wait until Jackson sees how I organized our "Fast Food Fun Nights".

As I replace the large raspberry photo with the week nine photo of a medium green olive, I marvel at the changes the babies underwent in their first two months. From an orange seed to an olive, I'm proud to facilitate this miracle for my best friends. My tummy is now even more noticeable. I plan to encourage a shopping trip with Kennedy on Saturday for real maternity clothes.

On Monday morning, after my daily routine with morning sickness in the restroom, I update our weekly baby photo on the refrigerator. A prune, that's right, week ten and our babies are now the size of a prune. I secure this visual representation of our little ones in the refrigerator frame. Jackson spends minutes many times each week looking at these photos and bragging about the size of his sons. Kennedy likes to inform him she feels strongly I'm carrying daughters. I keep my opinion on this matter to myself.

Next, I pose for my side views of my pregnancy belly while holding my week ten sign. With each week, I look more and more forward to gracing Kennedy with the photo book gift at the end of the surrogacy.

While on my laptop this afternoon, I decide we need to brainstorm baby names. Needing two of them, we must be even more creative than most parents. I type a quick heading on my Mac and print it out, then hang it in the place of honor on the refrigerator above the current green olive size of our baby. With my pen, I place "Jax, Meridian, Riley, and Ryan" on the list. As these will not be my babies, I'm not sure if Jackson and Kennedy will want my input in naming the twins. I plan to add to the list. They may do what they want with my ideas.

Taylor
At Dr. Wilson's Office, Thursday, October 6th

Today's session focuses on my continued fear of carrying and delivering twins. When prompted, I share. "I am not an average woman. I worry because I am tiny, I might not carry the twins to term or they will be too small. I read a lot about all the changes pregnancy causes on a body. I worry with twins, I will gain more weight that I will struggle to lose later. I worry my risk factors will rise with each month as they attempt to grow inside my little frame. I'm an enormous baby when it comes to pain. Now, instead of delivering one baby, I need to deliver two. Will my labor be longer and more painful?" I sigh, dramatically. "When I look for answers online, most information is for a woman over five feet tall. I know women gave birth for centuries, but I'm a wimp and this freaks me out with twins." I gasp for breath. A small weight lifts from my chest, having shared my many fears. My worries are still present. I look forward to Dr. Wilson guiding me.

"All expecting couples fear the unknown," she states. "Each of your fears is warranted. You must not dwell on these thoughts. Remind yourself of your positive obstetric visits. Your physician hasn't expressed concerns or restricted your activities. You are healthy." She waits for me to agree. "You cannot avoid pain during delivery. Informing yourself of all procedures and accepting while there will be pain, once the babies arrive, you'll soon forget it."

I scan my notes before continuing. "I realize baby size is determined by the size of the parents at birth, but I do not know what I weighed. I assume I was little. Jackson doesn't remember his birth weight and, as he doesn't speak to his parents, I'm not sure we will ever know what we weighed." I look at the doctor for guidance.

"Let's start with birthweight. Do you know where your birth certificate is?" I nod. "It contains information to help you find your birthweight. If your weight is not on it, you may contact the hospital in which you were born. Jackson can do the same for his birth weight."

"May I borrow an ink pen to make these notes in my notebook?" I ask.

"At your next exam, discuss gaining weight, your small size, possible complications and treatments, and your birthing plan with ways to avoid pain. The nurses and obstetrician will help," Dr. Wilson encourages. "Your youth and continued exercise might assist with carrying the twins. It's important you remember that most twins deliver earlier than single pregnancies. Information is power."

As we close, I am to continue with my research, reading, and openly communicate with my physician, Kennedy, and Jackson.

Once home, I slide the fireproof safe from under my bed, wiggle the key in the lock, and open it to reveal my treasured items. My fingers fumble through the file folders, searching for my legal documents.

Found them.

I flip by the Mustang title, my teaching license, and…

Ah-ha, here it is.

As I hold it, my hands tremble. My original birth certificate, as well as several copies, were lost over the years of my youth. My mother and grandmother requested new copies each time I needed to enroll in school, transfer custody, and get my driver's license. In high school, I secured my own copy from the state. I always keep it safe and near me.

My eyes scan left to right, reading the information, looking for my birthweight. It's not among the information recorded. I see my mother's name, while my father's name is absent. This certificate is a billboard, announcing my lack of a father. A door deep in my belly opens, revealing the empty chasm I locked away in my youth. I've never had a father figure. The empty rectangle is a flashing neon sign.

I'm incomplete.

I've always been incomplete.

I'll always be incomplete.

I shake my head to clear unhealthy thoughts.

I don't need a dad. Jackson's father, Gerald, is all I need.

Not finding my birthweight, I now need to request my medical records from the hospital. *At least the hospital name is on this certificate.* I open a search engine on my phone and search for the hospital. I print the contact information. I'll sign a release form at my next physician's appointment. I suppose it will take several weeks or maybe even a couple months, but I should get the information before I deliver the end of April.

Crap!

I can't sign a release at Dr. Harrison's office.

To them I'm Kennedy Hayes. I can't request a birth record for Taylor Taft at their office. *I need to be more careful. I can't slip up and reveal our fraud.*

I use a search engine to find then print a medical release form. I request the records sent directly to me.

64

IT'S A GOOD THING HUMANS DON'T HAVE TO SHOP FOR THEIR CHILDREN

Taylor

In mid-November, Kennedy remains home with Jackson and me for today's noon Chiefs game versus The Panthers. Seems Isaac and Madison plan to meet to discuss their marriage today. Kennedy, though present, is withdrawn. It's clear to me she doesn't want to be here.

In the second half, she naps on one end of the sofa while I sit at the other end. Jackson and I focus all our attention on the close game. While she sleeps, we try to quiet our cheers and groans.

Jackson immediately notices my sudden change in position, as well as my alertness. My hands cover my entire belly. I crane my neck as I focus on the sensation I just experienced.

"Feeling sick?" Jackson inquires nervously.

Kennedy raises her head from the pillow to see what causes our focus to turn from the game.

"Not sick," I answer, while still trying to decipher the sensation I experienced.

There it is again. What could it be?

It isn't nausea, not gas. It feels like butterflies fluttering for a few seconds.

As fast as it starts, it ends.

"You're scaring me," Kennedy says.

"I felt a flutter for a few seconds," I announce. "Then a minute later I felt it again."

Jackson's perplexed face tilts to the left. His eyes rove me up and down a moment before he pops up from his seat and darts to his bedroom.

Great, more weird avoidance of me.

I glance at Kennedy, and she simply shrugs before returning her attention to the TV commercials.

Jackson reappears, flipping through their copy of What to Expect When You're Expecting. "I remember reading about this," he claims, flipping forward and back through the book. "I even highlighted it because it's an important milestone in our pregnancy."

"There it is again," I announce, my hand jumping near the location of the slight sensation.

"Can you feel it?" Kennedy questions.

"Not with my hand," I answer. "It's a flutter inside. It's so weird. I wish I could describe it to you better."

"Ah-ha," Jackson cheers. He slides his book with the highlighted section towards me. "You are feeling the babies move." Turning to Kennedy, he says, "She's feeling our babies move!"

Kennedy quickly scurries closer to me on the sofa. "Really?" She asks. "You can feel the babies move?" Her hand moves towards my belly, but hesitantly pulls back at the last moment.

"I wish you could feel it on the outside," I state.

"The book states it's early for you to experience this, but not unheard of in tiny women," Jackson recites after taking his book back upstairs. "We should be able to feel baby movement on the outside by about the fifth month."

"Do you think we might feel it earlier, since she's feeling the flutters earlier?" Kennedy inquires.

"We'll have to wait and see," I answer.

The next day, my belly full of fast food, I settle on the sofa for a movie, hoping Jackson might join me. His trip to the restroom, not a short one, I open my iPad and check my email. I unsubscribe from three spam emails, then smile as I see the next email is from Elizabeth and Gerald. I glance up the stairs, listening intently. I don't hear Jackson, so I open the email from his parents.

I smile as I read about Elizabeth's recent painting class and projects. I wish she knew how to send me a pic in an email or text. I love to see her art. Next, I read about Gerald's road trip in his vintage car.

"Anything important?" Jackson's deep, masculine voice startles me.

I confessed to him I kept in touch with his parents over the years. After the initial shock wore off, he became genuinely interested in catching up on the lives of his parents. Unfortunately, he relies on my contact with them to spy. I hope through my sharing, he will eventually reach out to them. After all this time, his parents would love to hear from him. I'm not sure how they would welcome Kennedy back, but I know they regret their handling of the situation years ago. I hope I can mend this relationship during my time here. The news of new grandbabies will make them so happy.

This morning sucks. After thirty minutes in the bathroom, I crawl back into bed, exhausted. For two hours, I alternate between sleeping and hurling. Finally, my stomach seems calm enough. I emerge from my bedroom, grabbing water from the refrigerator. Closing the door, I realize I need to change out the picture on the fridge and take pics of my belly. I pull the picture of the palm of my hand from my pregnancy book and hang it on the fridge door.

The twins are now the size of my palm. I stare at my palm for a moment, marveling at their size.

Wait!

Could they be the size of Jackson's palm?

His is much larger than mine. The fear of two large babies growing inside me still scares me.

I'm not as excited as usual to pose for my baby belly photos today. My excessive vomiting takes a lot out of me. I prop the iPad on my dresser, write on my chalkboard, then pose. A small smile dawns on my face as I imagine Kennedy and Jackson's reaction to the photo book when it arrives after the twins are born. A gift nine-months in the making will allow them to revisit the pregnancy and perhaps share with the twins when they're older.

I'm not sure how I feel about that. Do I want the twins to ever know me as anything other than their aunt? Will Kennedy or Jackson want to tell them the truth?

I grab my notebook and make a note to discuss this with Dr. Wilson and my friends.

Later, checking my email before I attempt my afternoon nap, I skim the top three emails in my inbox. A squeal escapes me, as my eyes read the subject of the second email, I'm glad no one is home to witness my excitement. I quickly open the email and read it out loud.

From: Middle Tennessee Pomskies
Subject: Pick of the Litter

Congratulations! You are at the top of our waiting list. It is your turn to pick your Pomsky from Shadow's litter. Please look at the five photos of Shadow's litter on our Facebook page or our website. I will call you in the next day or two to discuss questions you might have and secure your pick from this litter.

Congratulations on becoming a new fur baby parent.

I reread the email, then dart to their Facebook page. I find Shadow's litter has three absolutely adorable females and two very handsome males. I spend a couple minutes on each photo on my tablet. I zoom in and then out.

How will I ever be able to decide?

The cuteness level is too much to take. The thought of an afternoon nap evaporates. I rise to pull out a notebook and pen. I need a plan to help me choose my future fur baby. I must make a list of questions, as well as pros and cons, to help me choose.

Pomsky Picking
Male or Female?
Eye color
Markings? Face, Back, Legs

I can only come up with three items to consider in choosing my puppy. As I've never had a dog of my own, I need to ask Jackson and Kennedy to see if they have any insight into male vs. female dogs. Eye color is simple; I want two blue eyes. That narrows it down to Aggie, Maddie, or Mortie. Now, if I choose a male, my decision is made. Looking at the facial markings, all three have black and white masks. Maddie's face is all black except for her white snout. Aggie's black fur around her eyes with small white ovals where eyebrows would be and white cheeks to her snout are very striking. I especially love the white eyebrows. Mortie's mask of almost entirely black with only white near his ears, causes him to look strong and perhaps a bit vicious. I find this decision difficult and table it for now.

I glance at my clock, sigh, then revisit the idea of a nap to quickly pass the time until my friends return home to assist in my decision. My mind spins with pros and cons of each puppy. It's a good thing humans don't have to shop for their children.

On the first Monday of December, my breath heads to the Caribbean while I stare at the manilla envelope in today's mail. My thumb slides back and forth over the return address; it's the hospital in which I was born. This is it. Someone safely tucked the details of my birth inside.

I try to open the envelope several times throughout the afternoon. I don't understand my hesitancy. I know who my mom is; I know no father is mentioned. I know I was a healthy baby. I just don't know my birthweight.

As it seems is our new normal, Kennedy is at Madison's tonight. Jackson and I dart out quickly to secure our high in calorie and carb dinner. As we eat in the living room, I cannot ignore the large envelope on the coffee table.

"Jackson, will you help me open my medical records?" I ask, barely above a whisper.

He places his food on the end table beside his recliner before taking the manilla envelope in hand.

"I don't think you need help to open it," he informs me. "But if you want me to open and browse through it before you, I will." He pauses, waiting for my nod. First, he pinches the metal prongs together, and he rips the flap open. Next, he scans each page. A smirk upon his face, he releases a few hmms and wows.

I realize he tries to annoy me. "Jackson please," I plead. "Any surprises? How much did I weigh?" I wring my hands in front of me.

"Perfectly healthy baby girl," He announces, sliding the photocopies my direction. "I didn't see a weight, but I wasn't reading every word. You look."

I accept the offered papers. I read every word and every handwritten note. As I expected, there are no surprises. I find what I'm looking for.

"I weighed a whopping six pounds two ounces," I proudly inform Jackson. Seems right, I am short and petite now and was then, too.

"I doubt I was that tiny," Jackson laughs.

I witness something in his eyes before he hides it from me. He wants to know his birthweight, but because of Kennedy, he thinks he can't reach out to his parents. I want to let him know I'm trying to bring Elizabeth and Gerald back into his life. I'm slowly mending the feud between them and getting all parties under one roof for the first time in over three years. I can't tell him yet. I must keep my plans a secret for now. Asking for Jackson's birthweight from Elizabeth will be tricky. I need this information, so I make a mental note to come up with a plan.

Soon, my yummy yet greasy fast food haunts me. I moan and clutch my chest as heartburn slowly climbs my esophagus, burning every inch on its way up. As this is not a new symptom, Jackson fetches relief from the kitchen.

"The twins may have a full head of hair after all," Jackson teases as he extends the bottle of Tums my way.

While I wait for my relief to take effect, I grab my iPad to distract me. I open email, glance to ensure Jackson focuses on the TV again, then type.

Elizabeth,

I'm reaching out for your help in closing a bet. I believe I have mentioned that Jackson and Kennedy's neighbor Martha is expecting baby number five. You may recall she is the sister of my bartender friend, Jorge. I know I have mentioned him to you. Anyway, the topic of birthweight came up. We have created a pool, each putting in five dollars. The person who weighed the most will win the pot of over $50. I didn't know mine and Jackson didn't know his. I've sent for my medical records to uncover my weight. How big was Jackson? Inquiring minds want to know. I promise to email more soon.

Thanks,
Taylor

65

YOU ARE ONE-HUNDRED PERCENT NERD

Taylor

I smile at the calendar. *Today is the day; it's finally December 7th. Today is the sonogram that will hopefully divulge the sex of the twins.* I'm excited, Kennedy is excited, and Jackson is a nervous wreck. It's cute. I'm very excited for the two of them.

Jackson meets me in the parking lot as usual for the appointment. "Ready for this?" he asks.

"Are you ready for this?" I counter.

He shakes his head, and we walk into the three-story physician's office building. "The good news is, we know there are two babies in here." I rub my tummy as I speak. "No more surprise babies. Just finding out if they will pee sitting down or standing up."

Jackson sputters. He wraps his arm around my shoulders, pulling me in for a side-hug. "You're a dork," he says for the millionth time.

"Good news," I reply. "Your children will be fifty-percent my genes. The nerd and dork genes are dominant. Are you prepared?" I tease.

"I can only hope I have a brainiac daughter just like you."

Jackson's words hit me hard. When I daydream of Jackson and

Kennedy's twins, I do not consider they might look like, or act like me. I plan to be an active participant in their lives, but I hadn't considered I might look at a reflection of myself.

I need to address this in my next session with Dr. Wilson.

Dr. Harrison records the usual vitals into my chart on his tablet, as the nurse and technician ready the ultrasound equipment and prepare my exposed belly. Jackson holds my hand as he bends to whisper in my ear. "Thank you for sharing this with me."

Why would he say that?

I'm his surrogate. It's my job to share every step of the pregnancy with the two of them. I tried to encourage Kennedy to attend today's appointment. Her hesitation perplexes me. Friends may attend appointments with expecting mothers. It happens all the time.

With jelly on my belly, the tech maneuvers the sensor over my ever-growing girth. Jackson and I anxiously stare at the black and white shadows on the monitor. Our full attention takes in the arms, legs, heads, and bellies as pointed out by the technician. The twins, no longer resembling beans, look like babies now. The tech concentrates on one particular area, rolling the device this way and that. Eventually, he pauses, taking a screenshot with the keyboard. Focusing on the second baby, he repeats the same task. It takes much longer before the tech takes a screenshot on this baby.

The nurse wipes the jelly from my basketball-sized abdomen while the tech prints a few pictures, handing them to Dr. Harrison before leaving the room with equipment in tow. I glance nervously at Jackson. He glues his eyes to the ultrasound pictures in front of Dr. Harrison as if he can decipher them from this distance. I squeeze his hand, drawing his attention.

"There are only three possible outcomes," I whisper. "Thirty-three percent chance of two boys, thirty-three percent chance of two girls, and thirty-three percent chance of one boy and one girl."

Bending to my ear, Jackson whispers, "You are one-hundred

percent nerd." He places a feather-light kiss on my forehead before standing upright, facing Dr. Harrison.

The skin of my forehead tingles where he kissed me. I realize we're playing the part of a married couple for the doctor's benefit, but I'm not sure how I feel about his kiss.

"The results are in," Dr. Harrison announces while fanning the printed pictures in the air. "Are you sure you want to know? Many enjoy the surprise on the day they give birth."

"We are positive," I firmly state for both of us.

Dr. Harrison is unaware that I am actually a surrogate and not the real Kennedy Hayes. It is important that Kennedy and Jackson know the sex of the babies in order to continue to bond with them.

"Jackson," Dr. Harrison addresses. "What are you hoping for?"

Jackson shakes his head. "I want two healthy children first and foremost. If I had a choice, I would like a son."

Dr. Harrison's grin widens, exposing his teeth. "You are having a son and a daughter." He proclaims. After our excitement wains, he explains, "You are carrying fraternal twins. They began as two eggs, and each have their own placenta. They are not identical twins."

I fight a snort. *Like we couldn't figure that out since one is a boy and the other a girl.*

This is perfect. A son for Jackson and a daughter for Kennedy. I couldn't have planned it better if I tried.

As we ride the elevator to the ground level, I compose a text to the baker at Jackson's store I met earlier this week. When I knew Kennedy would not be attending today's appointment, I arranged a gender reveal party for this evening. Reagan and Martha are prepping the house and food for me. We will all surprise Kennedy when she arrives home tonight. I only let Jackson in on the party as we sat in the waiting room before the appointment. He loves the idea.

ME
for gender reveal 1 boy & 1 girl

AMBER THE BAKER
Got it! Cake will be ready by 4

> **ME**
> you rock!

> **AMBER THE BAKER**
> Be sure to tell my boss that (winking emoji)

I chuckle. Jackson asks what I am laughing at. "I texted to order the cake for the party. I told Amber she rocks, and she asked me to be sure to tell her boss that."

Jackson chuckles, too. "I need to head back to the store for a bit. Can you handle the party prep without me?"

"Reagan and Martha plan to spend the afternoon on all the details. I just need you to pick up the cake at four and bring it home before Kennedy leaves work today," I inform.

"I will be home by 4:30 with cake in hand," he vows.

I'm too excited to nap, but I must. I don't want to fall asleep at our party tonight.

Jackson arrives home, followed by the rest of the neighbors. Everyone anxiously awaits Kennedy.

> **ME**
> can't wait for you to get home

> **KENNEDY**
> on my way

I inform our guests Kennedy will be here soon. We place the cupcakes arranged like a cake in the center of the table. Half the cupcakes have pink and the other half have blue centers. The baker placed the cupcakes tightly together, forming a circle. A giant black question mark adorns their white icing tops. I never saw a cupcake-cake until the bakery showed it to me this week. It is perfect. It looks like a cake, but the cupcakes can easily pull apart and consumed.

At the sound of the garage door, everyone moves to the kitchen. We don't plan to hide in the dark and yell, "Surprise!" just stand here as she opens the door.

"I'm home!" Kennedy shouts as she opens the door between the garage and kitchen. She freezes at the sight of everyone waiting for her. "What's this?" She asks nervously.

"A gender-reveal party, silly," Madison answers, wrapping her in a hug. "Taylor and Jackson wanted to surprise you with a party." Kennedy smiles nervously at our group as she removes her coat and places her purse with keys on the counter.

"Thank you for the party," Kennedy says. "But I can't wait until after dinner to find out. I need to know now."

Jackson and I laugh; we expected this. We each grab a cupcake from opposite sides of the cake and hand them to Kennedy. We order Kennedy and our guests to wait until everyone has a cupcake before eating them.

"On the count of three," Jackson announces with a raised voice. While Kennedy has two cupcakes, everyone else will only find the sex of one baby when they bite to the center of their cupcakes. Jackson's eyes remain on Kennedy while I look to everyone else for a reaction. "One, two, three!"

Reagan, Martha, and Kennedy simply break their cupcakes in half to reveal the pink and blue centers. Everyone else bites their way toward the colored centers. Cheers and murmurs erupt from our guests' cupcake-filled mouths. Kennedy hugs Madison excitedly. Reagan and Martha congratulate Jackson. I watch as everyone animatedly discusses how perfect a baby boy and girl will be.

66

TWO JACKSON JUNIORS

Taylor

On Thursday, I awake from my afternoon catnap slowly sitting up. While I wait for my body to adjust, I snag my phone from the coffee-table. My alerts notify of three Facebook messages, one snap on Snap Chat, and a text from Kennedy.

I read the text first, finding Kennedy will be at Madison's again this evening. *I guess Jackson and I will continue working through our fast-food list.* I mentally tally she spent four evenings of the last seven with Madison. It seems Madison's marriage struggles are more than she can handle. I may try to stay awake until Kennedy comes home tonight to get an update on the situation. *Maybe I can assist Madison, too.*

Later, I decide to take advantage of the forty-five-degree day and venture out for a walk. As I round the corner, I notice Madison pulling into her driveway. She is home early, and I plan to take advantage of this opportunity. Keeping a steady pace, soon I arrive at Madison's door. Ringing the bell, I attempt to organize my questions while I wait.

"Hi," Madison greets. "Come on in."

I assumed all the houses in the neighborhood to be similar on the inside. I find Madison's interior style is industrial design. Exposed brick walls, exposed metal pipes and ductwork, with the distressed wood beams, transform this typical two-story suburban home to look like a downtown loft.

Madison escorts me to the kitchen area, and we sit at the island. "Want a drink?" she offers.

"May I refill my water bottle from my walk?" I ask her.

It's time; I need to let her know why I'm here.

"I'm glad you're home early today; I need to ask you a few things," I awkwardly start. Of Kennedy's friends, Madison is the one I know the least about. "Kennedy spends many evenings here. I just wanted to ask you if she might want to avoid me." *There. My big worry is out in the open.* "I worry that my constant morning sickness reminds her of her struggles with eating disorders. I'm pregnant with her children, but she is pulling away from me. She no longer texts me during the day, we no longer watch movies or TV together, and she spends most of her free time with you."

Madison rises, moving to the opposite side of the island. We now face each other. "I told her she was spending too much time here. She insisted she wanted to help me." Madison shakes her head. "I'm not aware of any reason she might avoid you. I truly believe she wants to be here, so I am not so lonely while separated from Isaac. She is acting like a counselor for me."

I breathe a sigh of relief. "Thank you. I'm so sorry I overreacted. I just had to make sure she wasn't suffering a setback because of me. She worked so hard to overcome the anorexia and bulimia; I would never forgive myself if I was a trigger for her."

I have intruded enough. I rise to leave. "Thanks again."

Madison walks me to the door. "I will encourage Kennedy to stay home more," Madison shares.

At home, I rest on the sofa until Jackson arrives home. I browse social media, then move to my emails. While reading, I excitedly click on a new message from Elizabeth. I look forward to our communication. As my eyes scan left to right, I spit water from my mouth, spraying across the room.

Fuck!

Ten pounds!
Ten pounds? Jackson weighed ten pounds at birth.
Oh, hell no!
I have two Jackson Juniors inside me.
No way am I giving birth to two ten-pound babies.

Elizabeth continues to share that Gerald weighed nearly twelve pounds.

What have I gotten myself into?
I'm so fucking screwed!

This is information I should have researched prior to fully committing to this pregnancy. I can't take pain. Realizing now the twins could be large, scares the Dickens out of me.

The bigger the babies, the bigger the pain.
I can't undo this now.
Crap! Crap! Crap!

I add this topic to my list for my next visit with Dr. Wilson.

I am too tired for a ride to fetch fast food tonight, so we order pizza for delivery. I have no energy. I take twenty minutes to ingest my two pieces of pizza.

College basketball keeps Jackson entertained as I place my feet on the coffee table and lazily lie on three throw pillows.

"I'd like to try something," I mention during a commercial break. Jackson looks at me for more details. "I read that if I drink orange juice and lay down, then you can feel the babies move."

This sparks Jackson's interest. He hops from the recliner to fetch me a drink.

"Guess that is a yes," I tease.

I slowly sip the juice as Jackson anxiously watches.

"It isn't instantaneous. I will let you know when the show starts."

Finished with my drink, I lie down, and we continue watching basketball. I giggle every time I catch Jackson staring at my belly. I hope this works; it would suck if I got his hopes up for nothing.

"Want me to fill your water?" Jackson offers at the next commercial break.

"No, I'll be up all night if I drink anymore," I reply. That's when the sugary orange juice kicks in.

Pow!

"Jackson it's happening!" I call to the kitchen.

Jackson jogs to my side, drops to his knees, and stares intently at my stomach.

I take his right hand, placing it in the area of the first kick. I lay my hand on the other side of my belly and rub. This time I feel a kick on my side.

"Put your other hand over here," I direct.

It happens.

"Whoa!" Jackson pulls his hands away, one flying to cover his mouth. "Did you feel that? I mean, I know you did. How weird does it feel?"

"Put your hands back. You are missing some more kicks," I encourage. "Both are moving now."

Jackson looks like a boy on Christmas morning. "They are really moving now. Orange juice must be like a double shot expresso for babies."

At 9:30, I announce it's time for me to head to bed. I've had an eventful day. Jackson assists my slow, clumsy rise from the sofa, and I fill my water bottle before climbing into bed. Although my entire body is ready to sleep, the two tiny humans are still on a sugar high. I move from position to position while rubbing my baby bump, hoping to lull them to sleep. They continue their soccer match for thirty more minutes before finally winding down so I might sleep.

The next afternoon's task is researching possible Pomsky names. I could keep her name Aggie, but I want to look at other possibilities. I open a new document on my Mac. At the top, I type "Possible Pomsky Names" then type "1. Aggie". I set up auto-numbering, then move to my iPad to search the internet for names. I type "Husky names" in the browser. I click on the top site and browse the names. I continue this on several more sites. I add Denali, Yukon, Mako, Aspen, Aurora, Luna, Indigo, Sasha, Kyra, Kira, and a few others.

I type "wolf names" into the search engine and the second site excites me. The names are dire wolves, the mythological-like dogs, adopted by the Stark children on HBO's *Game of Thrones*. I'm a huge *GOT* fan. The names include: Ghost, Lady, Summer, Nymeria, Shaggy Dog, and Grey Wind. I quickly move my curser to number two on my list and insert Nymeria, Ghost, and Lady. This moves all other names farther down the list of possibilities. I circle Nymeria, as Arya Stark is a favorite character of mine.

67

THE CONFESSION

Taylor
At Dr. Wilson's Office, Thurs., Dec. 15th

"Your journal is open. What shall we discuss today?" Dr. Wilson inquires, pointing at my open notebook in my lap.

"I'm concerned about Kennedy," I inform. "She spends three or four nights a week at Madison's house instead of spending the evening with Jackson and me." I close my notebook. "Madison's husband has moved out, and Kennedy said she was helping Madison cope. It has been several months now, and I fear there is more to the situation." I rise from my chair and pace the office. "She opts not to attend the OB appointments with me. I invite her multiple times. I mean, these are her babies, and this is her pregnancy. She doesn't seem as interested as she was the first few weeks." I pause, placing my hands on the back of my chair. "I feel she her pull away from all of us. I don't know of anything we did to cause it. Will she magically return for the birth of the twins and be involved? Will she even come to the hospital for the birth? I just have no idea what is going on or how she will react."

"Have you discussed your concerns with Kennedy?" Dr. Wilson asks.

"I've tried to catch her a few times at the YMCA after my workouts, but she's tied up or away from her desk." I sigh. "Often, she texts us she won't be home because she is going to Madison's, so I can't talk to her then." My hands perch on the back of my neck as my elbows jut out from my cheeks. "I talked to Madison about it. She assured me Kennedy is not lapsing into her eating disorders and not upset with Jackson or me that she is aware of. She apologized for consuming so many of Kennedy's evenings." I shake my head. "I thought living with her during the pregnancy would be a great opportunity for her. I thought she would enjoy every experience with me. I never imagined she would leave me alone with Jackson while carrying her babies." I lower my arms to my sides and resume my seat. "Am I being oversensitive? Is it my hormones and lack of sleep? Or did I set unrealistic expectations?"

She offers me no answers but suggests actions I might take to remedy the situation. I can't deny she makes good points. As she is also Kennedy's therapist, I wonder if she knows the real reason Kennedy spends so much time with Madison. I realize she can't share it with me, just as she won't share my session with Jackson or Kennedy. Although we resolve nothing during today's session, I do feel better about everything and plan to talk to Kennedy soon.

Kennedy
At Dr. Wilson's Office

Dr. Wilson asks, "Kennedy, have you noticed any tension in Taylor or Jackson?"

I do not respond, so she continues browsing my journal and asking questions. She moves on to awkward moments, I observed. "Why do you think Taylor freezes, then cries like that? Why do you think

Jackson leaves the room? Can you think of anything that might cause these disturbing reactions?"

My tears stream down my cheeks as my words trap in my throat. Dr. Wilson continues to encourage me to respond. "Remember, this is a safe place Kennedy, you can tell me anything; I am here to help you. I don't share our work with Jackson and Taylor, just as I don't divulge their sessions to you." She pauses and I nod my understanding. "What are you thinking? You mention spending many evenings with Madison. Why do you enjoy your time with her? What do you discuss? How do you feel? How does your time with Madison differ from your evenings at home?"

"Why is that? Have you discussed these feelings with Jackson or Taylor? How do you think Jackson and Taylor feel about your spending your evenings with Madison?" The doctor continues to pry for me to share more.

I confess, "Sometimes I can't look them in the eyes. I don't like the way I feel when I see them struggle. I've asked too much of them. I asked Taylor to give up a year of her life to give me a baby. I wanted a baby so bad; It is all I could think of. I thought of some ideas, like the insurance fraud, that are very selfish of me to carry out. I've resorted to committing crimes. I am that desperate for a baby." My diarrhea of the mouth shows no signs of stopping.

"In talking with Madison, I realize I am very lonely in my life. Granted, Taylor now lives with us. Jackson and I are so comfortable with each other, yet I feel alone. I actually look forward to seeing Madison; I enjoy spending time with her. We just lie around and watch TV. I feel alive again in her presence. I am finding I think about Madison more than I think about becoming a mother." I worry about what this statement says about me. I cannot turn around now. I will be a mother of twins; there is no way to change that.

"You mention committing crimes, other than insurance fraud, what crime have you committed? Kennedy, you stated you feel guilty when you are around your husband and surrogate. You stated you can't take the hurt in their eyes. Why are they hurting?"

This answer hurts the most; I can't admit it yet. I cannot take the guilt I bear for hurting the people that love me the most. They knew my every secret, yet I violated their trust.

"In order to move forward, we need to work through these feelings. Let's try this, close your eyes, breath in and now out. One more time, breath in and now out, open your eyes. Now, Kennedy, what did you do?"

I stand, placing my hands on the back of my neck before I begin. I answer honestly about my actions during the conception of our babies. "At the time, I desperately wanted a baby. It's all I could think about morning, noon, and night. We did extensive research, we took every precaution we could to ensure we conceived. Taylor calculated our ovulation window. I read online that the window can be 2-4 days and that sperm lives inside the body for a couple of days. We planned to attempt 'The Deed' twice-a-day for three days. If it had been up to me, we would have tried twice-a-day for five days. I wanted a baby more than anything. I was so blinded by my desire that I chose to take it into my own hands."

Dr. Wilson passes a glass of water to me.

I open up, and I share everything. *Everything.* I couldn't stop the words if I wanted to. I have locked these feelings away so deep; they have festered; they have grown, and now they demand to be confessed. I speak of my actions the night before we started 'The Deed'. I share my observations of Taylor and Jackson in the months following. I realize I caused their discomfort and pain. I felt if I fled to Madison's, they wouldn't hurt. Madison needed a friend when Isaac left, but it became so much more.

"I stole prescription sleeping pills from Madison's bathroom. I fixed Taylor and Jackson several glasses of wine one evening, and I spiked the last one." I roll my head, attempting to release the tension in my neck.

"Taylor became relaxed. She lay her head on the back of the sofa while slumping down. Jackson started shaking his head, as if trying to clear the cobwebs out of his brain. I encouraged Taylor to lie down on the sofa. I asked if she was hot. She said yes so, I helped her remove some clothes." I avoid the doctor's eyes. I do not want to see the horror in them. I return to my chair.

"You know Jackson and I don't have sex. You know I just can't allow myself to relax and be in the moment. But that night I was in the moment. With Jackson and Taylor as my puppets, I played out the sex I wished I could enjoy. I had to tell them what to do. I had to raise my voice some, but they were so out of it, they complied. As I watched and directed, my husband and my best friend had sex. In their haze, they were hesitant, but I kept persuading them. While I stood behind the sofa, Taylor had tears rolling down her cheeks just before she orgasmed. Jackson didn't last much longer."

I chance a glance from my hands in my lap, up through my lashes, to Dr. Wilson. Her thin lips form a fine line, tears threaten to spill from her eyes, and she frantically records notes onto her notepad.

"It wasn't easy coaxing each of them to their beds. Taylor was a limp doll. We fell a few times, but finally made it to her room. I pulled a vibrator from her bedside table and laid it on the bed so she would think she used it before bed that night. Jackson could walk, but his rambling hurt. He tried to ask why; he tried to ask what he did. I told him it was a dream several times until he drifted off to sleep." I stand again, leaning on the back of my chair, my hands folded tightly in front of me.

"The next morning Taylor texted her temperature rose, so we began attempting 'The Deed'. I never spoke of that night. Neither of them asked about it the next day. It was awkward, but because we were performing 'The Deed', they assumed that was the source of discomfort."

"Sometimes, Taylor freezes in place, gets upset, then leaves the room for a while. She doesn't ask about it, she doesn't act different towards me. I think she wonders but doesn't know. Jackson doesn't freeze like Taylor. He gets a deer-in-the-headlights look and darts to the bedroom for a half-hour or so. He has withdrawn a bit. He doesn't tease Taylor as much, but he hasn't asked about it or anything." I sigh my confession now out in the light of day.

"And how does that make you feel?" Dr. Wilson whispers.

"I feel guilty, sick, and I hate myself. I hate I am this selfish. I hate I am so greedy that Taylor moving to KC, quitting her job, agreeing to carry my baby, agreeing to commit insurance fraud, and agreeing to sacrifice her body to give me a baby were not enough. I hate I can't give Jackson the sex he needs, the sex he deserves as my husband. I hate that even under duress, the two of them could orgasm together. I hate I violated the two people that love me most to get what I thought I wanted more than anything," I yell, wiping sweat from my brow.

"Do you still want a baby?" When I do not respond, more questions follow. "Do you still want to be married to Jackson? Do you still want to be friends with Taylor? What do you think would happen if you told them what you did?" Dr. Wilson pries, even though I refuse to answer.

"Do they talk about that night with you?" I ask. This question has haunted my every visit with Dr. Wilson since that night.

"I can't share our private sessions with you, Kennedy. I can't tell you if they are hurting or not. What do you think they feel?" The good doctor is ever in control. She shares nothing she shouldn't. Our conversation continues and I describe what my friends might feel.

As our time is over, Dr. Wilson prompts me to journal this week. "We need to uncover what you want. Has what you want changed? When we know where you want to go, then we can work on steps to get there."

68

A CALL BACK

Taylor

My new year starts with my new puppy's arrival on January Second. While playing together on the floor, my cell phone vibrates.

JORGE
home yet?

ME
yes

JORGE
can I call?

ME
yes

Moments pass before a FaceTime call from Jorge arrives. When I answer, the first words I hear are not hello or hi.

"Hey dork, turn the camera around so I can see your new puppy," he demands.

"And here I thought you called to talk to me." I attempt to inflict guilt upon my friend for not caring to speak to me. However, Jorge shows no shame. We talk for over forty minutes as I follow the puppy around the house with my phone for him. I finally let Jorge go, so I can take my new puppy to the backyard to potty.

I return my phone to my pocket, pick up Nymeria, then approach the backdoor. I bend down, ring the sleigh bells I hung on a post by the door, and announce to Nymeria, "It's time to potty." I ring the bells one more time and say, "Time to potty," again before we head outside. I read online that these bells allow dogs to alert owners they need to go out.

With the thin leash attached to my tiny puppy's collar, I roam the backyard with her. As she rarely leaves my side, I take a chance, drop the leash, then waddle around the yard, allowing her to follow me. I become short of breath quickly and sit on the grass. Immediately, Nymeria stops running. She walks towards me but stops and squats.

"Yay!" I cheer. *My puppy is a genius.* We've gone outside twice, and she pottied both times. No accidents in her first three hours that she has been in her new home. When within arm's length, I scoop her into my lap, cuddle, and praise her lovingly.

"What are you doing on the ground?" Jackson's deep voice startles us.

Nymeria barks her tiny puppy bark. She scrambles around my side to peek towards the voice that spooked us.

"Come here, come here pretty girl," Jackson encourages sweetly as he bends to his knees near the deck. He pats his thigh and continues his sweet coaxing. "Nymeria."

I turn to find Jackson on all fours, slowly crawling toward us. Nymeria tucks into my side, cautiously observing this new human in our midst.

"It's okay," I encourage. "Go."

I gently push her towards Jackson. Nymeria takes three hesitant steps before squeaking out another petite Pomsky puppy bark.

"She's telling you she is in control and this is her yard," I inform.

I already observe a sassy, alpha demeanor in my cuddly fur baby.

As Jackson nears even closer, Nymeria squeaks out three barks. Her front paws hop off the grass with each bark. Jackson pauses, and she sits. Fighting the urge to pee, I cannot take this drawn-out introduction. I scoop up Nymeria and hand her to Jackson as I quickly scurry to the bathroom.

When I return to the living room, Jackson is lying on the sofa with Nymeria lying on his chest, sleepily.

"I'm gonna call her Nia. Nymeria has too many syllables," he announces, looking to me for an argument.

"Let's shorten it to Nya instead of Nia," I counter. Jackson expected a major debate from me on this point. "I noticed long ago you struggle with three and four syllable names. You call your wife Ken instead of wasting time on Kennedy," I tease.

Nya yawns a big, exhausted puppy yawn, stretches her tiny four-pound body out, then lays her head on Jackson's chest.

"Shh," Jackson warns. "It's our nap time." I place the TV remote in Jackson's hand, grab my iPad and curl up in the chair to read.

Thirty minutes pass before I hear the garage door signal Kennedy's arrival. I rise, quietly slip into the garage, and let Kennedy know that Jackson and the puppy are sleeping on the sofa. I show her several pictures I snapped with my phone of the two napping.

"Well, nap time is over as soon as I lay my eyes on her," Kennedy muses. "I need my puppy loves, too."

To Kennedy's dismay, Nya and Jackson are in the backyard playing when we enter the house. I smile to myself. It's a good call by Jackson; my puppy should potty before meeting another human.

In late January, a knock on the door breaks my typical afternoon routine. Nya barks three times. I rise from the sofa to see a woman through the peep-hole. She doesn't seem to be dangerous, so I carefully open the door.

"Hi," I greet the stranger, and Nya peeks her head through my legs.

She smiles sweetly at me. "You must be Taylor," she says. "I'm visiting Martha; I'm Rosalynn."

"Jorge's Rosalynn," I announce. "Come in, come in."

At my excitement, Nya barks and begs me to pick her up.

"Are you sure it's not a bad time?" She inquires hesitantly.

"I was just reading on the sofa," I inform, motioning Rosalynn to sit in the living room.

Nya cuddles close on my lap, cautiously eyeing our visitor.

"Jorge made me promise to drop by. He wants more pictures of your Buddha belly," Rosalynn nervously explains. "His words, not mine."

I'm seated on the end of the sofa nearest her in the recliner. "What brings you to KC?" I ask.

Nya now begs Rosalynn to hold her.

"May I?" Rosalynn asks.

I pass my tiny Pomsky over. Nya licks her hands.

"I had an audition this morning," Rosalynn explains. "I'm hoping to have a call-back for tomorrow. I'm too nervous to sit alone at Martha's, so I came to distract myself while keeping you company. Jorge couldn't find coverage for the bar, so he couldn't travel with me. I'm grateful Martha insisted I stay with them instead of a hotel."

"So, how do you think this morning's audition went?"

"I don't want to jinx it; I'm very superstitious," Rosalynn explains. "I did my best, so now I wait to see if it was good enough for them."

"I will think good thoughts for you," I say. "Is this a traveling group or a KC production?" Selfishly, I hope it is a KC-based production, and this means Jorge and Rosalynn might move to Kansas City. I like my new neighbor friends, but I enjoy my phone calls with Jorge more.

"It's a local company that stages four performances per year. Besides those performances, they book many community appearances for festivals and fundraisers. I will need to move nearby. Jorge and I discussed his relocation so we can live closer to his sister, his nieces, and his nephews," Rosalynn answers. She looks up, a big smile on her face. "Nothing is set in stone yet. But fingers crossed, it will all work out."

I cannot contain my joy at hearing her news. "I'm sure Martha will be overjoyed to have Jorge closer."

"It would mean less phone time between Jorge and you, as well."

Rosalynn's words ring true, but I can't hide my worry that she is not as understanding of our friendship as Jorge claims she is.

"I must admit," she intrudes on my worries. "I was jealous when Jorge spoke of you the first couple of times." She tilts her head and smiles at me. "It opened my eyes to my actions in New York. I left him, started a new life, and went out with others. It wasn't until he mentioned meeting you that I realized how strong my feelings still were for him. I think I told myself the more I dated, the easier it would be to move on. In reality, I can never move on. It killed me to choose my dream career over my husband."

"You have nothing to be jealous of where I am concerned," I promise. "His heart has always been with you."

I watch tears pool in Rosalynn's eyes. "He told me you encouraged him to insist on a visit to New York. You are the reason we are back together." With her free hand, she wipes the tears from her cheeks. "I can never thank you enough."

Loud chimes puncture our quiet conversation. Rosalynn quickly answers her cellphone. She excuses herself to the kitchen to take the call. I can hear Rosalynn's words from the kitchen. When she ends the call, I pretend I did not eavesdrop.

"Yes!" Rosalynn cheers in the kitchen. She quickly covers her mouth, worried her excitement and raised voice might be too much.

"Good news?" I ask.

"I got a call back. I dance again tomorrow morning." As her body dances around the kitchen, her eyes gleam with joy.

Ever analytical, I query, "How many dancers get a call back?"

Placing her hand on my arm, she answers. "Four dancers. Two men and two women."

Wow!

"You have a fifty percent chance, then." *There is now a fifty percent* chance Jorge might move to KC. My close friend might live minutes instead of hours away. "You've got this."

"I really think I do. It's a contemporary dance group. That's my specialty." She bounces with each word. "I really, really want this one. Jorge and I have reunited, and I think it's meant to be."

I can't help but smile at this. "Should you call Jorge?" I urge.

"Shit! Thank you, I'm so scattered. He will kill me if I don't call him." Rosalynn taps a few buttons on her phone. She holds her phone up at arm's length from her.

"Mi corazón," Jorge greets. "Hey, Taylor."

It's a FaceTime call. I wave to him.

"I got a call-back!" Rosalynn sings.

"Turn the camera around. I need to see you right now," Jorge requests. "No offense to Taylor, but this is *big* news."

I quietly fade to the living room, giving this private moment to the two of them. I'm so excited. I hope she will get the spot, they will move here, and will slide right into our friendship circle.

Rosalynn strides towards me, phone extended, Jorge's voice flowing from the speaker. "Nya, Nya," he calls.

Nya lifts her tired puppy head from my lap, turning her head from side to side. "You are the most precious puppy ever," he coos. "I can't wait to come and visit you myself. We'll play in the yard and go for walks."

Nya's ears perk up and she barks her agreement before looking to me for confirmation that we are going on a walk.

"Okay, I gotta go. Time to get ready for work," he announces.

"Oh, no you don't," I protest. "You don't FaceTime in my house and hang-up without saying one word to me."

"Sorry," he says. "Can I call you on my drive to work?" I agree to his concession but request no FaceTime. I look a mess; the pregnancy is taking its toll on me.

69

A DEMON

Taylor

At the end of February, as usual, the sound of the rising garage door signals my alone time, complete for the day. Not that Nya isn't a great distraction, but human interaction is lacking in my daily routine. Nya waddles as her little tail excitedly wags towards the garage entrance. I ask her to sit, which she does with tail still brushing against the tile floor. When Jackson enters, she immediately raises her front paws as if doggy-paddling in the air. This is how she begs for anything and everything. Right now, she wants his full attention.

"There's my little girl," Jackson greets, sweeping Nya into his arms. Her little puppy tongue places kiss after kiss on his cheek as her front paws rest on his shoulder. "What did you two do today?" He baby-talks to her with eyes on me.

"The usual: lots of naps, a few playtimes in the backyard, and a session focused on training," I answer.

Jackson chuckles as Nya refuses to stop slathering her kisses on his cheek. He lowers her to the floor, stating he wants to see what his smart little puppy learned today. He grabs some training treats from the pantry and places them in my palm.

"Nya, sit," I request firmly, and she complies. I reward her with praises and a treat. "Shake," I request, and Nya raises her left paw to my open hand. Again, I praise her, and reward with a treat. "Lay down."

Nya, still seated, uses her front two paws paddling in the air to beg.

"Nya, lay down," I repeat, she complies, and I reward her with a chew bone. It's her favorite treat.

Jackson lowers himself to lie beside Nya on the kitchen floor. With one hand, he rubs her from ears to back to curly tail while praising her for how smart she is. I imagine this will be like Jackson's routine once the twins arrive. He will come home and ask about their day and praising them while peppering them with kisses and cuddles. I enjoy witnessing the stress of his work day melt away while interacting with Nya in the evenings.

"A large package arrived from Amazon for you today. I left it by the front door," I inform Jackson.

He hops up quickly from Nya and her bone to retrieve the box. Nya places a paw on her bone to protect it, while her little head and perky ears assess Jackson's movements closely. Jackson deftly carries the oversized box to the kitchen counter, then uses a box-knife from his work slacks to open it. I shake my head at the fact I had to slide the box from the porch to the living room as it was too large for me to maneuver.

"I bought you something," Jackson states matter-of-factly.

I try to decipher whether he is speaking to me or to Nya as he reaches into the large brown box to reveal its contents. He proudly holds a long, snake-like, stuffed object nearly as tall as he is.

"It's not much to look at like this. Follow me," Jackson prompts, striding to my bedroom. He removes the protective plastic covering and displays the pillow on my bed, forming a capital C. "It's a pregnancy body pillow," he proudly announces. "The reviews claim it allows a pregnant woman to sleep more comfortably. Hop up here and try it out." He holds a picture-flyer showing the pose to use.

I'm frozen, speechless, in the doorway. Jackson not only bought me a gift, but he researched it. He listened to my constant complaints of inability to sleep in any one position for any length of time. He heard I had a problem, and he remedied it without my asking him.

I flinch, startled, when Jackson places a hand on my shoulder. "Hey, you okay?" he asks, concern on his face.

I nod.

"C'mon, climb on the bed and try the pillow," he encourages.

This is not a simple task in my current state. I'm in shock by his act of kindness, not that Jackson isn't a kind person. He went above-and-beyond for me. I sit on the end, pushing off the floor with my tippy-toes to slide my body further onto the bed. I use my arms and legs to slide towards the top. I ask to see the picture again, then position myself snuggly in the C-pillow. The lower curve between my knees comforts my ever-widening pelvis. The top curve, I snuggle to my chest and squeeze with my head propped on the pillow. I marvel at the simple shape of the body pillow and its ability to comfort my pregnant body.

I smile awkwardly at Jackson. "Thank you, it is perfect." My quivering voice signals my battle with approaching tears. "You shouldn't have, but I am very glad you did."

Jackson offers me his extended hand to assist in my extrication from the bed. "What are we eating tonight?" he asks, before ascending the stairs to change from his work clothes.

"It's your night to choose," I answer. "I've had a calm day, morning sickness-wise, so anything goes tonight."

"Let's order pizza. I feel like staying in," he announces.

Nya rings the front door bells on her post, signaling she wants to go outside.

"Patience," I encourage. "We will go for a walk when Jackson comes back down."

I slowly squat in an attempt not to tip over and scoop her up. I let her out the backdoor in case she really needs a potty break before we order food and take our evening walk. She quickly learned we walk when Jackson is home each night, usually after dinner. Our walks are her favorite time of the day.

"Up for orange juice tonight?" Jackson hopefully asks after our walk.

I can't tell him no. This is the only way he can physically connect with the twins right now. So, in bed tonight, I'll remain awake, waiting for the twins to burn off the extra sugar again. It doesn't weird me out now to have Jackson's hands on my belly, and I've learned to drink less OJ, with the same results. After several powerful kicks, I decide to share even more with Jackson.

"Can I show you something straight out of *Alien*?" I ask.

Jackson nods. I lift my t-shirt to reveal most of my large baby bump.

"Wait for it. Wait for it."

"That's a foot! I see a foot!" Jackson shouts.

In bed the other night, the twins were moving about, trying to get comfy, and my nightshirt was scrunched above my belly. I found I could see their body parts as they pressed on the inside of my belly. At this marvelous discovery, I knew Jackson and Kennedy, if she ever stayed home, would enjoy the interaction.

"It looks like a demon has possessed your stomach." Jackson cannot get enough. He talks to the babies and rubs where they press.

Although I am now more comfortable with Jackson's focus on my stomach, when he bends down to kiss my belly, I gasp and tears well up in my eyes. At my reaction, he apologizes, believing he crossed a line. I wave, trying to express it's okay as words escape me. I cannot categorize the emotions flooding me. Jackson attempted to show love to his baby. I know that was his intent. With his kiss, my breathing escalated, my stomach fluttered, and I... *I wanted. I want a man to worship me as he does his unborn babies. I want a man, my soul mate, to share every day and start a family with. I crave tender kisses, touches, and words. I crave intimacy. The question is, who am I craving?* My confused brain worries I might crave Jackson.

I quickly check my emotions. "I'm sorry. It's these stupid pregnancy hormones and I'm tired." I need us to move on from it. "There's a foot," I point out.

Body parts appear from time to time. We quickly try to guess what we see pressed to my stomach. The kicks are stronger, as the twins are much larger now. Occasionally, they press on my ribs and lungs, making it difficult to breathe.

An hour later, I call it a night. I struggle to find a comfortable position, even with my new body pillow. My thoughts float to my longing for a husband of my own to share my pregnancy with. I imagine the two of us watching the baby kick from the inside. *He lays with me now as the twins continue emulating Riverdance. My husband caresses my baby bump, talking calmly, encouraging the babies to sleep so I might sleep.* In dreaming of a perfect husband, I realize I wouldn't sleep alone each night; he would be here when I wake to nibble and pee in the night. He'd also be here for my morning bouts of nausea. I realize Jackson supports me as much as he can in our situation. I still long desperately for my happily ever after. I hope to find a husband, a father, and a soul mate of my own to start my life with. As the twins slow their movements, I drift off.

70

MR. PERFECT

Taylor
At Dr. Wilson's Office, Thurs., Mar. 9th

"My dreams of a family consume my thoughts daily. I fear they cause me to cling to the men in my life desperately," I confess.

Dr. Wilson nods before asking, "When you are in a relationship, do you see that man in your dreams of a family?"

Cocking my head to the side, I ponder over my visions of family and future. "I don't. When I envisioned my family, John was never the father figure."

"As we discussed in previous sessions, you are not trying to change these men. You hope they will wake up and change on their own," Dr. Wilson says. "Did you make the list of traits you dream of in a spouse and father of your children?" When I nod yes, she continues. "Did you make the pros and cons lists of your past three boyfriends?" Again, I nod. She passes an orange highlighter to me. "Please highlight the traits that match those on your list of a dream spouse."

It only takes a moment to complete this task. There is not much for me to highlight.

"Now, think back to the day you met these guys and your first date with each." Dr. Wilson gives me a minute. "Now look at your dream list. Were there any signs they might be the one you are dreaming of?"

At the frat party, John attempted to be the center of attention. He seemed very concerned about how others saw him. On our first date, we watched a movie at his place, a movie he chose. He ordered pizza without asking my preferences for toppings. The entire date, he never asked about me.

I do not analyze the other men. I know I jumped in feet first, completely forgetting my preferences, my goals, and my future dreams. "It seems I'm so desperate to not be alone, I…"

Dr. Wilson pats my knee. "This is a break-through. From now on, what will you do differently?"

"I can't take a checklist with me," I chuckle. "I could create a note on my phone that I could glance at from time-to-time. I could sneak a peek to keep me mindful of my hopes and dreams."

Dr. Wilson interrupts, "I do not think you need a list with you at all times. You can create one if you'd like. But you must remember, no one is perfect. Your dream of a spouse and father is perfect in your mind. Reality will differ." She pauses for a quick sip of water on her side table. "As you spend time with a man, it is important that you compromise. Relationships are based on give-and-take. In the past, you made all the sacrifices. In the future, assess your relationship from time-to-time. Ensure your happiness, stand firm on items important to you, make sure both of you compromise and work toward a shared goal."

"I've started a notebook for my life after I give birth," I inform Dr. Wilson. "I'm making lists of things I want to do, goals for one and five years, and now I will add relationship reminders and goals from today's session."

Our time ends. I wave goodbye as I exit the office. My heart is light. I have renewed hope for future relationships. I need to thank Kennedy again for suggesting I see Dr. Wilson. I am pleased with the results I am attaining.

Later, it is time to start dinner, but I'm craving appetizers. I popped by Jackson's store earlier this afternoon. When a pregnant, hungry woman shops, she purchases way too much. I plan on leftovers the rest of the week for lunches.

I start by placing cheese, diced tomatoes, and a splash of milk in the microwave for a minute, then stir. I repeat this over-and-over until the cheese entirely melts. While I wait for each minute to pass, I preheat the oven and pull other items out to prepare next. I pour the cheese dip in the slow cooker on warm.

I heat little hotdogs in KC Masterpiece Barbecue Sauce on the stove before placing them in the other slow cooker. I set the marinara sauce on the counter to warm to room temperature. My "Rock Out" playlist wails from the living room speaker. I sing along to Nickelback's *Something in Your Mouth* as I move from task to task in the kitchen. Alone in the house, the volume is higher than it should be while I sing and dance with no one watching. *I love this song.* I realize the lyrics are not favorable for women. I like what I like. This playlist contains explicit lyrics and songs I can't let others know I love.

As Five Finger Death Punch's *Burn MF* blares, I pause to ensure I didn't forget anything. I have two more to place in the oven when Jackson and Kennedy arrive home. My preparations complete, I thrash around the kitchen island, screaming along with Ivan Moody. At this moment, I'm not pregnant with twins, I'm not a surrogate, and I'm not a prim and proper adult. I thrash, scream, and cuss as stress evaporates from my body. This song and these lyrics free me.

Spinning and thrashing near the refrigerator, I instantly freeze. Jackson leans against the garage entryway. His tie off, his cuffs unbuttoned, and his big-ass grin inform me he didn't just walk in. My left fingertips touch my lower lip as my right hand pauses the playlist on my phone on the island.

"Sorry," I whisper in Jackson's direction without making eye contact.

He strides past me into the kitchen, peeks in each slow cooker, then announces, "For a few minutes, I was transported to The Sprint Center for a fabulous rock concert." Despite his attempt at seriousness, he breaks into laughter at his last words.

Regrouping, he continues his teasing, "I'm not sure how Dr. Harrison would feel about your dance moves while carrying twins."

Jackson grabs a bottle of water from the door of the fridge. "And I've read babies can hear voices in-utero. Maybe heavy metal and you yelling 'mother-fucker' over-and-over is frowned upon for a surrogate."

"I plan to expose your twins to everything, Kennedy and you don't. They can't be sixteen and only exposed to the oldies you prefer," I inform. "As their aunt, I will take them to concerts, rated-R movies, and feed them copious amounts of sugar."

Jackson shakes his head at me. "I expect nothing less from Aunt Taylor." He motions towards the oven. "What's for dinner?"

"I'm craving munchies," I explain. "We have chips with cheese dip, little barbecue hotdogs, mozzarella sticks, and potato skins."

"Craving?" He mocks. "Isn't a craving for one, maybe two things? You've planned an entire buffet. Are we entertaining friends tonight?"

"Whatever," I snap. "Go change your work clothes. I'm putting the mozzarella sticks and potato skins in the oven." I look his way. "We eat in ten minutes, with or without Kennedy. I'm starving." I hear Jackson's laughter fade as he climbs the stairs.

A pril finally arrives; it seemed the last month of pregnancy would never arrive. I slowly pad my way to my bathroom and lean over the stool. My slow movements do little to calm my morning sickness. I no longer attempt to sip water and nibble on saltines to soothe my stomach while lying in bed. I've learned I cannot prevent the inevitable. After a few minutes, I start my day by rinsing my mouth and face, brushing my hair, then leaving my room in search of breakfast. Today, I choose a bowl of Cheerios and sit at the island to eat.

I open my phone to read today's news and social media, finding two unread texts.

JORGE
good morning

> text when you are up

ME
> what's up?

In between spoonfuls of my cereal, I look for Jorge's reply but see none. I place my empty bowl in the sink as the front doorbell rings. Nya barks at the intrusion. *Who could that be?* No one visits here during the day. *Maybe it's a delivery.* I make my way to the front door, peek through the peephole, and squeal as I fumble with the locks.

"Jorge!" I squeal as I pull the door open. "You're here!" I throw my arms around his waist, pulling him into an awkward-pregnant-belly-hug. I forgot he planned to be in KC on Monday.

"Hey, easy squirt," he teases. "I don't want you to puke on me."

I playfully swat his biceps. This causes Nya to bark protectively from between my legs. "I've already been sick this morning. I should be okay for an hour to two," I inform him. "So, are you officially living here now?"

"May I come in?" Jorge asks. I pull him by his hand into the living room, pausing as he scoops up Nya. "We will stay with Martha this week, and our apartment will be ready on Saturday."

I can't contain my joy at this news. With Kennedy spending so much time helping the newly separated Madison, I've needed a friend to hang and chat with. He is so easy to be with. Jorge will fill my friendship void.

"Tell me all the details about your job and the apartment," I urge.

We settle into the sofa and Jorge shares everything.

"I plan to work at the family restaurant," Jorge explains. "This will allow Martha and James more time with kids and the new baby. I worked at the restaurant until we moved to Chicago, so it is nothing new. Rosalynn is very busy with rehearsals and appearances during the day, nights, and weekends, so my work hours won't be a problem."

As he speaks, I can't help the wide smile on my face. *He's here. He is really in Kansas City. My best friend is no longer hundreds of miles away.* My heart is happy.

"Spill it," Jorge orders. "Why are you smiling?"

"I just imagine myself sitting at a table in the restaurant, enjoying a delicious meal, and you chit-chatting with me as you pass by from time to time," I explain.

"Your entire world revolves around food now, doesn't it?" he teases.

"Food and the nearest bathroom," I correct, laughing.

71

DONUTS VS. PEANUT BUTTER

Taylor

By late afternoon, the warm aroma of chicken and noodles swarms throughout the house. Cuddled under a blanket, Nya asleep at my feet, I shut off the TV and open my Kindle. I'm transported to Denver, Colorado, for more escapades of India Savage and her gang.

As is usual when I read, time passes quickly. Kennedy emerges from the garage, causing Nya to flop from the sofa to the floor, before running to greet her. I rise much slower to avoid upsetting my stomach and the babies.

"I should take her out," I inform Kennedy.

"Let me do it. You get right back on that sofa," Kennedy orders. "You fixed dinner; it smells divine. I will take her out."

The two skip to the door and outside, as I tumble back into my comfy position on the sofa. Returning from the yard, Kennedy rewards Nya with a treat before looking my way.

"Need a drink or a snack?" she asks.

I start to shake my head but decide a snack would be smart. Hours flew by since I last nibbled. I ask for some pretzels and water. Kennedy delivers them to me on her way upstairs to change from her work clothes. I laugh as Nya attempts to climb the first step to follow her. Deciding the climb un-scalable, she returns to me, whines, and I lift her to my lap.

At seven, Kennedy and I move to the kitchen to put the finishing touches on dinner. I turn off the slow cooker while Kennedy pulls plates and bowls from a nearby cabinet. I pull the mashed potatoes from the refrigerator. I will wait for Jackson before microwaving them. As I carry the salt and pepper to the table, the sound of the garage door announces his arrival.

"Hi," Jackson mumbles as he walks straight to his bedroom to change.

I guess today was a rough one at the grocery store. I ask Kennedy if she should go check on him, and she informs me he will be fine.

He would probably be fine quicker if he could vent about his day while he changes his clothes. I scramble for a plan to cheer him up. I ring the bells, announce to Nya it's time to potty, and help her outside. I carry her up the stairs and let her down at the top. Nya looks at me, then hearing a noise goes, looking for Jackson. *Puppy cuddles and licks might cheer him up.*

Jackson's mood appears cheerier upon his return, carrying Nya to the bottom of the stairs before letting her down. She follows on his heels as he joins us in the kitchen. I place a ladle in the slow cooker and a large spoon in the potatoes, then turn and signal dinner is ready. Kennedy opts for a salad while Jackson and I fix our plates. I place my chicken and noodles in a bowl and my potatoes on a plate. I notice Jackson piles potatoes on his plate, with chicken and noodles on top.

As we eat, he is too quiet. Kennedy chats about this thing and that, but seems oblivious to his mood. I share my puppy stories from the day, and this draws a slight smile. Not able to avoid it any longer, I ask, "How work was today?"

"You used mom's recipe," Jackson states, avoiding eye contact while continuing to eat.

Crap! Crap! Crap!

I'm so stupid.

Elizabeth's homemade chicken and noodles are simple and delicious. I fell in love with them while I lived with The Hayes's my last year of high school. I felt like a warm, comfort-food meal today. *Carbs, carbs, and more carbs.* I drove to the store to secure the four ingredients, then hurried home excitedly. I enjoy good food, now I almost worship it. In my excitement at fixing the meal I craved, I didn't think how Jackson might feel about eating his mom's recipe. Life would be so much easier if he would just arrange a meeting. I know they are ready to move past this disagreement. They miss their son, and I know he misses them, too. He is more stubborn than I am. *Dammit, Kennedy, help me here!*

"I'm sorry," I begin. "I had a craving. I didn't stop to think."

"It's delicious," Jackson replies. "Don't be sorry. I just forgot how much I loved her food. It's bringing back a lot of memories."

I reach across the table to pat his arm. *Now is not the time for me to encourage a truce.* Perhaps these chicken and noodles will open Jackson up to the possibility of discussing his parents.

Jackson smiles up at me. "Thank you for craving chicken and noodles."

We never discuss Jackson's day at the store and the reason he came home sullen. Jackson contributes to our conversations the rest of the evening and plays with Nya. While we watch TV, Nya rings the bells by the backdoor. Jackson and I go crazy.

"I can't believe she learned to use the bells so soon," I cheer.

"We have the smartest Pomsky puppy alive," Jackson declares before he takes her outside.

He awards Nya three treats for ringing the bell.

"Jackson, she will be obese if we spoil her," I tease.

On Saturday, Kennedy and I decide to eat at our neighbor's restaurant. Martha, acting as hostess, walks us toward the back, behind the bar and around a corner. Balloons, gifts, and "Surprise!" greet us. Madison, Reagan, Martha, and several ladies from Kennedy's YMCA stand around a large square table. *It's a baby shower for Kennedy. Why didn't they include me in the planning? It's not a shower for me; I'm just the surrogate.*

I'm thrilled when Reagan announces we will eat, then open the gifts. *This pregnant woman is starving; it's a constant situation for me.* Kennedy chooses a seat by Madison, so I select the only remaining seat between Reagan and Martha. Before I know it, we finish our scrumptious meal, and we move on to the gifts.

I document gifts received on each card as Kennedy opens them. She receives several matching boy and girl newborn outfits, diapers, and baby books to document milestones. For the last present, Martha's husband pushes out a large, wrapped box. A group went in together and purchased a double stroller. Kennedy needs this stroller; she will have her hands full with two little ones for many years to come. A smile warmly, realizing I can use the stroller when I babysit so Jackson and Kennedy can go out to eat for adult time. I could take them on walks, to the park, or even shopping next to Kennedy as she pushes a shopping cart.

All gifts open, the moment I looked forward to for the past an hour-and-a-half for arrives. It's cake time. I constantly crave sugar and carbs. I reward myself with two pieces claiming I am eating for two babies after all; this causes everyone to laugh.

"Kennedy, please share an update on the arrival of the twins?" Reagan urges.

"Our induction is scheduled for May 6th," Kennedy shares.

Ever the nurse, Reagan shares, "Most twins arrive early. I can't believe your babies haven't chosen to emerge into the world by now."

As I hurry to spread crunchy peanut butter onto my two slices of toast, the patio door slides open.

"Ready?" Jorge asks.

"I just need to eat my toast, then I am ready."

I turn finding, Jorge holds a familiar bakery bag.

"Is that what I think it is?" I query.

"Two iced donuts from your favorite grocery store," he proudly professes. "I figure I need to keep my pregnant helper happy and energized for my moving day."

I look from my toast to his bakery bag, then back to my toast. Sensing my dilemma with wasting good food, Jorge offers, "I'll eat the toast if you want the donuts I selected for you."

I quickly trade breakfasts. We eat as Nya whimpers at our feet for attention, clean our breakfast mess, take Nya potty, and then head out.

Our task begins with Jorge lugging armloads of boxes from Reagan's SUV up two flights of stairs, as I unpack the boxes in the kitchen. They used newspapers to pack the glass items, so I run them through the dishwasher prior to placing them in cabinets. I hope Rosalynn won't mind where I place everything. Jorge claims she isn't picky, but I can't imagine another woman organizing my kitchen in my absence. With rehearsals this week and a few public appearances, she asked me to assist Jorge with unpacking for her. I organize the pantry, place towels in drawers, place pans in the lower cabinets, and the freshly cleaned dishes in the upper cabinets.

"What should I unpack next?" I ask, on Jorge's next trip in.

He suggests the bathrooms. He assists carrying three boxes into the main bathroom so I may begin. I feel like an intruder handling their personal items. I tell myself Rosalynn is exhausted at night, so every little bit I do is helpful.

"Let's call it a day," Jorge suggests, leaning on the open bathroom door.

I glance at my phone, finding it is almost three. The day flew by. It seems like a moment ago, we took our lunch break.

As Jorge drives me home, I feel the day's exertion take its toll on my body. I might not have lifted boxes, but I bent, squatted, and stood all day. My aching muscles cry for a warm soak in the tub.

"Same time tomorrow?" Jorge asks, helping me from the SUV and into the house. "Tomorrow's my last day off, then I start at the restaurant."

"Your return excited Martha and James."

"James will have more time with their kids. I'm glad it worked out for all of us," Jorge smiles proudly. "Get some rest. Rosalynn and I will pick you up about 6:30."

72

ALTERNATE UNIVERSE

Taylor

Just out of my barely warm-but-safe-for-the-baby bath, I scoop up Nya, and we crash on the sofa.

My eyes flutter open to the vision of Jackson standing over me with Nya in his arms, lapping at his cheek and neck.

"Hey, sleepy," he greets.

I slowly slide to a semi-upright position near the arm of the sofa. Jackson doesn't hide his shit-eating-grin.

"What did you do?"

He is up to something ornery; he has no poker face.

"Look at your phone." Is all he says, carrying Nya up to change his clothes.

I snag my phone from my pocket. I have a new text from Jackson. It's a picture. He took a picture of Nya sleeping on my chest while I napped. I can't be mad at him. It is a tender moment. *I need to frame this one.* My large pregnancy belly looms prominently as I am horizontal. Nya snuggles on my chest with her head propped on my belly bump, and my puffy face is peaceful in sleep. *I love this snapshot. I'm glad he recorded this moment in time for me.* Nya naps beside me in the recliner or at my feet on the sofa most afternoons. This is the only time that I know of that she napped on my chest.

Slowly peeling myself from the sofa, I make my way to the kitchen. I peek in the slow cooker at the chicken swimming in KC Masterpiece Barbecue sauce. The sweet aroma excites my taste buds. "Almost time," I tell my rumbling tummy. I check and double check that I have all the ingredients for my barbecue chicken pizza. The salad is chilling, drinks are cold, everything anxiously awaiting the arrival of our guests. I'm a bit nervous about tonight. They've met Jorge, although they haven't spent an entire evening together without a large group. Adding more stress to this situation, I'm still not sure if Kennedy is upset with Jackson, me, or why she is with Madison more than us. *I hope she engages in our conversations tonight.*

Nya's tinkling bells break my thoughts.

"Time to go potty?" I ask as I approach her at the back door. She darts into the yard when I open the door. I waddle out much slower behind her as she runs to the fence, then back. Next, she runs in a large circle around me before she squats to potty.

"Good girl." I turn back towards the house.

Nya barks at me. When I turn to face her again, she crouches low to the ground, taunting me to chase her. I take one step towards her. She sprints, circling me twice. She barks once, before running toward the fence again. It is clear she doesn't want to go back in the house, so I sit on the steps to the deck. I marvel at her sudden burst of energy. I chuckle to myself, knowing she will crash hard this evening for a nap. *I don't need a burst of energy to make me need a nap these days.*

"Here they are," Jackson calls, stepping through the back door.

Nya immediately runs full speed to greet him. I am often jealous my dog prefers Jackson over me in the evening.

"Nya, what are you doing?" he coos, scooping her up. "Taylor, Jorge should be here in ten minutes."

Crap!

I lost track of time with Nya's playful spirit in the back yard. Jackson extends an arm to assist my cumbersome rise from the steps.

"I need a crane." I tease, and Jackson chuckles.

Nya barks, insisting on his full attention once again.

I'm washing my hands at the kitchen sink, when the doorbell rings, signaling the arrival of Jorge and Rosalynn. *They're early.*

"I've got it," Jackson hollers from the living room as Kennedy descends the stairs to join me in the kitchen.

I dry my hands while Jackson escorts our guests to the kitchen.

"Plan on introducing us?" Jorge taunts.

I throw my dishtowel at his head. Of course, he snags it prior to its collision with his face.

"Rosalynn," I greet begin. "This is Kennedy and Jackson." I motion towards our hosts. "Jackson and Kennedy, this is Rosalynn, Jorge's better half," I tease.

"Hey, now," Jorge chides teasingly.

"Hello," Rosalynn greets. "Thanks for having us over tonight."

Nya begs Jorge to pick her up with her usual doggy-paddling in the air. As my four friends exchange greetings, I begin my pizza prep.

"How may I assist you?" Jackson asks.

"I have it all under control, but you can make sure I don't burn the pizza when it is in the oven," I inform.

I roll the dough on two pizza stones, top it with KC Masterpiece, spread the marinated shredded chicken from the slow cooker, then three types of shredded cheese on top before placing it in the oven.

Turning to my friends, I state, "It's easy enough for me. The hard part is setting a timer and not burning it." I point to Jackson. "You are to pull it out when the timer goes off or before the cheese browns."

"Let's move to the living room until dinner is ready," Kennedy encourages.

Rosalynn and Jorge sit on the sofa with me while Jackson and Kennedy take the recliners. Nya begs Jorge to lift her to his lap, and Rosalynn oohs-and-ahhs over her. Of course, Nya loves the attention and begs for more.

Conversation flows easily among the five of us. I wonder why I even worried about it this afternoon. Before I know it, the pizza timer signals it is time to eat. We move to the table. Jackson pulls the pizzas from the oven, slices each, then carries one to the center of the table

Kennedy set earlier. Kennedy carries a water and tea pitcher to the table.

Conversation continues as we eat. They love my pizza. Rosalynn talks about her dancing and upcoming appearances. Jorge animatedly describes his shifts at the restaurant. It feels good to see my important people getting along. I've shared so many things about each of them with the others. I'm glad our worlds are finally intertwining.

Jackson and Jorge escort Nya to the backyard when she rings the bells as we women load the dishwasher. While in the backyard, I overhear Jackson informing Jorge, I overdid it today. Together, they vow to ensure I rest more until the twins arrive. Upon their return, I gift Nya with a treat for taking care of her business by ringing the bells, then we move into the living room to visit.

I struggle to open my eyes when I feel warm lips on my forehead.

"Goodnight, sleepy momma," Jorge teases.

I take in the room. Everyone is standing. Kennedy and Rosalynn are near the front door while Jorge and Jackson act as a forklift to help me from the recliner. Jackson keeps his arm around my waist as I say my goodbyes to Jorge and Rosalynn. *I can't believe I fell asleep.* I look at my phone. It is only eight-thirty. *These twins are sure making me into a wimp.*

Kennedy fills my water bottle as Jackson escorts me to the bathroom and then into bed.

"You overdid it today," he states. "You need to take it easy."

Kennedy places my water on the bedside table.

"I think we should limit your activities to short walks, lots of naps, and allowing us to wait on you hand-and-foot until the big day," Jackson says.

I realize he politely orders me to slow down for the rest of this pregnancy. I know he has the twins and my best interests at heart, but my hormones get the best of me and tears flow. I fan my face in an attempt to keep them at bay.

"Hey," Jackson attempts to calm me. "Don't cry. I'm not mad that you helped Jorge and Rosalynn move today. You've read everything I have. You know, these last few weeks are hard. You can't do everything you did in the first two trimesters. It's time to slow down and enjoy the pampering for once." I nod, cuddle into my pillow, and quickly fall asleep.

I do my best to slow down, but the second afternoon in May, I can no longer take it. I sneak outside for a short walk with Nya. Last week, Dr. Harrison assigned me to modified bedrest. I'm to limit my time not in bed or the recliner to two hours a day; that's two hours of bathroom time, showers, preparing meals, and that is about it. I've watched mindless daytime television, visited the movie channels, binge-watched Netflix and Hulu, and can take it no more. I need fresh air. I vow three blocks down, then back is all I will walk and at a very slow pace.

Nya's excitement at finally walking during the day with me is contagious. She darts right and left as I leisurely stroll on the sidewalk. I notice Isaac's truck in Madison's driveway. As I near, he waves me over to him. Isaac has never been my favorite person. I can't imagine what he and Madison are going through so, I decide to approach for a moment.

"Can I ask a favor?" Isaac reluctantly asks. I sense he understands my hesitation based on our past interactions. "I need to grab a few items from our house. I would really appreciate it if you walked with me and witness what I remove. I don't want Madison to claim to her lawyer I took items I shouldn't have and didn't."

"I guess I can spare a few minutes," I agree. "I'm supposed to be on bedrest, so I can't help long."

Isaac promises it will only take five minutes. As I begin to squat, he quickly scoops Nya up and places her in my arms. I'm in shock.

Did Isaac, Mr. Male Chauvinistic Pig, just sense the difficulty I have bending at my size and help me?

Wow! I must be in an alternate universe.

As I follow him, Nya in my arms, to the main bedroom to fill his suitcase, I take in his appearance. He is very unkempt; it's easy to see he is suffering during this separation. His hair needs washed and cut, his stubble is a little longer than is in style, his clothes wrinkled, and the dark circles under his eyes announce his lack of sleep.

"Madison has a new lover and will move out in the next month. At that time, I will move back into the house." Isaac claims, as he removes clothes from the closet, throwing them into his suitcase. "It seems futile to pack anymore items, but I need them for work."

When his suitcase is full, we walk out the front door.

"Why don't you come over for a drink?" I invite, even though I can't indulge with him. "Jackson will be home soon. You can stay and visit while I go to Martha's."

Hours later, I return after having my baby fix until the twins arrive later this week. Jackson meets me in the kitchen.

"I insisted Isaac stay. He passed out, so I put him in my bedroom because I wanted him to be close to a bathroom in case he pukes. I figure I will sleep on the sofa, and Kennedy will climb into bed with you when she comes home."

I nod and smile. I knew Isaac needed a friend tonight.

"I didn't think he was drunk until he said something about Kennedy and Madison being lovers," Jackson chuckles.

I quirk my head, my eyes squinting as I replay his words.

The next morning, I help fix a light breakfast for all of us. To my surprise, Kennedy didn't come home last night but arrives as we eat.

Isaac doesn't try to lower his voice. "She spent the night...I told you," he reminds Jackson.

73

STAR WARS DAY

Taylor

> KENNEDY
> be ready @ 5

> ME
> I remember

> KENNEDY
> (thumbs up emoji)

> ME
> craving French fries

> KENNEDY
> (laughing emoji)

Tonight is the night. Jackson asked to take us out to eat and to a movie. For two weeks I've fought going stir-crazy in the house all day. I'm too large to bend over, so cleaning and exercising are out. I struggle to play with Nya; this kills me. She is so cute and at a very playful stage. I attempt to sit on the floor for a while every day and play tug-of-war and fetch with her. Afterward, my rising from the floor is a struggle. Dr. Harrison believes everything is just as it should be, but he requested total-bedrest this week. I'm to stand or walk only to the bathroom. Sitting and horizontal relaxing are now my day-job.

Netflix and Hulu binge-watching fill my days. Premium channels and On Demand entertain me, too. Daytime TV is not my style. If only it was fall, I could watch all the holiday movies on the Hallmark Channel.

At 4:45, I attempt to pee one more time before the car ride. I pose in front of my mirror. I'm wearing my totally awesome Star Wars white t-shirt. A young Luke Skywalker and Princess Leia peek through the white fabric low on my enormous belly. The Star Wars twins peek out with swords in hand. Once baggy, the shirt now clings everywhere. I pair it with red leggings and flip-flops. They are the only shoes I can put on without help. I added Luke and Leia to our baby names brainstorming list, but Kennedy refuses to humor me by naming her twins to appease my Star Wars infatuation. I need to wear Star Wars attire today. It's May the Fourth. I always celebrate Star Wars Day and "May the Fourth be with you". *I'm a proud nerd.*

Promptly at five, we pile into Jackson's Impala. Kennedy occupies the passenger seat because I chose the backseat. As I let out a loud exhale, Jackson's eyes glance at me in the rearview mirror.

"I'm okay," I assure him. "The twins make it hard to breathe."

Kennedy turns the radio down and shares funny stories from the YMCA today on our drive. I beg her to stop. I don't want to laugh because I might pee my pants.

Without warning, a deafening crash surrounds me. My body shifts sharply to the left; my head hits the window. I struggle to open my heavy eyelids as a constant car-horn blares. Blinking rapidly, I slowly check my surroundings. I call to Jackson and Kennedy in the front seat with no response. I must focus hard to open my door. I attempt to climb out, but my safety belt restrains me. My shaking hands fumble with the release.

Shit!

I will myself to calm down. I call again to Jackson and Kennedy. I breathe in-and-out a few times to steady myself. After a few moments, I'm now able to unlatch my seatbelt and exit the car.

Standing on wobbly legs outside with an incessant ringing in my ears, I observe a red sports car smashed into the passenger side of the Impala. Taking in the crumpled metal of the cars, my head pounds, and my eyes attempt to focus as I shakily pull open Jackson's door. Broken glass crunches under my flip-flops and the shrieking sound of metal on metal only ends when the door opens all the way.

"Jackson!" I shout.

My shaking hands shoot to my head, hoping to ease the pain. It's then I notice the pain in my lower back. Fear consumes me as bile rises into my mouth. A deflated air-bag dangles from the steering wheel; Jackson's head slumps slightly as his nose and lips bleed.

"Jackson," I call quieter this time. I shake his left arm. "Jackson!" His head snaps up and eyes pop open. "Jackson, are you okay?" I cry hysterically.

"Fuck!" Jackson yells, taking in the entire scene. His head whips to me. "Are you okay?" as he inquires, he unlatches his belt and rises from the driver's seat.

"My head hurts, but the twins and I are okay," I answer. "I can't get Kennedy to answer me. I called to the two of you as I got out of the backseat." My trembling hands caress my abdomen protectively as I speak, my back-pain eases, and my head continues to pound.

"Let's walk over to that hill and sit you down. We need to get you out of the street," Jackson states. He places his left hand on the small of my back. Instantly, he pulls his arm away. "Shit!" Inspecting his wrist, he claims, "I think it's broken."

"I'll walk myself to the hill and sit while you pull Kennedy from the wreckage," I inform him.

The world moves in slow motion as I watch Jackson round the front of the Impala. I feel I'm walking through a movie and not my real life. The hood is bent inward from the passenger side. With the crumpled metal of the red car attached to ours, Jackson must walk around it, too. He pulls the other driver's head off the horn, leaning him back in his seat.

"Taylor, go sit down in the grass!" Jackson shouts at me. I jolt from my frozen stance and nod, turning toward the grass, my lower back pain returning.

I take two steps.

Crap!

I'm peeing. Stupid maternity bladder.

I spin toward Jackson; he is yelling at Kennedy. The red car is still connected to the passenger door of our car. A gut-wrenching scream punctures the scene. Jackson's eyes dart to me. It's me; I'm screaming. The other driver stirs. Jackson attempts to calm him, while trying to arouse Kennedy. Sirens approach. I turn towards their sound, frantically waving my arms.

Two police cars followed by an ambulance park. First-responders scramble toward the wreckage, shouting orders as broken glass shards shatter further beneath their steps. A medic asks if I was involved in the accident. He dabs at my bleeding scalp, while waving his partner in my direction.

"I'm fine, please go help my friends. We can't get to Kennedy, and she won't wake up."

He refuses, stating the officers are there.

In a voice that resembles a demon, I shout, "Leave me alone! She needs you. The other driver needs you. I'm standing, walking, and fine, other than I wet myself."

The EMT examines my legs. "The fluid is still trickling. I believe her water broke," he announces to his partner. "Mam, we need to help you onto the gurney; you are in labor."

The two men lower the bed, lock the wheels, and help lay me upon it. I listen as the tall blonde-haired, blue-eyed EMT radios for a second ambulance to the scene. To distract myself from the pain, I take in his navy T-shirt with the EMT emblem on the left chest and a stethoscope draped around his neck.

My hands tremble as they secure the railings and move me toward the ambulance.

"I need to tell Jackson. He needs to know. I can't leave without him," I cry.

Worried I might become hysterical, they agree to fetch Jackson for me prior to loading me into the ambulance. As the dark-haired medic, wearing blue latex gloves, takes and records my vitals, I watch the blonde approach the twisted metal to address Jackson.

I observe as a firetruck arrives and the firefighters help extricate the other driver before they work to remove Kennedy. Hate for the other driver seeps through me. He hurt my friends, ruined our night, and caused the pain in my head and back.

Even from this distance, I sense Jackson's turmoil in choosing whether to stay with his wife or come check on me and his children. I quietly chant, "please choose me, please choose me." Panic and fear overwhelm me as I realize I'm in labor; the twins will arrive soon. The thought of experiencing labor and delivery on my own physically makes me sick. As I heave, the dark-haired EMT quickly retrieves a basin for me.

Jackson's hand securely tugs my hair back while I vomit. "Easy, easy, I'm here. It's all good." Wiping my mouth, I notice he still holds his left wrist gently to his chest.

"He has a broken wrist. Please help him," I beg of the EMT.

He surveys Jackson, asks questions, and examines his wrist tenderly.

"She may be correct," the medic asserts. "You should ride with us to the hospital. We can get your wrist fixed in time to help her through labor."

"Labor?" Jackson pales. "You're in labor?"

The EMT explains my current situation to Jackson. "You can ride with us to the hospital, and your other friend will follow in the next ambulance," he suggests to Jackson.

Jackson looks over his shoulder at the same moment that what I assume is the jaws-of-life, pries the passenger side open to extricate Kennedy. The blonde medic returns and the two waste no time in loading me into the ambulance, then encourage Jackson to climb in. Jackson looks to Kennedy, then to me, to Kennedy, then back to me. He climbs inside, the doors close, and we are on our way to the hospital. The birth of the twins becomes more real with each passing minute.

"My head hurts," I mention to the EMT. "My back hurts, too." I take a mental inventory of my body from head-to-toe.

"I will inform the staff at the hospital. I will let them decide if meds are needed." He stops documenting on my chart, looking me in the eye. "I don't want to give you anything that will change the treatment the obstetrician plans for you." He pats my shoulder. "Hang on for five minutes. We're getting closer."

74

HEARTRATES DROP

Taylor

At the hospital, Jackson is escorted in one direction while I am wheeled onto the elevator toward the obstetrics ward. *Alone again. I cannot deliver these twins alone.* When I ask where they took Jackson, I am assured he will join me as soon as he can.

Nurses escort me into a labor room, one asks me questions, as another prepares the bed and room for me, while a third lays out a pad and gown for me. They scurry about quickly this way and that, I stand stone-still, scared of the impending delivery and pain.

"I'm Taylor Taft, my physician is Dr. Harrison at North Kansas City Hospital. I'm carrying twins, and my induction is scheduled for tomorrow." I rattle off my answers to her questions. This nurse adds the ambulance notes to my file, while I am helped into my hospital gown, and assisted onto the large pad on my new bed.

Fuck! Fuck! Fuck!

I gave my real name and not Kennedy's. Dr. Harrison has my records under Kennedy Hayes. Pain sears through my lower back interrupting my thoughts. *Make it stop.* I attempt to focus on my shallow breaths to distract from the pain radiating under me.

"A contraction?" Nurse Adams, according to her name badge, questions.

"My back," I moan as I slide my hand to my lower back.

"Concentrate on your breathing. This is back labor, it will pass. Breathe." Nurse Adams pats my exposed arm. I scan her large frame, noticing her curly, black hair is gorgeous and perfect for her long face.

When the back-pain eases, I realize only Nurse Adams remains in the room. She secures fetal monitors to my abdomen. As she adjusts the sensors, I hear the wispy, thump-thump of a baby's rapidly beating heart. A few adjustments on the other sensor and now two hearts are beating. It sounds like a steady drum rhythm; their sounds calm me.

A new short, stout, red-haired nurse peeks her head through the door, "Taylor?"

"That's me." I confirm.

"I am Nurse Johnson, and I'm told Jackson is on his way up from the ER." Her sweet smile conveys all is well as she joins Nurse Adams.

Soon I will not be alone.

The nurses hover. My vitals are taken, they use a test strip to ensure amniotic fluid is indeed leaking. Then, I am informed Dr. Harding is on duty and will be in soon. Nurse Adams exits while Nurse Johnson remains with me.

Suddenly, my door swings wide open and a female doctor enters. This sandy-haired, athletically built, tall woman couldn't be more than thirty-years-old. If she weren't confidently wearing the white doctor's coat, I would have questioned her.

"Taylor, look what I found in the hallway," the doctor teases, swinging an arm toward Jackson then laughs. "I am Dr. Harding. We failed to reach Dr. Harrison, so I will fill in until we do." She tugs on the requisite blue plastic gloves. Next, she encourages me to slide to the end of the bed and place my feet in the stirrups. I sigh deeply then awkwardly attempt to slide and scoot my whale-sized body down to follow her requests.

Jackson moves to my left side, taking my hand in his. He kisses my forehead, keeping eyes on the doctor and her assessment. His left wrist is wrapped.

"Is it broken?" I ask the last word ending in a grimace.

"Sorry," Dr. Magnussen says. "Just checking for dilation."

Jackson squeezes my hand while attempting to smile supportively to me. "Just a sprain," he says.

The doctor pats my knees, encouraging me to scoot back up the bed and get comfortable. Nurse Johnson makes notes on my chart, as the doctor explains I am four centimeters dilated. At the knowledge that my contractions should start soon, I begin worrying even more about the pain. *I can't even rip bandages off because the glue hurts the skin as it rips away. How will I ever endure the pain heading my way now?*

Jackson's eyes dart quickly to mine. I understand his stress of needing to be with both Kennedy and me at the hospital. But this look is different.

Whispering in my ear he states, "You used your own name."

I turn my head, looking into his eyes, "It's okay. She is downstairs and I'm here. It needs to be this way." Jackson nods.

When we are alone, I explain. "At the ambulance, I wasn't thinking. I gave them my name, so now I need to use it." As he rubs my arm, I continue, "We can't both use the same name and insurance in the same hospital. It wouldn't work. I'm sorry. I know this will be expensive. I'll help pay the hospital bills," I offer.

Jackson shakes his head. I know he won't allow me to help financially. They will have tens of thousands of dollars in hospital bills now. *Life is so unfair.*

Jackson's words intrude on my spiraling thoughts. "Car insurance will be responsible since it was a car accident."

A large weight lifts from my chest. It's a tiny bright side to this tragic night.

The nurses and Dr. Harding return, scurrying around me again. As I glance at the wall clock reading it is now 10:15.

"I'm sorry I didn't grab your hospital bag from the car," Jackson apologizes.

In all the commotion, I don't blame him.

All heads turn to the monitor when the heartbeats begin to slow. Dr. Harding rattles off orders to the nurses around the room. I pull my attention from Jackson to the doctor.

"Taylor, the babies' heart rates are dropping. They are in distress; we need to deliver now. We will start prepping you for a C-section." Dr. Harding speaks as if this is an everyday occurrence.

Nurse Adams announces, "Jackson, there's a call at the nurse's station about your friend also in the accident, then we will prepare you for the surgery." Jackson kisses my cheek and immediately leaves.

75

DARKNESS SETTLES IN

Taylor

"The babies?" I cannot even form a sentence; fear clogs my throat. Tears well in my eyes as sharp pain forms in my lower back. I cringe, moving my hands to massage the area.

"The babies need us to hurry, this happens sometimes. We move quick and the three of you'll be just fine. You are experiencing back labor. The pain comes and goes, right?" Dr. Harding inquires.

I nod yes. *I'm scared*. Dr. Harrison discussed the possibility of C-section with us at more than one appointment. I thought the fact I carried the twins full-term meant we were out of the woods. I told myself the twins were perfect, and my pregnancy was perfect.

Nurses scurry here and there. An IV starts and my chart updates. An anesthesiologist enters to discuss my medical history and explain the spinal I'll receive in the operating room. A nurse with razor and a tub of water in hand prepares to shave the surgical area. She smiles at me and claims my continued waxing made her task very easy. I attempt to smile through my panic.

"Easy now," Nurse Adams coos, rubbing my forearm. "We need

mom to remain calm so the babies remain calm." *Like I can flip a switch and turn my stress off.* "Deep breaths in then out. Relax yourself." A whimper escapes as tears increase. "We perform C-sections many times a day, you have nothing to worry about."

"The babies heart rate dropped. They might…" I cannot speak the horror I imagine in my mind.

"Yes, they dropped, but we can still monitor them. We are concerned, but everyone is okay." She attempts to calm me with information. "A calm mom will help us get you and the twins through this."

"I need Jackson," I announce. "I can't do this without him. Where is he?" Nurse Adams exits to check on the twins' father. I lie, staring at the door, willing him to return.

Moments pass and still with no Jackson. Dr. Harding enters and announces they will move me to the OR now. I begin to freak out.

Jackson!

I need Jackson.

We can't go to surgery without him. I cannot deal without him. He is my rock. I can't face the dangers in the operating room alone.

Nurse Adams and Johnson flank my bed as I'm pushed through the ward into a hall towards an elevator.

I will not get in the elevator without him. I can't!

"Jackson, we can't go without Jackson!" I yell. My head turns to each nurse, pleading they understand and take me to Jackson first.

As the elevator doors close, I feel I am being buried alive. I can't breathe. I clasp my chest. My eyes plead for help, for Jackson, for breath.

"Taylor, we need you to calm down," A male nurse I hadn't noticed near the foot of my bed encourages. Sensing my extreme panic, he yells at me. "Taylor! You need to take long deep breaths! The babies need you!" Now having my attention, he calms his voice. "Jackson will meet us at the OR. You need to focus on your breathing and the twins. Can you do that for us?"

"You promise Jackson will meet us?" I ask.

When all three nurses nod yes, I attempt to slow my breathing. I close my eyes and think of Jackson and Kennedy holding the twins later tonight. I attempt to count to three with each breath. I find I can only hold them for a two-count. I think of Nya in my lap, licking my face. *In one, two; out one, two.* I imagine the twins in their bassinets napping at home. *In one, two; out one, two.* I think of Jackson and Kennedy with all their friends, welcoming the twins home. *In one, two; out one, two.*

"About time you got here."

I open my eyes to Jackson, dressed in scrubs and a hairnet. I would have laughed at the sight if I didn't have to see the anguish written all over his face.

"You made it," I greet. "Are you ready for this?" I extend my hand, seeking his for comfort.

Jackson smiles a genuine smile. "The real question is, are you ready for this?" He takes my hand, raises it to his mouth, and kisses my knuckles as we are escorted into the surgical area.

The team moves quickly around as Jackson stands at my head looking down at me. "Kennedy?" I ask.

"They are still working with her. I had to give her history to a nurse. They suspect internal bleeding, and they need to operate." He attempts to smile.

I see through his armor. Her injuries are worse than he's telling me. I see the tears, attempting to build in his exhausted eyes. He's trying to be there for both of us. He's torn between the two women that need him most.

"Let's deliver these twins, so you can go share the good news with her." I try to calm his nerves.

As instructed, Jackson stands in front of me, as I sit, holding both my hands as they perform the spinal tap in my back. I whimper but do not move at the poke of the needle. *I'm such a wimp when it comes to pain.* When I'm instructed to carefully lie back down, I can't move.

"I can't, my body won't move." I don't try to hide this panic.

"That was fast," the anesthetist says, as the team lays me down and positions my arms straight out on the boards to the sides. A screen of material is draped up from my neck. Jackson is given a stool to sit at the left side of my head.

"I can't believe you whimpered and you're taking the wimpy way out with a C-section," he teases.

I prepare to inform him of all I endured in the last nine months, but the team begins talking and I understand the procedure begins.

"Taylor, do you feel this?" I reply no to all the prompts.

I relax knowing I am good and numb.

"You will feel some pressure," Doctor Harding states, placing the scalpel and beginning.

I look at Jackson. He stares admiringly at me. Moments pass, a nurse asks if Jackson would like to watch. He shakes his head no.

"Yes, he does," I firmly correct, and they lower one side of the drape.

"You need to see this miracle," I say, looking him in his brown eyes.

I watch the emotions flood his face. He pales and when he draws his hand to his mouth, I wonder if it is in ah or to hold back vomit. He has a very weak stomach for blood and needles.

"You okay, dad?" I ask, stifling my need to giggle.

He smiles at me quickly before looking back at my mid-section.

I listen for any words or sounds to clue me in on what is happening. I feel slight tugging and shifting occasionally. A cry slices into the almost silent room. I breathe a deep sigh. *One twin is out and crying. One more to go.*

"Which..." I start to ask.

Jackson interrupts me, "A boy." He can't pull his eyes from the baby.

A big brother. Every girl needs a big brother to protect her. Another cry jars my thoughts.

"A girl," Jackson states before I can ask.

I watch as Jackson looks to one baby then the other. Back and forth like watching a tennis match. I smile. I am pleased I successfully delivered these healthy gifts to Jackson and Kennedy.

Suddenly, I feel light headed.

"Taylor?" A male voice calls from far away. "Taylor!"

I close my eyes.

I feel so weak.

Darkness overtakes me.

76

MY WORK HERE IS DONE

Taylor

"Welcome back," a male nurse greets as I struggle to open my heavy eyes.

I take in my surroundings. The wall at the foot of the bed contains clipboards and a gigantic clock, signaling it is 1:00 a.m. Two occupied beds line the wall to my right. On my left, a tall, thin brown-haired nurse holds my wrist, taking my pulse. His dark-rimmed glasses add character to his lightly freckled face. "You're in recovery. Dr. Harding and your handsome man accompanied the twins to the nursery." His name tag informs his name is Reggie.

"Healthy?" My dry voice rasps.

"Very healthy. They have an impressive set of lungs on them. Their loud cries sang to us as they rolled toward the nursery," Nurse Reggie smiles.

I attempt to itch my nose. My arms won't move. I attempt to lift my head, but nothing seems to work.

"The spinal will wear off slowly. What do you need?" he asks.

I explain my cheeks and nose itch. He uses a cool, damp cloth to wash my entire face. "Nurse Reggie?" I ask.

He shakes my hand even though I can't feel it yet. "I'm Reginald, I prefer Reggie." He shrugs, tilting his head slightly.

"Where did Jackson go?" I ask.

"He is with the twins in the nursery," Reggie assures me. "You'll remain in recovery for forty more minutes. Then you'll join the rest of your family."

My family. Not really.

I'm their friend, but they are a family.

A family of four.

My work here is done.

As soon as I recover, I will need to find a place of my own. *I'm a mother that is not a mother.* I get to be the aunt in name only. My thoughts are interrupted as Dr. Harding approaches.

"I tucked away the twins in the nursery with dad watching over them protectively," she reports, a wide smile upon her face. "Your son weighed seven pounds and your daughter weighed six pounds, two ounces." She pats my arm; I observe rather than feel it. "You did good, mom. They are the biggest twins we have delivered at this hospital since I've been here. You gave us a bit of a scare in the OR, your vitals dropped, and you passed out. We quickly closed you up, and your vitals came back up. How do you feel?"

"Lonely," I answer.

The doctor and Nurse Reggie laugh.

"We will get you to your family as soon as we can. Let Reggie know if you need anything or feel anything weird." She looks at my chart and informs me about thirty-five minutes more in recovery.

"My face really itches," I state.

In my attempt to itch, this time my hand flinches a bit, but I still can't lift it.

"I will send in the anesthetist," Dr. Harding informs as Nurse Reggie wipes my entire face again with the cloth.

They walk away, exchanging words I cannot hear.

I concentrate on wiggling my toes and twitching my fingers. I can now bend my arm. My movements are heavy and sluggish, but I have regained motion. I itch my nose with the back of my hand, then scratch my cheeks.

Nurse Reggie returns to my side as the anesthetist arrives. After I show my ability to move my extremities, I am told my face is breaking out with hives. *That explains my itching.* I am apparently allergic to a medication in the spinal, so they order a shot to counteract the reaction. The anesthetist claims he will check in later tonight before waving goodbye. Next to me, Nurse Reggie inputs orders on his tablet.

I stare straight ahead at the clock, willing the hands to move faster.

I need to see Jackson; I need to see the babies.

My shot arrives. I'm thankful when it enters through the IV instead of inflicting the pain into my hip. Moments later, my itching lessens. Thank goodness I no longer want to rip the skin and nose off my face.

If my calculations are right, I am in the last five minutes of my imprisonment, referred to as recovery. Nurse Reggie is on the phone at a desk area. The other two beds were now empty. I am alone. No TV. No music. These forty minutes have been pure torture. *Why wasn't Jackson here to keep me company?* If I had my phone or iPad, I could read.

Three minutes.

Get off the phone Reggie. You need to help me escape soon.

Get off the phone.

A timer signals. Reggie silences it as he ends his call.

"Time's up," He cheers my way.

Finally.

I hope he pushes me fast to OB.

But he picks up a phone again.

Crap!

I can't wheel myself out of here in the bed.

Nurse Reggie, you are killing me.

He quickly hangs up and approaches. "OB nurses are on their way to fetch you."

I thank him and train my eyes on the door.

"Yay!" escapes as two nurses enter.

They smile knowingly at me. Reggie places my chart near my legs and wishes me luck.

"You have the most adorable twins," the curly-haired Nurse

Adams informs me. "They cried all the way to the nursery, but when we picked them up to weigh them, they stopped."

"Not a peep from them since," the shorter Nurse Johnson claims. "They are so big, and you are so little. Did you have a rough pregnancy?"

As they push me toward the goal, I quickly answer her question. I am a bit calmer this elevator ride than the previous.

I need to see the twins. I feel a pain in my chest aching for them. Anticipation builds with every florescent light we pass in the hallway.

"I haven't been able to see the babies yet. Is that normal?" I ask.

"No," Nurse Johnson answers, baffled.

"It is my understanding you had complications at the end of the surgery," Nurse Adams states. "Perhaps that is why you weren't given the opportunity. We will hurry to settle you in a room and introduce you to your twins."

As we slightly turn left to enter the OB ward, Jackson exits the doors urgent in his walk. He freezes at seeing me. He stands in his street clothes, holding the door open. Concern floods my body.

Where was he headed?

What is wrong?

Kennedy?

I completely forgot about her surgery. I lay selfishly in recovery. *I should have asked Reggie for an update on her condition.*

"How is Kennedy?" I ask as the nurses wheel me toward my room with Jackson beside me.

His face tells me all I need to know.

"I've been called down to see her," he admits. "They wouldn't give me an update over the phone." He rings his hands, then runs them through his hair as I am lifted into my new bed.

"Go then," I order. "Go tell her about the twins. Find out when she can come see us. Then hurry back to me."

The thought of spending more time alone in bed does not thrill me. I know he needs to be with his wife, too. I am sure Kennedy is scared and going crazy with worry about her twins.

"Jackson, I am fine. Go." I hope my tone masks my lies.

He nods and exits my room. Sobs escape as my body shakes. In his absence, I cannot hide my fear.

"Last I heard," Nurse Johnson explains. "Your friend went to surgery to stop the internal bleeding." Looking at her watch, she continues, "That was over an hour ago."

Glancing at the large clock on the wall, I see it is 1:55.

"Jackson spreads himself thin between the twins and going down to your friend. He wants to be in two places at once," Nurse Adams shares.

I take in my room as they take my vitals, update my chart, and settle me in. In my shock of the accident and impending labor, I didn't look around the last time I was in here. They cover the walls in a soft apricot color. They mounted a TV in the far-left corner of the room. The bathroom door is open. I see another door inside there, too. They built shelves into the wall straight in front of me. I see a closet-like door at the end of them. I have a set of drawers to my left and the typical over-the-bed rolling table on the right. A small sofa bench is built in under the window and a chair is in the right corner near the head of my bed. *I better like it. This will be my room for a couple of days.*

Nurse Johnson leaves the room. I ask Nurse Adams to hand me my cellphone. My lock screen reads it's 2:00 a.m. on May Fifth. I quickly send a text before I can talk myself out of it.

> ME
>
> I need you
>
> I had a baby
>
> Please come to Liberty Hospital at 7pm tonight
>
> & If possible can you help me for a week or 2?

77

MY BABIES BUT YOUR BOOBS

Taylor

Nurse Adams pushes buttons on my IV pump. "Do you have names picked out for your twins?" she asks, making small talk.

I simply nod yes. I don't want to divulge the names in case Kennedy or Jackson have changed their minds.

Tears over take me; I can't blame these on hormones. My time in the cozy family of three has come to an end. After months of company, I'm alone again. Although Kennedy and I struggled during the pregnancy, Jackson and I grew very close. I will miss our short evening walks, trips to sneak fast food, as well as times watching football games and ESPN. I hiccup.

"Look who I have," Nurse Johnson announces. "Time to meet mommy." She wheels a bassinet in front and another behind her. My eyes take in the soft blue and pale pink hats. She parks the beds to the side and turns to me. "Are you ready to hold your twins?"

I should say no. Kennedy and Jackson should hold them before I do. It's not my place, but I cannot fight the overwhelming need to cuddle them to my chest. I nod.

"Little man, here is your mommy." She places the tiny bundle in the crook of my right arm. His small face is bright red as his fist nears his mouth and he sucks. Something washes over me from head to toe. "Little princess, here is your mommy." She places the slightly smaller bundle in my left arm.

As I stare at the pair of perfect angels, I hear the familiar sound of a camera shutter. I look up to find Nurse Adams snapping pictures with her cellphone. "I'll text you the pics. I couldn't let you miss saving this moment for eternity."

I look back at the bundles of joy wiggling in my arms. They're sucking on fist and thumb.

"I think they are ready if you would like to nurse," Nurse Adams says as she opens her tablet. "Were you planning on formula or nursing? I don't see it on your chart."

Nurse Johnson reminds her we were the car accident that started labor, and this wasn't our planned hospital. Four eyes look to me for an answer. The problem is, I don't know the answer. I can't answer. Kennedy is still undecided. She claimed she wanted formula, so I could get back to my life sooner and they could feed the twins. Jackson and I had lobbied for nursing, explaining the health benefits and that with pumping, they could still feed the twins.

"If you are unsure, you could nurse now and switch to formula," the nurses states.

An overwhelming desire floods through me. "I want to try nursing," I reply.

The nurses run through the procedures, common positions to hold, and some of the first-time complications. They help tuck one baby to the first breast where he quickly latches on. A hiss passes through my lips at the discomfort. I'm assured that will pass with time. I marvel as Baby Boy Hayes nurses as if there is no tomorrow. The nurses move to assist with my other breast. They arrange pillows, then lower the baby. She doesn't latch on as easily. When I'm encouraged to rub her cheek near her lips, I laugh. It seems with twins nursing at the same time, this cannot be accomplished. Nurse Adams shows the rubbing of the cheek to stimulate sucking. It works, and I again hiss as Baby Girl Hayes nurses.

I look from one baby to the other. I'm in heaven. Two tiny babies are feeding in my arms. As I gaze in wonder, I do not witness Jackson slipping into the room and around the curtain. When the nurses excuse themselves, promising to return in ten minutes, I glance up. My eyes find Jackson's.

"I'm so sorry," I stammer. "They were hungry, the nurses needed an answer, and I..."

"It's perfect," Jackson assures me. He moves to sit on the bed near me. He reaches to caress one baby cheek, then moves to the other. "They are too perfect."

I tear my eyes from the twins to find Jackson beaming at his children. Not wanting to ruin this tender moment, I struggle with wanting to ask about Kennedy, or waiting. Moments pass as we listen and giggle at the rooting sounds Baby Boy Hayes makes as he chows down. Baby Girl Hayes seems to have fallen asleep. I now struggle with the fact my hands are under two babies, and I can't move. I feel I should assist with removing her from my breast and burp her, but I can't.

"Jackson," I interrupt the moment. "Can you fetch a nurse? I need help."

His eyes dart to mine. "I can help. What do you need?"

I purse my lips to the side, debating his offer of help. "I think I need to remove her and burp her." He looks to his daughter, still latched to my breast, then right back at me.

He quickly presses the page-a-nurse button on my bedrail, blushing. He turns away from the three of us.

"Should I burp her now?" I ask when the nurse arrives.

Nurse Adams shows me how carefully inserting a finger between my nipple and the baby's lips eases her off and calls for Jackson to come burp his daughter. He turns around, witnesses my exposed breast and darts to the nurse's side to take his daughter. She instructs him on proper burping methods, then turns back to me to remove the still nursing baby boy. Jackson keeps his back to me as he coos to his daughter while patting her back. I'm instructed to rub the lanolin ointment on my nipples to prevent chapping, then cover back up before burping Baby Boy Hayes. Nurse Adams shuts off the call light, then leaves us alone again.

"Jackson," I call, but he doesn't turn around. "The coast is clear. I'm all covered up," I inform him.

Now he turns around.

"You don't have to turn away. These are your babies."

"They may be my babies, but those are your boobs," he counters.

"I can't feed them both without another set of arms. Until Kennedy gets to come up here, I need you to help me." The reaction on his face alerts me something is wrong. "Tell me," I demand.

"Kennedy is in surgery," he states before elaborating, his eyes on his daughter. "This is her second surgery. They thought they stopped the bleeding after the first surgery." He moves his daughter from one arm to the other. "Complications arose, and she is back in surgery. Therefore I was called back downstairs as you moved to recovery."

"Jackson, I'm so sorry." My words are not enough, and I know it. "You should go to her. She needs you. We are safe, fed, and will probably sleep for the next hour or two. Go to her." I reach my free arm towards him.

"They promised to call the minute she is out of surgery. The nurses' desk will come get me then." He steps towards my bed. "I need to be here with the three of you now. I can't do anything but sit in the surgical waiting room down there."

He gently hands me his daughter, then scoops up his son from my arms. Proud papa beams at his son. I sense he isn't telling me everything, but I don't pry. He needs the babies to occupy his thoughts as he waits. I will grant him this.

78

A QUEEN

Taylor

Nurse Johnson peeks her head in after knocking. "Sorry to interrupt," she approaches my bedside. She quickly records my vitals. "Your IV will beep soon. Page us and we will change it out." Smiling at Jackson, then to me, she clutches her chest. "Too precious. Need anything?"

"I'm starving," I confess. "We wrecked on the way to dinner, then with the birth of the twins... I didn't eat."

I look at the wall clock noting it is 3:15. *I should be asleep instead of ordering dinner.*

"I'll put in an order for two meals," Nurse Johnson promises as she leaves.

"I'm not hungry," Jackson states.

"You'll need your strength to hold your twins all day," she reminds him.

"I just can't get enough of them," Jackson confesses, sitting beside me. "How will I ever get anything done at home?"

"Oh, you'll get plenty done," I inform him. "There will be baby laundry, changing dirty diapers, and midnight feedings."

"With you nursing, I won't have to worry about the nighttime feedings," Jackson argues.

"Someone needs to carry the twins downstairs and wake me," I claim. "C-section, remember? Stairs will be a challenge for a couple of weeks."

Is this why Kennedy decided on formula? With the nursery across from the main suite upstairs and my room downstairs, nursing doesn't make much sense.

"Speaking of diapers," Jackson teases. "When and how do we change theirs?" He looks at me as if I have all the answers.

"Let's ask the nurse when dinner arrives," I answer, causing him to laugh out loud.

This startles Baby Boy Hayes and he cries. Jackson coos as he pulls him tighter to his chest and rocks from side-to-side. It amazes me how easily being a dad comes to him. *He's a natural.*

Moments pass as we take turns holding each baby. When our food arrives, my plate contains dry toast, crackers, a banana, and Jell-O. They deliver chicken strips and French fries to Jackson. When I offer to trade him, the nurse informs me I am on a modified diet because of my surgery. Tomorrow, my meals will improve. I accept my pre-approved meal and nibble.

"Let me hold the twins while you eat," Jackson offers.

"I need the babies in the nursery for a few tests and a fresh diaper," Nurse Adams informs. "I'll bring them back as soon as we finish," she promises, assisting Jackson in placing them in the beds and wheeling them out the door.

"I should go watch through the window," Jackson strides towards the door.

"Please, stay and eat with me," I beg. "I hate being alone in the hospital. The recovery room was excruciating. You need to eat, so stay and eat with me. Please."

Jackson returns to his chair and eats. With each bite, he moans or comments on how delicious his meal it. "How's your dinner?" he teases. He even waves French fries in front of my face.

"Cruel. I gave you two healthy, rather large babies, and you return the favor by making me miserable," I tease back.

I want nothing more than to steal a fry or chicken strip. But I vow to be a good patient, so I can break out of here as soon as possible.

I attempt to adjust myself on the pillows, wincing at the pain in my abdomen. Jackson hops to my side, assisting in positioning the pillows behind my head. I wiggle slightly, trying to adjust my hips and legs into a more comfortable position. I hide my pain from Jackson. *He has enough on his mind, worrying about Kennedy.*

I use the remote to find something to watch on TV. Jackson pushes the page-a-nurse button without my noticing. Nurse Adams returns. As she places our trays near the sink, she asks how many French fries I ate.

"I didn't eat any," I state.

Looking at me, she tilts her head to the side, trying to assess my honesty. "Why is ketchup on your gown?" she inquires.

I look down, then point to Jackson. "He teased my by waving fries in front of my face," I explain.

Hands on her hips, feet wide apart, she lectures Jackson. "You must treat the mother of your twins like a queen instead of tormenting her."

I enjoy listening and watching him blush immensely.

She turns off the call light. "Need anything?" she inquires.

"She's in pain," Jackson states.

I turn to him, realizing I didn't hide it as well as I thought. While carrying the trays out, she states she will return with pain meds.

"You weren't going to admit you were in pain, were you?" Jackson asks knowingly.

"I'm a wimp. I figured I was overreacting to the pain," I confess.

Jackson shakes his head at me. He rats me out to the nurse when she returns with pain meds and a water pitcher.

"You need to tell us of every ache and pain," she scolds. "We will decide if it's time to medicate or not. Remember, a happy, healthy mom will keep the babies happy and healthy."

Again, with the baby guilt. I feel they use the twins to get me to behave way too much in this facility. *It works, though. I will do anything to help the twins, just as I will do anything for their parents.*

"The twins will be back in a minute, and you should try to get some sleep," she urges as she changes out my IV bag.

"Jackson," I whisper after she leaves. "How I am supposed to sleep. I can't roll over. They take my vitals every hour, I hurt, the twins are too cute to put down, and I need to know Kennedy is out of surgery."

"The twins can sleep in their beds near mine. I will check on Kennedy and you throughout the night. You better follow the nurse's orders and rest, or they will withhold the French fries tomorrow," he chuckles.

"I will try to sleep, if you promise to wake me to fill me in on Kennedy's condition, when you return," I offer.

The pain meds help whisk me quickly to sleep.

As I wake, my eyes focus on the clock. *It's 4:30.* I glance around the room. I see no Jackson, and I see no twins. As panic sets in, I page the nurse.

"May I go for a walk?" I ask.

"Your catheter will be removed later this morning, then you can start walking in the hallways," she states.

"I'm going crazy lying around so much. I really need out of this bed," I beg.

"Now is the time to rest. When you go home with the twins, you won't have as many helping hands," she reminds me.

I understand. I don't like it, but I acquiesce.

"Jackson is down with Kennedy; he left about thirty minutes ago. The twins are sound asleep in the nursery, and you need sleep, too," she informs me as she leaves, dimming the lights again.

The next time I awake, I find I'm still alone, my pain has returned, and it is now 5:00. Before I press to page a nurse, she appears at my door.

"Good, you're awake. It's time for you to nurse and take a pain pill."

"I was just about to page you for one," I admit as I try to sit up.

"Wait," Nurse Adams orders as she quickly uses the controls on the side of the bed to adjust the incline to a sitting position.

It hurts, and I groan as I adjust my hips and bottom.

"You need to take it easy. Your stomach muscles will take months to strengthen again."

She pushes the pill cup in front of me, then my glass of water. Being the good little patient I am, I comply.

"Would you happen to know where Jackson is?" I ask, afraid of her answer.

"He's standing at the nursery window watching the twins sleep," she smiles. It's clear she thinks this is sweet.

"The twins should eat soon. Would you like me to bring them in?" she asks.

I nod. She records my vitals in my chart before leaving.

79

UP CLOSE AND PERSONAL WITH MY BREAST

Jackson
At the Same Time Near the Nursery

I stand, peeking through nursery windows, watching the nurses flitter from one infant to another. My twins sleep side-by-side, soundly near the window. *Taylor thinks I'm still with Kennedy.*

A nurse approaches my side.

"Jackson, a gentleman approached the front desk requesting to visit with you or Taylor."

"Where is he now?" I ask, scanning the area. "Who is he?"

"His name is Howard Buchanan. He is still at the front entrance," the nurse informs.

"Can he come to me, or must I go to him?" I question, running my hands through my hair, worrying it might be the neighbors coming to visit.

"If you agree to see him, I can have them buzz him back," she offers.

I stare at my babies while I wait for Howard Buchanan to arrive.

"Twins?" a deep male voice asks.

I nod, not taking my eyes off my perfect little daughter and son to take in the stranger beside me.

"I regret contacting you with all you are going through, but I needed to see you. I needed you to know."

I face him as he continues.

"I cannot apologize enough for what my son did to your family. My son, David, was the other driver," he explains.

Heat floods my body and bile climbs my throat.

"I'm told you assisted him on site, then directed the medics to assist him. Thank you for that." I can see the inner turmoil he battles. "I will not make excuses for his actions last night. I've attempted to reach him for years. Last night was the final straw. I've contacted my lawyer."

I'm not sure what to say or feel. *His son, the drunk driver, ruined our night. He ruined our lives. Kennedy may not make it. He may have ended my marriage and left my twins without their mother. The man in front of me is not to blame; he didn't cause my pain.*

"I will draw up paper work to convert David's trust fund into two funds for your twins," he announces, matter-of-factly. He speaks of this money as if it will not burden him to give it up. "Maybe this will be drastic enough to change my son's destructive behaviors. Of course, his auto insurance will cover hospital expenses for your entire family." He looks back at my twins, a smile on his face. "Hopefully, you will allow me to set up the trust funds to protect the future of your twins. A small token from my family to yours."

With that, he passes me a business card. "I hope you will contact me when your family returns home." He shifts his weight from one foot to the other. "I remember taking David home from the hospital for the first time. His whole life was in front of him. Where did it all go so wrong?"

His conversation jumps again. "Might I ask for your contact information?" I pull my work card from my wallet and share it.

Howard thanks me, shakes my hand, and promises to be in touch in a couple of weeks. I stare in disbelief as he leaves the unit.

The nearby day nurse informs me, "Howard Buchanan is on the hospital board. He is on many boards in the North Kansas City and Liberty area. It's a shame his son is not more like him. My husband is an officer and has mentioned many times how David has been in trouble with the law."

Her unsolicited words validate Howard is truly honest in his intentions.

Trust funds? My twins will have trust funds.

Taylor

Later, Jackson and the nurse wheel the babies into my room. I search his face for any news on Kennedy's status.

"Which one first?" Jackson asks me.

I shrug. I'm not sure it matters. He kisses his son on the forehead before passing him to me.

"I need your help," I state, as the nurse has left, yet again. "Can you place a pillow under my arm?" I remember his apprehension at my bared chest, so I try to ease his discomfort. "Great, now hand me the blanket from his bed." I point as I make the request. I place the extra blanket over my shoulder and his son before I pull down my gown, tickle his plump cheek, and he latches on. The baby's suckling sounds fill the room.

"That was quick," Jackson chuckles. "He has quite an appetite."

I nod. "Please start a stopwatch on your phone to monitor the time for us. Then you can place a pillow under my other arm, hand me a blanket, and pass me the next baby."

When he offers the baby girl to me, I realize I don't have a free hand to help her latch on.

"Jackson, I can't..." *How do I ask this?* "I need another hand." I tilt my head apologetically his way. "I know it makes you uncomfortable, but she needs to nurse, and I can't help her latch on without a hand." I take in Jackson's frozen stature. "If you tickle her cheek to perk her up and help slip her under the blanket, maybe she can latch on by herself."

If not, I fear Jackson will have to get up close and personal with my breast.

It works.

Baby Girl Hayes takes my nipple and quickly starts nursing.

"She isn't as loud as he is when she eats. Already the proper little lady," I tease.

"Why does it hurt?" Jackson asks from the nearby chair. "You wince a bit as they begin."

"The nurses state it takes a while for my nipples to toughen up," I reply, knowing my answer embarrasses him.

"I'm sorry I asked." Jackson says, shaking his head.

"Hey, it's okay," I comfort. "You are their dad. You need to be involved. We were unconventional in their conception. We will have to be unconventional in nursing them, too." I smile his way. "I need your help and don't want you to feel uncomfortable in helping me."

He nods. I know his discomfort is not over, but hopefully it will be easier.

Several silent moments pass. I listen for the nursing babies, trying to ignore the elephant in the room.

"I think they are done." My words puncture the air. "Will you stop the timer for me?" I prompt Jackson as I attempt to find a plan to detach the babies.

"Okay, so I need to place my finger inside the corner of her mouth so she lets go, right?" Jackson hesitantly asks. When I nod, he says, "I will just slip my finger under the blanket." He then does so before continuing. "I will slide down her cheek, and.."

And just like that, he lifts his daughter from under the blanket and I cover myself before I unlatch his son.

Jackson burps his daughter, cooing softly again. "I wish I had a way to burp both at once," He admits, and I chuckle.

When both burp tiny baby burps, I hand Jackson his son. He rocks to-and-fro while talking to both babies. I page my nurse as I take in the love Jackson shares with his twins. The nurse peeks in.

"My face is very itchy again," I inform her.

The nurse asks questions about this while searching my chart. "Here it is. Oh, you had an allergic reaction. I need to page a doctor, but we will get you more meds for that. Hang in there," she says, observing as both my hands itch my cheeks and rub my nose.

80

I WON'T TAKE NO FOR AN ANSWER

Taylor

"For tiny babies, they quickly wear out his arms," Jackson shares, ten minutes later.

"Bring them here. I will hold them to take my mind off my itchiness," I offer.

He relinquishes one to me. "You need a free hand to itch with," he claims.

I'm not naïve. I know he can't bear the thought of not holding at least one of them at all times. The events of the past eight hours hitting him, Jackson sinks into the nearby chair. Both he and his daughter are asleep in said chair when the nurse returns with my allergy medicine.

"Ah," she marvels as she takes in the sight. "Want me to snap a pic?" she whispers.

I nod. She carefully clasps my phone from the table and snaps a couple of pictures for me.

"Perfect."

She shows me the pictures she took on my phone. Then she inserts the medication into my IV and discards the syringe.

I stare at the photo. A teardrop glides down my cheek at the sight. *Indeed, it is perfect.* She slips out after she dims the lights.

I close my eyes, hoping to join Jackson and his twins in sleep, but it alludes me. My mind races to Kennedy and her surgeries. The last time I saw her, she sat lifeless and belted in the car. I'm unsure of her condition now as her twins now wait to meet her. I worry about Jackson, and his worrying about being in two places at once with all of us. *No sleep for me.* I need to ask Jackson for an update. I need to know what he knows. I grab my cellphone from the mattress at my hip.

I'm never going to be able to sleep. I fed the twins, now they sleep, and my pain is managed. The lights, although low, distract me. The sound of nurses and machines are faint but can be heard in my room, and this hospital bed is not comfortable. I want to roll on my side, but with my C-section sutures, I cannot. I flip through the channels available on the mounted television set, finding nothing of interest and turn it off. I randomly scroll through my phone. I pull up the pictures the nurses took of us. I smile as I witness the proud father Jackson instantly morphed into holding the twins.

As I continue scrolling through the photos on my Google Photos App, I find my stages of pregnancy photos I took throughout the surrogacy. I realize I should order the photo book so I can gift it to Kennedy and Jackson. I visit a couple of websites until I find the type of picture book I desire. I upload the photos. I didn't realize I took this many pictures over the last nine months. I glance through my creation two times prior to submitting my final order. I arrange for it to be express shipped to Kennedy's house. It's forecast to arrive in five days. *Perfect. I'll be in here two nights, so we should be home before it arrives. They will be so surprised.*

The alarm on my IV pole wakes Jackson. I press the call button, trying not to laugh at his confusion.

"Can you manage to hold them both?" I ask, and he gladly holds his twins.

The nurse shuts off my alarm before she fetches a new IV. I ask if I can have more pain meds. She checks the chart, nods, and heads out. Jackson looks at the clock to see how long he slept.

"Jackson," I can wait no longer; I won't rest until I know. "How is Kennedy? You haven't updated me."

Jackson looks from baby to baby before looking at me.

"She's out of surgery, in critical condition, and they are monitoring her closely." His soulful, exhausted eyes tell me he's honest.

"Have you told her about the twins? What did she say?" I ask.

Tears.

Tears. He is crying.

Our pillar of strength, our protector, is crying silent tears.

"She has not regained consciousness. Not at the crash site. Not in the ambulance. And not since she arrived at the hospital." Voicing her situation out loud crushes him.

I move to stand, but wince when reminded of my current weakness. Quickly, I page the nurse.

"Can you wheel the twins to the nursery for a bit?" I murmur.

The nurse doesn't ask questions. She simply moves each baby one at a time to a bed, then exits, pulling the door shut on her way through.

"Come here," I command.

Jackson refuses at first, but at my insistence, he sits at my side. I take his hands in mine. I struggle to find words to comfort him; I struggle for words of hope. I pull on his hands, signaling him to come closer. I tug again. This time, he complies. I wrap my arms around him and tuck his head on my shoulder. I can sense him trying to be gentle. He tries not to cause me pain even as he hurts. I hold him, allowing him to let out all that he holds inside.

"I am so sorry, I..." I pause to calm my shaking voice. I need to be strong for him in this moment. "She's a fighter. Don't give up on her. She wants the twins. She will do everything she can to get to be with them."

I believe my words but know medically she can't control the damage she sustained. Her body is weak because of her years of eating disorders. I can only hope and pray that she is strong enough to pull through. I need her to pull through for Jackson, for the twins, and for me. *I need her.*

I rub my hands up and down Jackson's back. "Should I ask the nurses to get us an update?"

Jackson wipes his eyes on my gown.

"No news is good news, right?" *I need to shut up. He doesn't need me to add to his worry. I'm sure he's worried enough about his wife already.*

"They promised to call with any changes," Jackson says.

I can't see how an update would hurt. I press the call button. *I need an update.*

When the nurse appears, I ask, "May I go see Kennedy in a wheelchair? I need to see my friend, to encourage her, to tell her about the twins." I please.

"I don't think you should," she states.

I decide I won't take no for an answer.

"I need to see my best friend. I need to talk to her. She needs to hear my voice. I must tell her about the babies..." Tears adorn my cheeks, my voice shakes, and I struggle to catch my breath. "I need to talk to her one more time. One more time, please." I clear my tears with a disgusted swipe. "Please, help me. I have to see her one more time."

Jackson attempts to soothe me. The nurse tries, too.

The car ride cannot be the last time I see my best friend. Our stupid conversations on the road cannot be our last words to each other. She can't leave me here with her children and her husband. We had a plan. I carried her babies; she is a mother now. They need her; I need her.

"Let me see what I can arrange," the nurse says, grasping my hand.

As she leaves, Jackson moves back to sit on the bed.

"Don't get your hopes up. They're only looking out for your safety, keeping you in bed to recover." He swipes tears from my cheeks with his thumbs, smiling gently. "I can go down and get us an update." He offers.

"Let's see what she finds out first," I counter.

We sit in silence, waiting. Unable to bear it, I turn the TV on for a distraction. I watch as the clock moves from 9:15 to 9:20 to 9:25. With each passing minute, I realize my hope of seeing Kennedy dwindles. Jackson excuses himself to the restroom. I can hear the running water.

I startle at the knock on the door before the nurse reenters. "It took a lot of convincing, but I think it's a go." Her smile reaches from ear-to-ear.

Jackson exits the restroom, finding me clapping. He looks at the nurse, then back at me. I nod to let him know I get to go for a wheelchair ride.

"I need to remove your catheter before you go," the nurse informs.

Jackson excuses himself to check on the twins while the catheter comes out.

"It's not a pleasant procedure, but I'm glad to be rid of it," I state.

"You may think differently when you have to climb from the bed, walk to the restroom, sit, and then stand again before climbing back into bed," the nurse warns.

As cheery as she was to tell me I could go to Kennedy, her comments now seem cruel. I'm in pain, and I know I just had a C-section. I don't need a step-by-step account of my future pains. I mentally attempt to prepare myself for my journey and visit with Kennedy.

81

YOU WERE RIGHT AND I WAS WRONG

Taylor

Kennedy's nurse greets us in the hallway, then signals a nearby doctor to join us. They escort us to a private waiting room. As the lights flick on, I see four chairs along the wall, a side table with a lamp, a TV mounted on a far wall, and pamphlets scattered on a coffee-table. I'm wheeled near a chair; they prompt Jackson to sit next to me. The latching of the door sends an ominous chill through my body.

"I am Dr. Peterson," she greets, shaking my hand with no accompanying smile. "Kennedy has not improved since we last spoke." She directs toward Jackson. *Apparently, Jackson had already met this physician.* "Extensive tests show no brain activity." Taking my hand, then Jackson's too, she kneels in front of us. "Kennedy is brain-dead, she is on life support, and will not improve."

"Jackson, I must inquire again. Does Kennedy have any other living relatives?" Dr. Peterson asks.

He shakes his head, and she takes the seat next to him.

"As her spouse, there are hard decisions you must make," she states. "With no living will on file, Jackson, you must decide whether or not to keep Kennedy on life support. As the nurses mentioned to you earlier, if you consider organ donation, Kennedy's passing may assist others and give the gift of life despite this tragedy."

As they continue talking, my mind drifts. *Girl Scout Camp each summer with Kennedy, our sleepovers, our double dates, driving off to college together, her wedding day...*

How will I go on without her?
Who will I call when I need to vent?
Who will I call when I need advice?
Who will I talk to when I need a good cry?
Who will I share my good news with?
How will I live each day with the twins I carried for her?

"Are you ready?" Nurse Jacobs asks from behind my wheelchair.

I cannot speak; I nod. As I am wheeled closer to my best friend, I struggle to accept her fate, our fate. *I should help Jackson make his difficult decision, but I can't.* I am exhausted physically and emotionally. Every breath I take feels like I'm running a marathon.

How can I be this exhausted?

"You will have five minutes," she explains. "If alarms sound, you need to leave the room immediately to allow room for staff to treat Kennedy."

I agree, and Nurse Jacobs wheels me to Kennedy's bedside while she remains in the corner of the room.

Cables, chords, and tubes cover her face, neck, chest, and arms. The wispy sound of the ventilator provides a steady rhythm, joined by beeps of several other monitors. I can see her heartbeats represented by hopping red lines on the monitor.

"Hey Ken," I greet, unsure where to begin. I have so much I want to say. "I had to break a lot of rules to come see you. They tried to keep us apart. I had to inform them no one keeps best friends apart." I force a chuckle. "The twins are strong, healthy, alert, and perfect in every way. You should see Jackson hold them both. He was made to be a dad. They're waiting for you to name them. I'm getting pretty tired of referring to them as baby girl and baby boy. So, you better hurry, wake up, and come visit them." I want to rise from my wheelchair. I long to touch her face and whisper in her ear. But I can't. I can't stand; I can't lean towards her. All I can do is lightly touch her hand.

"Ken, I'm so sorry. You shouldn't be lying here. This is not how it should be. This isn't what we planned. Jackson needs you, the twins need you, and I...I need you. I realize you've been through so much already. I know you are weak. But we need you to fight, and you need to wake up."

My voice is too loud, too bossy, too emotional. I regroup. I squeeze her hand, then continue in a whisper. "You are my best friend, you are my sister, and I will love you forever. I know you want to give up. I know you are weak, tired, and hurting." Pausing, I wipe my eyes, trying to prepare to say goodbye. "I promise to tell the twins all about you, our adventures as children, and your love for their father. I'll try to take care of Jackson for you." I groan. "Ken, this is not what we planned. You weren't supposed to leave us. I wasn't supposed to raise the twins. And..."

A frustrated wail escapes my throat.

"And..." I close my eyes. "I wasn't supposed to fall in love with your husband. I'm so sorry. I hope you know that. I'll do my best for you. I love you and I will miss you always."

I wave my hands frantically to signal to the nurse that I am ready to leave. I'm a blubbering mess. As the nurse pushes me from the room with my eyes closed, I ponder my confession to Kennedy. *I'm not sure where my confession came from.* While spilling my heart to her for the final time...those words and those feelings just spilled out.

I told my best friend I love her husband.

I just told my best friend I am in love with her husband!

When? How?

I'm a horrible best friend.

"I am exhausted," I inform Jackson with a raspy voice, unable to make eye contact. "I will meet you back in my room. Take your time."

I pathetically wave over my right shoulder as the nurse wheels me away.

I hope Jackson will take a long time with Kennedy. I need time to wrap my head around my true feelings, my loss of my best friend, and my betrayal of my best friend. Maybe Jackson needs to stay away until dinner.

I cry. I cry, and I cry, and I cry. I'm a spectacle with my puffy eyes and my blotchy cheeks. This time, it's not from my allergic reaction.

Jackson

I hesitantly approach the head of Kennedy's bed with all the tubes, wires, and monitors. As I settle in the bedside chair, I listen to the steady sound of the respirator and heart monitors. As much as I would like to sit here quietly, I need to press on.

"Ken, I fucked up. I let our conversation distract my driving. I should have recognized that the guy wasn't slowing down at the stoplight. I didn't protect you, and I will pay for that for the rest of my life."

Hot tears stream down my cheeks. I long to be anywhere but here. I want to escape, but I need to do this.

"I wish you could meet the twins. They are all we dreamed of and more. How Taylor carried the two of them inside her still baffles me; they're so big." I sigh deeply as I caress the back of her hand.

"I've been thinking a lot about our fight the other night." I close my eyes and draw in a long breath. "I know I over-reacted when you spilled your heart to me. I think it was a mixture of shock and my own denial. I should have encouraged you to seek what makes you happy. That is all I ever hoped for you. That one day you could not be so hard on yourself and allow yourself to be happy." I chuckle hollowly. "I guess I always assumed it would be with me. I'm glad you found Madison, and I'm sorry that now it has been cut short."

"You were right about Taylor. I know I denied it and blew up at you for suggesting it. You were so right. I was fooling myself. I fought it daily. I told myself she was my sister to explain the pull, the constant draw towards her. I don't have to tell you how magnetic she is. You saw it even better than I did. You begged me to go to her, to tell her how I felt. That thought scared me to death at the time. But now," I sigh, thinking of the last ten hours. "You should have seen her when the twins' heart rates dropped, and she was told she needed a C-section. She was scared but not for her. She was scared for the twins. She looks so natural with them in her arms."

"She hasn't slept much, but she threw all sorts of attitude to break all the rules to come see you. There's no stopping her when she wants something." I laugh at the memory.

"Ken, I love you and I will always love you. I can see now how much you loved me. You laid it all on the line the other night. You told me to get my shit together and open my eyes to what was right in front of me. You were so right. The fact that I understand I love her does not change the way I've always loved you. You were right; we grew apart. You and I were best friends and roommates. We were not a married couple; we never were. I don't regret our time together, please know that. I am so sorry it's gonna end this way. You should be moving on with Madison, not lying here. You don't deserve this."

"I need to make a choice, since you have no one else. I know what you want. I only hope I'm man enough to follow through for you. I can't do it right now, but I promise to try soon. Thank you for chewing my ass out. I love you." With my sleeve, I wipe my face. I squeeze her hand one more time and place a kiss on her forehead before I head for the comfort of my twins.

82

OURS

Taylor

"Taylor's back," Nurse Jacobs announces to the new shift of OB nurses as we enter the ward. She hands me off, pats me on the shoulder, and leaves without a word.

No words could comfort me from the goodbye downstairs.

Upon returning to my room, I'm assisted to the restroom. *I'll never take the ability to use the bathroom for granted again.* Two nurses escort and maneuver me with the precision of a team of Navy SEALs. I painfully rise from the wheelchair to the stool. They even lower my hospital-issued underwear for me. I am allowed the privacy of a closed door, but I'm ordered to call as soon as I am done. The simple task of rising from the stool and reaching for my underwear is painful and brings tears back to my eyes. Unsuccessful, I remain on the stool and call to my nurses. They assist me to rise, pull up my underwear, then stand at the sink, and wash my hands. Back in the wheelchair, the nurses assist me painfully back into my hospital bed. One nurse leaves while the other fusses over my IV tube and blankets.

I'm tucked cozy in my hospital bed, my thoughts on losing

Kennedy forever, when the most welcome sight in the world enters my room. They roll the twins to my bedside. One is crying while the other is sucking her thumb.

"I know you are exhausted, but let's feed the little ones, then you can crash," a new nurse cheerfully offers.

She is tall, like five-foot ten inches tall and skinny, like model skinny. Her curly, long blonde hair secured in a ponytail at the nape of her neck. Her smile, if I weren't physically and mentally spent, would have been contagious. I can tell she is as sweet as she looks. Her youthful energy bubbles from her every pore. She assists me in appeasing the crying baby boy to nurse, then attaches the self-soothing baby girl on my other nipple. As she adjusts the pillows to provide me even more support, she wipes a stray tear from my cheek.

"Even on our darkest day, God gifts us with light." She looks from my puffy eyes down to the two little miracles at my breast, before she waves and bounces out of my room.

With my hands full of nursing twins, I glance at the clock. It's almost noon. I estimate I slept two hours overnight. *I guess exhaustion is to be expected.* I close my eyes, allowing the slurping sounds to lull me to sleep.

I jump at the sensation of dropping one of the babies. My eyes flash open. Jackson cradles his daughter to his chest. My reaction has startled his son, who lets go and cries. I cover my exposed chest and cuddle the crying baby. I attempt to rock and bounce to soothe him, but with my abdominal pain, I cannot.

Instead, I use my familiar voice to comfort him. "Hey now, it's okay. No need to cry. I'm here. Easy, that's a good boy."

His cries subside, and he burps loudly on my shoulder.

"That's my boy," Jackson proclaims.

I stifle my laugh in hopes not to cause more baby boy tears.

Jackson looks much older than his twenty-four years. *The lack of sleep and emotional stress take their toll.*

I suggest Jackson hold both babies and he obliges, as my peppy nurse enters, carrying my food tray. She stops dead in her tracks at the sight of Jackson and the twins. Even in his exhausted state, it is a precious sight to see. She places my tray within my reach and quickly exits the room, pulling the door closed behind her.

As I nibble on peanut butter toast and wash it down with cran-grape juice, I decide I can wait no longer. Jackson is holding his two babies. Maybe they can make our conversation easier on him.

"Jackson," I gently begin. "What did you decide?"

His eyes move from his children to me. He shakes his head.

Am I to interpret that as, "No, I don't want to talk about this?"

Should I press my luck or drop it?

"I haven't decided," he confesses. Sitting, he repositions the twins side-by-side on his left arm and lap. His free right-hand tugs their caps down and caresses their exposed fingers. "I know what my decision needs to be. I just can't…"

Just can't what?

Just can't say it out loud?

Just can't do it?

Just can't do it by myself?

I know he needs my help. I just don't know how to suggest it or do it.

"I wish I could hug you now," I blurt.

Where did that come from?

Why would I say that out loud?

Seems they removed my filter with the birth of the twins.

"I just feel chained to this bed. I can't rock the twins. I require two nurses to assist in the bathroom, and in your moment of need…I feel so useless." Before Jackson can speak, I keep going. "I can help. I just need to know what you need. I am… I need… I am a little out of it and need guidance. I am not one-hundred percent at the moment, but I want to help, so let me."

"There is nothing you can do." His words pierce right through me. "I mean, as her only living, legal relative, I have to make the decision." He tickles baby cheeks, causing sucking motions from their mouths. He smiles. "You are helping; the twins are helping. Escaping up here with the three of you helps. It allows me time to think, time to focus on the future…" He lifts the babies and lightly kisses each forehead. "I know what I should do, but what do you think she would want me to do?"

I take a deep breath. "Kennedy wouldn't want to live on machines. She wouldn't want a life dependent upon electricity and constant hospital care. She would want us to let her go, Jackson." I lay my heavy head back on a pillow, unable to hold it up any longer. "You already knew this, didn't you?" Jackson nods. "I can help you make it official. I would like to be by your side." *Riding in a wheelchair back down is not a journey I want to repeat, but I would for him.*

A thought pops in my head. "We could ask the doctor to come up here to us. The twins and I could be here for you."

Jackson nods. "Let me think about it." He moves one baby in each arm, then stands, walking towards me. "We need to officially name the twins. We've wasted enough time." He passes his daughter back to me. "I know you've got to be tired; I am." His free hand rubs the back of his neck. "Should we stay with Carter and Cameron?"

Fuck!

It's starting already. The life planned with Kennedy is shifting to me. I don't want to over-step my bounds. I don't know what my role is now. I have no desire to replace Kennedy.

"Taylor," Jackson calls. "I'm open to any ideas you might have. I love the name Carter for our son but have never been sold on Cameron for our daughter."

OUR son?

OUR daughter?

Crap! Crap! Crap!

"Kennedy," I whisper.

Where did that come from?

"I know. But I don't want to…"

"Let's name her Kennedy," I interject, still whispering.

Jackson nods, a smile upon his face. "Carter and Kennedy, I like it." He looks at me for confirmation. "So, we need to tell the nurses we are ready. Carter and Kennedy, it will be."

A weight releases from my heart. *My friend will live on.*

A large yawn overtakes me.

"It's time to finish your lunch to make you healthy and strong, then sleep. I need you at one-hundred percent so we can take Carter and Kennedy home soon." Jackson's words warm my heart while scaring me to death. As I finish my food, I mull over his words. *Our son. Our daughter. We take them home.* I guess genetically they are my children, too. We used my eggs and his sperm to conceive. I spent the entire pregnancy preparing to think of the twins as niece and nephew; it seems weird to shift to calling them son and daughter now. As for the house, it has been my home for several months now; I suppose it could be for a few more as we cope with our new reality.

83

PHONE CALL

Taylor

Hours pass. I don't remember falling asleep. I didn't feel my bed lowering to a horizontal position. To my side, the twins lie in the bassinets, tucked tightly beside a sleeping Jackson on the sofa at the window. I can hear his light snores. Not wanting to disturb him, I don't raise the head of my bed.

As I lie flat on my back, I keep my head turned towards the three sleeping Hayeses on the far side of my hospital room. We all need sleep; we need more sleep. But the uncomfortable urge that roused me from sleep grows with each passing minute. I give in to my need, and I press the nurse call button.

My peppy nurse quietly slips into the room and my bedside. She must have been in earlier to know we were all asleep.

"I need to go to the bathroom, my face is very itchy again, and my pain is back," I whisper.

Peppy nurse nods and turns off the call button before exiting. A few moments later, she returns with another nurse to assist. They raise the head of my bed, then offer me my pain pills and a glass of water.

Peppy nurse informs me my IV almost ran out while I slept. They turned it off to keep the alarm from disturbing me, but couldn't remove it until I woke. She pushes my allergy medicine through the IV.

Crap! If she removes the IV, then the allergy medicine becomes a shot. And shots hurt. Double crap!

Lost in my thoughts, I'm not prepared when she removes the IV from the back of my hand.

FUCK! That hurts!

Jackson jumps up from his slumber. The twins startle in their cribs.

I must have said that out loud. So much for letting them sleep.

While Jackson soothes the twins, the nurses lower the side rail and assist me from the bed. I slide my feet ever so slowly as the nurses flank my sides. The short trek to the restroom feels like ten miles. I'm proud to say I don't cuss or cry as I lower myself onto the toilet. I remain seated a bit longer than necessary, trying to devise a plan to stand again, avoiding pain. When I realize pain is inevitable, I call for my nurses to assist. By the time I am safely back in my bed, tears advertise my discomfort. Before leaving, the nurses record my vitals.

"Sorry, I woke you."

I marvel at Jackson's ability to lift and hold the babies. When I nurse, I need a pillow to help me support them. *Mental note: I need to research recovery timelines for a C-section.*

"I think Carter is hungry again." Jackson approaches my bedside. I peer at the fist-sucking infant. "Seems he is perpetually hungry," Jackson adds.

As he passes his son to me, I'm still hung up on hearing him refer to the baby as Carter. *Carter and Kennedy, they now have names. No longer Baby Boy and Baby Girl Hayes, at least in our minds.*

"Help get me settled, then you should go get the paperwork for us to legally name the babies," I prompt.

Jackson tucks a pillow under Carter and places a blanket over my shoulder. He repeats the same for Baby Kennedy's side. Next, he starts a timer on my phone and leans it against my water glass so I can monitor it. Jackson bends down and kisses me on the forehead, then walks out. I sit reeling at his gesture. *A sweet kiss to the forehead.*

What was that about?

When the next nurse enters the room, Jackson naps on the sofa with the twins asleep on his chest. I motion for him to approach my side.

"Would it be possible to ask Dr. Peterson to visit us in my room this afternoon so we don't have to go back downstairs?" I whisper.

The nurse offers to check into it for me.

With the paperwork filed for the babies' birth certificates, now Jackson needs to talk to Kennedy's doctor. I hope he'll understand why I asked for Dr. Peterson to visit us. He is stuck in limbo. He hangs on to Kennedy as he tries to start a life with his children. He won't be better overnight, but he needs to start the grieving process. The twins will be here for him every step of the way.

The next knock on my door an hour later brings Dr. Peterson into the room. She greets each of us and coos at the babies we hold.

Wasting no time, she jumps right to the point. "Jackson, have you made a decision?"

Jackson nods. "I knew my decision immediately; I just needed time to accept it." He bends and kisses Baby Kennedy on her cheek. "Kennedy would not want to be kept alive by artificial means, and I think she would want to donate any of her organs that might help others."

Dr. Peterson nods her understanding. She peeks her head out the door; more staff join us. They walk Jackson through paperwork and signatures. Dr. Peterson inquires if we want to visit Kennedy one more time. I leave this to Jackson. *If he does, I'll go with him.*

"I said my goodbyes earlier, as did Taylor," Jackson's voice cracks as he tries to respond. "When?"

"The tests for organ viability and typing for the database will occur by 7:00 this evening," the staff informs.

No more words are needed. This conversation seals Kennedy's fate. My best friend, Jackson's wife, will finally be free by 7:00 tonight. As I lose my battle with my tears, I lift Carter to my cheek.

Jackson passes Baby Kennedy to me, stating he needs to go make a call. I quickly take his daughter. His warm brown eyes share this will be a difficult phone call.

Is he reaching out to his parents?
Please say it's so.
He needs them now; I need them now. They need to meet their grandkids.
Please, please, please, let him be calling his parents.
I don't think he would call the neighbors. Although they're close, having the six of them here for Kennedy and then with the twins would be very taxing. I'm sure they will help in our mourning process, but not today.

I avoid interrogating him upon his return. Instead, I motion for him to take a baby. He takes both babies. "I'm okay," He shares with me. "I called Madison. They were very close lately. I felt she should visit before…"

"Yes, I agree." I'm shocked he called Madison. Kennedy spent four to five nights a week there for several months now. "The others?"

"I asked her not to phone the others. I'll contact them soon." Clearly ending this conversation, Jackson asks, "When will your dinner tray arrive?"

84

BLINDSIDED

Taylor

After dinner, the twins return to the nursery, and the nurses encourage Jackson to take me for a walk. I'm given a robe to keep me warm, and they secured my socks with the grippy-side down. I cringe in pain as I leave the bed. Once I'm upright, the pain fades. I tolerate slight pain, meandering up and down the obstetric hallway. We pause at the nursery window to peer at the other babies living with Jackson's.

Scratch that.
Living with ours.
Living with mine.
My babies? Jackson and I really need to talk.

On our next lap, at my turtle's pace, I ask Jackson, "Will you hire a nanny to help with the twins?" I keep my eyes focused ahead down the hallway and my hand on the railing.

"Do you want a nanny?" He inquires, stopping in front of me and lifting my chin so our eyes meet. "We have much to discuss. I have a few ideas," he adds.

"Want to talk as we walk?" I ask.

"We'll talk back in your room with Carter and Kennedy in our arms," Jackson states.

Jackson holds Carter lengthwise in his lap. The baby's eyes open for a moment. Jackson softly coos to his son. I notice his dark hair is a bit shaggier from the long day. "It's going to be tough. We need to create an entirely new plan." Jackson jumps into our life outside the hospital discussion. "Kennedy and I asked many favors of you. I don't plan to ask a favor now; I want to know what you want." He lifts Carter up to coo some more, then lays him back on his legs. "You are their mother. Even the birth certificate states this. Would you like to help me raise our children?" He pulls his eyes from his son to witness my reaction. "I mean, I know you planned to resume your life when you recovered from the delivery. I would totally understand if you need to go live your life. I don't want to guilt…"

"Stop," I interject. "You aren't guilting me into anything." *That being said, what do I want?* "Several times today, I struggled to think of the twins as mine. I drilled it into my head for nine months that these were Kennedy's twins, not mine. It seems weird to realize they are mine. My children created with my eggs. I am head-over-heels in love with them. From the moment I first heard their cries in the OR, loving them was easy." I sip my water through the flexible straw, talking and emotions dry my throat. "In Kennedy's absence, I want the opportunity to help in raising the twins. I didn't have a mom or a dad; I will not willingly inflict that on any child."

"So, we agree we will raise the twins together as their parents," Jackson summarizes. When I nod, he states, "We can iron out the specifics in the upcoming weeks."

My mind races. *The two of us living together. The twins calling us mommy and daddy. What will the neighbors think of this? What will the twin's teachers and friends think of our situation? Will I live in Jackson's home? Will we live separately and have joint custody?*

We have much to iron out, indeed.

At 7:15, Nurse Adams slips into my room.

"I'm glad the night shift has returned," I state, greeting her with a smile.

She smiles a muted smile. "This is our chaplain," she informs.

Now I understand Nurse Adams's mood. *This is not a pleasant OB visit; this is a counseling session for our heavy thoughts.*

The chaplain begins with small talk, asking about the twins, their names, and how I am recovering. A knock on the door interrupts our conversation.

"May I join you?" a female voice questions from the hall.

Jackson rises, walks around the curtain toward the door, then returns with his arm around the shoulders of Madison. He introduces Madison to the chaplain. Her pale face wears large red blotches. She's in a sweat shirt and yoga pants. *This is not put-together Madison with never a hair out of place.* Jackson escorts her to the chair near my bed and passes her little Kennedy to hold. I welcome her with my smile, as words fail me yet again.

Fifteen relaxed, but emotional minutes of conversation pass before the chaplain asks us to join hands for a prayer. I grasp Madison with my right hand and Jackson with my left. Jackson holds onto the chaplain's hand across my bed. The chaplain and Madison finish out our circle. The minister's poignant words speak of the end of Kennedy's life on earth and the start of her life in heaven.

After the chaplain excuses himself from the room, reminding us he is always available, Jackson slips Carter from my arms.

"I'm glad he stopped by. I think we needed his guidance to end this emotional day."

I cringe at Jackson's words. My nerves and regret over the text I sent haunts me. I'd like to blame it on my hormones or the pain meds, but it is a text I tried to send many times before.

"Thank you for thinking of me and inviting me to be here," Madison murmurs, as she passes little Kennedy to me.

"Why don't you plan to come over tomorrow night to help us settle in at the house?" Jackson invites.

"Don't jinx it, they still need to assess everything before they will discharge me tomorrow afternoon," I scold.

I need out of this prison. I want my clothes, my blankets, and my own bed. My cellphone vibrates on my side table. Madison slips out the door while I read my text.

ELIZABETH
We're walking in hospital now

ME
C ya soon

Should I confess to Jackson now?
Does he need a moment to compose himself before they enter?
Or is a surprise the best tactic?

"Earth to Taylor," Jackson waves his free hand in front of my face. "Where'd you go just now?"

I fold under the pressure. "Jackson, I'm so sorry. I did something…"

Three knocks on the door, then the sound of Nurse Adams's voice announcing visitors cuts off my confession.

"You lied!" Gerald's excited voice announces. "You didn't have a baby; you had two babies."

My eyes freeze on Jackson. He stands like a statue beside me while his parents' attention is firmly on the babies. I pass Carter to Elizabeth. *Or did she take him from me?* She fills the empty chair before her baby coos and chatter begins.

"Jackson," I prompt. Turning to me, I cannot decipher his reaction. "Can Gerald hold her?"

Jackson leans low to whisper near my ear, "I'm mad, but thank you." Then he turns, offering his daughter to his father.

Mad.

He said, "I'm mad." I knew he would be.

"But thank you." Does that mean it's a good mad or a bad mad? Does 'thank you' mean he is happy I invited them?

He is not giving me anything to work with here.

"So, Miss Taylor," Elizabeth feigns anger. "You have some explaining to do. You text us out of the blue stating you had a baby, you are in Liberty Hospital, and you need us to come help you for a week or two." Her attention returns to Carter. "Oh yes, she did. Your mommy kept a secret and used a text to spill the beans. Silly mommy." She baby talks, expecting a reaction.

"When we met at The Smokehouse?" Gerald lets the rest of his question dangle.

"Yes, I was pregnant then," I confess. Inside, I feel like I'm confessing to murdering someone. *I never wanted to hide it from them.* They are the closest thing I have ever had to parents. "But there is more to the story."

It's at this moment that Jackson pushes the button on my side rail to page a nurse. Panic floods to my core, and bile rises to the back of my throat. *He's mad. What is he doing? Is he leaving? Is he asking for the twins to go to the nursery so he can yell?*

Crap! I didn't think this through.

Jackson meets the nurse at the door. "May we get another chair in our room?"

As he follows the nurse from the room, I release the breath I didn't know I was holding. Elizabeth squeezes my hand; she senses my nerves at Jackson's reaction to this forced reunion. Jackson returns with another large chair.

"Here, dad, sit," Jackson orders with his hand on his father's shoulder. Gerald tries to argue that he sat the entire ride to Kansas City, so Jackson should sit. "I'm going to sit right here." Jackson sits on my bed. He reaches out to take my hand in his. Elizabeth's eyes widen, witnessing this act.

"I need to apologize," I blurt. "I texted you to come see my babies, knowing Jackson would be here. I blind-sided all three of you. In a moment of weakness, I decided to end this riff."

Jackson wastes no time. "Mom, Dad, Taylor and I are going to tell you a rather long story. We will start at the end, as that is the most important part, then we will fill in the blanks. I," he pauses, looking at me for support. I pat his forearm and nod. "I mean, we need you to hear all of it before you ask questions or interrupt, okay?"

Gerald and Elizabeth nod. At this moment, I imagine they think Jackson and I had an affair, and these are his twins since Kennedy is not here. *Oh, what they must think of me right now.*

"Last night, at five, Taylor, Kennedy, and I were headed out to eat. We planned to celebrate Taylor carrying the twins full term and enjoy a great meal before our lives became hectic with babies. On our way to the restaurant, as I pulled through a green light, a drunk driver collided with our car. I was driving, Taylor in the backseat, and Kennedy in the passenger seat." His voice cracks.

I hop in. "The impact point was the passenger door, Kennedy's door."

85

ADOPTED DAUGHTER

Taylor

Emotions somewhat in check, Jackson continues. "Taylor opened her door then yelled to wake me up. I got out and went to help Kennedy. Taylor's water broke, so the EMTs drove the two of us here, while the fire department extricated Kennedy." At his mother's audible gasp, Jackson pauses, and Gerald reaches for his wife. "Taylor was in active labor when Kennedy arrived at the hospital. The babies were in distress, so she was prepped for a C-section. When Taylor went to recovery and the twins to the nursery, I signed forms for Kennedy to have surgery to stop her internal bleeding." Jackson releases my hand and stands. "Taylor and the twins got settled here while Kennedy had a second surgery."

"It was a long emotional night," I add, hoping to give Jackson some support in this emotionally tragic story.

"This morning, Taylor decided she needed to go down. She paged nurses, insisting they wheel her down to see Kennedy. She didn't take no for an answer." Jackson's Adam's apple visibly bobs.

"We found Kennedy on life support with no brain activity." I venture on; we need to get it all out. "Jackson is her only relative…"

"No!" Elizabeth cries. "You had to make the decision?" She quickly passes Carter to me and embraces her son. "Honey, I am so sorry. You shouldn't have had to do that on your own."

"I wasn't alone. Taylor and the twins were here. They helped me," Jackson admits.

Elizabeth sits on my bed, a hand on Jackson's and one brushing Carter's blue cap.

Jackson continues, "Kennedy passed away about 7:30 tonight. I asked for her organs to be harvested, hoping to help others. Kennedy would have wanted it that way."

The sight of tears in Jackson's eyes cripple me. I cannot stand to see him relive this entire day. I know letting out his emotions, talking about it, and having loved ones near will help us mourn. It hurts; the pain is still fresh.

The four of us reflect in silence, our eyes on the tiniest two in the room. With Kennedy sucking on her tiny fist, I realize I need to nurse soon. "Um, I think it's time to nurse again." I don't want to interrupt the silence.

"Okay, we will find a cup of coffee or something. You can text when you're done," Gerald suggests, wiping tears from under his glasses.

"Actually, dad, Taylor and I have a system." Turning to me, he asks, "They can stay; can't they?"

"Of course," I reply.

I sense Jackson embraces their presence. "Okay, let's do this."

I move Carter to my other side, remembering the nurses encouraged me to alternate the sides they feed on each time they nurse. Jackson places a baby blanket over my shoulder and places the pillow under my arm. I assist Carter in latching on. Elizabeth giggles at the loud rooting sound her grandson makes as he nurses.

Grandson.

They don't know these are really their grandkids yet. We need to move this story on.

Jackson passes Kennedy and a blanket to me, then secures a pillow for this side.

"Wow!" Elizabeth cheers. "You really have this down to a science."

"Almost twelve hours later, yes we do," I brag. "I know you are still grasping the tragic…"

Gerald interrupts, "We plan to stay for a week, or however long you need us to. We have much to learn and… mourn, but we are eager to hear about the twins now." He echoes my wants.

It's time to rock their worlds with some good news, too.

Unable to take the suspense any longer, Elizabeth asks, "Who is the father?"

"It's complicated," I answer.

Gerald and Elizabeth look from me to Jackson and back.

"Last spring, Kennedy and I planned to start our family. We met with adoption agencies and attempted to become foster parents. I won't get into the details now, but Kennedy wasn't able to carry a child." Jackson avoids the reasons behind this. His parents already know why. "Taylor came to visit us over The Fourth of July, and we asked if she might consider being a surrogate for us."

Elizabeth's sobs of joy erupt. "We are grandparents to twins," she announces to Gerald. The joy in their reactions warms my heart.

Jackson smiles at me.

"Anyway," Gerald prompts for more details.

"Of course, Taylor said yes. She moved into our spare bedroom, and we began the process."

Sensing Jackson's unease with this particular section of the story, I jump in. "We found we couldn't use Kennedy's eggs, so I volunteered for them to use mine. We became pregnant our first month. Nine months later, here we are." I'm sure we will have time to share more over the next week.

"Oh my," Elizabeth sighs, fanning her face.

I instruct Jackson to give her some of my water. Elizabeth assures us she is fine. She just needs a minute to process this. I look to Jackson in question as to what needs processed. I would have thought this the happier and easier news of the two items we had to share.

"Mom?" Jackson queries. "What don't you understand?"

Elizabeth replies, "I understand it all. The twins are truly my grandchildren. My son and my adopted daughter gave me two more grandchildren."

Yep, she understands. It sounds a bit sketchy, the way she refers to me as her adopted daughter.

"Perhaps we shouldn't refer to Taylor as our adopted daughter when we brag at church about our new grandchildren," Gerald teases.

Laughter abounds.

With nursing complete and burps out of the way, I look to Jackson. "You should officially introduce the twins to your parents," I inform him.

He sweeps his children into his arms. One at a time, he raises them to his lips, placing a kiss on their forehead.

In his best game show announcer voice, Jackson approaches his parents in their chairs. "Mom, Dad, let me introduce to you my oldest child, Carter Lewis Hayes." He passes his son to his father.

Elizabeth and Gerald say hello to Carter and welcome him to the family.

"And now, my second born, my little princess, Kennedy Hayes." He passes his daughter to Elizabeth.

As they greet and welcome her to their family, Elizabeth asks for her middle name.

"We thought if she had no middle name, she might use her maiden name as her middle name when she marries," I answer.

"She's barely twenty-four hours old, and you are already thinking of her married name?" Gerald teases. "Take it from your father, sons are definitely easier to raise than daughters."

I marvel at the ease with which Jackson is back in the fold with his parents. I envisioned an epic battle. Of course, we weren't in the hospital, Kennedy was involved, and Jackson was stubborn. Here in the hospital, in this tragic situation, with the precious twins, the family pulls together as family should.

Jackson

I ask my dad to walk with me to fetch a pop from the vending area. I share the conversation with Howard Buchanan and ask for his advice.

"With Kennedy's death and the twins' future up in air, could it be hush money? Guilt money? Is he doing this hoping I don't sue?" I run my hands through my hair. "I have no plans to sue. I just want medical bills to be covered so we can begin to heal and move on with our lives."

"There's nothing wrong with setting the babies up for future success," Dad encourages. "Think ahead to college and heaven forbid any future medical bills. I feel you should reach out to Howard or answer when he and the lawyer call. Get all the details, then discuss it with Taylor. As parents, this needs to be a mutual decision," he reminds me.

"When should I tell Taylor? She just gave birth, had a major surgery, and lost her best friend. I'm not sure how she is holding up so well, and I don't want to break her," I vent.

"She is strong. Do not keep this from her. It's better to tell her as soon as possible." Dad advises.

When we return to the room and my parents leave for their hotel, I tell Taylor everything about the stranger and the trust funds. I didn't predict her reaction.

"Can you imagine if your son caused a wreck, killing one and putting another into labor? He must feel helpless, like a bad parent. Can you imagine?" she asks.

I can't believe she feels empathy for a stranger.

"I would like to meet Howard. Next time he calls, can you arrange it?" she asks. "Did he tell me how much money is in the trust funds?"

I shake my head.

"If setting up the trust funds for the twins eases Howard's fatherly guilt, I think we should allow him this," she admits. "We will benefit from it as much as the twins will. Perhaps we might be able to help this father, too. I want to invite him over for dinner once we are settled in at home," she informs me.

Her strength astounds me. With all that is going on in our lives, with her surgery and her pain, along with losing her best friend, she now worries about this father and his pain.

86

THE VERTICAL BLINDS OPENED

Taylor

I behave like a perfect patient, and the doctor releases me on Sunday afternoon. As we round the corner, Jackson's home comes into view. A large sign with balloons attached graces the front lawn, welcoming Carter and Kennedy home.

"No, no, no," Jackson chants. "I told Madison not to tell the neighbors. I can't handle a party. This is not a time to party."

It might be easy to let his words upset me. The twins are to be celebrated. They are tiny, precious, bundle of joys. However, I completely understand Jackson's need for privacy. The passing of his wife at the same time his twins are born takes its toll.

"I will thank everyone for coming and send them on their way," I offer. "I'll fake fatigue." *Not that it would be much of a stretch.* I'm exhausted; the thought of relaxing on the sofa or in my bed is my only goal.

As Jackson pulls the Mustang into the garage, Gerald and Elizabeth park behind it in the driveway. Jackson opens my door for me and extends his arm to assist me to stand. I understand my pain will fade as I heal, but now it feels so intense tears come to my eyes. He chuckles at my cursing, reminding me soon the twins will repeat my every word. When I flip him off, he mentions I might regret that when the kindergarten teacher calls us in because Carter flips her off in front of the entire class.

Elizabeth offers to help me inside, while the men bring the twins and carriers in. I take her hand as she leads me into a home she has never seen. I don't allow myself to worry about this. I need to focus on sending our friends home.

We find balloons, plants, and food in the kitchen; otherwise, the house is empty.

"Shall we head to the sofa?" Elizabeth asks.

"Since I am standing, I think I will walk a bit before I crash," I reply, opening the card propped on a bottle of sparkling grape juice.

Welcome home Jackson, Taylor, Carter, and Little Kennedy,

We placed food in the refrigerator and freezer for this week. Know that we are thinking of you all. We are only a text or phone call away. We promise to do our best to allow you time to grieve and settle into a routine. Remember, your friends are nearby to help in any way.

Love,
Tyler, Reagan, James, Martha, Madison, Jorge, Rosalynn

P.S. Nya is at Martha's house-No hurry.

I breathe a sigh of relief. We can relax tonight with no need to pass the babies around while we mourn. We cannot put it off forever; the time will come, just not tonight.

I ask Elizabeth to assist me to my bathroom as the men enter car seats in tow. My reflection in the dresser mirror gives me pause. Exhaustion carves my features, my hair is in a straggly ponytail. I turn sideways. My figure did not change as I imagined it would with the birth of the twins. *I guess my waistline is a bit smaller, but it's still large.* My thoughts fly to Carter and Kennedy; my loss of a waistline is totally worth it.

I emerge from my room to find Gerald, Jackson, and the twins on the sofa watching a sports program. In the kitchen, Elizabeth warms up a dish left by the thoughtful neighbors. I assist by moving the plants from the island but am reprimanded by Elizabeth.

"Too heavy. You aren't supposed to lift," Elizabeth chides, removing the plant from my hands.

Jackson darts to my side with Carter in his arms. "You need to follow directions. We don't want to delay your recovery; the twins need a healthy mommy."

Mommy?
Did he just refer to me as mommy?
I am their biological mother.
Kennedy was to be mommy; now I'll be the mommy.

"Hey," Jackson places his free arm around my shoulders. "Don't be upset. We just want you to take it easy."

I pull my eyes from my wringing hands to meet his. I fight the urge to cry.

"I'm too tired to cry," I whisper.

"Mom, can you hold Carter for me?" Jackson asks. He returns to me and guides me to the living room. "Let's get you comfy. Once you eat and the twins nurse, I think you need to rest. Mom and I can handle dinner, cleanup, and the twins. You need rest."

Jackson's words, although very sweet and caring, make me feel weak. *I feel like a failure. Woman have given birth for centuries and continued to work at home and in the fields immediately. I, on the other hand, am exhausted, in pain, and have no desire to do anything.*

I wake to the sounds of a fussy Carter. Elizabeth tries to soothe him while bouncing him side to side. I glance around the room; I must have fallen asleep.

"Now, you've done it. You woke up your mommy," Elizabeth teases Carter. "I kept your dinner warm for you, but I am afraid this little guy needs to eat first."

I wiggle around on the sofa, trying to find a comfy position. Sensing my discomfort, Gerald rises and suggests I use the recliner. Jackson helps me from my position, then into the recliner. He places pillows in my lap and extra blankets nearby before delivering an anxious Carter to me. No coaxing necessary, he loudly latches on. Kennedy, on the other hand, sleeps soundly. Jackson attempts to wake her as he carries her toward me. I encourage him to rub her cheek near her lips. Moments later, she is ready to nurse.

"Want me to feed you?" Jackson sweetly offers.

As tempting as it is to my now growling stomach, I pass on his offer.

"I knew you were exhausted. You need to rest more," he states.

I should take care of him; not him taking care of me. He just lost his wife; he is mourning. He must have a million things to do. Tomorrow, I need to jump in and help him.

While I eat my dinner Elizabeth saved for me, the grandparents burp then cuddle the twins. At 9:00, Gerald suggests it's time for them to head to the hotel, so we can turn in for the night. It takes me a minute to extricate myself from the recliner to hug them goodbye. They urge me not to get up, but I assure them I need to pee, and I'm ready for bed. They thank me for bringing their family back together, and I thank them for their help with the twins.

Jackson raps lightly on the bathroom door. "Everything okay?"

"Yeah," I quickly respond. "It just takes me a minute because it hurts."

Slowly sliding my feet with each step, I pad into my bedroom. "I've moved the bassinets in here so the twins will be closer to you tonight," Jackson explains. "I've made up the sofa. I'll leave the door cracked so I can come and help."

I hadn't come up with a plan for the midnight feedings. *It seems Jackson thought of everything.*

Jackson

"Let's sit on the deck while they sleep," I say to my parents on Monday. I tried to find a moment to speak with them earlier, but we were busy with funeral arrangements and helping Taylor with the twins. I found it hard to find a moment alone. I carry the baby monitor out with me just in case. Leaning against the wooden railing, facing my parents in their seats, the May breeze is welcome in the warm afternoon sun.

"I can't thank you enough for coming down to help us. I've leaned on you so much," I pause, swallowing hard.

I need to calm my shaky voice. I need to share something, and I need them to believe me. I cannot leave any room for doubt.

One more deep breath in and out.

"I'm in love with Taylor."

"We know," my mother replies.

I expected them to try to talk me out of it. I thought I would need to explain in detail the months leading up to today. I figured I would endure a famous lecture from my dad. His lectures often left me feeling lower than low and vowing to be a better man.

At my dumbstruck reaction, my mother explains. "It's apparent in all you do. It's easy to see in the way you are drawn to be near her and not just when the twins are around."

"What should I do? Should I tell her?" I pick at a torn cuticle. "How do I tell her?"

"I think she feels the same way," my mom claims.

I look up from the torn skin of my finger to judge her sincerity.

"With everything that occurred this week, the details that need taken care of, and the services ahead, you might consider waiting to tell her," Dad suggests, and I nod in agreement.

My dad is right; now is not the time. I feel I might explode, keeping it inside. The desire to profess my love grows stronger every day.

I share with my parents the conversation Kennedy and I had the night before the accident. I tell them everything about Kennedy going to Madison's, and Taylor and I on fast food runs and watching sports. I share Kennedy confessing her feelings for Madison, and not for me, along with Kennedy's urging me to tell Taylor I loved her. I'm honest about my refusal to see what she saw and my denial of my true feelings for Taylor during my talk with Kennedy.

Something opened up that night.

It's like the vertical blinds opened on a window in my mind.

Things are clearer.

87

SO, SHE LOVES ME

Taylor

"Did you halt the mail delivery while you were in the hospital?" Gerald inquires.

My eyes widen. We should have, but we did not.

"I'll walk Nya to the mailbox and back," Elizabeth offers quickly. "You need to rest and Gerald, you need to sit still so the twins can nap," she teases her husband.

When they return, Elizabeth releases Nya from her leash. She immediately darts to Gerald's feet. She stands on her hind legs to ensure the twins are safe in his care. Next, she whines at the side of the sofa, wanting me to lift her to my lap. This simple task requires planning on my part. One cannot simply bend over and pick up an eight-pound puppy two days after a C-section.

As I cuddle and coo Nya on the sofa, Elizabeth uses kitchen scissors to open a small package. She asks me if she should look inside or wait for Jackson. My eyes remain on Nya as I give Elizabeth permission to open it.

Sensing a change in her mood, Nya hops from the sofa to join her at the kitchen island. My eyes follow. Elizabeth wipes tears often as she turns page after page in a small book.

"Elizabeth?" I call to her.

Her eyes meet mine. "Your photobook arrived."

She need not say more; my gift for Kennedy and Jackson arrived. With the twins and losing Kennedy, I completely forgot about the surrogacy photobook I ordered for my best friends.

I attempt to stifle my sobs as Elizabeth joins me on the sofa. "I... I..." she stammers.

Elizabeth passes the photobook to me.

My fingers caress the dark green letters on the pale green cover. I trace each letter "Our Family Journey". I giggle at the first picture. My body no longer resembles the barely pregnant woman I see.

Elizabeth places her hand atop mine. "It's a magnificent gift." Her eyes lock on mine. "Jackson will love it." She brushes tears from my cheeks. "I love it; Gerald will love it. Thank you."

Her words, though true, do little to distract me from the fact Kennedy is not here to see the gift I created for her.

It's yet another item meant for Kennedy that is now mine.

I excuse myself to my bathroom to splash water on my face.

Jackson

Taylor sleeps in the recliner, Kennedy sleeping snuggly on her chest. Carter and I sit on the sofa, watching the end of a Royals game. His eyes are very heavy as his tummy is full. Internally, I debate waking Taylor up and moving her to her bedroom. The Royals are behind by one in the bottom of the ninth. I could pause the game, but I don't want to move. This is my first baseball game with my son.

I cheer quietly inside as the first Royals' batter walks. A faint groan escapes when batter number two strikes out. Back at the top of the order, the next batter rips a single up the middle. The fourth batter now stands at the plate with a full count. Here's the wind-up and the pitch...

"Jackson," Taylor mumbles in her sleep. "Jackson, I love you." It's barely a whisper, but I hear her.

Wait.

What?

She's asleep, right?

Her eyes are still shut; she hasn't moved. Baby Kennedy still sleeps on her chest.

Asleep. She's asleep. I decide to test the waters.

"Taylor," I murmur.

I witness no reaction, no eye movement, no words; she's sound asleep.

Was she dreaming, or was it a subconscious confession?

Exhausted physically and mentally, she is probably in a deep sleep.

Could she?

Would she?

I place Carter in his bassinet before lifting Kennedy from her mother's chest; Taylor does not stir. Remote in hand, I turn off the TV, realizing I didn't see how the game ended. It seems irrelevant now. My world has shifted; I must find out if it's real. I gently pat Taylor's wrist while calling to her. As much as I want to know immediately how she feels, she needs time. She is worth the wait. When I call to her a second time, she stirs.

With a stretch cut short by her groan and hands flying to her abdomen, she's awake. I'm ready for her pain to fade completely. I've always admired Taylor's strength. Seeing her weakened state causes me pain. I know she needs time to heal and exercise to strengthen her abdominals again. I'm not a patient man. If I could bear the pain for her, I would. Her body endured so much since August.

"Sorry, I fell asleep," Taylor murmurs groggily. I assist her in folding the recliner, then to stand. She glances at the twins and smiles. "The three of us fell asleep on you."

"I'd have it no other way," I admit. My thoughts on her dreamy admission. "You talked in your sleep."

Taylor's head jolts my way. "What did I say?"

I sense the panic in her voice.

Or am I trying to read too much into it?

"What were you dreaming?" I ask.

"We were having a picnic at the park for the twins' first birthday. The neighbors were there, so were your parents, your sister, and her kids," she explains, a broad smile upon her face and her eyes sparkling. "Carter threw a handful of cake at Kennedy; they were a mess from head to toe."

So, she loves me.

88

A SHIFT

Taylor

It's Sunday morning, Jackson's second day back at work. Elizabeth and Gerald are still in town, thank goodness. I climb from bed a bit easier this morning, my pain lessens with each passing day. I peek into the living room to ensure Elizabeth and Gerald are with the twins before I slip into the restroom. I enjoy a few extra minutes to freshen up; then stride toward the kitchen in search of breakfast. My appetite grows every day. I'm told it's because I need extra energy for nursing.

"Good morning," Gerald greets from the sofa as I walk by.

I return his greeting, noting he holds both twins in his lap. I climb upon a kitchen stool.

"How'd you sleep last night?" Elizabeth asks, sliding a plate of sausage and tater tots my way. As I rise, she pushes my shoulder down and fetches the ketchup for me.

I am very glad they put everything on hold to help Jackson with the funeral arrangements and me with the twins, but eventually I need to do everything on my own. *She pampers me too much; it will be a shock when they leave.*

"Tonight, the grandparents are babysitting while Jackson takes you out to eat," Elizabeth proclaims. Her hands fly up, palms towards me before I speak. "It's nothing fancy. You will be gone about an hour. If you nurse before you go, we're all set." Elizabeth's pride flashes like a neon sign.

I'm grateful, she took the initiative to arrange this, but panic overtakes me. The thought of leaving the twins overwhelms me. There is no doubt they will be well taken care of. I just don't think I'm ready to be that far away from them yet.

Sensing my nervousness, Elizabeth wraps her arm around my shoulders then whispers in my ear. "It's a big step. You can do it. If you need to, you can come back early."

I attempt to smile in her direction and nod. *I will try. I need to find a happy medium between my role as a mother and my own adult needs. Eventually, I'll get a babysitter to hang with friends or for my own appointments. I need to do this.*

The day quickly passes. Nursing every three hours leaves little time for more than eating and napping. After my shower, exhausted, I slept for two hours more. I decide to keep it simple in my preparations to go out tonight. I pull on red leggings with my St. Louis Cardinals Maternity T-shirt. Raising my arms to create my ponytail hurts my abdomen, so I opt for keeping it down, apply mascara, and lip gloss. I shrug at my reflection. I look like a new mother. *I don't need to impress anyone.*

"Ready?" Jackson queries as I enter the kitchen.

Elizabeth and Gerald hold the twins nearby. Elizabeth raises Carter's hand, helping him wave goodbye to us. I nod to Jackson, exiting to the garage before I lose my nerve.

Pulling from our neighborhood, Jackson places his hand on my knee. "They will be fine. Mom and Dad promise to text us updates often." He tries to assure me. I never imagined a mother's bond with babies could be this strong. *I now truly understand the term momma bear.*

"Promise me you will help me learn to be okay with this. I don't want to be a helicopter mom, I want a healthy equilibrium of family time and me time," I say, even though it is the last thing I want right now.

I need to be strong.

Dinner is delicious, and our conversation flows easily. Jackson shares stories from the store, along with customer and employee comments on the twins. He claims he pulled his cell phone out to show photos to everyone. I make a mental note to print some photos for him soon. Before I know it, dinner is over, and we pay the bill.

"Do you mind if we walk a bit?" I ask on the sidewalk just outside the restaurant. The fresh air feels good. I've been cooped up inside for a while now. "Not too long though, I need to get back to…"

Jackson squeezes my shoulders in understanding. He knows our time away weighs heavily on me. "You feeling, okay? In pain?" he asks.

I nod with a smile, signaling I'm okay as we slowly stroll around the shopping center. We walk and chat for a while, then sit on a bench overlooking a walking trail and small pond.

"It's been a crazy two weeks," he chuckles.

Quite the roller coaster ride of emotions, that is for sure. I cover my mouth with my hand as a long yawn escapes.

"I should get you back home," Jackson responds. "We've overdone it today."

"Please, just a bit longer," I plead. "I'm ready to be home, but I'm enjoying our little reprieve. We have had no time, just the two of us." I grasp his hand in mine, slide closer to him on the bench, and rest my head on his shoulder.

"We've been adjusting to this parent-thing pretty good, right?"

"Yes, I believe so. We haven't had to visit a pediatrician or ER yet," I quip.

"Nice, that's when we know we are messing up as parents in your book?" he teases. "I'm ready for my parents to go home. Don't get me wrong. I'm very glad you brought them to me, but I am ready for us to settle in to parenting on our own, too," he confesses. "Do you think you are strong enough to care for the twins while I'm at work? Or, I could work from home more than usual so I could help, too."

"I'm sure I can handle it. Women have for centuries. I've appreciated their help, but worry holding our babies as much as they have will spoil them."

When I smile up at Jackson, I see something in his eyes. *Something I cannot figure out.*

"I've..." He nervously clears his throat.

He turns sideways on the bench to face me, his knee bent between us. He takes both my hands in his.

"I need to tell you something. My parents want me to wait, but I can't hide it any longer."

Crap!

Is this what our dinner is really about?

Will he ask me to move out, get my own place, and split custody 50/50?

How will I be able to ride home with him after this?

Fearful tears fill my eyes in anticipation.

"I'm ready. Just say it," I urge, unable to take his drawn-out introduction.

"I love you."

Wait.

What?

He loves me? Loves me or LOVES me? How can I tell which one?

Feeling light-headed, I realize I'm holding my breath. I quickly release it. I raise my shaking hand to the side of my face.

"I know it seems sudden. I know there is a lot going on in our lives right now, but I've had these feelings for quite some time now." He tugs my hand from my face back into his hand on his knee. "Kennedy brought it to my attention. She encouraged me to tell you; she wanted me to tell you."

How can that be?

My best friend, his wife, wanted him to tell me he loved me?

Can my world be any crazier?

What am I supposed to do with this? I draw in a deep breath.

"Taylor, look at me," he prompts. "We've been friends most of our lives. We've shared good times and bad. Now, we are parenting together."

I nod.

"But it is the little things. I love the way you don't take crap from anyone, the way you express your love of foods, your love and knowledge of music, your loyalty to sports teams, your thirst for knowledge, the constant need to research anything you don't already know, and your constantly positive attitude. I love everything about you." He raises my hands to his lips, kissing one and then the other. "I love you."

"I…" I stutter, grasping for a reply. "I don't know…"

"You don't need to respond. Nothing needs to change. I couldn't live another day without telling you how I feel," Jackson confesses. "We need to focus on the twins, your recovery, and mourning now."

"I understand," I begin. "I know the feelings you mean. I just don't think we should act upon them now."

"That's why my parents encouraged me to wait a few months to tell you. But I'm afraid you might be ready to move out to your own place. I need you to know how I feel before you make any plans. I'm laying my cards out on the table along with my heart."

"Thank you for being honest with me. I feel we need to focus on Carter and Kennedy now. We need to visit with Dr. Wilson to work through our pain of losing Kennedy and the changing dynamic of our family." I pause, losing myself for a moment in Jackson's smile. "You are not scaring me away. I am a bit overwhelmed right now, and…"

"Taylor," Jackson interrupts. "I just needed to get it off my chest. Nothing needs to change. We are both overwhelmed right now. I just needed you to know where I am at in here." His splayed palm pats his chest near his heart. "Let's get you home. I'm sure the twins will need to nurse before you crash for the night."

With a hand on my elbow, he helps me stand. We walk hand in hand back to my car without speaking a word. We glance towards each other with content smiles upon our faces.

I like the comfortable routine we developed the past couple of weeks. I'm rethinking my plans for this year, as well as the rest of my life. I no longer want to get my own apartment in Kansas City. I think it's best if Jackson and I live under the same roof, at least until the twins are school age. I planned to reenter the dating world after I lost the baby weight. Now dating is no longer a priority. Seems with yet another car ride to dinner, my future path veered in an entirely new direction. I'm now more than just a friend to Jackson.

At the car, Jackson opens my door and helps me climb in before rounding to the driver's side. I place my hand on Jackson's before he can turn the key in the ignition.

"We're good, right?" I probe.

Jackson's warm smile conveys all I need to know.

"We're good; nothing has changed."

Nothing has changed. Seriously?

He confessed he loves me.

He confessed Kennedy encouraged him to profess his love for me.

Three little words change everything.

Showing you care is one thing, but saying these three little words out loud changes the game. When he spoke those three little words, I instantly felt a shift, a warm feeling deep in my core and in my heart. *We can pretend nothing has changed all we want, but I'm sure he knows as well as I do everything will change.*

89

MOM-MODE

Taylor

The doorbell wakes me from my nap. *Who could it be on a Wednesday?* I slowly rise from the sofa and glance at the sleeping twins in their nearby bassinets on my way to the front door. Through the peephole, I spy Dr. Wilson.

Did I forget an appointment?

"Hello," I greet.

"Taylor." Dr. Wilson wraps me in a gentle hug. "I'm so sorry. I read about Kennedy's passing in the paper. May I come in?"

I'm frozen in place. Seeing Dr. Wilson away from her office catches me off guard. She is here to talk about Kennedy's death.

I'm not strong enough to work through this now with her.

"Taylor," Dr. Wilson prompts. "If this is a bad time, I can come back."

"No!" I announce louder than needed. "Come in. I just woke up, so I am a little out of it," I confess, excusing my actions.

"Resting when the twins rest is important," Dr. Wilson states.

"How have you been feeling?" She seats herself on the end of the sofa nearest the still sleeping babies.

"Overwhelmed, but I'm sure all new mothers experience this." I check on the twins as I walk by. "Would you like a drink?"

Dr. Wilson shakes her head, then explains, "I won't stay long. I really stopped by to offer an individual and group session for Jackson and you in your home instead of my office. With the new babies, I realize it is not convenient for you to meet at my office." She glances at the twins. "Both of you experienced two life altering events; I would like to offer my services."

I hesitate to commit to an appointment. There is no schedule in my current life. With the twins feeding every three hours if they aren't napping, I can only guess what might occur in three-hour increments.

"I realize your schedule with the twins prevents planning. I'm flexible; I can plan to stop by on my way home. If I need to cuddle an adorable baby or change a diaper while here, I suppose I could bring myself to do so," she teases. Her fingers caress Carter's tiny hand.

"Jackson's parents just left today. I can't speak for him, but I'm sure we would both benefit from a session."

"Jackson is speaking with his parents?" she questions. "Hmm. I see we have more to discuss than I previously thought. Let's plan on me stopping by after four tomorrow. No need to clean, dress up, or prepare. Please, just go about your normal day with the babies."

I agree and walk Dr. Wilson to the door with the promise to talk tomorrow afternoon.

Taylor
Dr. Wilson at Taylor's Home-Group Session, Thursday, May 18th

Dr. Wilson sits in the recliner as Jackson and I sit side-by-side on the sofa. Carter soundly sleeps in her arms, while Jackson holds the sleeping Kennedy.

"Let's begin. I would like to focus today on the accident and losing

Kennedy, the adult Kennedy, that is." She smiles towards Baby Kennedy.

I begin by retelling my version of the accident and trip to the hospital. Jackson follows, adding his details I missed while in the OB department. Dr. Wilson asks about our feelings, our goodbye conversations with Kennedy, and her private funeral service. She asks what prompted us to choose the name Kennedy for our baby and how we feel about the constant reminder of our deceased wife and friend.

Jackson and I talk openly and easily with Dr. Wilson. At the end of the session, I'm exhausted but lighter. We agree to another visit next week. Dr. Wilson relinquishes Carter back to me and says good night.

With babies in our arms, Jackson carefully hugs me as the front door latches, whispering, "Thank you."

His words and hug catch me off guard.

"I needed the session with Dr. Wilson," he explains. "With returning to work and the twins, I've been too busy to mourn properly. She will help me heal instead of hiding my pain." Pulling back, he cups my jaw with his free hand. "She will help me work on items I swept to the back of my mind."

I hope my smile conveys I am glad to help, as words escape me at this moment.

I too have issues to discuss with Dr. Wilson in my private sessions. Jackson professing his love for me, Kennedy encouraging him to tell me he loves me, and my new role as a mother living with Jackson and the twins are atop my list.

Taylor
    Dr. Wilson at Taylor's Home-Individual Session, Friday, May 19th

"How are you adjusting to your unexpected role as a mother of twins?" Dr. Wilson directs after browsing her notes.

"I'm tired twenty-four-seven, otherwise it's great," I smirk. I know this is not the answer she looks for. "I struggle every day with the realization that this should have been Kennedy's role. I was to be moving out, finding a job, and entering the dating scene again." I pick at Nya's hair on my leggings. "I love the twins. Having held and nursed them, I can't imagine my life without them, but I feel guilty living the life planned for my best friend."

"Do you plan to re-enter the work force?"

"I can't imagine spending eight hours a day away from my babies. I know as they grow older, I may change my mind. I wasn't prepared for the immediate change that occurred the moment they entered the world. A switch flipped and mom-mode kicked in. I'm forever changed. It's not the perfect family I dreamed of, but it's perfect enough for me."

Dr. Wilson moves the conversation to our parental roles.

"Jackson and I decided I should stay in the same house and we will work together to raise the twins," I explain. "We plan to discuss it in more detail after a few months. We needed to focus on the twins and the funeral first."

"So, you are roommates raising your twins," she summarizes.

"When you put it that way, we sound stupid," I chuckle. "We're two close friends, both parents of the twins that agreed to put our feelings for each other on the back burner until we mourn the loss of Kennedy and settle into our roles as new parents," I rephrase.

"The two of you have shared your feelings for each other?" she inquires.

"Jackson told me he loves me," I inform. "I admitted I had feelings for him, too. I'm the one that suggested we wait. I was exhausted, sad, and accepting my motherhood. You know, a bit overwhelmed. I told him I needed time."

"What are your feelings for Jackson?"

"I love him," I admit with no hesitation.

Wow! That was easy. Why can't it be that easy to tell him how I feel?

"Have you shared this with him?"

"No, I fear when I do, things will escalate quickly. I want to be sure of our plans for the raising of our children. I want to understand how our friends might react. His parents already know Jackson's feelings, so I don't worry about their reaction." I fidget, trying to find a more comfortable position.

Dr. Wilson tips her head to the side. "Why are you grinning?"

"I've compared our current relationship to my dream list from our previous session," I confess.

Dr. Wilson speaks no words, yet encourages me to continue all the same. "We compromise, he cares about my feelings, he cares about my happiness, he listens to me, he chooses things he knows I like, we share similar interests, we share similar goals..." I can't contain my joy. "It's not perfect; we're not perfect. We work together. I'm hopeful, that's all." I shrug, still smiling.

"I see you have your journal open for our session today," Dr. Wilson notes. "Do you have something you would like to discuss?"

It's time. The moment has arrived. "It seems the evening before the accident, Kennedy approached Jackson... about me. She encouraged him to profess his love for me. Jackson denied his feelings, and they argued." I study Dr. Wilson's face. *I need to know if she is judging me. If she disapproves, and how she feels about this news.* I read nothing, so I continue. "Jackson did not approach me, the accident happened, the twins arrived, I texted Jackson's parents, and we welcomed the twins home from the hospital. Jackson confessed his love to me only recently. He says he talked to his parents about it. He claims after Kennedy said the words out loud, he started noticing his feelings and reactions to me. He realized he has been in love with me for months."

Dr. Wilson leans forward, placing her notepad and pen on the coffee-table. "When Jackson told you he loves you, how did you feel? What was your reaction?"

"I felt I was betraying Kennedy. I felt like I did something wrong, like I caused this," I confess. I relive the turmoil of the twenty-four hours following Jackson's "I love you."

"Do you feel the same way towards Jackson?" she asks.

"I've always loved him, as a friend, like a brother," I admit. "The flashes I experienced during my pregnancy made me worry my feelings were changing. I never fantasized about Jackson. I mean, I had a dream man in mind for my future spouse and father of my children, but I didn't think of...Jackson. We spent many evenings together while Kennedy went to Madison's. Nothing ever happened, but we grew very close. I never analyzed my true feelings. That all changed at the hospital. I needed him during the delivery. When he visited Kennedy, I felt lost. I thought it was the hormones and exhaustion, but my actual feelings surfaced."

90

KENNEDY'S CONFESSION

Taylor
Group Session At Dr. Wilson's Office, Monday, May 22nd

"Thank you for securing a sitter and meeting in my office today," Dr. Wilson greets. "I've asked a colleague to join us today. This is Dr. Jacobs."

"Dr. Jacobs, please meet Jackson Hayes and Taylor Taft." After shaking hands, we take our chairs.

"Are you leaving your practice or passing us off?" I question.

Why else would she have another professional sit in on our session?

"Our topic of today's session is delicate. I recently shared a situation with Dr. Jacobs. Through our discussion, we decided we should both be present today." Dr. Wilson assumes her usual chair, pulls out a manila file folder, and begins.

"As you are both aware, I met with the two of you and Kennedy individually throughout the surrogacy process. I did not share items from one session with the others, as privacy is vital in the therapy journey." She smiles at both of us before continuing. "The two of you shared a similar issue with me in your sessions. I have more information that now I can divulge with both of you."

My mind quickly flips through the many topics I shared with her in my sessions.

Which one would Jackson have also shared?

Think. Think. Think.

"As Jackson has signed a release of records for his deceased spouse, I can now share information I learned in Kennedy's sessions with both of you." She quickly sips her water, looking at Dr. Jacobs nervously. She holds patient notes in her hand as she continues. "During our many sessions, Kennedy shared in great detail a dinner that occurred on the evening of August Second."

I look from the doctor to Jackson to find out if he knows about this. It is clear he is as baffled as I am. I shrug and turn back to Dr. Wilson.

"This was the evening before you began ovulating and trying to conceive," Dr. Wilson reminds us. "Kennedy struggled with her actions for many months before confiding in me. I encouraged her to share her actions with the two of you. Her unwillingness to discuss it with you made my sessions with you more difficult for me. This is when I sought the counsel of my colleague." She motions toward the quiet Dr. Jacobs.

The more she talks, the more worried I become. *Kennedy took months to share this with her trusted therapist? If Kennedy struggled, it must be bad. She hadn't started visiting Madison this early. We were all nervous about performing 'The Deed'; nothing stands out about that night.*

"As I share this information with you, you will want to ask questions. Please let me share everything before we discuss." She waits for our agreement before starting. "Kennedy took medicine from a friend's house, and she slipped it into your drinks that evening. You might know the medication as GHB or roofies. She used your weakened state and lack of understanding to orchestrate intimacy between the two of you, hoping to create her baby. The flashes the two of you experienced resulted from her actions that evening."

The room spins, my stomach turns, and extreme heat climbs my spine. I rise from my chair next to Jackson and pace the shelved wall behind Dr. Wilson's desk. Memories rush back to me. *I woke up in the middle of the night to use the restroom... I was sore. I found my vibrator in my sheets with no batteries.* My hand covers my mouth. *I was sore the next day, but when my temperature spiked, I focused on 'The Deed' instead.* I breathe through my nose, fighting the urge to vomit. *The next three days were awkward, my mind consumed with the task at hand. The flashes started shortly after that. With Dr. Wilson's help, I found Kennedy's actions and words triggered the flashes. Dr. Wilson has known the truth for months and kept it from me.*

She kept it from us.

She knew.

I struggled, and she knew.

"I can't be here," I demand, striding toward the office door. I do not look at Dr. Wilson. I do not look at Jackson. *I can't.*

Dr. Jacobs follows me to the outer office. "Taylor, come with me." He motions to a hallway I hadn't noticed behind the reception desk.

I want fresh air. I want to ride with the top down and loud music. But I follow as directed.

"Take a seat."

I choose a seat on the far side of a small conference table. I grab a water bottle from the center and chug. I need to cool down.

"She knew," my raised voice announces. "For months I experienced flashes and worried I was fantasizing about my best friend's husband. I shared my pain with Dr. Wilson, and she knew why it was happening. How could she?"

Dr. Jacobs explains doctor-patient confidentiality ties every therapist's hands.

"Kennedy committed a crime. She...she raped me!" I gag. Hands over my mouth, I swallow the vomit. I cough as hot tears stain my cheeks. "She raped me. She raped Jackson. She drugged us. She stole medication. Doesn't that override fucking doctor-patient confidentiality?"

"Dr. Wilson explained to me by the time she found out from Kennedy, Jackson and you were less troubled by the flashes. If she believed you were in any danger, she would have shared information with authorities." He looks at me before resuming. "You were already pregnant with twins, the surrogacy progressing smoothly between the three of you, so divulging the truth might have created complications and stress in the arrangement and pregnancy."

"How could she?" I can't get the question out of my mind.

My chest tightens and my head pounds. A tumultuous storm swirls in my stomach, and vomit threatens every time I open my mouth. *Pain. I physically hurt.* "Why would Kennedy do this?"

"These are questions you will never have answered fully. Kennedy stated she desperately wanted a baby and thought this plan might work. Dr. Wilson can only share what Kennedy said in sessions. As Kennedy is no longer with us, you cannot confront her with your questions."

Dr. Jacobs slides his office chair further from the table and places his ankle over his knee. "Let's focus on Taylor. Besides, mad, how do you feel?"

Mad.

Mad?

I'm not mad, I'm livid, enraged, furious. Who wouldn't be?

I take a deep breath and focus on his question. "I feel violated. She drugged me. She slipped me a mother fucking roofie. She made…me…and Jackson…Oh my god!" My hand flies to my mouth. "I had sex with Jackson." I murmur behind my fingers.

"Violated by whom?" he queries.

"By Kennedy!" *Who the fuck else?* "Kennedy drugged Jackson just like me; he is as much a victim as I am."

Oh no!

She raped Jackson, her husband.

How will he cope?

A man being raped. He may struggle with his manhood.

What can I do?

What should I do?

"How can I help him?" I ask Dr. Jacobs.

"We need to focus on helping Taylor first. Dr. Wilson is helping Jackson," he says. "Let's do a role play. I'll pretend to be Kennedy; you confront me."

I don't think my mind takes over. "What the Fuck, Kennedy!" I yell. "What were you thinking? How could you do this to me? I volunteered to be your surrogate, I volunteered to donate my eggs, and this was not enough for you. You fucking drugged me and fucking raped me to create your precious little baby. You ruined all our years of friendship in your quest to be a mother. You lost your best friend and probably your husband to gain a baby. Was it worth it? Huh? Was it worth it? Does holding a baby make it worth losing us?" I cannot continue. My tears give way to hiccupping sobs.

My body quakes with this revelation. *Kennedy risked everything for motherhood. The motherhood that now belongs to me. She desired the tiny babies I cuddle and nurse. She truly lost everything. She never became a mother.*

I roll my shoulders and shake out my arms before I attempt to sit in the rolling office chair. I can't sit still; I stand again. I shake off my fury. I shake off my hate. "She wanted to be a mom so bad and now she will never be one. I want to hate her, but I can't. She died without ever seeing the twins—she never got to hold them. I did all of this for her; it isn't fair." I turn to face Dr. Jacobs. "It sucks. It all sucks. What she did… how she died… She overcame her eating disorders and was trying to find happiness."

"Taylor, you need to work with Dr. Wilson. You were dealt a large curve-ball today. You need time to heal. Dr. Wilson can help Jackson and you with what you learned today and how to move forward. You can trust her." I nod to Dr. Jacobs. "Shall we return to her office?"

I feel my eyes grow wide.
Return?
Return to…to Dr. Wilson's office?
Jackson's in there.
"Umm…"
How do I respond?
Should I want to go back? Or am I supposed to refuse?
I need to make sure Jackson is okay.
As I make my way back to Dr. Wilson's office, I worry about him.
How will this knowledge affect him?
Will it affect our relationship?
He told me he loves me; will that change now?

When my hand hesitates on the doorknob, Dr. Jacobs reaches past me to knock.

"Come in," Dr. Wilson beckons.

Jackson stands near the wall of shelves. Dr. Wilson remains in her chair. I return to my chair as Dr. Jacobs returns to his.

"Jackson," Dr. Wilson prompts. "Would you care to join us?"

Jackson complies, patting my shoulder as he walks in front of me. Seated, he turns to face me and grasps my hands.

"Are you okay?" he asks, his eyes pleading. "Please tell me we are okay?"

"We will be okay," I declare.

I don't one-hundred percent believe it, but I hope we'll be okay.

"We will need to work with Dr. Wilson." I squeeze his hands. "Nothing changed between us today."

I pull my hands into my lap as I turn to face Dr. Wilson again. "I'm sorry for my outburst earlier. I've had time to vent, and I understand now why you didn't share this when you first heard about it." She smiles a sad, knowing smile. "I'd like to meet again next week if you have an open appointment." I admit.

"It's important that the two of you journal this week. Journal reactions, feelings, anger, and fears about this session stir up. And if you feel up to it, talk to each other," Dr. Wilson prompts.

The two doctors talk with each of us, ensuring our mindset prior to letting us end this session. Jackson shakes Dr. Jacobs' hand and thanks him for his help before he places his hand in the small of my back to urge me to the door. As rage pulses through my veins, the warmth spreads from my back throughout my entire body.

I'm right, nothing changed today.
We are okay.

91

BEST FRIENDS

Taylor

"Taylor!" Jackson summons loudly from upstairs the next evening.

I recap my water bottle before attempting the epic struggle that is rising from the sofa post-cesarean. I peek at the sleeping twins before I slowly and painfully ascend the fourteen stairs from the living room to the second floor. *Jackson wouldn't require me to trudge upstairs if it wasn't important.* I pass the bathroom doorway as it is dark inside. The master bedroom door is open, but no lights are on. I notice light entering the hallway from the nursery. I place my hand on the door frame for support.

Jackson sits on his knees at the open nursery closet door. I see no spurting blood, signaling a need to yell at me.

"What's so important I had to climb the stairs?" I immediately regret my icy tone.

Jackson turns, rising to face me. "I'm so sorry, I didn't think. I just found the bag and reacted. Are you okay? Want to sit in the rocker? I should have brought it down to you."

I regret my words even more now seeing the sympathy on his face. "Never mind. What did you find?"

He grabs the extra-large duffle bag from the closet floor, places it on the changing table, and invites me to explore it on my own. I open the zipper flaps, revealing toiletries, clothes, and a handwritten note inside. I grab the notebook paper finding words on both sides. I immediately recognize Kennedy's handwriting. Jackson urges me to read it.

Jackson,
As you read this note, I am already gone. Please don't come for me, I'm only putting into action the situations we have previously discussed. You are in love with Taylor, and I'm in love with Madison. It's time we move forward. We were frozen in our marriage long enough. It's time for us to experience lust, passion, and true love. I'm taking everything I need with me. Please feel free to donate or trash anything I leave behind. I'm looking forward to the new-me and don't want old things to weigh me down.
I know together, Taylor and you will be perfect parents for the twins. I believe everything happens for a reason. Thus, the reason we couldn't use my eggs and used Taylor's is so the two of you could truly be together. It's written in the stars.
I needed the two of you to help me through the worst years of my life —now it is time for the two of you to move on.

Love Always,
Ken

Stunned, I glance into the duffle bag. I lift a prescription bottle. Turning it, I read the label. It belongs to Madison. Why does Kennedy have Madison's Rohypnol medicine? *That name sounds familiar.* I drop the bottle as if it burns my hand. *Oh my god! Roofies, this is the drug Kennedy slipped us that night.*

This was her go-bag. Kennedy planned to leave without a word just this note. My best friend didn't even tell me about her feelings for Madison. I moved in with Jackson and Kennedy to share the pregnancy and grow closer to my friends; instead Kennedy and I drifted apart.

Although Jackson shared his conversation with Kennedy about his love for me and her feelings for Madison, it still hurts to see her feelings in her handwriting. I hurt. *She betrayed me. She planned to leave me. She planned to leave the twins I worked so hard to create for her with me. She planned to leave her husband with me. In all her planning, she spoke not a word to me. She didn't even take the time to write me a note.* The hurt, betrayal, and violation cut through me. An open gaping chasm burns within me, heating my blood. Jackson approaches, reaching out for me. I raise my hands palm out. I can't. I need... I don't know what I need.

"I need time," I state as I slowly leave the nursery.

At the top of the stairs, the thought of a painful descent gives me pause. I decide to slide down the stairs on my bottom as if a young child. The pain is minimal, but pulling myself up to stand at the bottom causes me to groan.

I snag my phone and shut my bedroom door behind me. I shoot a text to Jackson.

> **ME**
> Taking a bath please keep an eye on the twins

As my warm bath fills, I reach out to a friend for help.

> **ME**
> Can you talk?

> **JORGE**
> Yes

I select the phone icon to call him.

"Hey, how's my favorite momma?" Jorge's deep voice greets.

"I..." My shaky voice rasps. I attempt to stop the tears.

"Taylor, what happened? Talk to me." Jorge urges concern, dripping from every word.

"Jackson and I found a duffle bag. Kennedy left a note." My words are choppy between my uncontrolled sobs. "She planned to leave Jackson and run away with Madison."

"Taylor, honey," Jorge tries to soothe me. "This doesn't change the accident. This doesn't change the fact you gave birth to two precious babies."

"She...she..." I suck in a sharp breath. "She was my best friend. I thought we were best friends." I swipe tears from my cheeks, thankful Jorge cannot see me now. "I thought we were close. She never told me about her feelings for Madison. She never told me she wanted to leave Jackson. She was my best friend, but I was not hers."

"I wish I was there. Are you alone? Where is Jackson?" he asks.

"I'm in my room, running a bath."

Crap! I turn off the water; its level is much deeper than I planned. "I found the roofies. She had the bottle of roofies in the bag. The roofies she used on Jackson and I." I shudder, thinking about Kennedy's action that night.

"I'm gonna soak in a warm bath and try to process everything again," I share.

"Taylor, your stitches, you can't."

"Fuck!" I shout. "This isn't fair. I can't drive, I can't go for a walk, and I can't take a hot bath," I rant.

"Taylor," Jackson's voice penetrates from the other side of my bedroom door. "Are you okay?"

I open the door, not wanting Jackson to worry. "It's Jorge." I point to the phone. "I'm just ranting. I promise, I am fine."

Jackson doesn't look convinced. Jorge's voice draws my attention back to the phone.

"Taylor, talk to Jackson. Share your feelings, and call Dr. Wilson if I need to," he encourages before saying goodbye.

I pat the bed beside me, prompting Jackson to sit. "I'm a mess. I can't go for a walk, I can't drive, I can't take a bath, and I can't have a drink."

Jackson places his arm around my shoulders, and we talk. We talk for hours. We talk as I nurse the twins, and we tuck them in bed. We talk as I fix a snack and climb into bed. Jackson lies beside me, arms around me. We talk until sleep rescues us.

92

TWINS, I AM YOUR MOTHER

Taylor
Two Years Later

"What time is it?" I ask the room.

"Twenty minutes after the last time you asked," Martha teases.

"We have five minutes," Elizabeth announces to everyone. "Taylor, might I have a moment?" She inquires, escorting me onto the balcony for a modicum of privacy.

I thought my nerves had reached a pinnacle; a private chat with Elizabeth escalates them even higher. Gerald and Elizabeth arrived with us three days ago to assist with the preparations and the twins. We shopped, dined, and even swam.

What will she discuss now, with less than five minutes until we start?
Why didn't she talk to me before now?

"You look beautiful, dear," Elizabeth says. "For many years now, Gerald and I have thought of you as our daughter. Today, you make that official." She dabs a tissue to the corner of each eye, not wanting her tears to ruin her makeup. "You brought our son back into our lives, you gave us two precious grandchildren, and today you give us the happiness and future we always dreamed of for Jackson." Trying not to crumple my dress, she gently hugs me. "We love you. We can't wait to share this special day with you. Welcome to our family."

Reagan answers a knock on the door. "It's time!" She echoes Tyler's words loud enough for all to hear.

Holding my hands between us, Elizabeth instructs me to take a few deep, calming breaths.

Reagan peeks her head onto the balcony, "Ladies, let's go."

The walk from our dressing room, down the elevator, and onto the patio takes an eternity.

"Kennedy, take your mommy's hand," Reagan encourages.

As Kennedy toddles towards me, I revel at her beauty. She wears a simple pale green sundress, and soft curls bounce in her thin light-brown hair. She doesn't look like my two-year-old today. My heart skips a beat, thinking of how fast she has grown and will continue to change with each passing year. I gasp as my eyes fall on her shoes. She is not wearing the pale green sandals I purchased for her. Instead, a new pair of white Converse adorn her chubby little feet. I bend to her level.

"Mommy loves your shoes," I point to her toes.

"Dada," she proudly says.

"Did Daddy buy those?" I ask my baby girl.

"Shh, Dada," she explains.

Seems Jackson took her shopping and helped her keep it a secret. She points her toe my way, so I can better study her new shoes.

"They look just like mommy's shoes," I tell Kennedy.

She lifts the hem of my dress in an attempt to see my shoes.

"Mommy's shoes are upstairs. Today I'm wearing different shoes." I wish I had on my Converse. I hate high heels. If I weren't so short and Jackson so tall, I could have worn flats. If I had my way, we would be in shorts in our backyard today. Jackson insisted and everyone favored his idea of a destination wedding.

Our guests are in their seats. Kennedy and I stand hand in hand. Our resort wedding coordinator signals us, and we start our walk. Woven mats of palm fronds line our way through the sandy beach. I smile, making eye contact with Jackson holding Carter near the arbor in front of our family and friends. I smile to Martha, Reagan, and Madison in the second row as they wave at Kennedy. Last, we pass Elizabeth and Gerald seated in the front row. Elizabeth smiles, still dabbing the corner of her eyes, and Gerald waves at Kennedy.

"Hi Papa," Kennedy says.

I position the two of us next to Jackson as he places Carter to stand beside him.

I opted to forgo the bouquet. I wanted the four of us to hold hands during the ceremony. My long eyelet lace maxi dress flows with the breeze as the officiant starts the ceremony.

I glance at my son in his tan Bermuda shorts and green Hawaiian shirt. Like his twin, he looks older than his two years. I note his feet aren't in the sandals I bought for him. Like his sister, he sports a new pair of white Converse. *Jackson was very busy shopping to surprise me.*

Looking up, I find Jackson smiling at me. I mouth, "I love you."

He returns the sentiment while squeezing my hand.

My mind drifts to the twin's first birthday. I rose early to decorate the house and yard for an amazing first birthday party.

I purchased a special outfit just for today. I pull on my fitted white t-shirt with large black and gold Star Wars font lettering across the top displaying a young Luke and Leia playing with light-sabers below it. It reads "Twins, I am your mother." I couldn't think of a better way to celebrate Star Wars Day and the twins' first birthday.

"You are such a dork," Jackson greets me in the kitchen, coffee in hand.

"Oh, please," I retort. "It's Star Wars Day; May the Fourth Be with You," I laugh. "I need to celebrate it."

Jackson simply shakes his head, smirking. My nerd side no longer surprises him.

We decorate the back yard with pink and blue balloons, streamers, and tablecloths. I purchased a large sheet cake with "Happy First Birthday Kennedy & Carter," in pink and blue icing along with small round cakes in pink and blue for each of them. Seated in their highchairs, we place a pink cake in front of Kennedy and a blue cake in front of Carter.

Carter wasted no time in grabbing a handful and moving it to his mouth. He paints his face a mess of blue icing and white cake crumbs. Kennedy merely pokes a finger into her cake and licks it off. She eats one fingertip at a time. Carter claps his messy hands together, letting cake and icing fly everywhere. He enjoys this spectacle and the attention we give him, so he repeats the action. Unfortunately, icing and cake land on Kennedy, her tray, and her cake. Not enjoying two blobs sticking to her cheek and brow; she cries. Jackson, wrapped around his little girl's finger, passes the video camera to his father and rescues Kennedy. He wipes the cake from her cheeks before lifting her from the high chair.

Later that night, when family and friends leave, and the exhausted twins are sound asleep in the nursery, Jackson approaches me in the living room with a glass of wine for each of us.

"You planned the perfect party," he says. "A toast to a fabulous first year and many more to follow." We clink glasses and sip. His eyes lock on mine; he places his wine on the coffee table. I feel he wants to tell me something, but he holds back. Tired from the decorating and party, I sip my wine quickly, hoping to soak in a hot bath before I turn in for the night.

"I'm going to check on the twins, then call it a night," I announce, taking my empty wine glass to the kitchen.

Jackson continues watching TV as I start up the stairs. The twins rest peacefully in their baby beds on opposite walls of the nursery. I turn the baby monitor on before placing a kiss on my fingertips, then to a cheek of Carter and Kennedy. I pause in the doorway, marveling at how hard they played all day and how fast they fell asleep. Carter almost fell asleep during his bath. He was so tired.

Jackson places his hand on my shoulder. Coaxing me out of the doorway, he shuts the door behind us. Jackson takes my hand, leading me toward his bedroom. I follow, assuming he has something to show me before I head down to my room for the night. In the main bedroom, he pulls me closer.

We stand nearly touching. My neck strains to look up, our height difference too great. He slowly closes the distance between us as I realize his heavy-lids and lust-filled molten brown eyes focus on my lips. His hand at my neck secures me as he presses his warm lips to mine. His kiss is gentle at first but morphs to feverish. His tongue caresses my lower lip, seeking an opening. With a will of its own, my mouth parts, allowing him the access he seeks.

My hands slide from his exposed forearms up to his shoulders. A moan escapes me when his free hand molds to my lower back, tugging me against him. His heated body warms mine. Breaking our kiss, he places his forehead on mine while we pant, struggling for breath.

"Jackson," I whisper.

"Shh," he quiets me. "I've imagined this kiss for a year now," he confesses. "I love you. I'm dying to share more with you. I'm ready to explore us."

His words mirror those we spoke just after the twins were born, when we agreed to put "us" on the back burner. We chose to explore our feelings after we acclimated to our new reality of losing Kennedy and parenting twins.

"We've had a great year." He continues pulling his forehead from mine and signaling for us to sit on his bed. "We're ready."

93

RESPONSIBLE PARENT

Taylor

My mind scrambles for words.
Ready?
Ready for what?

Our first kiss was everything I fantasized about this past year and then some.

Is he ready to sleep together?
I'm not sure I am ready for that tonight.

Our kiss proves our electric passion for each other. I stand in front of him, as he's seated on his bed; I move between his knees.

"I'm ready to explore us too, but I want to go slow." I swallow, my mouth suddenly very dry. "I need to go slow. We have too much on the line to jump into this."

Jackson nods his understanding.

To show my desire for him, I place feather-light kisses on his jaw. He places his hands on each side of my face, guiding my lips to his. This kiss is hotter than the first. Our hands explore arms, shoulders, ribs, hips, and chests.

I lift my legs to straddle his lap, aligning my pelvis with his. The heat from his cock exquisitely flows to my core. His hands on my hips grind me into him, and I moan. I continue the pressure as he moves his mouth to my jaw, then down my neck. His hot breath caresses my heated skin.

Still grinding, my pleasure rises.

"Jackson," I whisper breathily.

More. I want more.

As if reading my mind, he stands, and I wrap my legs around his waist. He pivots, placing one knee on the mattress, and lowers us. Lying above me on propped elbows, we are connected from our ribcage down to our toes. I long for the friction I lost.

"I need more. I need to feel you," I murmur, tugging at the hem of his shirt.

Jackson removes his shirt, then mine. I feel his skin on mine, his dark chest hair tickles me ever so lightly. As we kiss, my hands caress his strong back and shoulder muscles. He trails kisses to my ear, down my neck, and onto my bra-covered breasts. His warm, wet tongue probes between the cup of my bra and my bare breast. I whimper, unable to control my need. He slips a hand around my back to unclasp and remove my bra. I sigh as my exposed flesh tingles and nipples pucker.

Jackson licks, nips, and sucks one breast, then the other. I remain motionless, fighting my urge to writhe beneath him. My need for total contact supersedes the delicious sensations Jackson lavishes upon my breasts. My fingers fiddle with first his zipper then mine. A frustrated moan escapes my throat.

Jackson chuckles, stands at the edge of the bed, and removes his shorts and briefs. My eyes take in all of him. I'm distracted by his proud, hard cock stretching towards me. I don't notice as he removes my shorts and panties in one motion.

I reach for him, my primal need in control. My fingertips graze his abdomen, trailing down the smattering of short, dark hair leading down from his naval. At the base of his shaft, I grab curls and tug lightly. Jackson moans, fueling my actions. I wrap my hand around the base of his erection. Slowly, I tighten my grip as I glide my hand from base to tip and back. As I repeat the motion, Jackson's hips thrust forward and back. As I stroke him, I lightly trace the fingertips of my free hand around his soft tip. Jackson's piston-like movements become frantic.

"You must stop; I will not last long as it is," Jackson pleads, still moving against my hands.

I glide my hands up his chest. I'm restless, desperately longing to feel him inside me.

Birth control.

"Fuck!" I groan.

"I know; it feels…"

I have a nearly two-year-old condom in my room. Since he initiated, I hope Jackson is prepared. I'm momentarily distracted by one of his hands cupping my breast while the other lightly caresses my folds. My breath catches as his thumb rubs my swollen clit.

"Jackson," I moan. "Condom?"

An anguished moan rumbles from his chest.

I don't like the sound of that.

"Shit, I'm sorry."

Crap! Crap! Crap! We need to move slower; we're not prepared.

As parents of twins, we must be responsible adults. I'm too far gone to stop now, but I have two one-year-olds. *I can't handle another baby now.*

The angel and devil on each of my shoulders argue. I need to continue, but we should stop.

I also need to think of the twins, of Jackson, of our current situation, and what another pregnancy would add to that.

The devil on my shoulder wins. I grasp Jackson's swollen cock and plunge it towards my wet center. Jackson doesn't resist. I moan at the sensation of his thick cock stretching my inner walls. Slowly, he fills me.

I don't want slow; I need to be in control. I wrap my legs around his middle and shove to roll us over. Jackson complies. Now on top, I slowly rise and fall upon his magnificent length. I lean forward, placing my mouth on his. I suck his plump lower lip into my mouth and tug gently while grazing my teeth before releasing. I grind my pelvis against him after the next downward thrust. This motion places perfect friction on my very swollen nub. I selfishly continue the movements; it provides the friction I desperately desire. My hands on his chest cause my breasts to squeeze between my arms. My head falls back and my back arches as heat crawls up my spine.

"Close!" I cry, grasping his hands and placing them on my hips. "Help me, please," I pant.

Jackson guides my hips forward and back, again and again. I give in to the sensations. My core coils tight as I climb ever closer to the illustrious edge of the cliff.

"Don't stop," I demand in a whisper. "Almost... Yes!"

I plummet over the edge as my coil springs free. My core pulses; wave after wave of pleasure consumes me. Jackson maneuvers on top of me and continues pistoning. He extends the duration of my orgasm with his thrusts.

So...Damn...Good.

My orgasm wanes, my body relaxes, and I melt into the comforter. At the same time, Jackson's growling moan into my neck and shuddering signal his own release.

Our panting covers the white noise of the baby monitor as we're tangled around each other. Jackson nuzzles his nose to my neck. As our breathing slows, my brain turns back on.

"Crap," I whisper, swatting his shoulder. "We just had unprotected sex."

With my non-existent periods, I have no way of knowing if I might be in the ovulation portion of my cycle or not. *Triple Crap!* I intended for us to make-out only. I got carried away.

"Jackson," I whine as my forearm covers my eyes. "We're not very responsible."

Laughing, Jackson slides out, then onto his back next to me.

"It's not funny," I chide, swatting at his chest. "We're two single parents with twins. Our situation seems weird enough to outsiders as it is. We don't need another pregnancy to add to our scandal."

"My parents gave me their blessing," Jackson defends. "Our friends seem comfortable with us living together to raise our family. I don't see any scandal. We're two consenting adults. If we have another baby, that's our business." He rolls on his side, facing me, so I roll to face him.

"I hear you, but I'm not ready to have another baby anytime soon," I explain. "I have my hands full with Kennedy and Carter. Can you imagine caring for them if I'm experiencing morning sickness and tired all the time?"

He tucks hair behind my ear, leaving his palm on my jaw. "I love you." His statement is meant to shut me up. Any other time, I would fight back, but tonight I don't have the strength. "Need me to carry you to the bathroom?" He asks, sensing my weakened state.

I gather all my strength, freshen up in his bathroom, then exit, striding toward the stairs to my room.

"Uh-huh," Jackson says, grabbing my arm. "Tonight, you sleep with me." He grins a devilish grin, moving me to his bed.

I note he changed into pajamas and pulled the comforter back. I'm too tired to argue. I climb under the sheet and arrange the pillows. When Jackson climbs in, he pulls my back to his front. I stifle a giggle, realizing we're spooning.

I want to revel in the moment, recording it all to my memory, but I fall right to sleep.

Next, my mind recalls the twins' second Christmas.

I'm shocked to find Jackson purchased and wrapped a gift for each child, keeping it a secret from me. He passes the gifts to the twins at the same time, encouraging them to open. Carter rips right in, loving the destruction of wrapping paper that comes with gifts. Kennedy daintily picks at the paper piece by piece. Unable to endure her unwrapping, Jackson assists.

Kennedy pulls five wooden blocks from her tissue lined box at the same time Carter dumps two wooden blocks from his decimated box and paper. I watch as little fingers hover and point to the brightly painted blocks. Several moments pass before it clicks. Kennedy's blocks contain a m-a-r-r-y and Carter's blocks contain m-e.

"Marry me?" I whisper.

I swing my eyes up to Jackson, sitting behind the kids. He pulls the twins onto his lap and smiles towards me.

"Will you marry me?" he asks.

I stare at my adorable children and their handsome father in shock. I know I need to respond. My brain isn't firing directions to the rest of me. I release the breath I didn't realize I held.

"Really?" I seek confirmation as tears blur my vision.

Turning to Carter, Jackson says, "Ask mommy to marry me."

Carter wiggles free and toddles to me. "Momma," his chubby hand touches my cheek. "Dada." My son orders me to marry his father.

"Yes!" I announce. "Yes, I will marry you."

I shake away my memories, realizing I missed most of our ceremony. The officiant speaks of the importance of faith in a marriage with her heavy Mexican accent.

"Done Momma?" Kennedy questions.

My darling daughter inherited her father's patience. Our friends and family laugh at her interruption. I release Jackson's hand as I bend to pick up my little girl. I kiss her cherub nose, then whisper in her ear that we are almost done. I turn to Jackson. He lifts Carter and smiles at me.

"Ladies and gentlemen, I give you Mr. and Mrs. Hayes," the officiant pronounces.

Jackson leans in, kissing me while Carter pats my cheek. I pull away, laughing. *I love my family. I love my chaotic life. I have everything I ever hoped for in my future husband and family. Our start was not traditional, but we found love and happiness.*

The End

Help other readers find this book and give me a giant author hug —**please consider leaving a review on Amazon, Goodreads, Kobo, and BookBub**—a few words mean so much.

Check out my **Pinterest Boards** for my inspirations for characters, settings, and recipes.

ALSO BY HALEY RHOADES:

Ladies of the Links Series-

Ladies of Links #1 -- Gibson, Ladies of the Links #2 -- Christy, Ladies of the Links #3 – Brooks, Ladies of the Links #4 – Kirby, Ladies of the Links #5 -- Morgan

Boxers or Briefs

The Locals Series-

Tailgates & Truck Dates, Tailgates & Heartaches, Tailgates & First Dates, Tailgates & Twists of Fate

The 7 Deadly Sins Series-

Unbreakable, Unraveled, Unleashed,

Unexpected, Uncaged, Unmasked, Unhinged

Trivia Page

1.The first and last names of *ALL* characters in this book are the names of U.S. Presidents and First Ladies.

2.When my oldest son was born, we named him Carter. Without planning several of our friend group named our babies all born within 2 years with president's names. Like: Carter, Jefferson, Truman, Lincoln, Jackson, Madison, and Harrison.

3.It wasn't until I turned 46 that I was asked for my photo ID at a physician's office. (To prevent insurance fraud) I lived in 4 midwest states in 17 communities, so I've had my share of new-patient appointments.

4. My pen name is a combination of 2 of my paternal great-grandmothers' maiden names. (Haley and Rhoades)

ABOUT THE AUTHOR

Haley Rhoades's writing is another bucket-list item coming to fruition, just like meeting Stephen Tyler, Ozzie Smith, and skydiving. As she continues to write contemporary romance, she also writes sweet romance and young adult books under the name Brooklyn Bailey, as well as children's books under the name Gretchen Stephens. She plans to complete her remaining bucket-list items, including ghost-hunting, storm-chasing, and bungee jumping. She is a Netflix-binging, Converse-wearing, avidly-reading, traveling geek.

A team player, Haley thrived as her spouse's career moved the family of four, thirteen times to three states. One move occurred eleven days after a C-section. Now with two adult sons, Haley copes with her newly emptied nest by writing and spoiling Nala, her Pomsky. A fly on the wall might laugh as she talks aloud to her fur-baby all day long.

Haley's under five-foot, fun-size stature houses a full-size attitude. Her uber-competitiveness in all things entertains, frustrates, and challenges family and friends. Not one to shy away from a dare, she faces the consequences of a lost bet no matter the humiliation. Her fierce loyalty extends from family, to friends, to sports teams.

Haley's guilty pleasures are Lifetime and Hallmark movies. Her other loves include all things peanut butter, *Star Wars*, mathematics, and travel. Past day jobs vary tremendously from a radio DJ, to an elementary special-education para-professional, to a YMCA sports director, to a retail store accounting department, and finally a high school mathematics teacher.

Haley resides with her husband and fur-baby in the Des Moines area. This Missouri-born girl enjoys the diversity the Midwest offers.

Reach out on Facebook, Twitter, Instagram, or her website...she would love to connect with her readers.

- amazon.com/author/haleyrhoades
- goodreads.com/haleyrhoadesauthor
- bookbub.com/authors/haley-rhoades
- tiktok.com/@haleyrhoadesauthor
- facebook.com/AuthorHaleyRhoades
- instagram.com/haleyrhoadesauthor
- twitter.com/HaleyRhoadesBks
- pinterest.com/haleyrhoadesaut
- linkedin.com/in/haleyrhoadesauthor
- youtube.com/@haleyrhoadesbrooklynbaileyauth
- patreon.com/ginghamfrog